The Law of Inertia

S. Gonzales

Amberjack Publishing
New York | Idaho

AMBERJACK
PUBLISHING

Amberjack Publishing
1472 E. Iron Eagle Drive
Eagle, Idaho 83616
http://amberjackpublishing.com

This book is a work of fiction. Any references to real places are used fictitiously. Names, characters, fictitious places, and events are the products of the author's imagination, and any resemblance to actual persons, living or dead, places, or events is purely coincidental.

Publisher's Cataloging-in-Publication data
Names: Gonzales, S., 1992- author.
Title: The law of inertia / by S. Gonzales.
Description: Eagle, ID : Amberjack Publishing, [2018] | Summary: Told from multiple viewpoints, James seeks answers about his boyfriend Ash's suicide but the one most likely to have the answers, Ash's brother, Elliot, left town the day of Ash's funeral.
Identifiers: LCCN 2018006335 (print) | LCCN 2018014351 (ebook) | ISBN 9781944995881 (eBook) | ISBN 9781944995874 (pbk. : alk. paper)
Subjects: | CYAC: Brothers--Fiction. | Secrets--Fiction. | Gays--Fiction. | Friendship--Fiction. | Suicide--Fiction. | Foster children--Fiction.
Classification: LCC PZ7.1.G6532 (ebook) | LCC PZ7.1.G6532 Law 2018 (print) | DDC [Fic]--dc23
LC record available at https://lccn.loc.gov/2018006335

Cover Design: Stepheny Miller

23 22 21 20 19 18   1 2 3 4 5 6 7 8 9 10

For Lee, without whom:

my similes would be as awkward as a dog on a frozen pond,

my metaphors would be stagnant pools,

and this book would likely have never left Microsoft Word.

(P. S. Thanks for suggesting the above simile and metaphor.
Surprise!)

ASHTON

The first two times I tried to die, I survived.
But I'll tell you something only two people know.
When I did die, I wasn't trying to at all.

HIDE

ONE

Louise
September 2018

"Do you know how many Elliot Taylors there are in this damn country?"

As soon as those words came out of his mouth, the hot guy in the video had my attention.

I leaned back in my desk chair, turned the sound up on the clip, and called over my shoulder. "Hey. Look what Saras tagged me in."

Elliot Taylor, who was sprawled out on my unmade bed with one headphone in, snapped his head up to watch.

"I've spent most of the last year trying to find him. He's disappeared into nowhere, though. So I thought I'd ask strangers on the internet to help me. I have a message for Elliot Taylor. Dark hair, blue eyes, tall. Anyway, I know that's not super descriptive, but he'll know he's the right one when he sees me. I wanna talk to him about his brother, Ash."

I was too busy watching the clip, narrated by a slim Asian guy sitting crossed-legged on a picnic table, to notice Elliot's reaction to it at first.

It was only when Elliot sucked in his breath that he ended up on my radar. He was clutching his iPhone with white knuckles and staring at my laptop screen like the creepy girl from *The Ring* had appeared on it.

"I've needed to talk to him for a long time now, but he's conveniently dropped off the face of the earth," the guy in the video went on, fiddling with the drawstrings of his forest green hoodie. Going by his accent, he lived somewhere down south. "Ash was my best friend, and he killed himself last year. I think Elliot and I both know pieces of what happened on Ash's last day. If we collaborate, we might get the full story."

Elliot was breathing too loudly for my liking. He sounded like an emphysemic with a microphone. I raised an eyebrow at him. "You all good?"

In the background, the clip continued. "Elliot disappeared right after Ash's funeral. Nobody knows where he is or how to contact him. But I'd sure as hell like some closure. If you can share this video, or tag any Elliot Taylors, or anyone who might know an Elliot Taylor, you might be able to help me find him. And Elliot, if you're watching this, please. Talk to me. For both our sakes. You know where to find me."

The video cut off. Elliot didn't say a word. And this was Elliot. Silence wasn't really his thing. Plus, he'd barely blinked since the video began. Because *that* wasn't suspicious at all.

"Is it you?" I asked, spinning my chair around to face him.

He stared at the screen for a few more seconds before crashing back to reality. "No."

"*No?*" I repeated flatly. I wouldn't have bought that even if he was a good actor. Which, by the way, he was not.

"I've never seen that guy in my life."

Sure thing, Elliot. Totally. "Uh-huh. So why do you look like that?"

"Like what?" he asked. He turned back to his phone and flicked through it so quickly there was no way in hell he could read the screen.

Interesting. "You didn't tell me you had a brother," I said.

"I don't. I didn't."

"*Elliot.*"

"What? It's a common name, like the guy said."

"Tall, dark haired, blue eyed, Elliot Taylor—he even has your accent—okay, you're shaking."

"Tall is a stretch. And I'm *not* shaking. We have to go to work soon."

Oh, *masterful* subject change there.

Elliot and I worked at the same restaurant—Bruno's. We met there when he first moved to town. Back then, he'd been all quiet, withdrawn, and, in my opinion, mysterious. I'd started following him around like a pre-fame Kim Kardashian clinging to Paris Hilton as soon as I met him. We clicked straight away. Well, I clicked with him. Can clicking be one sided? Anyway, he realised he wasn't going to shake me, so he put up with me. Eventually, that tolerance turned into affection. Over a year later, and he loved me back. At least, I figured he must, because he spent half the week inviting himself over to hang, so.

"No," I said, shooting to my feet and standing to bar my doorway. I was a goalkeeper for three years. He could *try* getting past. "No, you stay right there."

Elliot gave me a weary look. "Louise, we'll be late." He tried to push his way past me. I stood my ground stubbornly though, and we had a Western film style standoff. At least, we did for three seconds, until Elliot ducked under my arms and darted down the hall. Okay, so maybe my football skills were rusty.

"*Elliot*," I called out, chasing him through the hall and downstairs, where I almost went tail up on the tiles.

In the lounge room he passed my abuela, who sat perched on the couch by a pedestal fan with one of her Spanish tabloid magazines. Abuela and I shared a borderline obsession with celebrities, only none of the ones she cared about spoke English. "Elliot," she said, lowering the magazine. "*No* running inside. You break something."

He stopped in his tracks, spun around, and gave her a grin. "Sorry, Chari—Louise is terrorising me." It's a testament to how into Elliot Abuela is that she let him call her Chari instead of Rosario. She thinks he's devastatingly handsome. Eh. To each their own.

She turned to me with large, accusing brown eyes. Oh, *hell* no. Abuela always took Elliot's side. She fell for charm way too easily. No one ever taught Abuela she didn't need a man when she was a little girl, and it made her weak. "*Louisa, eres tan mala que me vas a matar!*"

So, I could barely speak any Spanish, and half the time I didn't have the foggiest idea what my grandmother was on about. But in the six months that she'd been living with us, I'd become pretty good at figuring out the difference between her "I'm pretending to be angry" voice and her "I'm seriously pissed off with you" voice. This was one of the former. No big.

"We're going to work now," Elliot said, grabbing my wrist.

Abuela looked crestfallen. "You no stay for dinner?"

My Abuela was the epitome of a true Spanish housewife. Refer back to the aforementioned upbringing, if you will. Basically, she derived most of her self-worth from how fat we got off her cooking. The rest from how diligently she could stay on top of the grey hairs that highlighted her shoulder-length mane of thick, dark curls.

Nineteen-forties Spain didn't sound like it led the way in the girl-power movement, put it that way.

Mum, with her superhuman metabolism, scandalised Abuela by failing to get any larger than a size six, no matter how much she fed her. So inconsiderate of her, really. As for me, I lost the genetic lottery by inheriting Abuela's figure instead of Mum's. I put on three pounds if I even looked at *croquetas* for too long. A week or so ago, Abuela had pointed out with some sort of sick satisfaction that I'd gone up a dress size since she'd moved in with us. I still hadn't forgiven her for it. She could take her well-meaning compliments and shove them in—

"No time," Elliot said. He tried to pull me outside, but I yanked my hand back.

"I have to get my uniform, you idiot."

He tutted. "I'm not the one who made it halfway out the door before deciding to grab my uniform."

The sheer sass on this guy. I scowled at him and ran upstairs to change. As a general rule, I tried to spend as little time in the Bruno's uniform as possible. I mean, black trousers, closed shoes and a boxy, collared shirt the colour of a sewer rat? Adriana Lima herself couldn't make that work.

By the time I came back down, Elliot was in the middle of a cheerful conversation with Abuela about his flatmate and cousin, Bea, who was busy slugging through her first year of uni. Then, as soon as we left the house, he hijacked the conversation by launching into a story about some rude customer. No way had he conveniently forgotten about the video. Nice try, though.

I decided to give him a break and let it go.

For now, anyway.

TWO

Ash
March 2017

IF YOU ASK ME, life is like a string of dominos, placed with care to facilitate the journey towards a predetermined destination. Each moment is a single piece, and as it tips, it sets the next moment into motion. So you can't ever pinpoint where something begins. How do you say a story started with any one moment when that moment would never have happened if it weren't for the domino before it?

You might argue that some dominos are more important than others. Like one standing at a slight angle when all the others preceding it are in a ruler straight line. As soon as that domino tips, the course of your life alters.

If you prefer the latter, I suppose the moment that altered the course of my life occurred when I tried to kill myself at fourteen.

That single action changed everything. It collapsed the precarious Jenga tower that I had once called a family. Without it, Elliot would've never ended up in the hospital. Dad would never have lost custody of us. We wouldn't have spent the last two years being shuffled around town, sifting through various foster families.

At the time, I had no way of predicting the true implications of that one, desperate attempt at escape. If someone had warned me that all of the above would follow, I would've thought for certain it was the worst thing that could have happened.

In hindsight, I could see that if that particular domino hadn't tipped, nothing would have changed. The course of my life would've stayed in motion, hurtling towards a reality far worse than the one I lived in now—without it, we'd still be trapped at home. Or worse.

As it was, I still had a house to return to after school, even if it didn't feel like a home. And though I'd lost most of my friends, I still had James. Also, despite the lack of a functional family unit, I had Elliot around to keep me busy, like any good family member should.

And as much as I loved him, Lord, did he *ever* keep me busy.

Such as today, for example, towards the end of Maths. It was Tuesday, so Maths was my last class of the day. He attempted to call me twice, even though he *knew* I'd still be at school and couldn't answer without risking detention. My phone was set to vibrate, but I'd squeezed it into my pocket alongside my house keys, so it sounded less like a gentle notification and more like a chainsaw. On the other side of the room, James laughed at me, his mouth barely hidden behind his textbook. Oh, excellent. If James could hear the commotion all the way over there, I didn't stand a chance of remaining undetected.

Mr. Patricks, the worst teacher to be around while bending the rules—something I managed several times a week despite valiant efforts otherwise—whipped around. I hunched over my desk and acted like I was too lost in quadratic trinomials to notice the racket inside my jeans. Luck was on my side for once however, because, after shooting me a warning look, Mr. Patricks let it go.

On the way out of class, James hung back to talk to a group of guys from his football team. Rather than waiting for him like I usually would, I joined the sea of students as they headed down the hill. I was about to return Elliot's call when footsteps thudded behind me. I smiled to myself. James had caught up.

I slowed my pace, expecting him to fall into step beside me. Instead I was thrown forward with a grunt of surprise as an unexpected weight barrelled onto me. James let out a whoop of laughter from his perch on my back while I stumbled forward, nearly losing my balance on the slanted footpath.

"Get off me," I said, jumping to shake him off.

He wrapped his legs around my middle and pretended to crack a whip in the air. "Giddy-up," he ordered. The movement caused me to lurch forward again and a group of girls dodged sideways to avoid us. I offered them a sheepish grimace, then everything went black.

"James, get your hands off my face or I swear—"

"Follow my voice and thou shalt find the way. Onwards!"

"If I fall, I take no responsibility for—" I was cut off as James's hand slipped over my mouth. He managed to pull it away half a second before I went to bite him. "—injury."

Stumbling sideways beneath his weight, I held my arms out in front of me. One hand bounced against what I thought might've been a girl's chest, and I received a slap on my arm in return.

"I'm sorry, really sorry," I said to whoever was in front of me.

The ground beneath me shifted texture. Grass. I bucked, arching my back, and James removed his hands from my eyes to grab onto my shoulders for balance. Blinking into the sudden light, I glanced behind me to make sure the way was clear, then threw us backwards. James hit the lawn hard beneath me, his school bag only somewhat cushioning his impact. I rolled off him, ripped my bag from my back and brandished it as a weapon.

James raised an arm to ward it off, laughing helplessly. "Stop, Ash, I surrender. I'm at your mercy."

"You idiot; you made me molest someone."

He cackled. "That wasn't a girl; it was just Caleb Crosier."

I threw my bag at his face, and it bounced off his crossed arms. He held out his hands, weak from laughing. "Help me up," he said.

"Help yourself up."

I returned to the crowd of retreating students, and James joined my side seconds later, struggling to hoist his bag on his back. "We need to get you distracted," he announced.

"Is that so?"

"You've been mopey all day," he said, throwing his arm across my shoulders, "and I know it's over Gemma. So I'm staging an intervention."

We veered left after exiting the grounds. On Tuesdays and Thursdays, the only evenings James didn't have football or athletics practice, we walked home together. The short way if our schedules were full for the night, the long way if we preferred to extend our time together. We never had to voice the decision out loud; it was always one we appeared to agree on.

"What does an intervention involve?" I asked as James hopped up to balance on the brick trimming that bordered the street. "Are you intending to tie me up in a room of naked women and make me move on?"

James pulled a face. "I'm having shit-all to do with a torture chamber like that," he said. "If that's what you're hoping for, you can ask someone else."

"You're not being very supportive," I said. "I'm aching. An empty shell. And you won't even do one small thing for me?"

"Can I wear a blindfold?" The street came to an end, and James jumped onto the pavement, hitting the ground only inches from me.

"You can do whatever you would like. No judgement."

"We could try anger relief? Make a Gemma voodoo doll. Stab it, kill it 'til it's dead, burn it?"

"I get the sense you're more upset over this than I am," I said drily. "We broke up on good terms. You do know that, don't you?"

"Only 'cause you're gullible. No one breaks up with their boyfriend because their parents divorce. That's, like, the one time you *don't* wanna be alone."

If that comment had come from anyone else, it might have occurred to me to be offended. But he wasn't being nasty. He was just being James. And James wasn't one for sugar-coating harsh realities.

"I know it was an excuse," I said. "I don't mind, though. Things were fizzling out anyway."

"Then why are you all sulky?"

"I'm *not*. Can't I have a quiet day without a torrent of accusations?"

"Nope," James grinned, quickening his step to reach the creek. I hurried to match his pace along the beaten path, ducking under the low hanging branches of a weeping willow. He looked sideways at me, his face striped with alternating shadow and light. "Life's too short to be quiet. It's a waste of a day."

See, James felt that boys who liked girls had an easy time of things. He couldn't for the life of him ascertain why I didn't spend my time hopping from girl to girl like a bee perusing flowers, taking samples from each.

It made sense to an extent. If James had been interested, he would've had no shortage of girls queuing for his attention. He was one of those unfairly good-looking people. Having inherited the best features of both his parents, he'd burst into life with the universe's most mathematically symmetrical face, an adorable smile, and steel metabolism. As it was, he drew the "small town" card in the lottery of life, suffering from a drought of potential partners as a result.

Then there was me. My appearance wasn't an issue, even if I didn't belong in front of a camera the way James did. My standoffishness was the issue. Gemma had been a rarity; she'd snaked her way into my life so gradually I didn't realise what was happening in time to put my guard up. By the time I thought to erect any barriers, she knew me too well to care.

James, frustrated by my refusal to explore every fish in my vast sea when all he had to work with was an empty fish bowl, had adored her at first. Now, it seemed, he couldn't stand her. James might have been loyal, but he prioritised his loyalty. I'd been at the top of his hierarchy of companions since we were kids, so I was safe. With those unlucky enough to have a lower rank, he could be alarmingly fickle. Apparently Gemma was now on the bottom rung of the ladder.

The creek was growing wider now, the water rushing and crashing over the natural slope of the land in an imitation of white rapids. I stood on my tiptoes and grabbed a handful of leaves from the nearest tree, shredding them while we walked.

"Let's go to the beach soon," James said out of nowhere.

"What for? It's too cold to swim."

And even if it hadn't been too cold, I needed to invest in a pair of swimming trunks long enough to cover the full length of my thighs before we went anywhere near the water.

James shrugged. "We can chill there without swimming, can't we?"

We reached the spot where the creek rushed downhill in a mini waterfall to join the river. Here, you could either follow the path to the footbridge that crossed over—the recommended walking trail—or you could break the law like James and me, walking uphill and parallel to the river to cross the tracks on this side.

The station was on the far end of town, and not serviced often. Not many people wished to visit Rokewood Bend. We were merely a piece of pleasant scenery between more important destinations. Still, it wasn't wise to walk too close to the tracks. The trains along here travelled at high speed, shooting past every half-hour.

James and I were attuned to the sound of an approaching train due to many years of taking this route home. Today, the subtle vibrations on the ground alerted me that one was on its way. We cleared the tracks by several metres, treading along the overgrown grass instead.

"Tomorrow?" James suggested.

"Don't you have football?"

"Nah, it was cancelled."

That explained it. A night off was rare for James. No wonder he wanted to mix things up a little. "You want to go that badly?"

"I wanna go that badly."

"Well in that case," I said, hitching up my school bag, "Let's do it. Just for you."

"You're so generous," James said, placing a hand over his heart and falling to his knees in the grass.

I rolled my eyes and reached out a hand. He grabbed onto it and stayed on the ground, pulling me until I stumbled forwards. "Get *up*, the train's coming," I laughed, clasping onto him with both hands now.

He rose to his feet and I stepped backwards into an uneven patch of earth as I let go of him. Off-balance, I over-corrected, staggering sideways in the direction of the tracks.

At that moment, the train powered by. A sudden rush of air whipped me sideways like an undertow. The carriages flashed past too rapidly to see their contents. A blur of crimson, ochres and browns. The roaring vibrated in my veins, stunning me into stillness. It was barely a few feet from me.

I was far closer than I should have been, but not in any danger, so I wasn't expecting it when James grabbed my wrist and yanked me hard enough to jolt my arm from its socket. I fell backwards, and he caught me around the shoulders.

"*Ow*," I protested, barely able to hear myself over the rattling of metal against metal.

"Jesus Christ, Ash!" James yelled. His fingers dug into my upper arms like a bear trap, hard enough to bruise. I tried to shake him off, but he held me in place, pulling me into his chest.

All at once, the train passed, and we were thrown into silence. James, breathing heavily behind me, relaxed his grip. I wrestled free and swung around.

His eyes were wide with fury. "The hell was that?"

I shook my head, bewildered. I couldn't see why he was so upset. Trains are limited to their tracks, after all. It wasn't likely to swerve unexpectedly and bowl me down. "Settle down," I said. "I'm fine."

He stared at me for a long moment, scanning my face. "Normal people step *backwards* if they're that close to a

train," he said. "I swear you get off on this stuff or something."

We both knew what was upsetting him, even if he
couldn't bring himself to verbalise the thought. James had
been anxious and uneasy regarding my state of mind over
these past couple of years, ever since my attempt. He tended
to scrutinise me for signs that I wanted to harm myself, like
a storm chaser tracking patterns in the darkening clouds.

When I simply shrugged in response, he whipped away
from me and stalked across the tracks, muttering something
about "goddamn self-preservation." I sighed and hurried
after him. He pushed on without looking back until I called
out an apology, at which point he finally relented and hung
back until I reached him. Even still, he spent the remainder
of the walk sulking in silence.

James lived only one street over from me. It was one
of the few perks of moving in with Sue and Dom. Sure, it
was further from school than I was used to, and I'd stayed
with more welcoming families in my time, but the benefit of
living three minutes away from my best friend outweighed
all of the above and then some.

As we turned onto my street, James stole a glance at me.
"Are you okay?"

I laughed. "Honestly, yes. Are *you* okay?"

Of all things, he turned red. Embarrassment seemed like
a strange reaction to the question, but I'd take it over anger.

"Yeah," he said. "Sorry. I just . . ."

He trailed off, searching for the right words. I allowed
him to struggle for a few moments, then bumped my
shoulder against his. "It's good to know you care," I said, only
somewhat teasing.

James crossed his arms tight across his chest, unsmiling.
"Hey, Ash, do you . . . do you want—" He broke off, squinting
into the distance. "What's Elliot doing home already?"

I followed his gaze. Elliot was standing on the porch, watching us approach. I'd forgotten to call him back.

"Hi," I greeted him as James and I grew closer. "Why aren't you at work?"

"I took the afternoon off," Elliot said, hopping over the fence to meet us. "Had to sort something out. Are you free right now?"

I glanced at James, who shrugged, looking disappointed. "Go for it. I'll catch you tomorrow."

"All right," I said. I might have asked him to stay with Elliot and me, but something told me whatever Elliot had planned was out of the ordinary.

Intrigued, I joined my brother. Usually I'd be irritated by him taking additional time off work. He missed enough shifts due to hangovers as it was, and he could hardly afford to worsen his attendance rate. But something about his expression told me he might have a good reason for it today.

"We have to drive," he said, nodding towards his car.

"Where are we going?" I climbed straight into the passenger seat.

"Surprise."

"Is this the part where you take me to a dark alley to hack me into pieces?"

Elliot gave me a crooked smile, biting onto his lip piercing. The smile girls tended to lose their wits over. Sometimes I became jealous of Elliot's gene pool victory. We each possessed Dad's colouring—thick dark hair and blue eyes, although Elliot's were a darker, richer blue than mine. But facially, Elliot was the image of our mother, with high cheekbones, thick lips, and sharp, defined edges. I, on the other hand, resembled Dad. A heart shaped face, larger eyes than Elliot but thinner everything else. The similarities between Dad and me became quite pronounced when my hair was slicked back. Which was largely the reason why I wore it wavy and shaggy.

"All I'm saying is Sue and Dom will notice if I mysteri-
ously disappear," I added.

He scoffed. "Yeah, give them a week and they might
catch on."

Elliot and I had been in foster care for two years. Two
terrible years, but not nearly as terrible as the years preceding
them. In all fairness, it had its pros and cons. It all depended
on the family you ended up with. Elliot and I had worked
our way through quite a few. Too many foster parents gave
up on Elliot's extra-curricular activities and palmed the pair
of us onto someone else.

Our current carers, Sue and Dom, had requested to be
taken off the register about a month before they took us in.
They were too busy living their lives. But Alice called in a
favour and begged them to have us anyway. She'd been at her
wits end trying to find somewhere for us. Thanks to Elliot,
we'd burned bridges with every available family in town
already. There wasn't anyone else who *could* take us.

Sue and Dom minded their own business, as long as we
stayed alive. This suited Elliot fine. And as long as Elliot was
happy, I—well, I was okay, if nothing else.

We pulled over in a street I didn't recognise. I followed
Elliot out of the car, and we stopped outside a small, dark
grey house. Bewildered, I waited for an explanation.

"Okay, so," he said, spreading his arms out in a grand
gesture. "This house behind me is for rent. And I applied for
it."

"Oh." I was taken aback, but pleasantly so. Elliot recently
celebrated his eighteenth birthday, and he wasn't required
by law to stay in foster care anymore. He had a three-year
leeway, until he was twenty-one, to leave, but neither of us
was particularly invested in that idea. He'd been working full
time at the supermarket stocking shelves for a year, saving

everything he could to move out. The plan was for him to apply for guardianship of me first, in order to bring me with him. We had no intention of being separated. "Excellent. It's a lovely house."

"I got accepted."

"Wait, *what*?"

He grinned at the house, folded his arms, and shifted his centre of gravity to one side. "Better get used to the place. You'll be living there soon."

"Elliot!"

"Are you surprised?"

I took a step closer to the house and leaned on the concrete fence. "Am I surprised?" I asked, incredulous. "How could you possibly hide this? You need to apply for the CIA or something."

"I didn't want to get you excited until I knew for sure."

"When does the lease start?"

"Not for two months. But that works out for us anyway."

"Yeah. I guess there's a lot to organise," I said.

"We'll have to speak to Sue and Dom."

"Do they know you applied?"

"Nope."

"Oh."

"It's not like they can stop me," Elliot said. "I can do what I want."

"They can stop me though."

"They won't." Elliot was so confident in his reply that I couldn't help but feel at ease. "Alice knows I want guardianship. She's gonna help me with it. Don't even stress."

"Well, I'm not going to be the one bringing it up with Sue," I said.

"Yeah, yeah, I'll take this one. Don't worry your pretty little head, *mon poussin*."

Elliot, who remembered a lot more about our mum

than I did, liked to use the French pet names he'd grown up hearing on me. I'd never developed that habit myself—only the French would be sappy enough to think calling people things like 'my chick' was adorable, and I wanted nothing to do with it. "Call me that again and I might *stay* with Sue and Dom, *branleur*," I said.

Elliot grinned. "Wash your fucking mouth out with soap, *mon poussin*."

"Suck my dick," I shot back without hesitation. At the beginning of the year, when Gemma had first met Elliot, she'd told me I acted like a different person with him. I think she was mostly shocked at some of the things that came out of my mouth around him. Hearing her say that made me conscious of it, but it didn't affect my behaviour. Despite not being a child anymore, I suppose a part of me still wished to convince my big brother that I was his equal.

"*Ta mère est une pute*," Elliot said.

I rolled my eyes. "We have the same mother."

He gave up at this, clearly in too good a mood to invest himself in an argument. We climbed back in the car, wearing matching smiles, and I sent our cousin, Bea, a text.

We have a house!

She responded within the minute.

Where is it? When do you move in? Do you have a spare bed for when I visit?

I shared the message with Elliot, and he dictated a response to me with contagious excitement.

Finally, things were falling into place. *Finally.*

21

THREE

Louise
September 2018

Elliot buzzed around the table by the window, laughing with the couple sitting there. Another guaranteed generous tip, courtesy of Bruno's resident charmer.

If our waiters pocketed our own tips I bet Elliot's talent would've gotten him some resentment. Lucky for him, and even luckier for the rest of us, we pooled them, so his efforts won him countless brownie points night after night. It was probably why Joe'd promoted him to full-time almost straight away. The kid did me proud. Even though it wasn't me smashing the tips every night, he *was* my best friend, so it looked good on me by extension.

Even though he was able to turn on the charisma like a light switch around the customers, he hadn't spoken to me or Saras all night. Saras, who was bustling around preparing drinks, didn't seem to notice anything weird. I guessed all the little quirks Elliot had when he was bothered by something were only obvious to me. I'd known him long enough to catch onto them now. The way he was sucking on his small silver lip ring, and fiddling with his earlobe plugs, and running his fingers through the shortened hair on the sides of his head all screamed *something's wrong*. Like a language only Elliot and I could speak.

"Hey, Louise, I need to count the register," Saras said, shoving me aside with her hip. "Out the way."

"Yes, your majesty, right away, your majesty."

"You're such a cheeky shit," Saras smiled, grabbing out a handful of fifties while I stood guard. For what, exactly, it was hard to say; if a customer did decide to rob the register, I wasn't about to fight them. Not for a five-pounds-an-hour job.

"Ten," I said in response. "Six. Fifteen. Two-hundred-and-twenty-five."

Saras slammed down the half-counted wad of notes. "Do you have a death wish or something?"

I raised my eyebrows and set about sorting through the receipts.

"That's what I thought. Watch it or I'll make *you* count it."

"No, thank you," I said sweetly.

Saras went to school with me, and she'd started at Bruno's about a year ago, a while after I did. She was a regular Michelle Obama, taking everything she did seriously, even a cash-in-hand, casual secondary school job. I respected that. If someone tried to rob the register with *her* in charge of it, she'd defend it to the death. Which was probably one of the reasons Saras was a supervisor and I wasn't. Eh. *Que sera, sera.*

I leaned across the counter to tap Elliot on the shoulder

as he passed. "Hey you. Cheer up. You look like you have two days left to live. It's dragging down the mood."

Elliot pushed past me to dump the pile of plates in the kitchen, then poked his head out. "And the mood is usually so bright and upbeat," he said with more than a hint of sarcasm. "I *do* apologise."

Like I said, the *sass* on that guy. He was the president of Sass Island, situated in Smartass Bay.

"Lovebirds," Saras said, "you're cute and all, but if you make me lose count one more time I'm telling Joe it didn't add up and blaming it on Louise."

Elliot didn't even crack a smile before he disappeared back into the kitchen. Saras finally cottoned on that he was acting weird, and she lowered the bundle of notes. "He okay?"

"*Right*? He's acting weird, isn't he?"

"Slightly more so than usual," Saras said. "Want to go find out if everything's all good?"

"Actually," I said, lowering my voice, "I think I already know what the problem is. He was over at mine this afternoon, and—"

I had Saras's full attention now, the register count forgotten. "What did you two do?"

"What?" I asked. "Nothing. But remember when you—"

"*Tell me* you didn't have sex with Elliot, Louise."

Oh, *ew*. Because *that* was likely. It'd be practically incest. "Would you shut the hell up and let me finish?" I asked, balling up a receipt and throwing it at her face.

Elliot chose that moment to come back out of the kitchen, and I went silent. Saras nodded towards him. "Hey, Elliot, what's this I hear about you and Louise catching up without me? Where was my invite?"

She was only teasing, but he went totally white. "Louise, don't," he said, slowing to a stop. "Don't. Okay?"

Saras and I exchanged a glance as he stalked off to greet a new table. "Tell me," she whispered.

She didn't have to beg. "Remember that Facebook video you tagged me in? The 'Elliot Taylor' one?"

"Yeah?"

"He—okay, actually, he's watching us, so—*no, Saras, don't look at him*—I'll tell you later."

"Now."

"He finishes at nine. I'll tell you then."

"I can't wait 'til nine."

But she could, and she did.

I wondered if Elliot would hang around after close, trying to guilt us into giving him a lift home like usual. Instead, he was out the door at five past nine, shoving his headphones into his ears and melting into the night with only a hurried goodbye.

Saras and I waited until we were well out of earshot of the kitchen staff, then I summed up the afternoon. She listened, twirling her braid around a finger. Ooh, a hair twirl. Now I knew she was invested.

"So, you think this guy is trying to find *him*?" she asked, leaning her elbows on the counter while I wiped it down.

"Well if he isn't, then why's Elliot acting so weird? You should've seen his face when he saw the video."

"Okay, so, he has a brother?" Saras asked.

"*Had.* The guy killed himself."

"So, Elliot had a brother who killed himself, and he never mentioned it."

"Maybe?" I shrugged. "I mean, I'm not *totally* certain it's our Elliot."

"True. I mean, he did say it wasn't him. Why would he lie?"

She was right. It was far-fetched. Elliot might be private, but there was reserved, and then there was "witness protection program." People didn't hide dead brothers from their friends . . . right? Pretty sure that was a scientific fact.

"Well, that's what I was wondering."

Saras gathered the day's folders. "Well, if he *does* have a dead brother he's been hiding, I bet he'd be worried if there's someone trying to expose him."

I grabbed the cleaning gear and followed her to Joe's empty office. Joe was the manager and founder of Bruno's. Why he'd called it "Bruno's" and not "Joe's" was freaking beyond me. "Well he wasn't exactly little Mary sunshine tonight," I said.

"My point," Saras said, dropping the pile of folders on Joe's keyboard with a crash of collapsing plastic. "God. The poor guy. I wonder if that had anything to do with him moving here?"

"Who knows," I said as I locked up the cleaning cabinet. The door stuck open, and I gave it a kick, probably harder than I needed to.

We left the office together, silent until we'd passed the kitchen. "I think we should leave it alone," Saras said when we were at a safe clearance. "If it is him, and he wants to tell us, he will."

I thought about it. Like, on the one hand, she had a point. But I was curious. Who wouldn't be? I mean, this wasn't like someone trying to hide a speeding ticket, or an embarrassing childhood nickname. Hiding a dead family member was *weird*. "I guess. I'll try."

"Louise . . ." Saras sighed.

Okay, why did that sound like a warning? I said I'd try, didn't I?

Fine, *fine*, I'd drop it. I guessed it really wasn't any of my business.

Besides. It wasn't even my Elliot.
Surely.

I made it to Saturday before cracking. I, for one, was totally proud of myself for lasting that long. If only I could put this much discipline into my exercise routine, I'd be running marathons by Christmas.

I'd invited myself over to Elliot's. Bea worked on Saturday mornings, and I knew he preferred visitors to fill up the empty house. He wasn't into isolation. I wasn't sure when it'd become a tradition for me and Elliot to spend most of the weekend hogging each other's couches and talking about nothing, but I'd be lying if I said I minded.

Bea came through the front door around four in the evening, carrying three shopping bags in her hands, with a loaf of bread wedged under her armpit. I rushed to grab the loaf before she crushed it, but it was too late. She blew a curly lock of hair out of her reddened face. "Thanks, hon," she said, shaking her head at the state of the bread. "I didn't think that through."

Elliot and I followed her into the kitchen, where Elliot grabbed a bag and started putting away the food. "I prefer my bread squished, anyway," he said. "Makes sandwiches more interesting."

Bea grinned at me. "He speaks bullshit, but he knows the exact bullshit I want to hear."

I tried to help put the shopping away, but Bea swatted at me. "You, sit. Are you staying for dinner? I'm doing garlic pasta. Elliot, do you think you could dice me some tomatoes while you're over there, actually?"

Between Bea and Abuela, I should've had enough role models in my life to teach me the ins and outs of domestic bliss. Unfortunately, to Abuela's endless disappointment,

I was the kind of person who took store bought cookies to fundraisers after spending all night painstakingly baking chocolate chip bricks. She used to ask me how I planned on getting a boyfriend if I couldn't cook for him. At least, she did right up until I told her I planned on my husband being a stay-at-home dad, which almost gave her a coronary.

Elliot washed and chopped the tomatoes while Bea darted around the kitchen. Her peep-toe heels clacked on the kitchen floor, and her full, cherry-patterned skirt swished around like she was swing dancing. I could never decide if she reminded me more of Adele or Kat Von D. Today, there was even a bit of a Lana Del Rey vibe going on. But maybe that was because she'd redone her lip fillers recently.

"I need you two to teach me to cook," I said while I watched.

Bea snorted. "Sweet, no offense, but you're terrible at it."

"You're never letting me live the cookies down, are you?"

"No. No, I am not. You're going to be living off pizza and toast for the rest of your life."

"Not likely," I said. "I'm going to hire a personal chef with the millions I make from my very successful career."

Elliot looked up from his tomatoes and pointed the knife at me. "Ambition. That's what I like to see. I'm relying on your vague, unspecified future empire to take off, so I can get more tips by name-dropping you to customers."

"More like so you can take half of it when you guys marry," Bea said as she rummaged through an overhead cupboard.

Elliot shared an amused glance with me. Bea was convinced that we were entangled in a secret, passionate love affair. May I point out that this couldn't be further from the truth? The closest we'd come to a torrid romance was a solitary kiss at last year's Christmas party, and I'd been tipsy on the drinks I'd stolen from various aunts and uncles, so it totally didn't count. Like I said. Incest. Elliot was pretty, in a Nick Robinson in *The Fifth Wave* kind of way, but . . . Okay, call me old fashioned, but, self-declared feminist or not, I liked my guys square jawed, with a smouldering gaze, preferably in a leather jacket. The Zayn Malik, Colton Haynes, Trey Songz type. Don't blame me, blame evolution.

In the lounge room, I heard my phone go off. I hadn't realised it wasn't with me.

I went in search and found it sitting on the couch. Next to Elliot's.

And Elliot was in the other room.

After a few seconds' hesitation, I darted across the room and entered his password into his phone. I knew I shouldn't be doing it, and I felt the obligatory twinge of guilt, but I was way too curious not to. Besides, I wasn't going into his private messages or anything. I only wanted to see one thing. His YouTube history.

The moment I opened it, a sudden clanging in the kitchen sent me into a panic, and I exited the app and threw the phone back on the couch so hard it bounced. And . . . touchdown landed. Safe.

In the kitchen, Bea and Elliot laughed about something. Grabbing my own phone, I went back in to join them.

Elliot grinned when he saw me. The grin of someone who didn't have any worries. Who wasn't hiding anything. "Hey. Come here, I'll show you how to crush the garlic. I figure if we start now, your empire could be a restaurant chain in forty years."

It took every scrap of self-control I had not to admit what I'd seen on his phone. But somehow I got a hold of myself and went to his side. I acted casual, but while Elliot taught me to boil pasta, and all through dinner, and when Elliot flicked water at me as we did the dishes, I could only think of one thing.

The clip had been sitting right at the top of his "recently viewed" YouTube history.

Once I made it home, I found myself in my room, staring at my computer like a zombie. After an extended argument with myself, I decided watching the video one more time couldn't hurt.

It left me with a hollow feeling in my stomach. The guy in the clip looked miserable. He spent more time staring at the ground than making eye contact with the camera, and his voice was shaking for half of it.

It might not be my Elliot, I told myself doubtfully. *Why would he lie?*

In fact, that was bothering me more than anything. The thought that Elliot could look me in the eye and lie to me. If I never contacted this guy, I'd never know if Elliot was telling the truth after all. He might be totally innocent, and I'd spend the rest of my life secretly suspecting that he had this sordid, hidden past.

Well, when I thought of it like that, really, I owed it to our friendship to find out. Otherwise the suspicion was going to eat away at me. It would come between us sooner or later. I needed to nip it in the bud.

This was totally justifiable. I was actually being a *good* friend.

And so I convinced myself to write a private message. The link to the clip had been shared on Facebook by some Instagram-famous girl called Ellie Joy—doing her weekly humanitarian favour for cosmic-karma-brownie points, I guessed—so that was obviously a dead end. But as far as I could tell the YouTube version was the original, so I figured I'd message this guy through that. To be honest, it was the first time I'd realised people even *could* message through

YouTube. What a world of limitless possibilities we lived in.

LOU CASTELLANO:

Hi. You don't know me, but I was tagged in your video. I think I might know the Elliot you're looking for. Can we talk?

I didn't expect him to reply. I mean, the video had five hundred thousand views. He probably got people contacting him every day claiming to know an Elliot Taylor. His parents could've been more creative with his name, after all. So I was caught off guard when, fifteen minutes later, a small chiming sound signalled a response.

SEEKING ELLIOT:

Yeah. Can you call me?

There was a number listed beneath the message. I stared at it, chewing my lip.

I shouldn't do it.

I definitely shouldn't do it.

Maybe I just wouldn't respond. He'd never know who I was.

I'd gotten his hopes up now, though.

Who cared? He'd get these messages all the time.

No, I was going to leave it. I had to trust Elliot. Saras was right.

But . . .

The guy picked up on the second ring. "Hello?"

He was out of breath, and his voice sounded thin and strained. I got the feeling he was attempting to conceal how desperate he was.

"Hi," I said. "I . . . don't know your name."

"Oh. You're a girl."

And why did he seem so surprised? Male was not the default. Was he aware we lived in the twenty-first century? I bit down the lecture, figuring it probably wasn't the best way to make a first impression. "Yup?" I said instead, dipping into some of Elliot's sass.

"Sorry, I don't know why I said that," he said with a nervous laugh. "I don't . . . I just. Okay. Hi. I'm James."

"Hey. I'm Louise. I think you should try to breathe, James," I said, smiling.

"Yeah. I'm sorry. Sorry."

"It's fine. So, about Elliot . . ."

"*Yeah.*"

"Like I said, I think he's the same one. I mean, he won't admit it, but he saw your video and got really weird, so . . ."

"Do you have a picture of him?"

How had I not thought of that? I turned my phone on loudspeaker to flip through the gallery. "I think so," I said. "He doesn't have Facebook, but I'd have some group pictures." Actually, there was that hilarious one from the café, when Nikki pretended to wipe something off his forehead, so she could smear chocolate all over him. That wouldn't be too far back.

"He never had Facebook," James said. "It's half of why it's been so damn hard to find him."

"Who doesn't have Facebook, right?" I asked, still browsing my gallery. Note: Take less selfies. Or, at least, delete bad selfies once good selfie has been selected.

"I *know.*" He put on a mocking voice. "'It doesn't replace face-to-face interaction,' blah blah blah."

"'You guys might *think* it makes you closer, but knowing what someone had for dinner doesn't make you friends'," I quoted.

"Yeah!" James exclaimed. "That is *exactly* something he'd say."

I paused. Interesting. "He has short, dark hair, a lip piercing, and plugs in his earlobes, he can speak French—"

"He didn't have plugs when I knew him, but he had the lip piercing. And his mum was French."

"He said she died when he was twelve."

"Yeah. She did. Holy shit," James said. "You found him. You actually *found* him."

"I didn't find him. More stumbled across him," I said, returning the phone to my ear. "Elliot started at my work last year."

"He left town after Ash's funeral."

"The thing is, he never mentioned a brother."

James hesitated. "Ouch."

"Sorry."

"It's not your fault. So, where do you actually live?"

Where did *Elliot* live, he meant. "Conway."

"Conway? That's where his cousin lives."

"Bea?"

"Yeah, Bea."

"He lives with her."

"*What*?" He sounded outraged. "That *bitch*. The amount of times I've texted her asking if she knows where he is!"

I almost told him off for dissing Bea, then hesitated. If Bea was ignoring this guy, she must have a reason. Maybe I shouldn't be getting into an argument with him. I didn't know anything about him, after all. "Kind of sounds like Elliot doesn't want to talk to you."

"Right, kinda seems that way, huh?" James said wryly.

"Where do you live?"

"Rokewood Bend. You wouldn't know it. It'd fit on a postage stamp. It's on the coast."

"On the *south* coast? You're on the other end of bloody England!"

"Yeah. I can drive it in a day, though, I reckon. Can I have his address?"

"Um . . ." I trailed off. If there was one thing stranger

danger taught me, it was to not give out people's home addresses to random people on the internet. "Actually, I'll have to talk to him about it first. I can't just tell you where he lives."

James took a deep breath. "If he's lying to you about being the same Elliot, what makes you reckon he's gonna let you give me his address?"

"Well, I'm sorry, but I can't give it to you."

He was silent for so long that I checked the phone to make sure we were still connected. Then he spoke again in a thin voice. "Okay. Fair enough. But can you please message me once you've asked him? Even if he says no?"

I didn't see what harm it could do. "Yup. Sure. I think he'll definitely say no, though."

We disconnected, and I fell back onto my bed. The implications of the conversation were sinking in. Not only had Elliot lied to me several times over the last week, he'd hidden a huge part of his past from me. That was a lie of omission at best. The realisation made me feel empty and betrayed.

I'd have to get Elliot to admit everything to me himself. And not in his own time, like Saras suggested. He'd had over a year to tell the truth. If I left him to his own devices, he'd keep lying to me until the day he was too trapped to continue. Screw Sass Island. He was the king of Goddamn Liar Island.

I wasn't sure whether to feel offended that Elliot hadn't trusted me enough to tell me he'd had a brother, or concerned about what possible reason he could have to keep something like that from everyone.

What else was Elliot hiding?

FOUR

Ash
March 2017

It was a miserable day for the beach. When the weather was calm, the ocean was a crystal-clear blue-green, rolling with gentle waves. But as the wind picked up so did the water, and today it swelled into full, black hills that crashed against the nearby rocks, leaving a trail of froth in their wake.

James ambled ahead of me, unperturbed by the general greyness. He knelt to pick up a handful of sand and let the grains fly away with the wind, waiting until I reached his side. "I probably should've worn jeans," he said.

He only wore the compulsory polo shirt—our school's unsuccessful attempt at convincing everyone it was as prestigious as the private schools over in the city were—over black denim shorts that stopped above his knees. While jeans were my bottom of choice, James opted to bare his calves as often as he possibly could. He was exceptionally optimistic about the projected temperature when he dressed each morning. "You'll freeze," I said, removing my school jumper and passing it to him.

He waved a hand. "It's chill."

"Don't be stupid. It's far too cold."

"You need it."

"I'm not the one only wearing shorts."

That was James's fatal flaw. He considered himself a traditional heroic protagonist. Consequently, he resisted any and all of my attempts to treat him like a damsel, even if the distress was valid.

He accepted the jumper without further protest and pulled it on while we headed onto the rocky cliff-face bordering the second half of the beach. The jumper actually fit him, interestingly enough. Conversely, it hung off me like a potato sack. I wasn't slim the way James was, sleek-limbed and smooth-skinned. I was simply thin.

I hadn't always been this much smaller than James. As children, James latched onto the idea of us looking like twins due to our similar builds and dark, straight hair, ignoring the myriad of obvious physical differences.

Despite receiving a fifty-fifty mixed bag of genes, James identified with the Filipino side of his heritage. His dad took offense to this, but I could see James's point. He grew up speaking the language with his family, eating the family recipes his mum cooked, and visiting the Philippines to see relatives all the time. The greatest chance he'd had to associate with his German side was a goat-herder onesie he'd worn as a baby and seeing his grandparents every few years when they flew over for Christmas.

I'd always been able to relate to James on the whole "foreign parents" thing. As children, being bilingual had made us feel special. Maybe even, if we were honest, it made us feel a little better than everyone else. Although we'd never admit that out loud.

We stumbled our way over the rocks as they steadily became larger and taller, until we reached the base of a flat ledge that stood approximately ten feet above the ground. James stopped and looked up at it, determined. Oh, fantastic. He wanted us to scale it. What fun.

"Here," he said, stooping down on one knee.

"James, this is so sudden," I said, placing a hand over my chest.

With an eye roll, he clasped his hands together. "Come on."

I stepped into the makeshift foothold and he hoisted me over the ledge. Once steady, I hung over the edge and pulled James up to join me with a grunt. While he dusted pebbles off his knees, I shuffled back to the edge and sat with my legs dangling mid-air. My shoes scraped against the rock face, dislodging and scattering a thin layer of stone. I grinned to myself and tipped my head back.

James climbed to his feet to get a better view of the beach and stood beside me, his hair whipping around his forehead. "What are you happy about?" he asked, raising his voice to make himself heard. If the wind had been forceful on the sand, it was a borderline hurricane up here.

"Elliot applied for a house."

"And?"

I bumped my head against his thigh, breaking into a smile. "He got it."

James let out a whoop of excitement and fell to the ground, pulling me into a bear hug. "*Ash!* What the hell? That's amazing. How have you shut up about this all day?"

He rolled backwards, still holding me, and I landed on top of him, laughing. "Watch out—we'll fall," I protested, although I didn't truly care.

"Where is it? When do you move in?"

"About ten minutes from school, but in the other direction. And the lease starts in two months. So, yeah. If Elliot gets guardianship . . ."

"He will," James said, shuffling sideways to escape my pin.

My smile faltered. There was a good chance he would get guardianship, but still a sense of niggling doubt remained. A pervasive fear that he wouldn't, and I'd be left behind. I banished the thought. If it happened I'd deal with it then. For once, I reserved the right to be optimistic.

James sat up straight and pulled a face like he'd kissed a lime. "This means we won't be able to walk home together anymore."

"I think we'll survive."

"Speak for yourself. How am I gonna visit at night now?"

In truth, it would likely be good for him to have me further from his reach. Between his sporting and homework commitments, he had to work tirelessly to squeeze me in. Still, like water soaking into sand, whenever there was a miniscule crevice of spare time in his life, he filled it with me. And if there was no space, James shuffled and rearranged and made room. Failure was not on James's extensive to-do list.

"Get your license," I said, shifting onto my back while still lying down and sending my legs over the edge once more.

"You know I've still got four months."

"Stay the night then." My side pressed against James, our calves brushing together every few moments. "We can go to school in the mornings."

I swung my legs to get momentum and hauled myself back into a sitting position to find James giving me a funny look. "Sleepovers?" he asked. "What are we, ten?"

The mood between us bordered on uncomfortable. That alone was enough to make me pause. Awkward silences weren't a regular occurrence, and discomfort wasn't in our friendship's lexicon. I had the sudden certainty I was missing something.

As soon as he realised I was studying him, James directed his attention back out to sea. "Wouldn't you find it kinda weird?"

"Why would it be?"

The wind howled now, and the waves whipped into a grey and white frenzy. A sudden image of a cork bobbing on the waves before being hurled into the rocks flashed into my mind. The cork would survive it. But I wondered if a person would.

Then I wondered what those kind of thoughts said about me.

When I turned back to James with the intention of changing the subject, he was staring at me.

"I dunno," he said in a tone that told me he knew exactly what he meant.

I hesitated, unsure if I wanted to press the subject. The awkwardness that had settled over us shifted again, into a silence that was different—something new. Something undefinable. Intangible but undeniably there.

Our legs met in the middle again.

My senses pricked up.

There was something about his expression. I'd seen it on Gemma's face a few times. But never on James's.

We were pressed too closely together.

I'd held eye contact with him for several dangerous seconds now.

The waves stopped crashing, and the wind paused mid-wail, and the earth gave up turning.

I leapt to my feet so hastily I almost tripped. "Is that PE

assignment due tomorrow?" I asked, taking a step back.

James gaped at me as though I'd started speaking in tongues. "I'm not in your class."

"Right. Yes. Uh, it's due tomorrow." I neglected to mention it was only worth five percent of my grade, so I didn't actually intend to bother with it. "We should go."

"Sure." Without hesitation James lowered himself down the side of the rock until he was hanging on by the tips of his fingers, then dropped the remaining distance to the ground.

I got down on my knees and peeked over the edge. It hadn't seemed too high while scaling it, but now the distance to the ground made my legs weak.

"It's cool," James said. "It's not that far."

I gingerly inched down, then let go of the ledge. I hit the ground hard, my legs giving out. James darted forward to steady me. The moment his hand touched my shoulder, I yanked back as though I'd been electrocuted.

He blinked. "You okay?"

"Fine."

We started making our way back home. I made a point of hanging back by pretending to have trouble navigating the rocks, so James wouldn't notice my cheeks flushing.

I needed to collect myself and figure out what on God's green earth that moment on the rock was. Because, unless I was very much mistaken, James had wanted to kiss me.

FIVE

JAMES
September 2018

ACCORDING TO MY EMAILS, I'd only gotten one YouTube message that afternoon. Things were slowing down.

ADAM MARSDEN:
 I know a guy with dark hair and blue eyes called Elliot Taylor. He was dating my sister for a while over here in Kinsale. Maybe the same guy?

Nope. Sorry, Adam Marsden. Not him.

It was just another one of a billion messages. I'd been getting damn tired of receiving them, but I'd still contacted every one of them. Like, in case some sort of miracle happened, and I found him. The Real Elliot Taylor.

And a few hours ago, I found out miracles could happen after all. Who knew, right? I could finally start deleting the messages without needing to follow them up. With a grim smile, I mentally shot Adam Maslow a silent "thanks for trying," and sent his message straight into oblivion. Then I closed my laptop, crouched down in front of my desk and slid open the bottom drawer to fish out the shoe box I kept there.

The shoe box was only ever supposed to be a safe place to keep a couple of important things. Ash's affirmation pages, a few hard copy photos of us from primary school before Facebook was a thing, and an apology letter a teacher made him write to me once as kids, after he bit me during a play fight *(I am sory and I did not hurt you on perpos but I wish you did not tell the techer so I am verry mad at you)*. For an English genius, Ash's spelling skills had sucked when he was seven. Basically, the box stored mostly stuff Mum had hoarded on my behalf, and it didn't mean much to me back when he was alive, but I'd save it first in a house fire these days.

Then, when Callan changed everything that night a few months ago, shit got scrambled real quick. I needed a way to organise my thoughts. I'd decided to write what he told me in a notebook, so I wouldn't forget. Memories can be like a game of telephone sometimes, and the last thing I wanted was to mix up that kind of information down the track. And then the notebook had joined the shoe box.

My scribbling had gone from a single entry on page one, to so detailed I needed to buy a second book. I used it to keep everything straight, and I hoped no one ever found the thing. It was basically the Complete Guide to Finding Elliot Taylor. If anyone saw it, they'd think I'd lost the plot.

Maybe I had, hey? Off-the-wall stalker right here.

But it was useful, I thought as I pulled it out and flipped through the pages. One page listed the usernames of people who'd contacted me with the wrong Elliot. Another listed all the places he was likely to be—Conway had been crossed off that list back when Bea first told me she didn't know where he was. No way was I ever forgiving her for that—and another had a timeline. Everything I knew about what'd happened before, during, and after Ash's death. This timeline had been scribbled out and redone over and over again. Because it just. Didn't. Add. Up.

With a pissed-off frown, I found the tab for phone numbers. The numbers his friends had given me, and the numbers people online had tossed up. Ninety-eight percent of them had been dead ends. Only two hadn't. The first was when Elliot contacted Callan, and Callan was nice enough to give me the number. Or maybe he was sick of me harassing him. Maybe he was even a bit scared of what I might do to him if he didn't give me the damn number.

Either way, I got it. And Elliot had picked up, and I thought I'd *finally* be able to get some answers. Except he'd hung up on me straight away, and the phone number never worked again. And if *that* doesn't sound suspicious, I don't know what does. Who the hell is that terrified to talk to their dead brother's best friend? Guys with something to hide, that's who.

The other golden number, which I now highlighted, and circled, and underlined, and circled again, was this Louise girl's number. I'd had so many people tell me they knew an Elliot Taylor, especially once people started sharing my YouTube video around Facebook, that I hadn't expected her to be any help. But holy hell, had I been wrong. It was definitely my Elliot. But as awesome as it was to narrow down where he was—Bea. Conway. Thank God. I'd been worried he'd moved to the fucking Sahara for a while there—this was the tense part. If I pushed it too far, or Louise chickened out, I'd lose everything.

I didn't know where in Conway Bea lived, and it's not

like it was a small city. She wouldn't accept me on Facebook, she'd long stopped taking my calls, nothing came up when I Googled her—I'd tried as soon as I got off the phone with Louise—and the only people I knew of that would have anything to do with her were Louise, Elliot, and . . . and Ash. I needed Louise bad. She was my last hope, here.

Someone knocked on my door, and I slammed the notebook closed and shoved it in the shoebox. "Gimme a sec," I called out. I tried to put the shoebox back in the drawer quietly, but I was rushing, so it made a hell of a racket. Oh, smooth. Not suspicious at all.

I was still slumped crossed-legged on the floor when Mum peeked in. "Hi, *anak*," she said.

I went on the defensive straight up. That was her opening when she wanted to have a "conversation" with me. "What'd I do?"

She came in and closed the door behind her. Great, so it was gonna be one of those conversations she didn't want Dad to hear. Ramp the "fuck that" levels up to about an eight out of ten.

"I was at the shops, and I ran into Auntie Yvonne," she started. By Auntie Yvonne, she meant Wyatt's mother, an old friend of the family. Also, not an aunt. If I was blood related to every person Mum referred to as my 'auntie' we'd have to rent out a football stadium for family reunions.

"Yeah?"

"She told me Wyatt's applied to uni already."

Well *joy*. I could see where this was going. I played dumb. "Uh, yeah, I guess he would've."

"You didn't mention applying for uni."

Aaaannnd there it was. "Well, I haven't yet," I said.

The only sign that she disapproved of this at all was that single raised eyebrow. "James . . ."

"Mum . . ." I mimicked her warning tone.

"You know you could work as a bin man, and I'd be happy, as long as it was what you wanted. But you've always wanted uni. Talk to me."

I shuffled so I was facing my desk. "There's nothing to talk about. I'm still thinking about things. I'm not sure what I want."

"Last time I checked, you wanted to be a teacher."

I looked at the ground and shrugged.

"I never hear you talking about Wyatt, or Rick, or any of the boys anymore," she pressed.

"Not much to say about them."

"You never see them anymore. You don't even leave the *house*, James. I'm worried about you. It's been too long."

I could've told her to get off my case, but it probably would've earned me a whack over the side of the head. Instead, I tried to remember what I used to do, and why she was so convinced it was different now. To prove she was getting all twisted up over nothing.

Well, I used to do homework. A lot.

(Jesus Christ, you were a class A nerd.)

But I didn't spend much time on homework anymore, because really, who the hell cared? Why did it even matter if I got an A or a C, I figured? I'd rather spend my evenings having fun. Enjoying life.

Alright, what else? Football and athletics. But I'd quit them at the end of last year. It was taking up too much of my time. Way too much commitment.

Japanese lessons? Quit 'em. Not like I was ever gonna visit Japan, so why bother?

And I'd go see Ash. Which, obviously, wasn't on my calendar these days.

Basically, Mum was reading into things too much. She only thought I didn't do anything now 'cause I used to do so much. I'd just started to prioritise myself and what made me happy. That was all.

And I was about to tell her so, when it hit me smack in the face.

I hadn't replaced those activities with anything else.

Huh. No, seriously, *nothing* else.

I'd hacked away at my commitments like overgrown tree branches, one by one, to free up my days so I could . . . so I could . . . well, so I had more time to . . . what?

To *what?*

(*Come on, James. What are you doing with aallll that free time?*)

Mostly, I spent my time thinking about Ash.

No, that wasn't true, either.

I spent it thinking about Elliot.

And asking people about Elliot.

And brainstorming new ways to *find* Elliot.

Mum waited for my reply.

Finally, I settled on, "What's for dinner?"

She sighed. "Pancit."

The moment hung there, teetering. She could've pressed the point. Could've forced me to finish a tough conversation. One I wasn't super sure I was ready for yet.

But in the end, she decided to leave me alone without the third-degree.

Which was nice.

SIX

ASH
March 2017

MY FIRST THOUGHT WHEN I woke the next morning was that Elliot hadn't come home from his friend's the night before.

I had the unfortunate tendency of jolting awake if someone breathed too loudly. As a result, if the door had opened during the night, I would know, no matter how silent Elliot aimed to be. Sure enough, his unmade bed was empty. I tried his phone, but it went straight to voicemail.

No.

No, oh no, oh no.

Where was he? Why hadn't he come home?

He hadn't texted to say he'd sleep out. He always texted.

Oh God, *why wouldn't he pick up his phone?*

My hands trembled, and I forced myself to take several

deep breaths. It was fine. He'd simply gotten too drunk and fallen asleep. Logically, I knew it was the probable explanation. But logic couldn't stop me from imagining horrific scenarios.

Elliot lying in a hospital bed getting his stomach pumped.

Elliot lifeless in the passenger's seat of a wrecked car.

Elliot unconscious following a drunken brawl.

It was hard enough to force morbid images to the sidelines of my mind on a normal day. In times of crisis, those thoughts took centre stage like an understudy desperate for a solo.

I attempted to contact Dave, one of his best friends. He didn't pick up. Ryan, another friend, did answer, but he had stayed home all night. He suggested I try calling Dave.

With a racing heart, I sat in the middle of my bedroom floor, too weak to stand, and called Callan, the third member of their group.

To my extensive relief, he found Elliot asleep on his front porch with Dave. It was only after I made Callan vow to look after Elliot and bring him home safely that I calmed down enough to dress for school. If I hurried, I could still get my attendance ticked off for second period. Overall, it was a successful morning.

I was the only one in the house when I finally did leave. Sue and Dom were likely to be blissfully unaware Elliot had gone out at all, let alone that he hadn't come back. They both worked odd hours, and often didn't return until late in the evening. Elliot loved the freedom of flying beneath our carer's radars. It made me uneasy, though.

After signing in at the office, with a quick greeting towards the receptionist—one of the only school staff members who actually liked me—I warily made my way to Mr Patricks's maths class. I'd forgotten it was Thursday, and

I'd have to face my least favourite teacher that morning. I paused outside the door to peek in. Mr. Patricks had his back to me. He'd recently shaved off his hair, leaving behind a bald, dark brown canvas. At least I could be certain he didn't have eyes hiding in the back of his head, watching me. Back when he'd sported an afro, I could never be quite sure.

James sat towards the front of the room, staring straight through the whiteboard with half-closed eyes. When he noticed me in the doorway, he lit up, awake once more.

A naïve part of me had hoped Mr. Patricks would continue the lesson. Though he kept talking about trinomials without even a break in his thought train, his voice grew closer. He was following me while he spoke. I slumped in my seat and dug through my bag, pretending I couldn't see him even as he stopped before me.

"Glad we have the pleasure of your company today, Ashton," Mr. Patricks said, tapping the edge of his ruler on the desk in front of me, before putting down a blank worksheet.

I raised my eyes to look at him. "Family emergency," I said dully.

"You have an awful lot of those."

"My life's a soap opera sometimes." The words, fuelled by the frustration of that morning, came out before I could rein them in. A couple of Gemma's friends, Natasha and Kristy, tittered.

Behind them, so did Wyatt.

My cheeks burned, and I sank in my seat. Wyatt had been my first big crush, back when I was about twelve or so. I'd liked him in the hopeful, obsessive, naïve way you only feel that very first time your heart ever chooses someone. Of course, I kept it to myself. I was torn between hoping it wasn't real—that I wasn't *really* the only one I knew with feelings for a boy, just as everyone else started noticing girls—and praying that a miracle would occur, and he'd tell me he liked me too.

He didn't. In fact, he was one of the first friends to blend themselves into the background when I ended up in hospital. My heart healed eventually, and I'd had multiple crushes since him—on guys *and* girls. But even now I found it difficult to see him without that residual pang of rejection. Like an afterimage that never properly fades.

Mr. Patricks glanced at them and then back to me. I struggled not to let my expression twist into a resentful glare. Didn't he have better things to do than pick on me? For example, educating the students who actually wanted to be here? "They don't think you're funny, Ashton," he said. "They're laughing at you, not with you."

There was nothing I could say without either being falsely sweet or starting a fight, neither of which options I had any inclination to do. Instead, I averted my eyes. My head began to spin, and the class felt suddenly distant. Foggy. *Just fast-forward*, I thought. *He'll leave you alone soon. You aren't here anymore so you can't hear him.*

"You should wipe that smirk off your face." He'd at least lowered his voice somewhat now, careful not to let his lecture distract the other students. Unfortunately, it was too late for that. They were hyenas watching the lion feast. "You're a smart kid, but you never put in any *effort*, Ashton."

Smart? What was he basing that on? A few essay awards I won in year six and seven? My primary school report card? I doubted he knew about either.

And I resented being called kid.

Mr. Patricks droned on, "—showed up to school more than twice a week you might actually be able to achieve something . . ."

That was a vast exaggeration. I missed one lesson a week at the most.

Don't retaliate, the voice in my head urged. *He'll stop soon. Don't provoke him.*

Across the room, James watched us, his face cloudy. My attention focussed on him. As long I could see him, I felt somewhat centred.

"Are you even listening to me? Or is it in one ear, out the other?"

James rose and quietly made his way to the whiteboard, where he seized an eraser. Keeping his eye on Mr. Patricks, he slunk back to his desk. He'd moved so casually no one even noticed him. They were too busy watching me.

"Ashton? *Ashton.*"

I tore my gaze away from James and chewed on my lip, annoyed and embarrassed. Most of the class was watching us now, despite Mr. Patricks's attempts at keeping quiet. I was quite certain the ones who weren't watching were at least listening in.

Mr. Patricks wasn't going to ease his questioning until I responded. I had stage fright, though. I wanted to be left alone. Why couldn't he just let me be invisible? Why did he always have to draw everyone's attention to me? Why did he like everybody except me?

I imagined curling up into an impenetrable ball, small and solid and unremarkable.

A sudden movement at the front of the classroom, behind Mr. Patricks's back, preceded a flurry of tumbling and crashing as the neat pile of books and electronic equipment on the teacher's desk went flying onto the floor. Mr. Patricks's laptop, a sleek MacBook that travelled everywhere he did, teetered on the edge of the desk precariously for a moment, before toppling over and hitting the carpeted floor with a cringe-inducing crunch.

The class was completely silent. Mr. Patricks stared at the mess on the floor. A brief, hysterical fancy that he was trying to figure out a way to blame it on me flashed across my mind.

He snapped out of his trance and stormed over to his desk. On the floor lay a lone whiteboard eraser. From its position it was impossible to tell if it was involved in the chaos, or if it'd simply fallen from the board. But I had an inkling.

"Did anyone see what happened?" Mr. Patricks asked the class, bewildered. Someone must have noticed James launch the eraser at the desk, but no one offered any explanation. Mr. Patricks was a well-liked teacher, but he wasn't likely to win a popularity contest involving James.

James affected innocence with the rest of the class, a convincing display of confusion and empathy on his face, safe in the knowledge that no one was going to sacrifice him.

One of the girls hurried to the front of the classroom to help Mr. Patricks to gather his books. They discovered—to Mr. Patricks's dismay—that the laptop no longer turned on. I found it hard to force false sympathy, so I opted to turn my attention to the desk.

When the bell rang, James made a beeline for me. "What a tool," he said under his breath, brushing his fingers against my elbow so briefly it could've been unintentional.

I glanced at his hand as it returned to his side and pictured us on the rock the day before. His leg bumping against mine. "You didn't have to break his laptop."

He shrugged, unconcerned. "I was aiming for a distraction. If he wants to keep his shit in a dangerous pile that's his business, not mine."

We stopped, facing each other, and the students parted around us as they moved to their various classes. I smiled grudgingly. "Thanks anyway."

"He needs to learn not to mess with you. He's losing a beloved item every time he does it from now on 'til he puts two and two together."

"That seems somewhat drastic."

"Just classical conditioning. No one's allowed to bother you but me."

"I can handle him next time," I said. "But thank you."

James grinned. "You couldn't stand up for yourself if an ant picked a fight. You are *the* most timid person I've ever met."

Well, I didn't agree with that. Not exactly.

Back in the day, I'd been anything but timid. In fact, out of James and I, I used to be the one who talked incessantly. The one who dominated group conversations and made jokes at my own expense. Then, when I was fourteen, and things with Dad were at their worst, I lost most of that spark.

As I thought about it, I supposed I'd always viewed this as a temporary withdrawal. A coping mechanism, to handle my life falling apart around me. But that had been two years ago, and I was still quiet. I still tried to avoid conflict and conversations with anyone who wasn't James or Elliot. I still had no friends other than James.

Did this define me now?

I could still be that boisterous, confident person from the start of secondary school, couldn't I?

"I can be assertive," I insisted.

His laugh was closer to a scoff than anything. "Yeah, 'kay, Ash."

I folded my arms and looked at him for a long time. I *could* be. Just because I chose not to didn't mean I lacked the ability. His words, even if they were meant to be teasing, offended me. James's smile faded, becoming uncertain as my expression hardened.

"I'll see you tonight," I said, starting down the hallway.

I counted to five before allowing myself to look back. James hovered where I'd left him, staring ahead with a knitted brow. He caught me looking at him, and I turned away before he asked me any silent questions.

SEVEN

Ash
March 2017

A SCOWL WAS PAINTED onto James's face throughout the walk home. He seemed reluctant to talk about the reason for its presence, however, despite my extensive prodding. When we arrived at the park and discovered it abandoned—surprising, given the mild weather that day—we wandered onto the playground to talk, and he finally gave into my persistent questioning.

"I'm pissed off at Chemistry," he said as he climbed onto the main platform of the jungle gym, letting his legs hang down the slide. "Turns out I only got a B for the practical report last week." He hooked his wrists behind the platform bars to keep himself in place.

I stepped onto the base of the slide and gingerly walked my way up. "I would be over the moon with a B," I said. "I don't remember the last time I saw one of those."

Well, I could. It was around the time I exchanged homework for housework, studying for cooking, and perfect attendance for surviving the morning. Anybody who considered it an unwise exchange had surely never experienced a threat to their basic needs. Maslow understood, though. If he had still been alive, he would have made an exceptional teacher.

"Yeah, but you don't try," James said. "No offense."

"None taken. Your parents know you tried, at least. They shouldn't be too irritated."

"It's not about my parents." He extended his arms to allow his body to slip. "I wanna do well for me."

"You *do* do well." I'd reached the top now and I clasped onto the bar, my hand narrowly missing James's. "Excuse me," I said, ducking around him to reach the platform. It was a narrow squeeze, but he shifted over to let me pass.

He flipped in place to face me, resting on his knees at the slide's entrance, still gripping the pole for balance. "Can't you let me vent without being all encouraging?"

I shuffled forwards and sat inches from him. "Fine. You're pathetic. An idiot. You'll never get anywhere. A B? You don't spell academic with a *B*, James. Or achievement, or aptitude, or—"

"Thanks, Ash," James said drily. "That's super helpful."

I shoved him gently, and he made a spectacle of losing his grip on the bar, slipping backwards. I grabbed onto his hands and held him suspended.

"Let me go," he moaned, arching back. "I don't want to live anymore."

"All right."

He travelled down the remainder of the slide with a pitiful look, and I followed suit, bumping against him softly at the end.

"You weren't supposed to actually let me go," he said,

turning away from me.

I nudged his back with my foot. "And now you've learned not to trust me. Now that's sorted . . ." Jumping over him, I landed on the bark chips and strolled away.

Faster than a mouse's heartbeat, he shot past me onto the grass and vaulted forwards, landing in a handstand. I tipped my head on the side as I approached him in amusement, attempting to meet his eyes. "You have too much energy," I said, as he tumbled forwards in a heap.

He splayed out like a starfish, bringing one leg up at the knee. "I wanna run 'til I forget about science."

I lay down beside him, close enough that our arms touched. James's energy seeped away all at once, and when he dropped his leg down straight it ended up pressed against mine. I wasn't sure if it was an accident.

He stared at the sky with his lips parted, his outside arm thrown carelessly across his forehead. The position left his fingers curled only inches from me. Experimentally, I let my head roll to one side, making contact with his hand.

We remained frozen until James's fingers shifted, displacing a few locks of my hair. It could have been an absentminded movement. If not for the silence, heavy with tension, I would have assumed it was nothing more.

My thoughts kept ending up in the same place, no matter which path they started down. Our almost-kiss the day before. I'd been replaying it in my mind periodically, trying to determine if I was jumping to conclusions. Now I was certain I hadn't been. There was something beneath the surface here, and it excited me.

Not because I had feelings for James, to clarify. Rather, it was a mixture of a few things, not all of them flattering. Admittedly, the idea that James could desire me was a welcome boost to my rock-bottom self-esteem, and a selfish part of me was tempted to encourage it. Even if James was likely so desperate he'd find a stick figure attractive if he thought it might return those feelings. Not to mention, I'd never experienced this form of attention from a guy before. I wanted to explore it, to find out what it was like to hold a guy's hand, kiss his lips, run my fingers through his hair.

I wasn't considering the implications that kissing James could have for our friendship. Foresight never had been my forte.

The air was so still we could almost have been indoors. It was one of those ethereal afternoons. Like I'd jumped out of my own life and gotten a sample of someone else's. The night was cold, but it was a soft cold. The kind that almost has a taste of its own. It seeped into every breath, filling me up right to the bottom of my lungs.

Lazy in this inexplicable happiness, I stretched out on the grass. My free hand fell, and I hooked my thumb beneath the waistband of my jeans. James's stare landed on the small section of skin the movement exposed. I lifted my chin pointedly, so he couldn't miss that I'd caught him.

Kiss me, I willed him. *Go on. I'll let you.*

At that moment my phone vibrated. It was Callan. I sat up as I answered, so quickly my head became light. "Hello?"

"Hey, Ash." He was yelling, his voice high-pitched. Oh, excellent. They were drunk. Again. "You . . . you need to come fetch—" He broke off, laughing with someone. "Get your brother. He's locked in the bathroom. He's *gone.*"

James studied me with an air of concern, and I beckoned him with a tilt of my head while I stood up. "Yes, all right. Fine. I'll be there in ten."

James sighed. "Elliot?"

"Of course. He's at Callan's still."

"At least he's nearby."

We arrived at Callan's to discover a house party well underway, despite the early hour. I hesitated at the porch, self-conscious, but James ploughed through the open front door. I hurried on his trail.

Inside, we were assaulted by a blast of deafening dubstep and suffocated by cigarette smoke. A group of college students stepped out of our way as we entered, but they didn't acknowledge us beyond that courtesy. On the couches a number of year thirteens, at least two of whom had been on various sports teams with James, called out to him. He nodded back at them but remained alongside me.

James glided through the house with the easy grace of someone who could assume everyone he met would instantly adore him. I stuck close behind him, allowing his presence to shield me.

We checked the bathroom first, but it was empty. James allowed me a few seconds to utter some choice words regarding my brother, then we launched into our search. Thankfully we found Elliot within minutes, cheerleading a game of centurion between Dave and Callan.

He reached out to me as we drew closer, beckoning me to sit beside him. "*Ash*," he slurred, raising his voice over the music. "I almost won. But I threw up. And they wouldn't let me keep going."

"It's the rules," Dave said. A beep sounded from his phone, and he and Callan tipped back a shot of beer simultaneously.

"Time to go?" I asked Elliot, without much hope.

"Fuck no. Most people aren't even here yet."

James shrugged at me. I folded my arms. "Callan said you were throwing up badly."

Elliot nodded, unconcerned. "Nothing I can't handle."

"Come on, Elliot."

His attention wandered to the countdown now, apparently finished with the conversation. "If you want to drink, join us. If not, shoo. Drink!" he directed the last part at Dave and Callan, who raised their shot glasses in sync as the timer sounded. Eighty-eight minutes. Eighty-eight shots and counting. We were lucky attendees at the match of the year, no doubt.

James and I gave up, turning to leave. I was relieved to be on our way, to be honest. The atrocious music, the stench of beer and smoke and the overbearing heat of too many bodies invoked a state of tension. We'd made it as far as the hallway, the front door within arm's reach, when one of James's football friends, Rick, grasped onto James to talk, thwarting my escape mission.

I hovered, hoping James would read my body language and cut the conversation short. They had commenced the topic of mid-term heats when I realised we were unlikely to escape in the foreseeable future. Initially, I took out my phone and pretended to text. As though I was too busy speaking to my many other friends to notice I was left out of James and Rick's conversation. That worked for approximately ten seconds, then the familiar anxiety crept up on me. *You look awkward,* it told me. *It's obvious you're following James around like an imprinted duckling. Give him some space. Stop being so dependent. It's embarrassing.*

Once upon a time, James's friends had been my friends. Years ago, before I'd tried to kill myself. It turns out people find it somewhat difficult to be around you when they're monitoring each word they utter to prevent exacerbating your symptoms. I suppose it didn't help that I hadn't presented as the chirpiest canary in the cage. So *our* friends gradually became James's friends, and my many friends became friend—in the singular. A fact that I was fine with when I wasn't stuck standing around them, pretending it didn't matter to me that I no longer mattered to them.

Remaining resolutely collected, I took a deep breath, excused myself, and headed straight down the hallway to

Callan's room. It was off-limits to guests, but I was certain that didn't apply to me. I'd known him since I was three, after all.

The second I closed the door my heart rate calmed. I sat on the edge of the bed, relieved to be in my own company, the noise and heat of the rest of the house muffled by the bedroom walls that formed my fortress.

Once I collected myself, the shame set in. *Timid.* James was right. He always was. For all the time I spent envying James's social success, I did a pathetic performance of attempting to raise myself back to his level. Who couldn't even spend ten minutes at a house party?

Why couldn't Callan have left me out of this? I'd been enjoying myself at the park. Suddenly, the memory of what James and I had been doing when Callan called sprang into my mind. What had that been? Where might we have ended up had my phone stayed silent? *Probably nowhere*, I realised. *You'd never be brave enough.*

A knock caused me to startle, wrenching me out of my thoughts. James peeked around the edge of the door, then entered, closing it behind him. "Hey. You okay?"

I stared at him without speaking. Out of nowhere, I was overcome with a wild urge to demonstrate that I could be confident and self-assured too. Before I could weigh up the potential consequences, I got to my feet.

James hesitated, one corner of his mouth lifting. "What?" he asked. I approached him. His chest rose and fell as he took in a nervous breath. "What's the matter?"

I dragged it out, standing in front of him without a word. James was on edge. He ran his tongue over his lips, breaking eye contact.

Pulsing with adrenaline, I let the moment hang for a second longer and then stepped forward, stopping immediately before James. He was stunned now, frozen into place. I scanned his face in an effort to gauge his emotions.

I wanted to do this, to reassure myself that I could still be fearless. But I couldn't bring myself to close the last few inches of space between us without a nudge.

Then James sucked in a breath through parted lips. And at that moment, I understood. If I did this, if I kissed him, it would throw the trajectory of our friendship entirely off course. Towards what, I didn't know. But I was certain the new direction would be irreversible.

I shouldn't.

But the mixture of worry and hope on James's face would have been obvious even to someone who hadn't known him for ten years. He wanted me to kiss him. Badly.

And I wanted him to want it.

All at once, he stepped forward and lifted his chin, and I cupped my hands around the back of his head, pulling him in to crash his lips against mine. I kissed him hard. He tasted salty and sweet, a mixture of skin and lemonade.

When my tongue brushed against his, he made an involuntary noise. It sent a pang straight into my lower stomach.

Suddenly, I forgot this was my best friend I was making out with. All I could think about was the fact that the mouth pressed against mine belonged to a guy. Giving into the heat of things, I forced James backwards until we crashed into the wardrobe.

James's knees buckled, and he squeezed his eyes closed. "I—I, um . . ."

I had no idea what he was trying to spit out. I pulled away to give him a chance to finish the thought, but it appeared he didn't have any idea either.

"Is this okay?" I asked. He responded with a faint nod, and I kissed him again.

When we finally tore apart, his eyes betrayed a hint of confusion. "I . . ." he tried, "I didn't think you—"

My hands wandered down to his waist, then his hips, and he broke off mid-sentence, threading his fingers through my hair instead.

I didn't want to talk, or think this through, or give myself any reason to doubt myself. I knew how bewildered James must have been, and what he would likely be taking from this, but, shamefully, I was too lost to mind.

My head was floating now, dizzy and light, like the oxygen in my veins had transformed to helium. I dug my fingers into the skin of his lower back, slipping under his shirt. His skin was softer than I'd expected. He pulled away, pausing me. "Someone could walk in on us," he whispered, steering me away from the wardrobe.

By that point I couldn't have cared less if the walls in the house lost their opacity and the whole party saw us. Both of us ignoring James's warning, we collapsed on Callan's bed in a tangle of arms and legs. I grabbed James's shirt in handfuls, lifting it to expose his flat stomach. My own stomach swooped and my fists tightened, and I leaned forward to kiss his skin.

Then, out of nowhere, he tensed and sat upright, toppling me backwards to the floor. "*Stop*," he said. "Don't. I'm not having sex with you."

I let out a startled, breathless laugh. "I never asked you to?"

He pulled his shirt down with shaking hands. "That wasn't funny."

"Who's laughing?" I asked, resting my elbows on the edge of the bed.

He shuffled away from me. His face was flushed, his demeanour flustered. "What was that? Explain that to me."

"Well, pretty sure it was us making out."

"You know what I mean," he snapped. "Why'd you kiss me?"

I thought carefully, exploring my feelings for the most honest answer. "Because I could."

It sounded harsher out loud than it had in my head. Perhaps that wasn't such a bad thing, however. At least it wouldn't lead James into thinking the kiss was something it wasn't.

He studied me in disbelief, but I kept my composure. When I didn't offer any further explanation, he pressed his lips in a thin line. "Was that . . . just you proving you're assertive?"

I didn't know the answer to that yet. So I didn't provide one.

His lip curled, and he left without another word, slamming the door.

Alone, I ran my hands through my hair to tame it again. He'd always been one to overreact. The positive thing about James was that he forgave as quickly as he riled up. Instead of going after him, I focussed on organising my own thoughts. Why I'd done what I'd done.

Well, wasn't that the question of the century.

To prove myself, I supposed.

To see what it was like, yes.

To feel attractive? Oh yes.

Hmm. This was what they called a rebound, wasn't it?

In that case, it wasn't the kindest thing I'd ever done. Playing around with James for my own gain.

Now that I thought about it, it was utterly cruel.

I dwelled in the guilt briefly, but it was banished by a startled laugh as the reality of what'd happened came to light.

I'd *kissed* a guy.

And he'd kissed me back.

When I left the room, James was nowhere to be found. I decided I'd wait until school the next day to speak to him in order to give him the chance to cool down.

I just wasn't certain if I was eager to hear what he had to say or wary of it.

EIGHT

Louise
September 2018

IT TOOK ME A few days to get up the courage to bring James up to Elliot. I waited until we were alone in my room, me sitting at my desk chipping away at a chemistry practical and Elliot reading a book he'd stolen from my shelf. *The Langoliers.* I'd never read the thing, and I could not be less interested in what a Langolier was. Pretty sure it was the name of a group of crime-fighters. Unless I was thinking of a Musketeer. Either way, he'd nabbed the same book the last three visits. One of these days I'd just give it to him.

I snuck a peek at him. He was chewing on his lip ring with a serious expression, totally focussed on the book. He didn't even notice me look.

"I think you should talk to James," I said, keeping my tone casual.

Elliot dropped the book to his chest and set his jaw. "Louise, I told you I don't know him. It's a different Elliot, okay?"

Interesting that he knew who I was referring to when I said James. Considering James had never mentioned his own name in the video. *Caught you.* "Yes, you do."

Elliot didn't seem to have realised his mistake. "No, I don't."

Eurgh, there was something so dirty about being lied to when I knew the truth. Looking at Elliot's honest face, and going by his firm tone, I would've believed him if I didn't know better. It made me wonder how many times he'd lied to my face before now. I'd thought I could read him better than that. I'd thought we trusted each other.

"Look. I know it's you," I said, trying to keep my tone unaccusing. For whatever reason, he clearly didn't feel like he could talk to me. He needed to know he could. Somehow, I didn't think self-righteously demanding information would help my cause there. "So let's skip this part. I want to make sure you're okay."

Elliot picked the book back up and pursed his lips. Well, he wasn't denying it anymore. I should be able to coax him into a proper answer. I reminded myself that even if he was a lying shit, he was a lying shit with a dead brother. And if a friend's got a dead brother, you make sure you're there for them. That's what Abuela always said. Well, something vaguely along those lines, anyway.

"I can't even imagine how hard it would've been," I said. "It was bad enough when Abuelo died. And he was . . . you know. Old."

I wasn't handling this with as much grace as I'd aimed for. The corner of Elliot's mouth turned up, though he still refused to look at me. Good to know my lack of tact was so amusing.

S. Gonzales

"Sorry," I said finally, turning back to my desk. After a minute or so of more silence I glanced at him. He was on his side now, facing the wall.

I bit my lip, suddenly guilty. I'd upset him. But I wasn't much good with comforting people. Especially not when it was my fault they needed comforting. "Don't be mad at me," I said. "Please. I didn't mean to pry or anything. It's just . . . you've never told any of us. So I thought maybe you could use someone to talk about it with."

He ignored me. Okay, so clearly not. Feeling all tangled up, I went back to my homework. I had the report almost completed by the time Elliot sat up, wiped his eyes with the back of his hand, and silently left for work.

I waited until he'd been gone for a few minutes then sent a quick message to James.

LOU CASTELLANO:
So, he really doesn't want to talk. I'm sorry. I don't know what else I can do. Do you think you could tell me what you do know, though? I'm not in a position to find out anything if I barely understand what's going on.

Two hours later, he replied.

SEEKING ELLIOT:
Where do I even start? Ash was two years younger than Elliot. Ash was sixteen when he died. He and Elliot were pretty close, actually. They were in foster care because their mum died, and their dad was off the wall.

All I know is everything was going well. Elliot was about to leave care and rent a house, and Ash was gonna live with him. Then Elliot stopped speaking to Ash and moved without him, and Ash never knew why. Then Ash jumped off a bridge and Elliot left town. Bam. Like that. I saw him at Ash's funeral and he didn't even cry.

Wouldn't talk to me, just walked away from me.

Two years younger than Elliot. Elliot's brother would've been my age.

That was so weird to think of. Like, would we have gotten along? Maybe the three of us would've formed a little group. Or would he have just been Elliot's brother, in the background like Nikki's sister was to me? Maybe he would've been all chiselled and leather-jacket wearing, and I would've developed a crush on him and made a thousand excuses to go to Elliot's, so I could run into him.

Guess I'd never know now.

It seemed so unfair that I'd never get the chance to get to know him. Could you even really mourn the loss of a friendship that was only a potential at most? Wasn't that kind of like missing a limb you'd never had?

Yup. But I felt it either way. The way you feel it when you hear of a small child's death, and you think of all the people they would've affected in their lives, and how those people will never get the privilege of knowing them.

I wanted to know him, though. So I started the way any good detective of the twenty-first century starts researching-slash-stalking someone. Facebook.

I spent about half an hour trailing down random rabbit holes. Turns out I ran into the same problem James had mentioned. Taylor was way too common as a last name. Every man and his car was called Ash Taylor, apparently. But a quick scan through their profiles told me they were all well and truly alive.

That or they had a very devoted friend posting statuses about football scores and breakfast food on their behalf.

When I finally found him, it was only after I had the common sense to search for variations on "Ash." Ashley got me nowhere. Ditto for Asher. But Ashton struck gold.

I knew it was him as soon as I saw the posts on his profile. The page was locked down like Alcatraz; the links to friends and pictures were deactivated. All I could stalk was the profile picture and wall posts. But both were all I needed.

His wall was basically a memorial, with people posting personal messages and marking anniversaries. Mostly the anniversary of his death. The fourteenth of July, for the record. I scanned for a post by a James, but I didn't find one. I guessed that didn't mean much, though.

The profile picture was the second giveaway. A child, maybe four or so, in the arms of a curvy, wavy-haired woman who kind of looked like Nigella Lawson. They were giving each other identical, crinkle-faced smiles. I could see Elliot's genes in the kid instantly, from the light blue eyes to the thick dark hair to the heart shaped chin. This was Elliot's brother. For *sure*. I'd put any amount of money on it. Which meant that was Elliot's mother. It was the first time I'd seen a picture of her. She shared Elliot's full-faced, all-in grin. I bet if I could've been there when the photo was taken, she would've been giving out the high pitched, rapid-fire giggles that always got me laughing when they came from Elliot.

I wondered if Elliot thought about her every day. I wondered if he thought of his little brother.

How did you lose most of your family *without* thinking about it? I tried to imagine Abuela passing away and shuddered. Life would never feel "normal" again after something like that. No way.

The next thing I attempted was a Google search. This was less fruitful than the Facebook search. Ash must not have been an organised activity kinda guy. The only thing I could find was a brief mention in an old school newsletter from years back, when Ash and I had both been in year six. Going by what James and Elliot told me, it would've been about a year after his mother died. He'd placed first in some school-wide essay contest and had been entered in the state-wide heat at a secondary school level. So Ash had been a little nerd.

I could've stayed there all night, trawling for information about Ash, and, in turn, Elliot. But Abuela chose that moment to drag me downstairs for dinner. And you really couldn't put dinner as a low priority with Abuela. Not unless you wanted to hear comments about your weight and appetite for the next three weeks. So, reluctantly, I walked away.

This wasn't the last of it, I decided. I'd find out what was going on. What Elliot's life had been like before he came here. Now I had James, who didn't seem *too* much like a stalker, it'd be easy to put the pieces together.

Right?

NINE

Ash
March 2017

It wasn't until I passed Elliot's room and peeked around the cracked open door that I realised he wasn't awake yet. He was sprawled unconscious on the floor, tangled in the blankets that still half-lay on his bed, with a puddle of vomit next to his head.

I crouched next to him to check his breathing, then, satisfied, I wet a towel in the bathroom and wiped his chin. He moaned a little but didn't open his eyes. He was still fully dressed from the night before, his clothes drenched in the scent of alcohol and bonfire smoke. With difficulty I managed to strip him down to his underwear and haul him onto the bed, tucking the blankets underneath his clammy feet.

Elliot tried to speak while I cleaned the carpet. I couldn't interpret the mumbling though, so I tuned him out. It was at least twenty minutes before I was happy the carpet would remain stain free.

At this rate, the school would start contacting Sue and Dom whenever I missed class. Our school was quite lax about attendance. Unless you were one of the real losers, the ones who only came to smoke weed behind the gym one afternoon a week or to flirt with girls in the cafeteria, they gave you space. They didn't treat me like one of those guys. Not yet. But, bit by bit, I'd noticed things heading in that direction. It was in the knowing look in their eyes when I made a mistake. An "as usual" sigh, instead of an "are you okay?" questioning frown. The more they lost confidence in me, the less I believed I could redeem myself. So I stopped bothering.

Ashton Taylor: a walking self-fulfilling prophecy, a true product of general disdain.

Elliot's eyes were half open now. He looked terrible. "Ash?"

"Hmm?"

"Can you get me some water, please?"

I mentally crossed off any hopes of getting to school before third period and stalked down the hall. Sue sat at the kitchen table, sipping coffee and flicking through her iPad. I wasn't expecting her to still be here.

No matter how many pep-talks I gave myself about relaxing in my own home, the awkward silences made it impossible. It wasn't as though I'd never gotten along with a foster parent, but they'd historically had to approach me first. While at home, my every instinct told me to duck, whisper, tiptoe. To be the cobweb in the corner of the ceiling, not the blowfly begging to be exterminated. If I was going to have any sort of relationship with Sue and Dom, I desperately needed them to knock down the wall. Or at least give it a hard kick. *Anything*. But by all appearances, they didn't have time for that nonsense.

We locked eyes when I entered the room, and I wondered if she was going to tell me off for skipping class. Instead she sighed, disappointment ringing through the tension in the air, and opted to watch me silently.

I hated being watched. *Hated* it. It put me on edge, like being hunted, an attack imminent. I directed my attention to my task, allowing the running tap water to drown out the silence.

What was she thinking? What did she want me to do? Or not do? Should I not be in the kitchen? Should I be thanking her for the water?

On some level I knew Sue would find my worries ridiculous. But on another, more persistent level, I couldn't shake the constant fear that I was misstepping. After fourteen years of right morphing into wrong according to someone else's whim, it wasn't something I *could* easily shake. I'd been trained to second-guess. A perfect, nervous little puppet.

Her gaze stung my back as I left the kitchen. Once I was out of sight, my muscles relaxed. Safety in invisibility.

Elliot was unconscious again by the time I returned to his room. I considered leaving him to sleep, but my conscience riled up at the thought. With a sigh I gave him a gentle shake to rouse him. He spent a few disoriented seconds examining the room with bewilderment. Then his eyes focused on me, and he blinked into alertness. I handed him the water and was pleased that at least half of it made it down his throat. The rest soaked the comforter and his bare chest, causing him to wince from the cold.

"Thanks," he said, slumping.

"It's fine. I'll see you in a few hours, okay?"

"Don't go yet." He grabbed onto my arm as I tried to rise. "Stay for a second."

Grudgingly, I sat back on the bed. "Where did you end up last night?"

He narrowed his eyes and concentrated. "We were at Kaine's . . . but I think we went to Jenna's at some point. I remember her dog. I don't know, to be honest. It was a good night, though."

"It sounds like it. Do you need me to call you in sick today or can you manage?"

"I'll go in. I just need something to eat and I'll be fine."

I looked at him flatly. "Honestly. If you don't call in and you fall asleep they'll be furious."

"Trust me, *mon râleur*. You need to have more faith in me."

"Well, give me a reason to."

Elliot poked his tongue out at me, and I held up my middle finger in response, simultaneously blowing him a kiss as I stood.

I left the house without looking at Sue and all but ran to school. Halfway into third period I finally signed in at the front office. Instead of heading to class, I stole into the bathroom and texted James to meet me.

Hardly two minutes later the door swung open and James walked in. "You're lucky I had Ms. J today," he said. "She didn't give a shit. Doubt she'd even notice if I never went back."

"So, don't," I grinned.

On the outside, my performance of nonchalance was satisfactory. In truth, however, I was filled to the brim with the strangest mixture of anticipation, wariness, and excitement. I couldn't pinpoint exactly what it meant. But I did know if I didn't stay on top of it, I was in danger of spilling over.

I was still trying to come to terms with the fact that I'd actually kissed a guy. I'd really *done* it. I'd never come close to an opportunity to do it before.

Guys were, as a general rule, too dangerous in my opinion. With a girl you worried about misinterpreting her signals. With a guy, you were terrified of misinterpreting his entire sexual orientation. Both had their risks, but it was like comparing a school raffle to a national lottery. One has significantly better odds, and failure costs less.

Fine, so that was a generalisation. Chances were I'd flirted with a girl or two who didn't like guys in my time. But honestly, girls weren't as threatening in that respect. Get a queer girl's sexuality wrong, and at worst she'd correct you. Accidentally come onto the wrong straight guy, and you risked getting knocked out. Like the worst thing in the world you could do to a guy is like him.

So had I only kissed James because he was a safe bet?

If so, what did that say about me?

"Why are you just showing up now?" James tried to invoke a disapproving face, but the underlying fondness ruined the effect. Studying him, I noticed he appeared far more carefully assembled than he usually did. His hair was perfectly tousled, and he'd rolled the sleeves of his jumper up to his elbows, rather than haphazardly shoving them up like usual. Even his socks, peeking out between the tight cuffs of his jeans and his black Vans, matched. Another rarity for James.

I forced one of my own sleeves up to the elbow. "I had better things to do."

"Elliot came home, then?"

"At some point. I couldn't be too mad at him, though. I mean, I could've probably tried harder to bring him home the first time."

I meant for the words to steer the direction of the conversation. Looking at James, it appeared it'd had the desired effect. He was fidgeting, rolling the hem of his jumper between his fingers and darting his eyes around. It was a familiar tell. It meant his mind had turned into a tornado, his thoughts caught in the whirlwind. I knew if I let him be, he would stew on the issue, turn it into something ten times bigger than it was, then explode from the stress of it all within the week. Better to force it from him now.

"What's bothering you?" I asked, studying his face.

Something flashed in his expression. Guarded suspicion. A hint of hope, replaced by something resembling anger. "Why did you kiss me?"

I sat on the edge of the bathroom counter, crossing my legs at the ankle, pleased at his abruptness. But, simultaneously, I was cautious. So I put a guard up, keeping my tone light. "You looked like you wanted to be kissed."

His fingers were at it again on his shirt. "Mkay."

I couldn't prevent myself from breaking into a smile. "Because I wanted to. Is that what you're waiting to hear?"

"I'm confused." He folded his arms across his chest like he was trying to keep himself glued together. "Why would you wanna do that?"

Because I didn't want to be timid and afraid. Because I'd never kissed a guy before, even though I'd thought about it on a thousand occasions. Because it made me feel special, to know that he wanted to kiss me back.

All perfectly valid, if selfish, reasons, as far as I was concerned.

But I doubted James would agree. So I opted for a vaguer response. "Why do people usually want to kiss each other?"

"No. Don't bullshit me; you don't like guys."

Honestly, from the look on his face, you would've thought the possibility terrified him. "Don't I?" I asked, the picture of innocence.

"You just broke up with Gemma, for God's sake. You

were with her for five *months*."

"So?"

"What are you doing?" He slumped against the cubicle frame.

"I'm not doing anything."

"Is this you acting out?"

Now that hurt me. It must've shown in my expression for a brief second before I rearranged my features, because James softened at once.

"If you want to ask something," I said, "ask. I swear I'll tell the truth."

He hesitated, and we sat in silence. Then he spoke. "Okay. So, you're saying you like guys?"

"I haven't said much of anything yet."

"*Ash*."

I shrugged. "I haven't."

He opened his mouth to argue further, then caught himself. He took a deep breath and sat up straight, humouring me. "Fine. Then, do you like guys?"

My heart pounded. I chose my words carefully. "Not all of them."

"Do you like me?"

"You're my best friend."

He swallowed, his eyes growing darker. "Do you . . . have feelings for me?"

My inner monster urged me to take my time answering, to evaluate James's reaction, but I couldn't. It would be too cruel. "No. I don't."

James couldn't conceal his emotions like me. Though he fought to stay expressionless, the slump of his shoulders and the tilt of his head betrayed him. He was disappointed.

This surprised me. Honestly, I'd expected him to be confused or angry with me for messing with him, with our friendship. But hurt?

"Do you like me?" I asked with dawning wariness.

It was the first time the possibility had occurred to me. I knew he was attracted to me, but he was a teenage boy, for goodness' sake. More testosterone coursed through his veins than blood. Wanting to kiss someone did not automatically indicate feelings. Right?

"No," he said, a little too loudly.

I relaxed. Thank the lord. It was one thing to mess around with him if it was purely physical. But if he liked me, my actions yesterday would've been on a different plain of callousness altogether. Not to mention how awkward it could have made things. "Well, what's the problem?"

"I never said there was a problem."

I hopped off the sink, impassive. "Excellent."

I began to walk out of the bathroom, expecting James to be at my heels. When he called out after me, however, I turned to find that he hadn't moved an inch. I raised a questioning eyebrow.

He approached me silkily, like he was gliding rather than walking. Then, in one swift movement, he cupped his hands around my neck and pushed me against the tiled wall, meeting my lips with his.

I grunted in surprise, caught off-guard. As fast as he'd began, he pulled back, a satisfied glint in his eye. "Anyway," he said. "I was kinda in the middle of class so I'm gonna have to leave you."

Dumbfounded, I almost laughed. "Right."

"See you later."

All at once he was gone, and I was left touching my lips, wondering exactly what I'd gotten myself into here.

TEN

Ash
March 2017

When Mum died half a lifetime ago, Dad played "Ding Dong the Witch is Dead" on the stereo approximately five times a night for a week.

After I tried to kill myself four years later, Elliot blamed Dad. Then Dad tried to kill him.

Dad argues that he didn't mean to hurt him so badly. I personally think if you take something that far, you mean it, even if you don't realise you did.

Seeing Elliot lying in that hospital bed, broken and battered and unconscious from a cocktail of painkillers infuriated me. So much that I told everything. All of the family's secrets, blabbed out to a psychologist like they were pleasant childhood memories, not dangerous confessions that were never supposed to leave my lips. I wasn't scared, then. As far as I was concerned at that stage, I was going to kill myself as soon as I got the chance anyway, so if Dad killed me for revealing everything then he was saving me work.

But Dad didn't do a thing. He never got the chance to. In fact, I didn't see Dad again for a long time.

I didn't miss him the way I would have expected to. He was my dad, after all; weren't you supposed to want your family members around despite all their faults? When it was just Elliot and me, though, the deflating relief that accompanied Dad's absence far outweighed any nostalgia I held for his good days. The psychologist used to try to get me to talk about Dad. Mum as well. Apparently avoidance isn't healthy. As far as I was concerned, though, if thinking about my parents resulted in me curled up in a ball trying not to scream, that wasn't healthy either. So wherever I could help it, I forced them out of my words and my thoughts.

On the nights when Elliot went out with his friends, which was more often than not lately, the reality of our situation would hit me. He was all I had. If Elliot ever left, my family would be reduced to population: one.

The day after James kissed me in the bathroom, Elliot seemed to have no intention of going out, to my delight. The two of us sought refuge in his bedroom, safe from the awkward looks we'd receive from Sue and Dom in the lounge room.

Elliot hunched over his desk, working on some scenery sketch he didn't want me to look at, so I entertained myself by flicking through my phone.

"You doing anything tonight?" Elliot asked. He didn't take his eyes off the paper before him.

"Not really."

"I don't mind if you want to bail and see James or something."

Hearing James's name sent a pang through my lower stomach, and the memory of kissing him the day before flashed through my mind. It had been happening all day; every time I caught his eye without preparing myself, there it was. "Nah, I'm good."

He swivelled around on his chair and peeked at my phone. "Why do you even have Facebook? It's so much better to actually *see* your friends."

"Yes, well, at least when I talk to my friends, they remember it the next day," I said without looking up.

"*Touché.*"

Down the hall Sue and Dom clattered around in the kitchen. Dinner time. Elliot turned back to his drawing. His fingers went directly to fiddle with his lip ring. "Are you eating tonight for a change?"

"Um, no. I had a big lunch." I realised too late that Elliot was mouthing the excuse along with me. I glared at him. "I did."

"Oh yeah, what did you eat?"

I hesitated. A ham sandwich *was* big for me, but somehow I predicted Elliot wouldn't agree. My brain worked furiously to come up with a convincing meal, but it took too long.

Elliot sighed. "Okay, Ash."

I could tell he wanted to push the subject, but it was an argument we'd had a thousand times. One of these days, I felt sure that he'd stop bothering to ask. I ate dinner if and when I decided to, regardless of what Elliot said. It just so happened that my decision was usually to skip it.

Suddenly, Elliot stood up. "Come on," he said. "Let's go talk to Sue and Dom."

"What, *now?*" I asked, scrambling after him as he powered out of the room.

By the time I caught up with him he was already in the kitchen. Sue and Dom had started dinner. Chicken korma. There were no extra places set. They stared up at us in surprise, which faded into apprehension when they saw Elliot's face.

"So," he said, "I just wanted you two to know I have a house, and I'll be moving out in a couple of months."

Don't waste too much time beating around the bush there, Elliot.

Sue and Dom exchanged an unreadable glance. Elliot continued. "I've started applying for guardianship of Ash, so he'll be coming with me when I do."

Dom looked down at his dinner, and Sue laughed. "He absolutely will not." She barely even glanced at Elliot when she said it. As though what he'd said was so ridiculous it didn't even warrant attention.

Elliot folded his arms. He wore a no-nonsense expression, the sort that usually sent me straight into submission. "That's actually not your decision."

Sue placed her fork down. "It's Alice's decision. And I think she'll be very interested to hear how you spend most of your nights, don't you?"

"That has nothing to do with anything," Elliot said. "Who cares if I like to hang with my friends sometimes? I've got a steady job, I'm not on drugs, and he's my brother. They know he belongs with me."

"I can't think of a worse place for Ashton than alone in a house with you, Elliot," Sue said bluntly. I was stunned. While she'd never exactly been filled with affection for either of us, she hadn't expressed an opinion on Elliot's partying before.

"What, and you reckon he's so much better here?" Elliot shot back. "Because we have such a warm fuzzy family life going on? You don't even ask us to come to dinner anymore."

"Because you never want to join us," Sue said.

Dom looked at me and bit his lip. I avoided his eyes.

"Because it's awkward," Elliot raised his voice. "We know we're only here because you were forced into it."

I flushed red. Yes, but did Elliot have to say it? I preferred to ignore uncomfortable truths like that.

"You're here because the government wants you safe, in a house with carers who are present and sober and able to keep an eye on you," Sue said, unabashed. "I don't think you meet that criteria, Elliot. Sorry to burst your bubble."

"He doesn't need babysitting, he's sixteen," Elliot said. "What he needs is to be with family. He needs to belong somewhere that isn't completely transient."

Sue raised her eyebrows and began to eat again. "I'm not letting it happen. If you want to be with Ashton, you can stay. But if you leave, you're leaving without him."

An implicit dismissal. Our life-changing event was her meal interruption. I'd never hated a person as much in my life as I hated Sue in that moment. What gave her the right to try to separate me from Elliot? To arbitrarily decide I'd be better as a permanent unwelcome guest in her home than to live with *my brother*? Elliot and I needed each other. They didn't—*couldn't*—understand. Because they'd never bothered to get to know us or discover what we wanted.

Elliot gave her a dark, disgusted look and turned on his heel. I followed him until we were out of earshot. "Do you think she'll stop us?" I whispered as we hurried down the hallway.

He gritted his teeth and flicked a dismissive hand. "She can fucking try. We'll be fine, though. Alice even said they prefer not to separate family. They're fucking thrilled I want you to stay with me."

He grabbed his wallet off his desk, and I paused, frowning. "I thought you weren't going out tonight?"

"I'm not going *out* out, I'm just not staying in this damn house right now."

"Elliot—"

"Come on. We need some air."

If I didn't know him, I might have agreed. But I *did* know him, and an initial quick drive to seek some space would inevitably end at one of his friend's houses, unconscious on their kitchen floor. "I'm okay," I said.

"I want you to come." He paused so I knew the invitation was genuine. I offered him a fake smile and shook my head. "Okay. Fine. See you later, *mon poussin*."

With that he left, the slamming of the front door drowning out Sue's knowing laugh.

I floated to my bed in a numb haze and sent Bea a text.

What's up?

I sent out a silent plea. *Come on, Bea. I need someone to talk to. We can talk about the weather for all I care.*

Maybe cousin telepathy would prove successful here.

She never replied.

An hour later, I was still sitting there.

Often, when there wasn't much to distract me, I felt sick and scared for no reason at all. Worse was when there *was* a reason, but it was a silly little one that most people would brush off, and no matter how much I told myself it wasn't worth dwelling on it would bind me up like an insect in a spider's web. Then, for maybe an hour or so at a time, I'd forget about the Little Bad Thing. Until the nausea returned out of nowhere. Then I would remember why it was there, and suddenly the Little Bad Thing would be all I could think about again.

That night, the Little Bad Thing was Sue's threat. Each time I'd convinced myself that Elliot was in control, that he wouldn't leave me, the terrifying *what if* would spring back into existence and choke me. As long as I was by myself, the thoughts would continue to envelop me.

It wasn't that I couldn't be alone. I simply couldn't stand loneliness. With Elliot out, and James preoccupied with practice and assignments, and Sue and Dom doing their best to pretend I wasn't in the house, the loneliness was stifling. It ate away at me, tearing down my resilience piece by piece.

It always happened the same way, a familiar pattern I kept vowing I would break but never did. I'd remember my razor and push it out of my mind. Then I would attempt to distract myself, but nothing would work. Sooner or later, I'd end up staring into space, my thoughts uninteresting at best, morose at worst. Then my gaze would return to my razor of its own accord, and I'd tell myself no. *No.*

That's when my mind would fight back using the tool of warped perception. Time would stretch out like gum that refused to snap no matter how thin it was rendered. I'd beg myself to leave me alone, and then wonder if that made me crazy. Eventually my thoughts would stop making sense; I'd feel primal and desperate, and I'd crack.

That evening, I cracked.

Afterwards, I stood in the shower with my arms wrapped around my stomach and leaning against the tiled wall, hyperventilating and gritting my teeth. I didn't bother trying to wash my thigh; I allowed the shower stream to do that, not looking at the water as it ran red down my leg.

I despised it. If anyone knew, they'd hate me too. They'd assume I wanted attention and acknowledgement. All I desired, though, was to feel capable—in control. I could stand the persistent sting of an open wound. Anyone could. That was normal and human. It gave me a discernible cause and effect; the pain belonged to something. It was a neatly packaged suffering. Like colouring inside the lines. And it was such a relief to feel something so immediate and easily understood, even if it wasn't pleasant.

I still hated myself for it.

Before I left the bathroom, I tied my shirt firmly around my leg to stem the bleeding. The last thing I wanted was to run into Sue or Dom in the hallway with blood dripping down to my ankles. Even *their* distracted eyes wouldn't miss that. I threw a towel around my waist and entered the hallway.

My bedroom door was wide open.

I slowed my step, confused. I'd certainly closed it. Then James rolled forward on my bed, flashing me a grin. "Hey," he said. "Sorry. I couldn't be bothered going home just to come back, so I figured I'd wait for you to get out."

I secured the towel firmly around myself with one hand and retrieved a pair of sweatpants from the bedroom floor with the other. Did I look guilty? Could he tell what I'd been doing in the shower? "That's cool. What's up?"

"Bored. Wanna watch a film or play X-box?"

I was pleased, if a little surprised. James usually spent Saturday nights doing homework after his football games. Most of the time I couldn't even get a text out of him. "A film sounds fine," I said. "I need something that doesn't require brain cells."

He reached for the remote and it occurred to me I'd need to get dressed. James and I had known each other for too long for modesty to be an issue. But I couldn't allow him to catch a glimpse of my leg. I hesitated, then snatched up a fresh t-shirt and left the room. I shut myself in the bathroom, changed as swiftly as I could, and attempted to look casual. Hopefully James didn't notice the slight bulge under the left leg of my sweatpants. They were baggy enough to hide the makeshift bandage I'd created with the shirt, but I couldn't shake the paranoia.

James gave me a quizzical look as I re-joined him. "Uh,

'kay," he said with a forced laugh. "Are things gonna be weird now then?"

He thought I'd changed outside the room because of the kiss. "Don't be stupid," I said, climbing onto the bed. "It's only weird if you make it weird."

"Oh, great, no pressure." He started flicking through the films on my USB. Both of us kept our gazes fixed firmly on the TV screen.

It was too late. He'd made it weird.

He began chewing on his nails, a nervous habit that made me shudder. I wasn't sure what he was gnawing on— there was never anything there to chew. His nails were perpetually bitten to the quick, the skin surrounding his cuticles swollen and red, and peeling off in small shreds.

As soon as the nail biting began, I started a countdown from ten in my mind. I'd hit three when he spoke. Not a bad estimate. "So, just to clarify," he said, "are we pretending nothing happened?"

"Well, you clearly aren't." My thigh throbbed. I tried to ignore it.

"It's just . . . I was thinking it doesn't have to mean anything. We don't like each other, so it's not like it's risky. It could be fun."

I glanced sideways at him. "In other words, you're horny."

He groaned and fell against the wall. "*Always.*"

"Sorry to burst your bubble, but I don't have the energy for anything like that right now."

"I didn't come here because of that," he said hastily. "But . . . while we're on the topic . . ."

I wasn't sure I would have described that as a smooth transition through topics, but I spared him the grilling. In truth, I was glad he was here. I propped up a pillow behind my back while James started the film. Both of us sat stiffly throughout the beginning; myself due to physical discomfort, James, I imagined, due to mental. I might have tried to make conversation to set him at ease, but I couldn't pay attention to anything outside of my thigh. I'd pressed the blade harder than usual, and it *hurt*. It needed ice, or lotion, or something. Would it get infected?

I sighed in a mixture of unhappiness and frustration and leaned against James. He stiffened, then relaxed and let his head touch mine. The physical contact calmed me, to my surprise. I'd never been physically affectionate, with family *or* friends. Even Gemma and I hadn't made a habit of it. When we were dressed, anyway. The press of James's shoulder against mine had the same comforting effect a mug of strawberry Nesquik provided when I was little.

My eyes drooped after half an hour of this, and I realised I wasn't paying attention to the film.

It was me who turned sideways, but James was there to meet me. His kiss was gentle and chaste at first, then it deepened into something more urgent. I was lost in it until his hand pressed against my thigh, and a sharp pain sliced through my leg, punching me in the stomach. I somehow managed to squash my reaction to this, removing his hand with what I thought was impressive casualness.

He kept his hands to himself after this. He must have taken it as a rejection. Feeling guilty, I hooked one hand around the back of his neck and stroked his skin with my fingertips.

"So, what do you reckon?" he asked. "I don't mean we have to get serious or anything. But . . . you know."

I did know. I knew exactly what he was implying. But voicing the term "friends-with-benefits" out loud seemed too bold, even for James. So I spared him the clarification.

"I like this fine." I placed one more kiss on the corner of his mouth before returning to the film and settling against him.

This was a bad, terrible idea. No matter what I said, or what James said, kissing your friend did change things. And kissing them twice changed things for good. But logic was for forward thinkers, and I tended towards the "what do I want right this second" lifestyle. My habit of impulsiveness could be exceedingly self-sabotaging.

My phone vibrated. Bea.

Sorry I didn't reply! I was out to dinner. You still awake?

I was far too tired to talk, but I appreciated the response all the same. Better late than never.

I must have fallen asleep not long after this, because the next thing I knew, I woke up in pitch darkness. I'd been tucked into bed, the covers pulled up to my shoulders. The mattress buckled under a weight in front of me, bouncing a little. James, slipping his shoes back on. He shifted as I touched his arm. "I'm going," he said, and my heart sank. "I'll see you tomorrow."

I wanted to ask him to stay, to stave off the loneliness. But I couldn't do that. Instead I closed my eyes again and pretended to fall back asleep. James sat on my bed for a few seconds longer. A prickling on my neck told me he was looking at me. Without a word he pushed a lock of my hair off my face, then left.

Alone, I stared at my closed door.

ELEVEN

James
September 2018

AFTER SCHOOL I WENT to chill at our rock for a while. Even if it was kinda boring, and I didn't have anyone to chat to so it's not like I needed the privacy, I liked it there. It made things feel calm. Under control. Sometimes, if I got real lucky, being at the rock made me feel like Ash was nearby. Like he'd come around the corner any second. It probably wasn't super healthy, but what-the-hell-ever.

With the waves doing their white-noise thing in the background, I took inventory. Elliot was with Bea. Louise knew exactly where that was, but she wouldn't tell me. Maybe she'd open up eventually, but I couldn't count on it. I needed a plan B.

So, who else would know? Like, no one. Sue and Dom didn't know where Elliot was, so I doubted they'd know the address of his cousin. I'd even tried approaching Mary and Joseph, the holy foster parents of yesteryear, a few months back. They'd looked after Ash and Elliot before Sue and Dom, and they'd royally creeped me out. Too clean, too nice, too against swearing—and junk food, and long hair, and skinny jeans, and fun in general. Also it's hard to be buddy-buddy with people who think you're an unholy abomination, so. Yeah. Same as Sue and Dom, they didn't keep contact with Elliot.

There was still one shot, though. Callan had known Elliot even longer than I knew Ash. He would've met Bea a few times. Maybe he knew where she lived. Couldn't hurt to ask, anyhow.

I hitched up my school bag and went straight over to Callan's. I knew he'd finished his plumbing apprenticeship a few months earlier, and he was working full time, but it'd be after five when I got there. That should do.

Sure enough, he was home. And from the smell of things, had already gotten stuck into a joint. Figured. Some things changed in a year, but most stayed the same.

Callan answered the door with Dave. They seemed surprised to see me but invited me to join them in the lounge. Even offered me a spliff. Now, you can't fault that kind of hospitality. Guys were raised right.

"What's up?" Callan asked, flopping on the couch. He'd stripped out of his work uniform but didn't look like he'd showered yet. He was only wearing a vest and a pair of cotton shorts. "Haven't seen you around in ages, dude. How have you been?"

Ages. Not since the night at the party, a few months before. Not *that* long, but I guessed we saw each other more when Ash was alive. "Not bad. I actually came over to see if you knew something."

Callan cracked his knuckles, then took a deep drag. He

didn't seem to be in a rush here. "About Elliot again?"

I nodded.

"I dunno how much more I can tell you, mate. How many times have you grilled me now?"

"I'm trying to find Bea," I said. "I know she lives in Conway, but I don't know where. I was wondering—"

"Negative," Callan said, holding the spliff out. I waved a hand, and he shrugged. More for him. "Never been there."

Dave glanced between us. Wait, I recognised that look. He knew something. "How about you?" I prompted.

He cracked open a beer from the six pack on the table. "I know a couple'a things."

"I'm listening."

"I know Bea lives nowhere near the city. Kind of north-east, I think. In the suburbs."

Okay. Well, it wasn't an address, but it helped. Anything that narrowed things down helped. "Awesome. Thanks. And the other?"

Callan held out his hands, and Dave lobbed a beer at him. I'd always been told not to drink and smoke at the same time, but what did I know? I wasn't a seasoned pro like these guys, so I didn't say shit.

"The other," Dave said, "is Elliot really doesn't wanna be bothered."

Yeah, and fire's hot. "Mm. Tell me something I don't know."

"No, like, really. Not just by you. By any of us. I tried to get him to come down for my birthday last year and he was the biggest prick about it. Reckons he's got new friends now. Reckons we were corrupting him."

Dave knocked back half a can in one go. I guessed he was pissed off at the snub.

Callan stared at him. "You didn't tell me that, man."

"Yeah, well, whatever. Fuck him, hey? It's not like we

had a gun to his head. If he doesn't wanna hang with us, that's his call." His tone didn't match his words, though. He seemed pretty bummed. I called that fair enough.

"When did he say this?"

"I dunno, like, last September-ish? I tried to touch base a couple months back, and the number was out of service."

"That's 'cause I tried to call him on it," I said.

Dave seemed surprised. "Oh. I thought it was so I wouldn't call again. Either way, though. He was acting fuckin' paranoid. Said some shit about the cops, and jail, and shit. You know, 'cause we're all basically on a one-way street to death row."

My heart started thudding so loudly I couldn't hear myself think. "What? The cops? Jail?"

Callan shot Dave a look. A *shut the fuck up* look. Then he shrugged at me like it was no big deal. "Like Dave said. Paranoid."

Like hell I was letting that one go. "Why would he go to jail?"

"He *wouldn't*," Callan said. "He just got obsessed with getting caught for shit towards the end there. He was getting all jumpy and shit. Then he told us he thought we'd end up getting him locked up or something, and left town right after. Think maybe he'd had a bit too much . . ." He mimed putting a joint to his lips, and Dave, taking a puff from the real spliff, cackled.

Callan turned the TV on and flicked to a replay of the weekend's football game. "Let him go, mate," he said to me. "That shit's all in the past. It was a shit time for all of us. Focus on exams. Go out some more. Have fun. Don't spend the rest of your life trying to find some douche who doesn't want anything to do with us. Yeah?"

I got where he was coming from. And it would've been so easy to agree, grab a beer, and hang with them for a while.

See some people, even if it wasn't my normal friend group (*ex-friend group, don't you mean?*).

But I couldn't let it go. Hadn't been able to let it go since Callan first told me some of the shit Elliot lied about. And now this? Nope. Fuck this. Something was definitely going on. And no way in hell could I just leave it. I had to know what happened with Ash and Elliot on that final day. Otherwise, it'd haunt me. I'd wonder for the rest of my life if it could've been prevented. If anyone deserved to pay for it.

And God only knew, I was getting real sick of wondering.

TWELVE

Ash
April 2017

"Sometimes I see a bug and I want to kill it, then I worry about reincarnation."

James looked up and hitched his schoolbag higher. ". . . Reincarnation?"

"Yes." I swatted at the dragonfly that had been circling my head since we left school. Rokewood Bend stood situated along an estuary. It made for pretty scenery, but the downside was the veritable plague of bugs that haunted the town season by season. "Like, what if a fly is, I don't know, Grandma Gladys coming over to say hi, then you squash her brains in, and the whole time she's thinking 'why, Ashton, why'?"

"Well, here's a tip," James said. "If you ever die and come back as a fly don't get up in my grill because I will murder the ever-loving shit out of you."

"That's cold."

"Well, if you wanna live you'd better get real good at writing messages with grains of rice or something 'cause I'm not going around the rest of my life refusing to kill anything just in case."

"Is it so awful to go through life without killing anything?"

"I've gotta to take out my frustration somehow," James said. He looked at my expression and scoffed. "Oh, come on, don't look at me like that. You eat meat."

We headed to the playground. These days we ended up at the park whenever we walked home together. Little by little, the time we spent with each other at school wasn't enough anymore.

"What changes?" I asked suddenly. "When you come out, I mean?"

James appeared surprised by the abrupt topic switch, but he didn't query it. "I dunno. It's different for everyone, I guess. I didn't change, I don't think. Did I?"

"You didn't. But did anything change *for* you?"

He slowed down, giving the question fair consideration. "When you haven't come out, most guys aren't looking out for your body language, so unless you start wearing a neon sign that says 'I'm into you,' they're not gonna read into anything. You could be in love with them, and they'd never even notice. Then once you come out it flips. Like, you can literally glance past a guy on your way to class, and he thinks you're coming onto him. And you wanna scream 'dude, just 'cause I like dicks does *not* mean I want yours'."

"I think I would've noticed if you'd flirted with me," I said, hopping onto the jungle gym platform.

James sat on the slide's base and buried the tips of his shoes in bark chips. "If you don't think I flirt with you, you're oblivious."

"Well, obviously you do *now*."

He shook his head and laughed.

Over the last few weeks, we'd been experimenting with the no-strings-attached arrangement James had suggested. And, to my surprise, it was sufficiently functional. As far as I could tell, it hadn't affected our friendship. But it set us free from all the nonsense. The labelling and the second-guessing and the expectations.

I sat at the top of the slide and lobbed a bark chip at the back of his head. He flipped around and tugged on my shoe, pulling me down the slide. I bumped into him at the end and positioned my bent knees either side of him.

"So." He grabbed the hem of my shirt. "Am I allowed to kiss you out here? There's no one around."

I nodded, and he leaned over me and pressed his lips to mine. He pinned my wrists above my head, further up the slide, and pressed himself flush against me. I was more than happy with this until he let go of one of my hands to touch my hips.

"*James.*" I wriggled away. "No. Nope."

"Because you're embarrassed?" He didn't seem impressed, but he removed his hand.

"No, because we're on a playground. It's sick," I laughed.

"We have plenty of options. There's the picnic bench, the grass—"

"And we're in public. There are things you don't do in public."

"Fair enough," he said. Relaxing, I let myself slide back down. He gave me a hopeful shrug. "What if we went back to yours, then?"

Now that was an option I could get on board with.

When we got back to my house Elliot called out to us from the lounge room. "Yo, Sue and Dom went out for dinner, so I'm thinking a film and nachos. You keen?"

"Definitely," I said, shooting James a playful look. He wasn't sure if I was joking at first, then when I headed toward the lounge room his face fell. I had to fight to keep from laughing.

I threw myself on the couch, and James slumped next to me, his arms folded over his leg.

"Suggestions?" Elliot asked, grabbing the remote.

"Comedy," James said.

"Horror," I said at the same time.

Elliot twisted his mouth then offered James an apologetic shrug. "Sorry, I'm in a horror mood too."

When the film began Elliot hopped to his feet. "I'll get the food ready."

"You'll miss the beginning," I protested.

"So? No one dies until at least half an hour into these things. All I'll miss is awkward, semi-hot people perving on each other. It just makes me wanna see them die faster."

"You have issues, do you realise?" I called after him as he disappeared into the kitchen.

There was a rustling of chip packets as Elliot rummaged through the pantry. I turned back to the TV, then noticed James staring at me in my peripheral vision. He shifted to bring his feet underneath him, and in the process brushed his shoulder against mine. It was only a simple movement, the slightest touch, but it was certainly deliberate. I trained my eyes ahead, outwardly calm, inwardly tumbling.

"I'm doing three layers," Elliot called out, "because I'm hungover and I'm worth it."

"You do that," I replied. "Don't let us hold you back."

James rested his elbow on the couch and dangled his little finger against my collarbone. I leaned into him.

"I won't," Elliot said over the crinkling plastic. "I don't have enough self-control to let a bit of judgement guilt me into making good choices."

Neither did I.

James's fingers moved now, trailing down the curve of my neck. I tipped my head back, my breath hitching. James examined me like I was a particularly interesting film twist.

"You own your faults," I said to Elliot. "I respect that about you."

Responding to my rather obvious enthusiasm, James's fingertips slipped down my throat, across my chest, down to my waist, before halting. He smirked and turned back to the TV. He left his hand where it was. A part of me knew we should stop, and that Elliot could surprise us at any moment. But that rational side was drowned out by the fact that I *wanted* it.

"What can I say? I'm a confident guy," Elliot's voice rang out. "Do you think a whole bag of cheese is reasonable? I mean, I think we can justify it here."

Slowly, like he was trying to make it look like an accident, James slid his hand under my shirt. I sank into the couch, my breathing growing thick, and checked the doorway. Elliot was still in the kitchen, clattering around. He couldn't see a thing. "Why not make it two bags?" I called out.

"We don't have two."

"Shame," I murmured. James stared ahead, feigning utter disinterest in the conversation, and in me. Absentmindedly, he ran a thumb across my hip bone. I exhaled long and slow, lifting my hips a little. The corner of James's mouth rose. Well, this was fantastic. If Elliot walked in now, even if James had pulled away, I'd have to put a pillow in my lap to hide it. If I had any sense, I'd stop this now and try to think unattractive thoughts. But that would involve having self-control.

"What?" Elliot yelled out. "Stop mumbling. I can barely

hear you."

"Nothing," I said, raising my voice and digging my own fingers into the couch. James was still only touching my hips, but my senses muddled. The room warped; the television sounded distant. The only things that existed were James and the heat pooling in my stomach.

"Do we still have that avocado?"

For friends with benefits, James and I had been treading precariously. We'd only recently started pushing the boundaries past kissing. Maybe because we were cautious about crossing some undefined line. But right now, I almost felt I wouldn't care if James never spoke to me again after this, as long as he kept going down the path his hand was suggesting. The pull of logic is weak when compared to the persuasive power of hormones.

James was watching me again now, biting his lower lip. He didn't seem entirely relaxed anymore either. But if he was mildly ruffled, I was falling to pieces.

"Ash?" Elliot called, and I spent a few seconds trying to organise my thoughts. Right. Avocado.

"I don't know," I forced out in a thin voice.

"Oh, never mind. I found it."

"Wonderful," I said sarcastically. James moved his hand further under my shirt, flattening his palm over my stomach.

"Don't give me your sass," Elliot replied. "I'm cooking for you, aren't I?"

"James," I hissed. The frustration was killing me.

"What?" he asked, the picture of innocence.

I gritted my teeth and looked behind me again. Thank God, Elliot was still nowhere in sight.

"What do you want?" James asked, leaning forward, resting all his weight on his free hand while the other kept brushing across my skin.

"*Stop.*"

"Stop?" He echoed, withdrawing his hand altogether.

I changed my mind instantly. "No. No, don't."

"Didn't you want to watch a film? Wasn't that more interesting?"

"No."

"Should *I* watch the film now?"

"*No.*"

"Better convince me fast, Ash. He'll be back in soon."

He was correct. The oven fan blew in the background.

"Can we go to my room?" I asked. James pressed his lips hard against mine and nodded so eagerly our foreheads nearly smashed together.

I called out a breathless excuse to Elliot in the kitchen and allowed James to pull me to the bedroom by my wrist. We kept the light off, kissing each other in the darkness with a desperate fervour as soon as the door was closed. James pulled my shirt over my head while walking me backwards. He directed me to sit on the edge of the bed and then straddled me, pushing my torso back onto the mattress. I clutched at the blanket above my head to anchor myself while James kissed down the centre of my chest, to my stomach, to just above my jeans.

When he unbuttoned them, I felt a brief rush of panic. It's not like I'd never done this before, but it *certainly* hadn't been with my best friend. While I'd quite liked the idea when it was me initiating it, I felt vulnerable with James steering. Would I know what to do? How far did he want to take this? Would it make things awkward if I cut him off?

He pulled my jeans off and rose back up to kiss my lips, the material of his jeans rough against my bare skin. "Is this okay?" he breathed, and my fears dimmed. I nodded, and he kissed my neck. With him fully clothed, all I could do in response was run my fingers through his hair.

I was so lost in the thick silkiness of his locks I took far too long to realise James had paused. I checked on him. He was staring at my thighs through the semi-darkness, tracing over one of the hardened ridges that covered them. I shot up and drew my legs away, but it was too late.

He raised accusing eyes. "You told me you'd stopped this."

I averted my gaze and gritted my teeth. "Don't be a mood killer," I muttered, holding my shirt in front of my chest. Suddenly I felt overexposed.

"*Ash.*" He sounded so let down, so disappointed, that I became defensive.

"They're just cuts. I'm not going to kill myself."

He scoffed. "Right. 'Cause I can believe that."

I shrugged and turned away from him. "I don't care if you believe it or not. It makes no difference to me."

"I'll tell Sue."

I stood up. "No, you won't."

We stared at each other, both of us defiant. He surrendered first, lowering his gaze. Predictable. He knew what I'd do if he told Sue.

Victorious, I pulled on my jeans. James remained staring at my legs, giving me the irrational, sickly sensation that he could see through my clothing. I pulled the blanket from my bed, wrapping it around myself. I hoped the message was clear: drop it.

He did. Biting his lip, he stood up and shrugged offhandedly. "Let's go back to the lounge room. Elliot's probably wondering."

We did, with me still wrapped in my makeshift cocoon. The plate of nachos sat steaming hot in the centre of the coffee table. James helped himself, but I just stared at it. "I'm not hungry," I said.

Elliot grinned. "I figured. If I thought you were actually gonna *eat* any of it, I would've made more."

It was unlike Elliot to joke about me skipping dinner. He *must* have been in a good mood. James pressed his lips together in a thin line but offered no comment.

Throughout the film, James appeared distracted and distant, not even pretending to smile at Elliot's running commentary. When he excused himself to go to the bathroom halfway through, Elliot raised an eyebrow after him. "What's his problem?"

Subconsciously, I raised my knees to my chest as though to hide the marks. "He's pissed off about school. Nothing big."

Elliot seemed sceptical, but he didn't press the topic. For a while I thought James would never return. When he finally re-emerged, he was wearing his shoes and his eyes were red-rimmed. "I'm gonna head off," he said. "It's getting late."

Hurt and anger fought for dominance in my mind. "You do that," I said, refusing to glance up from the television. According to my tone, anger had won.

James hesitated, and for a second, I wondered if he was going to stay anyway. Then he left.

Elliot and I both stared after him—Elliot, bewildered, I, crushed.

THIRTEEN

Louise
September 2018

Unseasonal heatwaves were probably my favourite thing. Bruno's closed every Sunday, so Elliot and I made it our business to drag our friends out of the house that day, given the unusually high temperature.

I set myself up on my beach towel, stretching out and daring the sun to do its worst. The lighter my skin was, the more my pimples showed. Which, obviously, hell no.

Rachael sat next to me, sharing my front-row seat to the increasingly competitive volleyball game the rest of the group was playing. A ball flew in our direction, and Rachael threw herself to one side to avoid its trajectory. Jacob chased after it, holding eye contact with Rachael. *Oh, so subtle, Jacob,* I thought. A regular Romeo.

Rachael smiled at him, then spoke to me without taking

her eyes off his six-pack. Honestly, this pervert right here. "We should probably be buckling down on assignments," she said. "Not chilling at the beach."

I sighed. Like, yup? But she didn't have to point it out. We were here now. Might as well enjoy it. "But chilling at the beach is so much more fun," I said.

"I don't know how you juggle everything while working." She turned back to me now. Behind her, Jacob continued to shoot her sideways glances between serves. They were basically eye-humping. "I'd fail."

"Just got to juggle. I'm passing, so."

"I need more than a pass if I'm gonna get into uni," she said, reapplying her sunscreen. She'd only put some on about twenty minutes ago, but I guessed she knew rubbing her hands all over her body was a good way to get Jacob's attention. Like she didn't already have ninety percent of it. Not that I blamed Jacob in that. Rachael looked great every day, but in a bikini, she channelled Yaya DaCosta.

"I'll worry about that later," I said. "I'm taking next year off."

"To work?"

"Work, travel. Work while travelling, maybe. See where the wind takes me," I said.

Rachael made a face. "I hate you."

"Hey, no one's stopping you from coming with me."

The volleyball game wrapped up, and Elliot and Nikki celebrated their win with zero grace, hugging each other and hurling taunts at Jacob and Liam. My kind of winners.

"You guys only won because Jacob was watching Rach more than the ball," Liam grumbled. Rachael went crimson, and I burst out laughing.

"No," Elliot said, grabbing Nikki's hand. "We won because Nicole is a tank."

"I'll take that as a compliment," Nikki said with a wink.

Elliot locked eyes with her for a few seconds, and I stopped smiling.

Let me clarify. It wasn't that I was *jealous*. Just, I'd be really offended if Elliot ever got with any of the other girls in our friend group. The whole reason nothing had come of me and him after the Christmas party, other than the incest thing, was that he didn't date friends. If he hooked up with Nikki, it meant that he'd lied, and the reason he'd pulled away was because he *did* date friends, just not friends that were *me*. And that felt a little personal. Not that I'd put it past Elliot to lie to me anymore.

But then Nikki followed the others into the water and Elliot launched himself onto Rachael's towel. "*Slaughtered* them," he proclaimed, more than a little proud of himself.

"I'm so impressed by your superior testosterone levels," I said. "Marry me. Please. Before my eggs dry up."

"Lou," Rachael said. "You're seventeen. Give them a minute before you write them off."

"I'd appreciate it if we could stop talking about egg expiries, if it's all the same to you two," Elliot said.

Rachael shrugged, stood up, and dusted sand off her exposed, flat stomach. "Works for me. I'm going in the water."

She headed straight to Jacob. Of course. He looked pretty impressed when she did.

I had a feeling our group was going to have a token couple pretty soon. Which was fine with me, so long as they didn't intend to hold any dramatic, group-dividing break-ups. Maybe we could get them to sign a prenup before dating to agree that no one would be forced to take sides if they *did* break up?

I watched them for a few seconds before giving Elliot a coy look. "I have a topic change. Your brother."

The good humour left his face. "So, how *is* your reproductive system?"

"Elliot."

He let out an impatient growl. "God, fine. *Fine.* The video was about me, okay? Are you happy?"

And, she *scores.* There it was. As much as I'd been sure it was him, it was weird to have him admit it. "Why didn't you tell anyone you had a brother?"

He picked up a handful of sand and let it sift through his fingers. "Maybe I don't want to talk about it, okay? I just want to get on with life."

Not that I was an expert in psychology, but . . . "I'm not sure that kind of avoidance is healthy."

Elliot rolled his eyes. "Well when *you* lose someone that close to you and *you* figure out the best way to deal with it, be sure to let me know, okay?"

With that he plastered a smile onto his face and stood up; the conversation was done.

Instead of following him like I usually would, I sat on the beach towel and buried the tips of my feet in loose sand. I felt separate from Elliot for the first time since I'd met him. We'd bonded so quickly and now I wasn't sure I could even trust him. Maybe I didn't know him at all.

He ran into the water and joined the others, slipping into their conversation as easily as if he'd initiated it. Rachael jumped on him, forcing him under the next wave as it swelled around the group. They came up gasping for air and laughing. Like people who'd known each other forever. This would've made me smile before. Now it seemed kind of false. Tainted. Knowing Elliot was hiding things from us.

We'd accepted him into our fold, laid out our own pasts to him without hesitating. Why hadn't he done the same?

How could anyone hide something so huge? He'd been hurting for years, and he'd never said a word. Not a single word.

Made me wonder what else we didn't know.

LOU CASTELLANO:

So. It's the same Elliot. I mean, duh, but he admitted it. And now I'm feeling guilty. Maybe I shouldn't be telling you all this. I mean, what do you think you're going to get out of talking to him? What good will it do? If he's gone to these lengths to move past everything maybe he needs us to let him. He hasn't been himself since this whole thing started. I feel like I'm stirring up all these horrible memories for him.

SEEKING ELLIOT:

Alright. I might as well lay it out on the table. Ash and I had a massive fight, then he jumped off a bridge a few hours later. I've spent over a year trying to deal with that guilt. But Elliot abandoning Ash, then moving out of town, and not crying at his funeral, and making sure I can't contact him . . . it's all super weird. And it's made me wonder what else went down on the day Ash jumped.

Put it this way. If Elliot did have something to do with it, then it would mean everything in the world for me to know. And if Elliot didn't talk to Ash then he probably doesn't even know we fought, and maybe he's spent this whole time wondering if it was his fault too. If it wasn't his fault, then he deserves to know it's mine.

I needed to talk to Saras.

At lunch, I left Rachael and Nikki and sought her out. Saras sat on the steps in front of the library with a bunch of girls who hemmed their dresses a little too short and were told off daily for wearing too much makeup. Like if the Kardashians were a group of seventeen-year-olds. I low-key worshipped them.

"Hey," I said as I approached her. "Do you think we could talk real quick?"

Her friends gave her curious looks as she stood up and followed me. "What about?" she asked.

"Elliot."

I summed up everything that had happened since the day I'd first seen the video, making Saras swear on her life she wouldn't tell Elliot what I knew. And if Saras swore on her life, she meant it.

When I was done, Saras chewed the inside of her cheek. "So, this guy thinks it was his fault?"

"Mm. And he thinks Elliot probably thinks it's *his* fault. And he wants to figure things out."

"Okay, but we're not talking about car insurance. We're talking about someone killing themselves. Isn't assigning blame the last thing anyone should be doing?"

She had a point. "True. But if Elliot's been beating himself up over something for the last year, don't you think it'll help him to hear there was other stuff going on?"

"And what if it turns out Elliot's right, and he *did* cause his brother to kill himself?"

"Then he won't be any worse off than he is now. And James will know he wasn't responsible. Which—"

Saras held up a hand to stop me. "Okay, Louise, I'm sorry but I couldn't care less about this James guy. *Elliot* is our friend. If we do something to hurt him that's not a good thing, whether it helps a stranger or not."

I folded my arms, annoyed because I so knew she was right. I'd kinda hoped she would help me justify what I was doing. Note to self. Stop relying on rational people to support your irrational wishes. We walked down the steps together and onto the oval, keeping to the perimeters to avoid the footballs being kicked indiscriminately around us.

"I won't tell him if it ended up being his fault," I said finally. "Then if it turns out he had nothing to do with it, I'll tell him what happened with James."

Saras sighed and pulled her long black hair into a pony-tail. "Do whatever you want. Just be careful. This is a land-mine if I ever saw one."

It was a landmine, but like that was gonna stop me. I'd just have to make sure not to step on any mines, wouldn't I?

It was hard to say why I'd become so obsessed with the truth. Partly because of James, partly because of curiosity about Elliot's past. But, in the weirdest way, I also wanted to know what happened to Ash for myself. Somehow the truth about a guy I'd never met, and never *would* meet, seemed to be important.

Instead of going back to mine after school, I went to Elliot's. For months, he'd been the person I went to when I was uneasy. Considering I'd only known him a little over a year, it was strange how quickly I'd forgotten how to deal with things without him. Sure, Lou. Rely on the guy who has turned out to be more unreliable than the butler in a murder mystery. What could go wrong *there*?

Bea was chopping potatoes in their kitchen when I got there. Her hair was in a bubble-gum pink coif, vibing Katy Perry *circa* 2011. One of these days it'd all fall out from all the dye, surely. "Hey, hon," she said without pausing. "How was school?"

"Shit," I said brightly. "Can't wait for it to be over."

"Uni isn't much better, unfortunately. Elliot's home. He's just in his room, I think."

I nodded, but instead of heading to him, I hovered in front of the counter.

Bea put the knife down and scooped the potatoes into a pot of boiling water. "What's up?" she asked, fishing through the fridge.

I lowered my voice. "Elliot told me. About Ash."

She emerged slowly, a bunch of leeks in hand. "Uh . . . what about Ash?" Her voice sounded strained. Right. Another landmine. I was talking about her dead cousin here.

"Well, that he existed, for a start. I was just wondering if everything's okay there. If Elliot needs any help. It seems like a weird thing to hide."

"Why do you think he'd need help?" She set about chopping the leeks. "Did he ask for it?"

I wasn't sure if that was a genuine question, or a hint to butt out where I wasn't needed. "No. But he's my friend. He shouldn't have to ask for help."

Bea was silent for a long time. She sliced the leeks, diced them, then spoke. "Did he . . . do you know what happened to Ash?"

"Yup. He killed himself."

She probably didn't need to cut the leeks quite that finely. They were bordering on being minced. But hey. I was no chef. You do you, Bea.

"Look, I'm sure he appreciates it," she said, "but bringing it up might be doing more harm than good. It changed everything for Elliot when Ash died. It uprooted his life. I think he moved here for a clean slate. Everyone deserves that shot, don't you think?"

Maybe she was right. In any case, it seemed like I was the only one in the world who thought it was healthy to talk about things that bothered you. Maybe it was a Spanish thing. "I guess . . ."

"Look, hon. He's doing much better now that he's here. And I want to keep it that way. So maybe just . . . let him come to you if he needs to talk. Otherwise, I'm not concerned."

I smiled, nodded, and went to find Elliot. He was reading on the bed, his headphones plugged in. When he saw me, he lowered the book and turned off the music, his pale blue eyes crinkling. It didn't matter that I was unannounced. Any time of the day, for any reason, he always wanted to see me. I loved him for that.

"Hey," he grinned, sitting on the edge of the bed. "To what do I owe the pleasure?"

Wordlessly, I approached him and wrapped him in a hug.

I wasn't sure if I agreed that blacklisting Ash as a topic was healthy, but I'd worry about that another day. For now, maybe all Elliot needed was to know that he had Bea, and he had me, and things would be okay. Even if he had hidden things from me, I didn't want to believe it was for a malicious reason.

Whatever he'd been before he moved here, right now, he was my best friend.

As far as I was concerned, nothing could, or would, change that.

FOURTEEN

Ash
April 2017

THE NEXT DAY EVERYONE seemed to share my mood. James didn't mention my cuts, but he remained distant. Even Mr. Patricks was cranky enough to snap at students other than me. For once, I was able to avoid his attention. Which was a small blessing, I supposed.

After taking attendance, Mr. Patricks made what appeared to be a grudging announcement. "So, some of you will remember this from the beginning of the term, but for the majority of you, who don't listen to a word I say, I want to remind you that from tomorrow, Thursdays and Fridays will end on RSE lessons with yours truly. I lost rock, paper, scissors over this."

"What's RSE?" Someone piped up.

"Relationship and Sex Education."

Oh *joy*.

"Now, I'm sure some of you already consider yourselves experts in the area," Mr. Patricks said drily, "but bear with me and you might learn something. At least make it painless for me, because this was not listed in my job description."

Gemma shot me a coy look from her seat, a few desks over. It was one of the first times since she dumped me that she'd properly acknowledged me. I caught her eye and gave her the smallest smile I could manage, sharing the private little joke. We weren't experts, but I happened to know neither of us were beginners anymore either. I turned back around to find James staring at me with an unimpressed expression.

James burst into the hallway the second the bell rang, heading straight to football practice, leaving me alone in his wake. With a sigh, I gathered my books and trudged home.

Things only worsened when I arrived to find Sue and Dom sitting at the kitchen table, deep in what appeared to be a serious conversation. I could only assume it involved me, because they fell silent the moment I entered.

Scowling, I stormed down the hall and threw my bag on the floor by my bed. I tried to distract myself on Facebook, then with X-box, and then even an attempt at homework, but I could still hear their hushed voices. Before too long, the only thing my mind could focus on was the possible content of that conversation.

I was grateful for the distraction when my phone buzzed in my lap. Until I read the message, that was.

James: You didn't tell me you and Gemma had sex.

Despite being completely alone, I blushed. Apparently our private glance hadn't been as subtle as I hoped.

It never came up?

The silence between our texts lagged.

Okay. Fair enough. So, you definitely like girls? Or did she make you realise you don't, haha?

Wait, was he genuinely irritated over this?

I like some girls. I like some guys. Can we not talk about this, please?

I waited for his reply, but it never came. I wasn't sure what he'd been implying. Surely he wasn't jealous of something that had happened before anything had begun between me and him? Mind, even if it'd been happening right now, it was still none of his business. I didn't owe him loyalty. He wasn't my boyfriend.

I was snapped out of my reverie when Elliot arrived home and came straight to my room.

"Yo," he said, his eyes gleaming as he jumped onto my bed. "So Alice called today. We'll be good to go soon. They're conducting checks, but I'm good. No criminal history, no health problems, and a couple of my managers are giving me a reference."

I gave a worried laugh. "Are you sure that's wise?"

He shot me a look. "*Yes*. They love me. They don't care if I go out the night before as long as I get through the shift fine, and I always do."

"When do Sue and Dom find out?"

"Well, they should've been told today I think."

Ah, that explained the serious conversation. "And what happens if they try to fight this?"

"Nothing'll happen, *mon poussin*," Elliot said, but he looked uncertain. My stomach flipped.

In the kitchen, Sue and Dom continued to talk. Distance distorted their voices, but the tone was unmistakable. Elliot rose to his feet and motioned for me to follow him. As quietly as possible, we inched down the hallway to eavesdrop.

Dom said something indiscernible.

Sue's response was clearer. "*No,*" she said in a raised voice. "I'm not leaving Ashton with him. He can't even look after himself."

"Ashton would look after him. I'm more worried about how Elliot would do alone."

"I'm not worried about Elliot."

"You're not?" Dom seemed flabbergasted.

"Elliot," Sue said, her voice growing dimmer as footsteps told me she crossed the room, "is a lost cause. There's nothing else we can do for him. He doesn't *want* to be helped. Ashton still has a chance. But not with his brother dragging him down."

Elliot and I exchanged a glance at this. He was pressing his lips together, clearly distressed. Worse, there was something else in his expression that looked an awful lot like resentment. Directed towards me.

I wanted to pull him away from the door, but it was like observing an accident. The masochist in me insisted on lingering, even if their words hit like calculated punches.

"We can't separate them."

"We damn well can. Our job is to look after the kids we have in our care. If Elliot wants to leave, we can't stop him."

"We should talk to him. Explain that—"

"Come off it, Dom, you just want the pay check he brings," Sue snapped. "You can't think he's better off with us."

"Better with us than by himself. He'll end up on the street."

"And what's going to change if he *does* stay longer?"

"Ashton will have left school and could get a job. They could support each other," Dom said.

"*Ashton* could have a future that doesn't involve looking

after a train wreck. If he's lucky."

"Okay," Elliot whispered, standing. I scurried after him, and we closed the door to his room behind us.

We stood in a tense silence for several seconds, then I reacted. Grabbing his pillow, I threw it as hard as I could at the door. *"Douche bags."*

"Sue is a piece of fucking shit," Elliot said, kicking his bedpost. "I can't . . . I can't believe she . . . and—"

"They can *watch* us." I whipped around. "'*Ashton could have a future,*' screw her. I *do* have a future. Regardless of if I'm trapped in this system or not."

"You do. And I'm not a fucking lost cause." Elliot sat down on the edge of his bed, wringing his hands before him. His eyes were welling up. I hadn't seen him like this in years. Not since we left home. The urge to wrap him in a hug conflicted with the sudden urge to burn the house down with Sue and Dom inside.

I sat beside him. "You're not. It's not true."

He cleared his throat and tried to reply. "I—They always. . ." he started, before trailing off.

"Always what?"

He shrugged with a bitter smile. "They always like you more than me. Everyone we've ever been with."

I didn't know what to say to that. Mostly because it was true. All Elliot wanted was for somebody to take an interest in him and put in the Herculean effort required to break through his protective shield. Isn't that what everyone wanted? To know that they're loved unconditionally, even when they messed up?

Instead, everyone rejected us.

Well, more specifically, they rejected Elliot.

Because it was *always* conditional.

"Screw them anyway," I said. "We have each other."

A tear escaped his eye and he brushed it away with a

furious grimace. He swore and stood up. I read his intentions straight away. "Don't," I said.

"I'm not staying here."

"You have to tonight. You'll give Sue ammunition otherwise."

"I'm sorry, but I can't."

"*Please.*"

He paused by the door. My heart leapt. He was going to listen to me for once. I should have known he wouldn't risk losing me. I almost dared to smile.

Then he strode over to his window and opened it. "They won't even know I'm gone," he said as he climbed out. "Not that they'd care anyway, right? As long as they have one kid who isn't a screw-up. Close my door behind you."

I wanted to beg him further, to tell him how desperately I needed him by my side for once, to offer me some comfort. Instead I stood with my hands hanging by my side, watching as he dropped to the ground and stormed away from the house.

There was nothing else to do. I returned to my own room, doing my best to ignore the fact that Sue and Dom were still discussing my lack of a future down the hall.

Alone, with only loneliness for company.

This was fine.

I could cope with this.

I was fine. Wasn't I?

Maybe not. No.

Why was I so pathetic? Why did I allow myself to be so dragged down? Why couldn't I lift my chin? Things weren't *that bad.*

Stop being dramatic, I urged myself. *Stop it stop it stop it.*

Not long after sunset, after an hour of stubborn resistance, I went in search of my razor.

It wasn't in the drawer.

Frowning, I looked in the drawer beneath it. *I must have put it there by mistake*, I reasoned. But it wasn't there either.

Fighting against the bubbling panic, I scanned the floor, behind the curtain, beneath the bed. Nothing. Had Sue or Dom discovered it somehow? Would they use it to take me away from Elliot? Was that part of their plan?

I sat on the bed and covered my mouth with shaking hands, trying to figure out what was happening. *Calm down*, I told myself. *So what if they did find it? You can come up with an excuse for it. And your wrists are clean. Besides. You've probably misplaced it.*

But where, exactly, had I put it? It had been there yesterday morning. I'd seen it when I grabbed my iPhone charger out.

Suddenly, a thought occurred to me. I whipped out my phone and sent James a text.

Did you go into my room last night?

He didn't reply. It was getting harder to breathe, and I forced myself to calm down. It only lasted a minute, and then I was hyperventilating. Sue and Dom couldn't find it. It wasn't fair. I just needed this one thing, this one piece of privacy. I just needed to be left alone. Why couldn't I have this? Why did everything always have to go wrong? Was I an idiot? Did I bring it on myself?

I wanted desperately, *desperately* to steal another razor from Sue's drawer and pry it apart. But if they *had* caught on I'd only be digging myself into a deeper hole by getting another.

I wanted to cry—*needed* to cry—but the sobs wouldn't come. My eyes burned with tears that refused to fully form. It was my body's favourite trick. It enjoyed causing me to ache, like a dam ready to overflow, and take away my only means of releasing the pressure. I was shaking harder now, and I paced around the room. My hands snaked up to cup the back of my own neck, pulling my head down towards my chest. God, God, no.

The knock on the door made me freeze. My breath caught in my throat, and my answer became trapped. I waited to be confronted, for my life to fall to pieces.

The door opened. But it wasn't Sue. It was James.

His hair was wet, though it wasn't raining outside. He must have been in the shower when I texted. Gently, he closed the door behind him, then turned to me and whispered, "It's not there anymore."

He was talking about my razor. I was midway through forming an indignant protest when I found myself enveloped in James's arms as he pulled me into a hard embrace.

"I'm sorry," he said. "I'm not mad at you. I just didn't know what to do. I'm not mad."

I was about to ask when he'd had the chance to find it when I remembered his extended absence during the film the night before.

"If you want to do it again, text me instead," he said. "Please. It doesn't matter what time it is or what I'm doing. I'll come."

I stared at the wall over his shoulder, words escaping me, and swallowed. This caused a lump to appear in my throat, and I buried my head in James's chest, scrunching the material of his shirt up in my fists. He threaded his fingers through my hair and rested his chin on the top of my head. Gradually my racing heart slowed, and my breathing grew steady. The lump disappeared. I took a deep breath and inhaled the familiar scent of his skin.

"Okay," I murmured, dizzy and lulled and grateful. "Okay."

FIFTEEN

Ash
April 2017

THE NEXT MORNING, ELLIOT still wasn't home. I stood in his room ready to scream in frustration as I commenced the task of tracking him down via the iPhone grapevine, then nearly had a heart attack when his door opened behind me. It wasn't Elliot, though. It was Sue.

I mentally raced through a list of excuses for his whereabouts, but Sue beat me to it. "Your brother's in hospital," she said. "He had an overdose last night. He's fine now, though."

It might as well have been Spanish for all the sense it made at first. "An overdose?" I repeated. "As in, on purpose?"

"No. With his friends."

"When did this happen?" I asked, tasting bile.

"About midnight."

"Why didn't you tell me sooner? Who's with him?"

Sue took a step back from me, her face a mixture of pity and defensiveness. "I didn't want you up all night before a school day. Dom and I were both with him overnight, but we've left him to get some sleep ourselves. He's *fine*," she said, and I had to fight to stay on top of the outrage bubbling up in my chest. She did this to him. She was responsible for this.

"Okay." I turned on my heel.

I hated how little she cared about Elliot. *Despised* it. He wasn't undeserving of protection just because he was eighteen. Why couldn't she pretend she wanted him, even if it was an obvious act? It was her fault he'd left last night at all. Now she'd abandoned him in a hospital bed.

I snatched up my schoolbag and stalked towards the front door.

"Where are you going?" Sue asked.

"School."

"Make sure you do."

"*I'm going to school, okay?*" I snapped, slamming the door behind me.

I walked straight to the hospital. I worried they'd take one look at my school jumper and turn me away, but to my relief the receptionist didn't ask any questions.

Being here was eerie. The stark white of the walls, the impersonal smell of disinfectant and disease, and the unnatural, too-cool temperature were familiar. They sang a song of misery, and fear, and vulnerability.

I'd only walked these halls once since my own admission at fourteen. That was when Elliot had given himself alcohol poisoning, while we were still in our last foster home. Our parents then had been deeply Christian, very strict, and two of the loveliest people I'd ever met. They'd put in their best efforts with us. Well, with me, at least. But they couldn't cope with Elliot's partying, so they'd let us go. I hadn't spoken to them since we'd left. I was conscious of bothering them, and they'd made no attempt to contact me, so that was that, I supposed.

As I said. It's always conditional.

I set my jaw and focussed on clearing my mind of those memories.

Elliot was lying in a stiff hospital bed, his dark hair matted from sweat and his blue eyes puffy and swollen. His good looks became marred enough when he got drunk. Now, they'd left the building. He looked more like a corpse than a heartthrob. An intravenous needle pumped some- thing unidentifiable into his hand, and a deep purple lump had formed on the side of his forehead. He must have fallen. Before the overdose or as a result of it, I didn't know. I made a mental note to call his friends and thank them profusely for having the sense to bring him in.

I hovered in the doorway, silent.

"I'm sorry," were his first words when he saw me.

"You said you'd be careful." I sounded like a whiny child.

"I didn't do it on purpose." He ran his tongue over cracked lips and I offered him my water bottle. He waved it away. "I'm gonna throw up," he said, pulling himself upright.

Wordlessly, I passed him the bucket.

He spent a few minutes bending over it, retching, but nothing came up. When he pulled away his eyes were tear- filled from the effort.

"You're going to die," I said. "Maybe not this time, but you are."

Elliot wiped his mouth and glared at me. "You're such an asshole."

"*I* am? One day you'll go to go see your friends, and I'll get dragged out of bed in the middle of the night to be told this time you didn't make it. I have nightmares about it all the time, and you're going to make them real."

The annoyance left Elliot's face. "I'm sorry."

"Okay."

"I am."

"Hmm."

"You should be at school."

"I'm staying here."

He nodded then smiled. "Good."

I sent a text to both James and Bea. James, to explain my absence. Bea, to inform her. Both asked if they should come. I told James it was family only. Elliot instructed me to tell Bea to stop being ridiculous and that she didn't need to spend two hundred pounds flying down to watch him throw up.

"I thought you didn't take drugs," I said later, selfishly ruining a period of comfortable silence. A naïve part of me still hoped that he'd assure me he didn't. That it was a stupid mistake. That he'd never do it again.

Instead, his expression clouded. "What, so now you're gonna stand there and judge me too? Fuck you, Ash. We can't all be fucking perfect, okay?"

He looked so angry, I almost riled up too. Then I remembered that Sue and Dom had been with him all night. I could only imagine how terrible they must have made him feel over this. There was little point making it worse. "I'm not judging you. But what if Alice finds out? What if she won't let me stay with you?"

"I'll tell them it was a one-off. An accident."

Now my worry for him gave way to resentment. We were so close, *so* close, and he was about to destroy our chances. Could he really not abstain from partying for one month? Did our chance of happiness matter that little to him? "What drugs do you do?"

"I don't *do* drugs," said Elliot, "I *did* drugs. Last night was an accident, and I feel like death right now, so could you get off my goddamn case? Please?"

I remained silent, wracked with fear and anxiety and trepidation. I wanted to believe him, but to me the speech was reminiscent of when he'd started drinking. He only got too drunk this once. It was always "just this once."

For the first time, I questioned the wisdom of moving out with Elliot. Would things get worse? What road *was* he heading down? Could I manage whatever came next?

Disgusted with myself, I pushed these thoughts out of my mind. I sounded like Sue. Elliot and I had to stay together. I needed him. I needed family. And if I gave up on him, who would he have left? What chance would he have if he didn't have one single person steadfastly on his side?

I'd figure things out. As long as we each had the other as a crutch, we'd fix things. We had to.

Mr. Patricks was less than thrilled to see me the next day, despite the fact that I managed to arrive on time. "And where were you yesterday, Ashton?" he asked as I entered the classroom with James walking beside me.

And once again I was the centre of attention. Some people smirked. Others, including Gemma and a few of my old friends, scanned me from head to toe, as though they were searching for evidence of—

Evidence of what? I thought. *That you're too stupid to be here? Or that you've turned into one of the guys who skip class to go smoke outside the local shops?*

I took a half-step backwards, as if I was trying to hide behind James. Maybe I was.

"Family stuff," I said. It was the safest answer, which is why I always resorted to it. No teacher wanted to press too hard after hearing this, in case they accidentally stumbled on something highly personal. No teacher except Mr. Patricks, that was. It seemed I'd used the excuse one too many times.

"Really?" he asked. "That's strange, because your family *called* the school yesterday to check that you were here. They were quite upset to hear you weren't."

Yes, I knew. Sue had called me, furious. I'd refused to leave the hospital until Elliot did, however. It didn't escape me that the single time she cared about my attendance at school was a ruse to ensure I wasn't there for Elliot when he needed me.

I shrugged. I intended it as a show of helplessness. Mr. Patricks took it as an act of defiance. "I assume you forgot about the maths quiz," he said with a bite to his tone. "If you bring in an excuse note signed by your parents I'll let you sit for a make-up in detention. If not, you're getting zero."

My maths grades weren't something I considered to be of paramount importance, so the threat itself didn't bother me. What bothered me was that the other kids in class were listening. I couldn't blame them for that. But still I despised proving them all right. For once, I'd relish the opportunity to surprise them. To prove I had some potential. Maybe even cause some of them to reassess me and wonder if I might not be all bad.

James, whose face had been growing darker as he listened beside me, opened his mouth to defend me. I shot him a pleading look. *Don't.* I desperately needed to return to my seat and be invisible. Away from the judgemental— or worse, *pitying*—stares of my classmates. Thankfully, James took the hint, and we went to our own desks quietly.

If I'd thought I saw too much of Mr. Patricks having him for both registration and Maths, being trapped in a room with him for an extra two lessons a week would rival

Roman Empire levels of torture. I could think of several ways I'd rather spend my afternoon than listen to my least favourite teacher describe genitalia. Such as performing brain surgery on myself with a chainsaw, for example.

"He let us pick our own seats," James said, beckoning me to the second to last row. "We're over here."

"You saved a seat for me yesterday?" Surprise and pleasure snuck into my tone against my will.

"Doesn't make any sense for me to share a desk with anyone else during sex-ed, does it?"

I didn't miss the connotation, and I sat down quickly, folding my arms to conceal my lap.

At the front of the classroom Mr. Patricks waited, wearing the same expression I imagined death row prisoners wore during their final ten minutes. "Alright, so I know you're all itching to get back into the birds and the bees," he said drily when we quietened, "but RSE doesn't just focus on that. It's also about your *inner* growth."

"So, STIs?" James murmured beside me, and I choked.

Mr. Patricks strolled across the front of the classroom with his hands behind his back. His thick lips were pursed while he thought. "I thought we could start with an exercise in opening up. Today you're going to write me a letter, and I want each one of you to tell me something that I don't know about you."

"Wonderful," I whispered. "Nice and corny."

Mr. Patricks glanced up at me with a hard expression. "Ashton, sounds like you must have been brainstorming during your break. Would you like to say yours out loud?"

I clasped my hands before me on the desk. "I would prefer not to."

For once, he didn't press it. Instead, he sat on the edge of his desk and allowed his legs to dangle. The effect was so startling I raised my eyebrows at James.

"That's fine," Mr. Patricks said. "I will, then."

The classroom buzzed with whispers, but they cut off as Mr. Patricks continued. "Something most of you don't know about me is that my father passed away a few days before the term began. I try not to bring my problems into the classroom, so I did my best to continue on as normal. But if I've been a bit more short-tempered than usual, I apologise."

You could have heard a mosquito land on the other end of the room it was so quiet. I don't think any of us were expecting to hear such a personal confession, but it got our attention anyway.

The silence was broken by a full volume guitar strum, followed by a cheesy keyboard riff as Mr. Patricks pressed play on the classroom stereo. I recognised the song. "Lord I Lift your Name on High." They'd made us sing it back in primary school.

"Jesus Christ," James muttered, not quietly enough.

"Yes, that's the guy," Mr. Patricks said, pointing at James with false enthusiasm. "Playing a few songs satisfies the Christian aspect of RSE. It was this or prayer-writing. If you'd prefer that . . ."

James held up his hands in surrender. Across the room I noticed Gemma point her index finger towards her temple and mime pulling a trigger. A couple of the football guys, Wyatt included, laughed. I didn't think it was a particularly funny joke. But then, I was rather more sensitive about the topic than the average student.

Two months or so ago, I might have been irritated to see anyone flirting with Gemma. A year before that, I probably would've been jealous of Gemma herself, given the way Wyatt was staring at her. But with James sitting next to me, shooting me that funny little half-smile—the one that made my stomach flip lately—I didn't feel anything except a warm glow. Gemma and Wyatt could strip each other naked and copulate on her desk right then and there, and I doubted I would even have torn my eyes away from James.

Still on his desk, Mr. Patricks made a sweeping gesture for us to start writing.

James was already scribbling away beside me. I leaned over to peek. *I'm good at a lot of things*, he'd written.

"That's not a secret, James," I stage whispered. "Everyone already knows that."

He swatted me away. "Fuck off, I'm not done yet."

I turned back to my own paper. What the hell could I write? Everyone around me was already bent over. No one else seemed to have any difficulty with the task. The thing was, however, everything Mr Patricks didn't know about me was too personal. He didn't know them for a reason.

Well, then, I supposed I'd have to write something personal. That was probably the point of the exercise, anyway.

I tapped my pen on the table, started writing, then stopped and crossed out the first sentence, losing my nerve. Then I regained it. I might as well be honest. It was unlikely to be the most scandalous letter Mr Patricks received.

Hi, Mr. Patricks.

Something you don't know about me is that I was off school yesterday because my brother overdosed and ended up in hospital, and I'm the only real family he has left, and I didn't want him to be alone.

Another thing you don't seem to know about me is I've never once slept in or skipped school because I don't want to be here or faked a sick day. Which is more than what I can say for most of the people in this class. There you go; two fun facts for the price of one.

I put my pen down, and James nodded towards the paper. I slid it across to him to read, and he passed me his.

I'm good at a lot of things, it said, *so I expect a lot from myself. When I'm in the middle of everything it feels manageable. I keep piling everything on, and I always fit it all in. But most nights I lie awake for hours freaking out about everything, like if I mess up one thing, I'll be letting everyone down. I don't like to complain, especially when I bring it on myself, but I'm scared of what will happen if I'm not the best at something. It's like I don't know who I am without that.*

Under the table I brushed my shoe over his, and he gave me a piercing look. "This is good, Ash," he whispered under his breath, and he pressed his leg against mine.

I prayed he didn't notice me blushing.

SIXTEEN

JAMES
October 2018

SEEKING ELLIOT:

You've been a massive help. If there's any chance you can find out the answer to a few things for me, I'll owe you for life.

1. Why did he leave Ash? One day they were moving out together, the next they weren't.

2. Did he speak to Ash on the day he died? If so, what about?

3. When did he find out Ash was dead?

4. What did he do the night Ash went missing?

So, I sounded like a stalker. Or a serial killer. Thank fuck Louise didn't seem to be the suspicious type. When this was all over, I was gonna send her a memo about catfishing. Girl could get in trouble trusting people this much.

I was surprised when she replied. She'd told me she was working tonight. Either she was on her break, or she was getting as into our information exchange as I was. Watson and Sherlock, going on adventures. Yay.

LOU CASTELLANO:
He says he didn't speak to Ash that day. He said he doubts Ash would've killed himself over an argument.

Oh, he didn't speak to Ash at all? Not at *all?* Well that was very interesting.

Well, Elliot, if you're so sure he didn't kill himself over an argument, then tell me what the hell happened. What happened in those few hours between our fight and his jump? Come on. I'm waiting.

Bit by bit, it was coming out. Any minute now, something was gonna give. It was surprisingly easy to blow holes in people's story when they underestimated how much you knew.

SEEKING ELLIOT:
Well, I'm not sure Elliot's in a position to comment on what Ash would've done, but anyway. If he says he didn't speak to him that day, I have my answer.

LOU CASTELLANO:
Just because Elliot didn't talk to him doesn't mean you should blame yourself. Besides, like I said. He doesn't think it would've been over a fight.

I sighed at my phone and shook it. Did Louise seriously believe that all of this was because I blamed myself? I'd have to be the most dysfunctional person *alive* to go to all these lengths to convince myself I was innocent. I already knew I was partly to blame. I'd come to terms with that a long time ago.

But I couldn't tell Louise that. Not yet. So I stuck to the narrative for a little longer.

SEEKING ELLIOT:

Elliot doesn't know the full story. He never even knew Ash was cutting. He didn't know anything about Ash's problems at school. Worse, he was the one causing half the problems Ash had at school. He spent most of his time smashed off his face, out with friends, coming home in the morning and needing Ash to look after him. I doubt he was sober often enough during those last few months to even notice anything was wrong. So excuse me if I sound rude, but yeah. I don't put much value on Elliot's opinion of Ash's suicide.

It was hard to hold back. I wanted to tell Louise everything. Just how shit of a brother Elliot was. How bad things had gotten. How much their foster parents had clearly favoured Ash. And how afraid I was that Elliot was more like their dad than Ash thought. But doing that would only lose her. Louise and I were playing a super risky game here. Only she didn't know it. For now, I needed to keep it that way.

LOU CASTELLANO:

I don't know what to say, James. I'm not suggesting you're lying, but Elliot doesn't drink. Like, ever. It's so weird to hear you describe him like this. I feel like I don't even know him.

Hah. She didn't. She didn't know the first thing about him.

I'd had zero intention to tell her anything yet. But now, suddenly, I wanted her to know. She needed to know Elliot wasn't innocent in all this. Was she ready for some harsh truths? Maybe it'd make her realise it was stupid to be blindly loyal to a guy who probably couldn't give a shit about her. How much could he care, after all, if he couldn't even keep his lies straight?

SEEKING ELLIOT:
By the way. Just so you know. He's lying to your face. He spoke to Ash right before he died.

SEVENTEEN

ASH
May 2017

"ASHTON, I NEED YOU to hang around for a second," Mr. Patricks said over the routine classroom chaos at the end of Wednesday afternoon.

James exchanged a glance with me. I waved him on as though my every muscle hadn't tightened in a sudden fight or flight response.

"I'll text you later, okay?" James asked, and I gave him history's most unconcerned nod of acknowledgement while I fought off approaching hyperventilation.

Mr. Patricks leaned against his desk and smiled awkwardly as the classroom emptied. In an effort to hide my trepidation, I sat on a desk at the front of the room, crossing my legs beneath me. It was one thing to be nervous or worried. It was another to look pathetic.

I expected Mr. Patricks to tell me off for sitting on the desk, but he ignored it. "I read your letter," he began.

I could predict the exact trajectory of this conversation. This happened every time I tried to share anything with an adult. They were never happy to just leave well enough alone. They always had to get others involved. He probably had Alice waiting in the office, ready to tell me I wasn't allowed to stay with Elliot anymore. The blood drained from my face. Why had I shared something so sensitive, and now, of all times? Why couldn't I have just told him I couldn't stomach the taste of liquorice, or something equally risk-free? "I didn't know there were going to be meetings," I said.

"There won't be meetings," Mr. Patricks said. "I just wanted a quick debrief with you." I didn't answer. He waited a few seconds and then continued. "I'm a teacher, but I'm also human. Sometimes I can be quick to make assumptions. Your letter, along with a few others, have highlighted that what I see of you all during class is never enough to assume I know the whole story."

I considered this. "I don't think you can ever know someone's full story. Even if you know them well. Unless they tell you."

"Well, I wanted to apologise for forgetting I don't know everything about you."

"It's cool." I knew I'd gone red, and I wanted to crawl inside of an Ashton-sized paper bag. I'd never had a teacher say sorry to me before. Or even speak to me one-on-one about a non-school related topic. It felt wrong. Like I should apologise for making him feel like he needed to say sorry.

"I'd like to apologise for not bothering to get to know you in the first place," he added.

That was taking it too far. I wanted to sink through the floor. "There's not much to know."

I'd preferred it when he'd been irritated by me. At least it was a familiar role.

"If there's ever something you'd like me to know, I want you to feel you can tell me," he said. "On the spot, or after class, or leave a note if you want. If there's anything you might need help with, or if you need extra patience one day, I'll listen."

"If you want to help . . ." I said cautiously, testing the waters.

"Yes?"

"I'd . . ." Did I dare? "I'd appreciate it if you'd try to ignore me a little more, please. Like the other teachers do. It makes things easier." Something flashed across his face. For some reason my answer seemed to have upset him. Things were growing more awkward by the second. Time for an emergency evacuation. "If that's okay, I mean. Whatever. Is there anything else, or . . .?"

He still seemed sad, but he pressed his lips together and nodded. "Yes. Don't worry about the maths quiz. I'll average out the rest of the students' grades and that'll be yours."

I could hardly believe my luck. "Thank you."

"Have a good night, Ashton."

I checked my phone as I left the classroom. There was a text waiting from James.

All good?

All good. I replied.

At home I headed immediately into the shower before Elliot had the chance to come home and use up all the hot water. As I turned off the taps I heard Sue talking to Dom outside, and I hovered uncertainly in the bathroom without making a sound. If they remained in the hallway for too long I'd have no choice other than to walk out in front of them, but I wanted to try my luck at waiting them out. To my relief their footsteps faded, and I took the chance to dart to my room.

I was being stupid, and I knew it, but I didn't want to face them and make uncomfortable eye contact, and determine if I was supposed to say something, or apologise for intruding on their conversation. On their house in general, I suppose. I was doing them a favour by minimising the impact of my existence on their lives.

Whenever Elliot came home, I relaxed, feeling less vulnerable. Since he'd returned from hospital, things had been better than I'd expected. He'd stopped going out. Instead, he spent the evenings with me, speaking or watching films or simply sitting in silence while we enjoyed each other's proximity.

Maybe the overdose was the wake-up call he'd so sorely needed. At least it seemed like he was going to be on his best behaviour until we moved out together. As far as I was concerned this was all worth the terror I'd felt when I found out he was in hospital. It was more than a fair payoff to have my brother back.

Which is why I was so caught off-guard to find Dave by Elliot's side when I came out to greet him that evening. Guilt sparked in Elliot's eyes, and I knew exactly why Dave was there. I'd seen this all before when Elliot had first started drinking. Except alcohol didn't cause that shameful slouch anymore. Which narrowed the likely vices down. "We're gonna be busy all night. Don't bother me, okay? If there's an emergency, text me."

I didn't reply. I only glared at him, my head spinning from the disappointment of the betrayal.

He noticed my expression and mirrored it. "*What?* What's the problem?"

When I didn't reply, he rolled his eyes, let Dave into his room, and closed the door behind them.

And that was that. I was unsure whether Dave had brought drugs with him or if Elliot kept some hidden in his room, but that was so *obviously* what they were doing. I clearly wasn't enough of a reason for him to stop. Sue and Dom might have been able to intervene, but if I involved them, they would inform Alice. I was helpless.

I slammed my door with as much force as I could muster. Sat there while Sue and Dom ate dinner, and Elliot and Dave laughed and chatted behind his closed door. Kept sitting while Sue and Dom cleaned up. And while Elliot and Dave exchanged hushed thoughts, breaking into laughter every few seconds. Sat while muffled thuds rang out from his room. Filling the passing hours with my thoughts.

I was in control. It would be okay. None of this was real, so it couldn't affect me.

But that wasn't working. Nothing was working. I was going to crack.

No, I'm not, I told myself. *I'm going to go to sleep and ignore it.*

I couldn't, though. My body was a bruise. Even contact with air was too much to bear. There was too much pressure, no release. No other way I could distract myself. Nothing else I could do to relieve it.

As quietly as I could I stole into the bathroom and shuffled through the contents of the cupboard. Each slight clash of metal and plastic rang out like dynamite. I paused every few seconds, certain that Sue or Dom would approach. No one came after me, though. Then I found what I was looking for. A half-used packet of disposable shaving razors.

Safely back in my room I held the blade between my fingers, examining its clean edge. It was my enemy and my temporary saviour at the same time. What a contrary little object.

At the back of my closet I found a jumper that was too

short for me. Balling it up as a rag, I slid out of my jeans and examined my newly-healed canvas. Then hesitated.

It was late at night now. I shouldn't bother anybody. This was my problem. It was mine to deal with.

I pressed the pad of a finger against the razor's edge and bit my lip. I promised James I'd call him.

But I didn't want to become a drain on him. What if he began to resent me?

No. I was leaving James out of this.

So why are you hesitating? The voice in my mind demanded.

Because I didn't *want* to do this. I just needed relief.

Goddamn it. Why was every option the wrong one as soon as I chose it?

More than anything, I didn't want to be alone.

I was so tired of being trapped with only my mind for company.

Please don't hate me, James, I thought. *I'm sorry.*

James picked up the phone on the second ring. "Ash?" His voice was gluggy with sleep, but he didn't sound annoyed.

"Hey," I said uncertainly, turning the blade.

"Hey?"

"I'm sorry, I know it's late. I just . . . wanted to say hey."

James was alert now. "Can I come over?"

"Yeah. If you want."

"I'll be five minutes. Unlock the front door, 'kay?"

"Yeah. Sure," I whispered, halfway across the house to do so already.

Back in my room I threw the destroyed plastic in the bin and placed the blade on the bedside table behind the lamp.

When James entered he kicked off his shoes and climbed onto my bed behind me, wrapping his arms around my chest. "I'm proud of you," he murmured against my ear.

The skin of his neck was cashmere against my cheek.

His presence snapped me out of my dreamlike state. I hugged him back as tightly as I could, overwhelmed with relief to have him there.

I crawled underneath the blankets while he got up to flick the light off. Back in bed, he pressed his body against mine, already shivering. "Fuck, it's freezing in here."

"Harden up," I teased.

James pulled back a little and used the space to stroke my hair, slow and methodical. My stomach swooped so violently that I thought I might pass out. "I've got an alarm set for five," he said. "My parents will murder me if they find out I didn't sleep at home."

"Excellent idea."

"I'm full of them." He pressed a kiss on the shell of my ear, light enough that I almost missed it.

I remained in his arms until my thoughts grew disoriented, giving way to various incomprehensible trains. It was funny, I realised in a moment of clarity. Usually I couldn't sleep until I'd changed positions twenty odd times. James running his fingers through my hair was the world's most effective sedative.

He stilled, and I thought he'd fallen asleep. He must have assumed the same about me, because his whisper was so faint it couldn't have possibly been meant for my ears. In the silence, though, I heard it as clearly as if he'd shouted. *You're so beautiful.*

My eyes flew open. I counted to ten, then rolled over to face him, throwing my arm over his back. He shifted closer, cuddling into me. I slipped my hand under his shirt and began to trace over his bare back, allowing my fingertip to carve a message into his skin. A message I'd never be confident enough to admit out loud. *I need you.*

It was the truth. And strangely, the thought didn't scare

me.

There wasn't much chance James could tell what I was writing. He probably didn't realise I was tracing letters at all. Nonetheless, when he furrowed a sleepy head into the curve of my neck, I kidded myself that maybe he'd understood me. If anyone could listen to my silence and hear the words I wanted to speak, it was him.

It was the first time in months I'd been so content, so *secure*. A voice at the back of my mind warned me not to let my guard down. I blocked it out.

See, the thing is, happiness is a whore. I've never met a more disloyal emotion in my life. Nothing like misery, which proposes to you on the first date. Yet, like a mistress I swear off every time, all happiness has to do is peek its head around the corner, contrite and apologetic, and I give myself over to it completely. It's transient and fleeting, and I know it won't still be in my bed the next morning, but while I have it, it's everything.

That night, it was everything.

EIGHTEEN

Ash
May 2017

James disappeared by the time I woke up. I hadn't even heard him leave. I rubbed the sleep from my eyes and touched the empty spot on my mattress, the one he'd occupied the night before. The memory of being in his arms, of what he'd said, came back to me.

Something had shifted. Whatever this was, it wasn't two friends experimenting anymore. If that's what it had ever been. I didn't know exactly what we were, but I was certain that if James came to me that day and said he was seeing someone I would be devastated. And I also knew the idea of kissing anyone else made me ill.

Were we together? James had never told me how he'd gotten with his ex. Had they formally decided they were monogamous, or had it just *happened?* Had it already *happened* with us? How did you know? Did he think we were together? I wasn't certain, but after last night I felt quite confident he wouldn't be against clarification attempts. I would ask then, I decided, and everything inside me somersaulted. Wow. I might have a boyfriend by the end of the day. Not just anyone. James. I might be with *James*.

I couldn't help myself. I had to share it with someone. Usually I'd tell anything exciting to James. Obviously, he was ruled out. And I was still annoyed at Elliot from last night, so he was no longer an option. Acting entirely on impulse, I sent through a text to Bea.

What would you say if I told you I had a boyfriend?

It was only after I sent it that I realised how bold that was. I'd basically come out to her. What if she had an issue with it? I stared at my phone, waiting for her answer, and I started to worry. What if she said something cruel? Or worse, what if she gave one of those noncommittal "I'm only pretending to be civil" responses? What if she told Elliot? I didn't expect her to mind, to be fair. She was about the most left-wing person in the country. But still. You never really knew, did you?

Her response gave me my answer.

I'd say send me a picture.

This was why I loved her. I felt dizzy with relief, and, relaxing, I allowed myself to get swept up in the excitement. I'd forgotten what feeling light was like.

What if I said you don't need a picture?

She responded immediately.

WHO ARE YOU DATING? Tell me everything!

I would. But she could wait. It would be wiser to check

in with James first. The humiliation would be quite difficult to swallow if I confirmed I was with him to Bea, only to find out he didn't see us that way.

James seemed listless when I arrived at school. Not as talkative as usual. It was more than likely due to me dragging him out of bed to trudge through the freezing cold. Still, his distance made me hesitate. Maybe I would leave it for a few hours. Or days. What was the rush?

Twenty minutes before the end of the lesson, James was excused to the bathroom. Three minutes later, my phone buzzed. I peeked at it when Mr. Patricks's back was turned. It was James, asking me to meet him.

I couldn't think why he'd want to do that. My instincts, ever pessimistic, were screaming that whatever was coming wouldn't be good, and I briefly flirted with the idea of ignoring the invitation and blaming Mr. Patricks. Curiosity got the better of me, though, and I decided to attempt to get out of class.

I wasn't full of optimism, given that asking to be excused at the same time as James would cause any of our teachers to laugh at us on a normal day, but to my surprise Mr. Patricks didn't hesitate to provide permission. It must have been part of his "fresh start" initiative.

James was pacing alone in the bathroom. I shut the door behind me and leaned against it, as though that would guarantee privacy.

"So," he started, playing with the hem of his shirt and standing in one place. "I've wanted to say this for a while, but I was too worried."

His whispered words from the night before came back to me and I exhaled. This could only go one way, surely. A thrill coursed through my veins, and I allowed myself a small smile. "Worried about what?"

"Well, since you've been cutting again, I've been . . . I

dunno, scared of doing something to make it worse."

My smile faltered as I tried to make sense of what he was saying. This wasn't where I'd expected the conversation to go. He studied me intently while he talked. He seemed afraid. "I wanna say first up that you should still come to me if you need help. I don't want this to affect that or our friendship. It can't affect it, can it? I mean, we've been friends our whole lives."

"Got something to spit out, *mon homme*?" I asked, my voice cold. I wasn't using the term fondly, and he knew that very well. I used French for one reason and one reason only: it lent itself wonderfully to sarcasm.

James hesitated, then hardened. "We need to stop what we're doing."

Inwardly, I broke. Outwardly, I merely raised and lowered my eyebrows in an unimpressed gesture. "That was anticlimactic. I'm supposed to cut myself over that? You underestimate me."

"Don't be mad at me, Ash."

I bristled. "I'm not mad. It doesn't bother me either way."

"Please tell me this won't make things awkward. We shouldn't have taken it as far as we did. It was stupid."

"It won't make things awkward," I lied.

I wanted to be left alone. *Needed* to be by myself. Would it be obvious that I wasn't okay if I went home? Probably. I tossed up the desire to save face against the desire to stare at the wall in silence. I'd have to survive recess, and lunch, and RSE was after lunch, *and* he would want to walk home. The thought of lasting the rest of the day was dizzying. "Is that all?" I asked.

"Well, I just . . . I want you to know it's not personal."

"*Okay*, James. It's fine."

James blinked, looking offended. *Offended.* I wanted to scream at him. "As long as you don't care."

"I don't."

"Good."

"It is."

Why was he still staring at me? What exactly did he expect me to say? Did he expect me to hang around and chat after effectively being dumped? To make some inane comment about the weather to clear the air? Without bothering to say goodbye, I stalked out of the bathroom and headed partway down the hall.

Why now? If he didn't want me, why had he let us carry on for so long? Hadn't he noticed I was getting too invested? Apparently, he was simply desperate. I'd thrown myself at him, and he'd gone for it because it was the only offer going.

Suddenly, I was walking back to the bathroom. I knew I was right, but I wanted to hear it from him because I was a masochist.

James was standing by the far wall hugging himself. He wiped a clenched palm hastily under his eyes when I entered, and I realised with a start that he was crying.

I hovered by the door, uncertain. "What's wrong?"

James's expression grew dark, and he turned to the wall to hide his face as a tear fell. "Fuck off."

"Well, no."

"You're going to stand there and make me say it?" he asked, gulping. "Screw you."

I was lost. "Okay, James, did you or did you not just end things with *me?*"

He turned around now, scanning me with puffy eyes. "You need me to say it?"

"Preferably, yes."

"Fine. I don't wanna keep going because it's hurting me. Because I like you, and I've liked you forever, okay? And I shouldn't have let us do anything, but I wanted to . . . I dunno. I was happy, so I didn't mind at first."

I blinked. "I don't understand. What didn't you mind?"

"That it didn't mean anything."

Was I following him correctly? Unwilling to jump to conclusions this time, I stepped through the doorway cautiously. "I think we may have some communication issues."

Another tear rolled down James's cheek, and he made no effort to wipe it away. He was waiting for me to continue. It was now or never. I started by stating the obvious. "All right, so I think I'm bi. I mean, I know I am. I am firmly bisexual."

James nodded uncertainly, looking at the wall behind me.

"Come on, James, you had to have figured that much out?"

"Go on."

I approached him the way someone might approach a bird that they were afraid would take flight any second. He remained perfectly still. I brushed his wet cheek with my thumb, my heart thudding so wildly I was afraid it might fail me. "It meant something to me."

James tore away from my touch and squeezed his eyes shut, tears glistening on his eyelashes like dew. "You said you didn't like me. You specifically said that."

"That's the fascinating thing about feelings," I said, leaning in. "They're not fixed."

He opened his eyes as I kissed him.

It was nothing like the way we'd kissed before. All of the others had been hungry, eager. This was gentle. A different sort of kiss.

The kind that resonates in your fingertips.

The kind that wraps itself around your soul and softens it.

When I pulled away, James burst into a smile so radiant that it planted itself on my own face.

"You've liked me forever?" I asked, touching my forehead

to his.

He laced his fingers through mine, skirting his thumb across the palm of my hand. He lifted his chin as though to kiss me, but merely brushed his lips, feather-light, against mine before replying. "Years. You knew, though."

For years? "I didn't."

"Are you sure? I thought I was so obvious."

"I'm sure," I smiled.

James studied me, squeezing my hand until it hurt. "So, what are you saying?"

"Come on, James."

"I know, I know, but I wanna hear you say it. Humour me here."

My cheeks flushed. "I have feelings for you. Are you happy?"

James pulled away from me and doubled over, wrapping his arms so tightly around his front that my first thought was that something was wrong. Then he straightened, crossed his clenched hands across his chest and threw his head back to look at the ceiling in an unashamed celebration.

I laughed with him, all the tension and fear replaced by a giddy, muddled ecstasy. When he was done, he grabbed me by the crook of the elbow and pulled me out of the bathroom. "Get your ass to the classroom," he scolded, shoving me towards the stairwell. "You've wasted valuable learning time."

"Whose fault is that?" I walked backwards up a few steps.

He hesitated by the bottom of the stairwell. "The bell's gonna go soon."

"Right. We should hurry."

"Yeah, we should."

"Definitely."

"Absolutely."

Instead we stood facing each other, grinning like absolute idiots until the bell went. We were forced to sprint back to Maths and gather our stuff before the next group of students filed in.

Mr. Patricks leaned a hand on the desk when we burst in, prepared to tell us off, but he took one look at our faces and closed his mouth. I hesitated, about to apologise, but instead I beamed at him, bounced on my toes, and scooped my books off my desk. He watched me with an incredulous expression, then, amazingly, smiled in return.

NINETEEN

LOUISE
October 2018

SEEKING ELLIOT:
He told me when Ash went missing that they hadn't spoken. But I found out later from their foster mum that the police found a call log between the two of them around the time he died. Elliot apparently told the police Ash called him and asked him to meet at the beach, but he was too drunk to go. If that's what happened, though, why does he keep lying about it? And why didn't he tell anyone that night?

"Okay, I'm sure of it," Elliot announced as he burst through the door.

I jumped and shoved my phone in my pocket. "Sure of what?"

"There's a club of people dedicated to making loud calls on otherwise peaceful public transport trips. I think they must allocate members on a rotating roster. They have the whole timetable covered." He threw his iPhone down on my bed and fell on top of it.

"What possible reason could they have for that?" I asked. My heart was playing the bongos somewhere in my chest. Hopefully he couldn't hear it.

Elliot gave me a dramatic, dark look. "Some people just want to watch the world burn."

Instead of replying, I stared at him, trying to conjure up an image of him drinking every night. I couldn't. He wasn't even a big coffee drinker, for God's sake. It was like picturing Emma Watson biting the head off a bat, or Ariana Grande moshing to death metal. Then I imagined that I'd gone missing, or Rachael, or Jacob, or Saras. Elliot would be a total wreck, I decided. He'd do everything he could to find us. He wouldn't hide information or brush off a search party in favour of a different kind of party.

So what did that mean? Was it possible James was lying?

Like, maybe. But he hadn't been lying about Elliot having a brother.

Only Elliot had lied about that.

Elliot, all perky and chirpy, didn't even notice the way I was looking at him. I tried not to let my feelings show on my face, but I knew they were. They always did. I wasn't one of those suave manipulators who could form a fake friendship with their worst enemy. My emotional control was more in the range of a four-year-old throwing a tantrum at bedtime. Something else I was going to go ahead and blame on Abuela's genes.

"So, I'm thinking Netflix. We have three hours. Suggestions?" He hung back over the edge of the bed and looked at me upside down while I sat on my desk chair.

"I thought tonight was your night off?"

"Mm, but Greg called in sick, and I'm greedy. Not going to buy a mansion sitting on my ass, am I?"

"Not going to buy a mansion working at Bruno's," I replied.

My phone buzzed. I ignored it.

"I'll be the new Bruno. Join you in usurping Joe. Open a chain of Bruno's. Take over the country. There's your empire right there."

"Why stop there?" I asked. "I see Bruno's going international."

I wondered what James had texted. My phone buzzed again.

"Interstellar. First piece-of-shit restaurant on Mars." Elliot grabbed my laptop and grinned at me. "Anyway. What show? Or are you feeling a film?"

Eurgh. I had to check it. I so didn't have the willpower for this. I made a note to never pick up smoking as I took out my phone. "I don't know. Whatever you feel like."

SEEKING ELLIOT:
Ash was my boyfriend.

SEEKING ELLIOT:
Elliot also left Ash right after finding out about us. Coincidentally. Maybe.

Ash had been his boyfriend? So that's why he was so determined to figure out what happened. No wonder he wasn't letting this go.

He'd been his *boyfriend*. His boyfriend had killed himself. I felt sick thinking about it. God—poor, poor James.

I'd never been more confused in my life. I kept oscillating between being on James's side and Elliot's. How could I be on James's side when I was supposed to be loyal to

Elliot? How could I be on Elliot's side when I was starting to think I couldn't trust him?

Scratch that. I *didn't* trust him. How could I keep blindly taking his side when he'd lied to my face repeatedly without flinching?

Had he turned on Ash for being gay? Or had he lied about that too?

Elliot finally noticed my expression. "What's wrong?" he asked, putting the laptop on my bed. He looked at me with his usual concern. Liar. Goddamn liar. He'd always come across as caring and loyal. He'd been so convincing.

"Did you disown your brother because he was gay?" I asked flatly.

"Oh my *God*, Louise," he said, slamming the laptop closed. "You have no idea when to leave things alone, do you?"

"*Did you?*" I asked, folding my arms.

"*No!* Jesus Christ."

"James seems to think you did."

Elliot looked to the ceiling. He was clearly trying to keep from exploding at me. Well, if he wanted a fight, I was ready for it. Then, he turned to look at me slowly. "How do *you* know that?"

I couldn't respond. I'd realised at the same time as him that I'd given myself away. I tucked one leg beneath me and stared at the ground. What was that about dodging land-mines?

"Are you talking to James?" he asked, sitting up straight. His face was red with anger.

There was no point denying it now. "Yes."

"Stop," he said. "If you give a shit about our friendship, you'll stop speaking to him. Now."

"You keep lying to me. You can't talk about keeping our friendship when you can't even tell me the truth."

Just like that, all the extra colour left his face, and then some. "What has he told you?"

"Enough. And his stories seem to be getting more and more inconsistent with yours. Why did you leave your brother if it wasn't over being gay?"

"You know what?" he asked. "That is actually none of your business. None of this is."

"It's James's business."

"Like hell it is. I can't *believe* you've been talking to him behind my back."

"You can't ignore him, Elliot! How heartless can you be? He's devastated."

"He has to move on. I have."

"You have not. What are you hiding?"

"Nothing," Elliot said, slamming a hand on the bed. "I just want to forget him, okay? Why can't everyone let the past stay where it belongs?"

"We're not asking you to exhume his body. Stop being so melodramatic."

"I'm not talking to him, Louise. Okay? Not *ever*. If you don't stop speaking to him, I'm done with you."

I gaped, stunned. Done with me? Was he really going there?

Why, exactly, was he so terrified of me talking to James? Enough to threaten me to force me to stop?

"What are you afraid of?" I asked, lowering my voice. "What happened that day?"

"What, when my brother died? He jumped off a bridge."

"Why?"

"Because he wanted to die."

"*Why*?"

"What do you mean 'why'?" Elliot snapped. "What is *wrong* with you?"

"Elliot," I said, "I love you. There is nothing in the world that you could say that will change that. If you need to talk to me, you can. I won't tell James."

I needed to know why he was so frightened. What did he do? How could I help him?

"You shouldn't have told him anything," he said. "Just . . . I can't. I can't do this. I'm going."

"Elliot, stop, please." I followed him out of my bedroom and through the hallway. "Talk to me. Tell me what's going on. I'm worried about you."

"Everything would've been fine if you'd minded your own business," he said, not even turning around. "If you're worried about me, *stop talking to him*."

Okay.

No, not okay.

I'd do it. He was right. It was none of my business.

But what was he hiding?

No. I had to trust him. If I couldn't trust him, what was the point?

Eurgh. They needed a rulebook for this kind of shit. Wasn't there some sort of self-help book I could buy? *He's Just Not That Into You Discovering His Secret Past?*

Elliot stormed straight down the road without looking back. I couldn't tell if it was in the direction of work or his house. Feeling like the worst friend in the world, I messaged James.

LOU CASTELLANO:
I told him I've been speaking to you. He was furious. I'm sorry I couldn't help you. I hope things work out for you, James.

I could feel eyes burning into my neck. I flipped around to find Abuela standing in the lounge room doorway, one over-plucked eyebrow raised in a silent question. "So much shouting," she said.

"He's angry at me."

"Why?"

Great. Here came the judgement. God forbid I do anything to make Elliot mad.

Or maybe that was just my guilt speaking.

"I have two friends," I said slowly. "If I make one happy, I make the other one unhappy."

Abuela nodded and sat down on the couch. I plopped down on the carpet and faced her, stretching out my legs. "Somebody always unhappy," she said. "You need to make yourself happy."

That surprised me. What, so her advice *wasn't* to totally ignore what I wanted in this?

Okay. Alright. I could roll with this. Then what would make me happy?

The truth.

I just wanted to know the truth.

To know who the hell my best friend was, because it was becoming abundantly clear I had no idea.

But at the same time, I didn't want to hurt him. Was my curiosity worth that?

And if I decided it was, what kind of friend did that make me?

My phone buzzed.

James had responded.

I opened the message with a heavy heart. A heart that jumped right up into my throat when I read what he had to say.

SEEKING ELLIOT:

Look. I know you care about Elliot. So I'll tell you this.

He's lying. He's lied about a lot of things. And bit by bit I'm figuring it all out. I'm going to the police unless something convinces me not to.

One way or another, he's gonna admit what happened that day.

I wanted to give him the benefit of the doubt before I involved them. But my patience is just about done.

LOU CASTELLANO:

The police? Why would you do that?

SEEKING ELLIOT:

I haven't been completely honest with you.

TWENTY

Ash
May 2017

STEP ONE. GET A boyfriend. Done.

Step two. Tell Elliot. Not done.

It's not that I cared to hide it. I simply didn't want to sit him down and inform him I was bisexual. Why make an event of it? I never had to sit anyone down and explain I was about to start dating girls. I just went ahead and did that. Compared to that, coming out in order to date James seemed like asking permission.

That settled it. I was going to tell Elliot about James. *Without* any precursory explanations. If he was surprised, let him be. If he was upset . . . Well. The thought of that made my stomach twist with fear, but it was a risk I was going to take. Despite the ever-present paranoia that Elliot *would* react badly, I didn't truly believe he would. He knew

James was gay, after all, and he never said a solitary word about that. So, in taking an inventory of the people I actually acknowledged the opinion of, there was Bea, who knew, James, who knew *very* well, and Elliot. Once Elliot knew, there completed my coming-out trifecta.

When I was younger, I'd been terrified of my own feelings. At one point I'd even vowed to only act on crushes I had on girls. These days, however, I couldn't have cared any less what everyone else in the world thought. Anybody who wasn't Bea, or James, or Elliot could figure it out in their own time, because I certainly didn't owe them any explanations.

I was lucky that James had already trodden the path of sin so thoroughly. That grass had been flat for years now. I already knew who the homophobes in town were, and that they were far outweighed by those who couldn't care less who slept with who. His risk had been a flying leap into an abyss, which rendered mine a calculated gamble at most.

The only aspect left to ascertain was the "when."

I was lost in thought about it while James and I watched a film. Which usually meant we spoke about whatever came to mind, or made out, or both, while we ignored whatever film was on.

I was about to seek James's opinion on telling Elliot about us, but the moment I turned to him, he cupped a hand around my chin and steered me to meet him in a soft kiss. When we parted James kept his hand lingering on my neck, stroking my jawline with such unabashed affection in his expression that I forgot about the film altogether.

"Why do you like me?" I asked.

With a laugh James detached from me and threw himself backwards on the mattress, allowing his arms to fall above his head while arching his neck. "James, *please*, shower me with compliments," he said.

"I'm serious."

"I *need* compliments—I *crave* them—they *fuel* me."

"I get it," I grinned.

"*Feed me.*" He rolled over and grasped at me.

"Okay, okay, I never asked." I kept smiling, but it was tinged with disappointment. I turned my attention back to the film.

In my peripheral, James studied me. I pretended not to notice.

"You make me laugh," he said. "And I don't have to try to censor myself around you. Like, with everyone else I'm putting on an act at least a bit. Making sure I say the right things and like the right things. You're probably the only person who lets me be who I wanna be. Even if it's mopey, or stressed, or mean." He put an arm across my chest. "And there's the obvious. You're gorgeous."

"I—"

"You *are*. And don't argue—you asked for compliments."

"I asked for clarification."

"Well, then, my clarification is I think you're hot as hell. And you *know* me. You know everything I've ever done wrong, and every embarrassing moment I've ever had, and you still wanna be around me."

"Of course I do," I said, shuffling around to rest my head on his shoulder. "You're the best person I know."

"That's another one. I get the feeling that if I could see myself the way you see me, I'd like what I was looking at."

I knew exactly what he meant.

"So, do you think you're fifty-fifty?" James asked suddenly. "You don't have a preference at all?"

"I'm not following."

"You know. For girls and guys."

Right. "I don't know. Maybe. It's hard to tell."

"How is it hard to tell? It's a simple question." James's

smile had drifted. This was why I hated discussing this with him. He appeared to consider my attraction to girls a personal insult.

"Well how would you like me to measure it?" I asked. "How many crushes I've had on each? Or should I try to rate how strongly I've felt about each one of them and average it out? I could start keeping a tally over what kind of porn I watch most. Mind you," I said, pretending to be deep in thought, "then I'd probably have to rate each orgasm out of ten to compare quality to quantity."

"Whatever." James didn't crack a smile.

"Why does it matter so much?"

"I dunno. If you like chicks more, then I'll feel weird. Like you're waiting to meet one you like more than me."

Right. As though the way I felt about James couldn't possibly be as valid as the way he felt about me. Because I didn't only like guys. What did he think I was? A straight person experimenting? Or did he hope I would deny how I felt about girls, so he could slot me into a file labelled "gay" and cease worrying that I'd realise I didn't like guys after all?

I attempted to view it as a compliment, to tell myself it was a good thing he didn't want to lose me. But instead I felt hurt.

I kept my tone light when I replied. "Since when are you so insecure?"

He chewed on his lower lip and shrugged.

"James," I said, inching closer. "I like you more than *anyone*. I'm not going to get distracted because a pretty girl shows up."

"Because I'm probably prettier anyway?" he joked, softening.

"Yes. Exactly."

The topic seemed to be over. We lapsed back into silence, and James stroked my hair. A habit he'd recently developed, and one I had nil objections towards. "You need a haircut," he murmured absently.

I knew that. But it would involve requesting money from Sue and Dom. I could probably ask Elliot to assist—usually he would have noticed himself. But lately he'd been quite distracted.

I didn't want to ask for money, because it would mean bothering Sue and Dom. One of the most relentless of the Little Bad Things was the persistent sense that my existence made life a little less enjoyable for those stuck with me. As far as I was concerned, the very worst thing I could be was a nuisance. But here I was. A constant nuisance.

Not even just for Sue and Dom. The only reason I was able to keep attending private school was because Dad had insisted on paying the bill until I graduated. I supposed it was his way of apologising. Which I despised for a variety of reasons. The first being that it was so much more difficult to hate someone while in debt to them. Another was the knowledge that, four times a year, a probably unwelcome bill served as a reminder of my existence to Dad. It would be the only time he had to bother with me. Sometimes, if I let myself think about it, I wondered if he resented me every time the school bills came in. If he regretted me.

Half-closing my eyes, I let James continue touching me for a while longer. Instead of asking James when we should inform Elliot about us, something else—the something I'd been working so diligently not to ponder—left my lips. "Elliot's still taking drugs."

He dropped his hand. "Shit. Seriously?"

"Yes. He's just changed the location. His friends come over here for it."

James seemed thoughtful. "So he doesn't just do it at parties?"

"No. It looks like one-on-one events these days."

I didn't have to explain the issue. Not only was this a direct threat to Elliot being appointed my guardian, it surpassed that. Was Elliot addicted to something? If not, would he end up that way? Was choosing to live with someone addicted to drugs the most idiotic decision I could ever make?

"When does he get home from work?" James asked.

"About an hour."

"He'd have a stash in his room, I bet."

"That seems likely."

"It'd be too bad if it wasn't there the next time he went to use, huh?"

James's face was alight, but I shrugged. "What good would that do? He can get more."

"Oh, long-term it won't do shit. But wouldn't you find it satisfying?"

I thought about it and broke into a grin. "Yes. Yes I would."

"Right then." James hopped to his feet and left the room. I ran after him.

It was odd going into Elliot's bedroom without him. Like we were breaking into a bank. His room looked the same in his absence; a few t-shirts balled up at the foot of his dresser, doodles decorating his desk, his laptop perched on the pillow of his unmade bed. Technically I wasn't seeing anything I couldn't see with him there. But it was an invasion of privacy either way.

James held no such reservations. Without hesitating he opened the top drawer of Elliot's desk and rifled through it. I watched him with a twinge of regret and guilt, then lowered to my knees to explore under the bed. Dust, a single shoe, a rolled-up pair of socks, a dog-eared book—nothing especially illegal in appearance.

James was sifting through the bottom drawer when

I emerged. I examined the room with a discerning eye, attempting to identify the best hiding spot.

As I scanned his desk, my eyes landed on his sketchbook. Several pages had been ripped out and scattered across the desk, some clean, others crumpled and discarded. Even his rejected pictures were impressive. He'd actually improved significantly. How many hours had we spent as children in his room, Elliot sketching, me reading? Even though Elliot had continued drawing, I'd abandoned reading years before. About the same time I'd moved on from my essay writing hobby at school. I simply became too jaded. I consumed one too many stories about happy, perfect kids leading, happy, perfect little lives with their happy, perfect families.

Thinking about reading in Elliot's room reminded me of living with Dad, which was certainly a dangerous thought process, so I cleared my mind and returned to the search. I checked inside his pencil case, rummaged through his chest of drawers, scanned the bottom of his wardrobe. James looked underneath his mattress and even did a quick sweep of the carpet in case there was a trap door—a move I personally felt was rather dramatic.

Then I placed a hand inside his pillowcase and ran into something that did not feel like feathers. Swallowing, I rescued a small zip-lock bag of opaque tan-coloured rocks. I studied it, bile rising in my throat.

James's eyes widened. "Found it," he said. He seemed apprehensive. I could see why. This wasn't marijuana, after all.

"How much do you think this would cost?" I asked.

"God knows. A lot, I reckon. Bet he hasn't saved much lately."

The first, desperate thought that came to mind was, *as long as he can still pay rent.* The second was an observation of how in denial I was. "All right, so what do we do with this?"

"We could try burning it," James laughed at his own wit.

"Hilarious," I side-eyed him. "But, honestly, what? We can't exactly flush it down the toilet."

"I mean, we could."

"Wouldn't that be bad for the environment?"

"I won't tell Greenpeace if you don't."

"Maybe we should Google it."

"Good idea." He pulled out his phone and spoke out loud, slow and exaggerated, while he typed. "Help: my brother's a crack head."

"Excellent. Thanks."

We moved to my room, shutting the door firmly behind me, and I placed the bag on my desk. James regarded it with suspicion, as though it were a time bomb, before setting his jaw and snatching it up. "I say we ditch it," he said, shoving the bag in his pocket. "Let's go."

"Wait, where? It's not like we can hide it in a bush."

James started walking, and I hurried after him. "In the river," he said under his breath when I caught up.

Sue and Dom sat in the lounge room reading. They both glanced up when James and I passed, but neither said a word. James offered them an awkward smile. I avoided eye contact.

Outside, James made a face. "They're like *American Gothic*."

"It feels less uncomfortable if you pretend you don't notice them."

"It wouldn't kill them to smile."

"I wouldn't know. I've never seen it happen."

James walked ahead of me, leading the way. The closer we drew to the river, the thicker and greener the grass became, and the more river moths swarmed around our heads. The bustling, traffic-laden sounds of the town faded, leaving only the chirps of birds in their wake.

We followed the dirt path that ran parallel to the river

below for five minutes before reaching the railway track. Here, James sat on the grass.

"What are you doing?" I asked.

"Waiting for the train. Trust me."

Without questioning him further, I sat next to him. We didn't touch at first—we tended not to make physical contact in public—but then his hand brushed the small of my back, and I leaned into him. "I hate this," I whispered.

He gave a heavy sigh and wrapped an arm around my shoulder. "It'll be okay. I promise."

The ground hummed. We pulled apart. The rumbling grew louder until the ground began to vibrate. We shuffled back from the tracks. The train flew by in a flash of colour and screeching sound and whipping wind.

When it passed, James stood up and followed the rails across the bridge. My ears rang in the gaping silence the train left behind as I went after him. I understood now. Trains came along every half an hour, so we knew we were safe to walk onto the railway bridge.

James had one hand covering his pocket, as though he was afraid someone would attempt to pickpocket him. The other hand brushed against my arm while we walked, me hopping between the slats, James balancing on the steel that formed the tracks.

When we reached the middle we stopped. With little ceremony or fanfare James pulled the bag out, stepped onto the railing and flung it over the edge. I gripped onto the barrier and hung over to watch. The wind caught it, tossing it on invisible waves as it fell, down, down, down.

The current was strong at this end of the river, close as we were to the mouth, and so the drugs would likely be swept out to sea within minutes. We'd done all we could.

"Now we just have to hope no one checks the cameras," James said.

"Hmm?"

"The cameras." He pointed up, and I spotted one, nestled underneath an iron arch above the centre of the bridge.

The blood drained from my face. "Why are there cameras? Do you think they'll see us?"

James started back. "They're not gonna check them. They're not there to catch people littering into the river."

"Why are they there?"

James didn't look at me. "Well . . . you know."

"No. I don't."

"Do you remember Mr. Olivers?"

The name wasn't a familiar one.

"The guy who jumped in front of the train last year?" James said.

Oh.

Oh.

James's voice was grim. "That's why."

I looked over my shoulder at the track. Against my will, I was picturing the middle-aged corner store manager standing by the railing, waiting for a train. "That's awful."

"Fucking gruesome is what it is."

"I agree." The thought of it made me feel sick. "At least he wouldn't have felt it. It would've been quick."

James, a few steps ahead of me now, gave an uncomfortable laugh. "Can we not talk about this, please?"

"Sorry." I waited a second, thinking about the man still. Had he regretted it as he went under? Or did he feel relief?

I tore my gaze away from the railing and headed after James.

It was several hours before Elliot noticed anything was amiss. James and I were watching YouTube videos on my bed when he burst in without knocking. We jumped apart, despite the fact that we hadn't been doing anything except bending our heads together to see the screen.

"Were you in my room?" Elliot asked. "And tell the fucking truth, because I need to know if it was you or Sue and Dom." His face was pale, his breathing erratic. He was terrified. And so he should have been. If Sue or Dom *had* found it, we would've been helpless to fix the situation.

"It was me," I said calmly, before turning my attention back to the laptop. James continued to stare at Elliot.

Elliot nodded. His relief lasted about two-point-five seconds, before switching straight to anger. "Okay, so what the hell did you do with it?"

"None of your business."

James bit his lip. I inwardly chastised myself for allowing him to stay. I should have known it wouldn't take Elliot long to find out.

"Like fuck it's none of my damn business, it's *mine*. Give it the fuck back."

"I can't. It's gone."

"Get it back."

"It's *gone*, Elliot. Properly gone."

He blinked a few times while he processed this. "Do you have any idea how much that cost?"

I snapped at this. "What the *hell* are you doing?" I got onto my knees, and James grabbed the laptop to stop it from falling.

"Fuck you, you self-righteous piece of shit," Elliot yelled. "What gives you the right to judge me? Like you have the right to go into my room *without me* and steal my shit!"

I'd never seen him so furious. I didn't know how else to react but shout back. "You're doing crack! What am I supposed to do, ignore that?"

Elliot slammed the door behind him and took a menacing step forward. "*Parle moins fort*," he hissed. Keep your voice down.

"*Combien de temps?*" I asked. How long?

James looked between us, bewildered. But we weren't censoring for his sake.

"*Deux-trois fois.*" Two or three times. "*Pas de problème.*"

"Actually, it's a *huge* problem," I said, abandoning French in my anger. "You're such an idiot."

"Fuck you. I know what I'm doing, okay? You need to stay the hell out of my life for once."

I was so furious I could have tackled him. Slammed him right to the floor. "Get out of my room."

He sucked in his cheeks. "You fucking owe me now. You're gonna pay me back for it."

"I don't owe you anything. Go to Callan's, do whatever you want. Have fun. Or, you know, as much fun as you *can* have without—"

He left the room, the slamming of the door cutting off my sentence. I stared after him and drew a trembling breath.

I was shaking. He'd never looked at me like that before.

Like he genuinely wanted to hurt me.

James pulled me into his chest and rested his chin on my forehead, encasing me. "Do you want me to stay tonight?" he murmured into my hair.

Do you need someone to babysit you and your razorblade? he meant. "No. It's fine." My words were muffled by the soft material of his school jumper.

Just as James kissed my head, the door burst open. We sprang apart, but it was pointless. Elliot stood still, his fury replaced by a flash of confusion.

James could hardly have looked more alarmed if Elliot had brandished a chainsaw. I leaned on one arm and gave my brother a carefully arranged look of mild irritation, the sort most people would direct at a barking dog or talentless busker. "I would appreciate it if you'd start knocking," I said. Elliot stayed silent. I widened my eyes and raised my shoulders. "*What?*"

"I'm going to Callan's," he said, giving me an unreadable look.

"Wonderful."

He slammed my door hard enough to make the walls rattle. James turned to me slowly. "I'm sorry," he said. He looked frightened.

"What for? That?" I scoffed. "I was meaning to tell him anyway."

"He seemed . . ." James trailed off.

Shocked? But that wasn't exactly surprising, was it? Shocked wasn't necessarily the same thing as upset. "It's fine. Really."

James still seemed bothered, so I kissed him. It was only a brief one, but he relaxed.

"I know you don't want people to see," he whispered.

"Let them see. You're not a secret."

He studied me as though looking for a sign I was lying. When he didn't find one, he turned back to the television, wearing the ghost of a smile. "What am I then?"

"My boyfriend. I think. Maybe?" My initial confidence faded as I realised we'd never actually discussed it.

James's beam almost left the boundaries of his face, and he glanced sideways at me. "Okay. Awesome."

I let my head fall on his shoulder. The moment was ruined, however, by the niggling worry at the back of my mind. Was Elliot horrified, or was he just surprised? I would text him to check, but I was still angry about the drugs, and I didn't want to provide him with the opportunity to make this argument about me.

There would be plenty of time to check in tomorrow, when he'd calmed down. I was confident everything would be okay.

After all, if nothing had come between us so far, what was there to worry about? We'd already been through the worst. Surely.

TWENTY-ONE

James
October 2018

The football team were practicing when I passed. Without me. Like they'd done all year.

They didn't need me. I didn't need them.

I didn't like to take the long walk home anymore. Unlike our rock, which I could stand, this route was painful for some reason.

The ghost of Ash walked by my side, taunting me. *Did you appreciate our walks, James? Did you watch me, filing memories away? Did you listen to every word I said? Or did you ignore me, rambling about assignments and languages and sports scores?*

Did I exist then as much as my absence exists now?

James?

Jaaammeess?

You're alone now, James.

I put up with it for today. I had to go to the bridge.

You weren't allowed to climb over the fence that ran parallel to the rail tracks. It guarded the river bank. A steep drop. Probably, back in the nineties before everyone got all anal about safety, people had slipped over the edge. To the water below. Or, more accurately, to the roots and bushes and rocks that lined the bank, and *then* to the water below.

Screw safety fences. They were only there to protect stupid people. I'd be able to scale to the bottom easy.

I hopped the fence and lowered my legs over the edge, finding a foothold in the earth. Gripping onto an exposed root—and giving it a tug first, because, as above, I was not one of the stupid people who fell down river banks—I began the climb down.

Athletics, at least, was something that'd always come easy to me. It only took me a few minutes 'til I landed, unharmed, on the grassy slope by the water.

Me and the river had a hostile relationship. Whenever I saw it, all I could see was Ash. I could picture it flooding his lungs, encasing his body, and dragging him downstream so forcefully that he couldn't fight back. I didn't wanna think he'd suffered. That left option number two. That he'd been unconscious when he hit. Which leads me to the hostile relationship I had with the rocks.

The water level was higher this year than it'd been when it'd happened, so they were underwater, hiding from me. But I knew what they'd done. They'd broken Ash's body. Snapped his back or crushed his head. They'd murdered him. Thinking of it (*snapping, crushing, crunching*) made me want to vomit. I almost did, retching, mouth metallic. But I got a grip. Straightened.

The police would return here soon. And we'd find out for sure, wouldn't we?

Had Elliot been here?

Had he stood on that bridge? Smiling? Had he dived into the water after Ash? Or was he the reason Ash was in the water? Had he been a reactor, or an instigator?

You knew what happened, Elliot, I thought. *You spoke to him. You saw him. You did something. And you hid it.*

But what? And why? *Why?*

The river kept running. It didn't give a shit. Nothing was gonna stop it from doing its thing. Not even the death of the world's most beautiful person had stopped it. The river was cold, and impersonal. Like the rest of nature. What did the world care about justice, and fairness, and love? What did it care about suffering? It just kept on moving. And it dragged us all along with it, whether we wanted to dig in our heels or not.

Unless you opted out. Like Ash did.

Opted being the operative word.

Maybe Ash had chosen to go. Maybe not.

We'd find out soon.

I knelt down and opened my bag. Pulled out my box of stalker-shame. It was damn good I had all this now, wasn't it? The police would be able to use this.

But first, I wanted to give Ash what belonged to him.

I took out the photo. Studied it, committed it to memory, then put it in the water.

The letter Ash wrote me. I gave that to the river too.

Then the affirmations. I pulled the pages out. Hesitated.

They belonged to Ash. The river should take them.

Instead, I read them.

Like he never would.

When I was finished, I held the pages to my chest and started crying. For fuck's sake, I thought I was done with that. Thank God I was alone.

With shaking hands, I pulled out my phone. I had half a

dozen messages from Louise. More and more frantic.

She really cared.

She deserved to know.

SEEKING ELLIOT:

I told you this was about guilt. I used to think things were straightforward. I had a fight with my boyfriend, my boyfriend was vulnerable, he jumped off a bridge.

But then a few months ago I was at a party and one of Elliot's old friends, Callan, recognised me. He was getting all soppy about Ash, then he said something about how bad Elliot took it, and I was drunk and angry, so I said Elliot didn't give a shit, and that he went out with his friends the night Ash went missing. And Callan looked at me like I was an idiot, and he said, "his brother had literally just died. How fucked up would that have been?"

So I got confused, and was like, "What do you mean? He told the police he had a party with you guys on that night."

And Callan said, "Yeah, he did, then he called me and said Ash jumped off a bridge, and he was freaking the fuck out. Obviously, he didn't come out."

I asked if he was sure he meant the night Ash went missing. And Callan said all he remembered was it was a Friday night. So it had to have been the night Ash went missing. And I was like, "No one knew Ash had killed himself yet that night, though?"

And Callan thought Elliot knew straight away because he was family. But he didn't, because the police didn't tell anyone that Ash was seen jumping. Even Sue and Dom didn't get told that a train driver saw Ash jump until the next day. So why would the police have told Elliot? And if they didn't, how did he know?

I thought about it, then I realised Elliot was lying. About everything. Something happened that night with Ash and Elliot.

So, here's what I do know. Ash and I figured out Elliot was doing some pretty heavy drugs. So we threw out what we found in his room. Then Elliot found out and went nuts at Ash. Same day, Elliot figured out Ash wasn't straight. Stopped speaking to him.

On the day he died, Ash called Elliot. Elliot denied receiving the phone call and told the police he was out with friends the night Ash died.

But he wasn't. And if he wasn't out drinking with friends, then why wasn't he out with the rest of us trying to find Ash?

Because he already knew Ash was dead. Not only that, but he knew how he'd died. When no one apart from a train driver and the police should've known.

Like, it could all be innocent. Maybe Elliot saw Ash kill himself or something.

But then why did he lie?

Why go out of his way to make sure he had an alibi? He had Callan tell the police he was at a party he never went to. Who the hell does that if they have nothing to hide?

Louise, I'm sorry. I know he's your best friend. But I wanna know what the fuck your best friend did to my boyfriend.

TWENTY-TWO

Ash
May 2017

ELLIOT AND I SPENT the next day going about our usual routine, me attending school, him dragging himself to work through a hungover haze. It wasn't particularly odd for him to head directly to his room following work, either, so when he did I thought nothing of it. Usually I'd join him uninvited, but today I was still feeling too uncomfortable about everything to take the initiative.

Then when I was brushing my teeth, he left his room to do the same, saw me in the bathroom, and went straight back inside. That was *certainly* not his usual behaviour. With growing trepidation I finished rinsing out my mouth and then knocked on his door. He didn't reply. I called out to him. He still didn't reply.

I stood by his room, stubbornly attempting to draw him

out, until Sue walked into the hallway. Silent as always, she looked me right in the eye. Defeated and worried, I slunk back into my room.

The next day was the same, if not worse. Elliot remained inside his room all morning, then returned there the moment he got home from work. He didn't invite any friends over, nor did he leave the house. I tried knocking on his door and texting several times, but it was as though I were trying to reach out from another dimension.

Finally, I resorted to listening for him to leave his room. When his gentle footsteps padded down the hallway later that night I pounced, cornering him as he entered the bathroom to shower. "What is going on?" I asked, placing a hand on each side of the doorframe. "You aren't honestly giving me the silent treatment, are you?"

The only sound came from Sue and Dom as they talked in the lounge room. Elliot turned on the shower and gave me a pointed look. I didn't budge. "Elliot?"

"Can I get some goddamn privacy?" he asked.

"Not until you tell me what the matter is."

He folded his arms. "Get out."

"No."

He set his jaw and then shoved me backwards. I stumbled into the hallway, unprepared, and he slammed the door in my face.

If I was bewildered then, it was nothing compared to how I felt as the days passed, and he continued to blatantly ignore my existence. He completely withdrew into himself, holing up in his room like a recluse.

I tried texting Callan, who had no better idea of what was happening than I did.

By the end of the week I even went as far as to ask Sue if she knew what was upsetting Elliot. After giving me a strange look, she simply said, "Not a clue. But it's nice, don't you think?"

I narrowed my eyes at her and walked away.

"To have him at home, I mean," she called out after me. I didn't dignify that with a response.

At the beginning of the following week I caught him as he came home from work. It wasn't the first time; I'd managed it once before, and he'd walked straight to his room as though he couldn't hear me begging him to speak. But this time I finally captured his attention. "Elliot, you have to talk to me. Please. I need to know what's happening with Alice."

He stopped walking and looked at me. His face was blank. He didn't reply, but he was listening. Encouraged, I continued. "You know. With . . . guardianship? Because aren't we supposed to move soon?"

He swallowed. "That's not happening anymore."

It was like the oxygen had evaporated out of the air. Of all the things I'd dreaded to hear, this hadn't even crossed my mind. Of course I was moving out with Elliot. That had always been our plan. No matter what else changed, that was the constant.

"What?" my voice asked from somewhere across the room. "What do you mean?"

"You're not coming with me. You're staying here."

But he couldn't leave me.

He was all I had left.

The last one.

He started the journey to his room again, his steps quick.

"Elliot, no," I said, chasing after him. "Stop. Please don't leave me here. *Please*."

He wouldn't meet my eye. My voice gained an octave. "What did I do? Is it because of . . . when I went into your room? I'm sorry. I shouldn't have done that. I won't do it again. I promise."

He entered his room and shut me outside. I pounded on the door. "Is it because of James? Is that why? *Talk to me. Why are you doing this? What did I do?*"

The door never reopened.

It didn't seem real. There was no devastation, or sobbing, or panicked hyperventilation. Just an empty feeling beneath my ribcage.

I would have taken tears if they'd been offered instead.

A few days later I found him carrying flattened boxes in from his car. His bedroom door remained closed, but I knew what was happening behind it now.

He was truly leaving me. And I didn't know why.

Each day I woke up praying that he would take it back. That he would assure me he was joking, and of course I was still going with him. Each day I was disappointed.

Eventually I stopped allowing my hope to build. I began drifting through the days, pretending everything was fine, to myself and everyone else.

James knew something was amiss, for all I denied it. I didn't want to tell him, though. For a myriad of reasons. I didn't want to verbalise what was happening, because that would make it appear more real. I was humiliated that I'd been so eager to move out with Elliot, only to have him reject me at the last second. Furthermore, I was plagued by the terror that James would think it was because of us . . . and guilt for wondering that myself.

I walked past Elliot's room one morning to find the door cracked open. I pushed it, half expecting to find him. Instead, I found nothing. Literally nothing. The room was bare.

Shell-shocked, I wandered into the kitchen in a daze. I found Sue drinking a cup of coffee. "When did Elliot leave?" I asked in a small voice.

"Yesterday, while you were at school."

Hah. He wasn't even living here yesterday when I'd gotten home. It was a testament to how absent he'd made himself over the last few weeks. I couldn't tell the difference between living with my brother and without him. Wasn't that utterly hilarious?

On my journey to school, I imagined Elliot lugging his worldly possessions out of the house while I sat in English class. Had he felt guilty at all? Sad? Regretful? *Anything*?

I texted Bea.

Elliot's gone.

He hadn't even said goodbye.

What do you mean he's gone?

Did he hate me that much?

He stopped speaking to me, except to tell me he didn't want me living with him and disappeared.

Bea attempted to ring me several times.

I didn't pick up. I didn't trust my voice.

In the same vein, I made little effort to speak throughout the rest of the day. I mostly sat and stared and thought.

James dialled up his cheerfulness in a vain ploy to pull me back into the present. But I wanted nothing to do with the present.

Was it just me now? Was I alone from now on? Was this it?

On the walk home, James's upbeat façade cracked. "What's wrong, Ash?"

"What do you mean?" I asked, shifting my school bag.

James shot me an impatient look. "You know what I mean. You've been down for ages. And you've been acting super weird all day. What's the matter?"

"Nothing's the matter," I said. "I've been tired. I haven't

been sleeping well."

"You promise that's all it is?"

"I promise," I said, my tone testy. "You don't need to babysit me, James. I'm fine."

James clearly didn't believe a word of it, but he dropped the subject. At least, until we passed Elliot's room at home. He'd noticed Elliot had disappeared lately—he wasn't slow, after all—but I'd told him he was out. Not implausible, knowing Elliot. But I couldn't make any excuses to cover up Elliot's empty bedroom.

James stopped and stared at it. "What the hell? Where's Elliot?"

"Oh. He's gone."

"What do you mean? Where is he?"

I shrugged. "I don't know. His new place, I guess."

"His new place? Wait, what? Are you saying he didn't get guardianship?"

The horror in James's tone was oddly comforting. Validating, in a way. To know that, for once, maybe I wasn't being dramatic. Maybe things actually were that bad.

I closed the door, blocking off Elliot's abandoned room. "He didn't want guardianship."

James stared at me. "What the hell?" he repeated. "What do you mean he didn't want it?"

What I mean, James, is he didn't want me *anymore,* I thought.

"He said I wasn't going to stay with him. That's it."

I started to head to my room, and James scrambled after me. "How long has this been going on?"

"Three weeks, give or take."

"Three *weeks*? Why didn't you tell me?"

I sat at my desk, my back to James. "I didn't want to talk about it."

"But what happened?"

"Honestly, I still don't want to talk about it."

"Was it because of us?"

I wish I knew for sure. "Possibly."

There were only two things it *could* be.

One: that my brother, who'd never had a bad word to say about James or his sexuality, was *that* against us that he'd leave me behind without a word.

Or he'd decided he had to choose between me and drugs. And I'd lost.

James nodded, biting his lip. Then he held out his arms and I went to him, climbing onto the bed. "He'll get over it," he said. "I *promise*."

Maybe.

Maybe, maybe, maybe.

Was it so surprising? Elliot hadn't asked for this. He'd only been sixteen when he got stuck with me. What sixteen-year-old would wish for such responsibility? He wanted his friends. To party with them, and have fun with them, and live his own life. I couldn't blame him for that. A small part of me was relieved, even, that he'd been brave enough to cut me loose if that was how he felt. I was a burden to enough people already without stifling his life too.

All I wanted was to stop bothering people.

James had to leave early to begin writing our English essay. He offered to stay, and I think he meant it, but I ushered him out. I didn't need to be looked after. More so; I didn't want him resenting me.

When he was gone, I lay flat on the floor, arms by my side, and existed. It was all I had the energy or inclination to do.

The temporary peace and stillness cocooned me while I lay safe in the silence. Nobody disturbed me. My phone buzzed a few times—probably James or Bea—but I ignored it. I would check the messages when I had the motivation.

Just a few more minutes. A little longer.

When four hours had passed I managed to haul myself off the floor and onto my bed, where I pulled my legs to my chest and waited for sleep. Tomorrow morning was still seven hours away. Thankfully, I didn't have to deal with it until then. I'd be ready to face it when it came. I was confident of that. But for now, I only had to sleep.

Morning came, and I didn't move. I scrunched up my face against the light and closed my eyes, willing time to rewind. It had arrived too quickly. I wasn't prepared. I needed another seven hours. Then perhaps seven more following that for good measure.

My phone blinked, displaying three messages from James the night before. I hugged my pillow and attempted to motivate myself into reaching for my phone. Or getting out of bed.

The door was a mile or so away. The bathroom three miles. The kitchen ten.

My legs were heavy as lead. My whole body felt like I had twenty-pound weights strapped to each limb.

I stared at the ceiling, defeated. What would happen if I stayed home that day? Sue and Dom wouldn't notice, and I doubted the school would contact them. Not over one day. I very rarely missed whole days. In fact, it was probably better that I remained at home. I would be able to start that essay rather than sitting at school being unproductive.

That settled it. I was staying here.

With a wave of relief, I sank back into the mattress. My eyes burned with exhaustion, but sleep didn't rescue me. It didn't matter. I was content to lie there.

I spent the rest of the morning doing just that, too fatigued to get out of bed. Around one in the afternoon, I summoned Herculean strength and dragged myself to the shower, but even then, I ended up sitting on the floor, letting the water rush over my passive body.

Needless to say, when James came to visit after football, I hadn't even started the essay.

"What's up?" James asked when I answered the door. "Why'd you ignore me all day?"

I hadn't even registered my phone buzzing. Now I thought about it, I'd forgotten to put it on charge. It was probably flat. I stepped aside to let James in. "I don't know. Maybe I'm coming down with something. I feel horrible."

We started down the hallway together. "Have you eaten?" James asked.

"I'm not hungry." I made a beeline for my bed and collapsed onto it.

James kneeled in front of me and rubbed my arm. "You're never hungry. You're probably fucking malnourished, you know. No wonder you feel like shit."

Fair point. "I haven't had much meat or anything in a while," I mused. "Maybe it's low iron."

"Been tired?"

"I feel like I haven't slept in a week."

"It's iron," James said with a firm nod.

I was satisfied with his diagnosis. Relieved, even. Iron would be a relatively easy fix. I'd be back to normal soon.

James brushed a stray lock of hair to the side of my forehead with a fond smile. "How about we put a film on and you can have a nap, then we'll see about dinner?"

He grabbed my laptop and climbed into bed beside me, and my tension melted away. James meant feeling wanted and as though there was no need to apologise for existing incorrectly.

I tried to focus on the laptop screen. My eyes drooped, though, and I gave into the urge to close them. Within minutes I was dead to the world.

TWENTY-THREE

Ash
June 2017

JAMES BECAME MY KEEPER. I don't think he realised it, but he did all the same. Every morning he sent me text after text to check that I was awake and coming to school. He always woke up ages before I did; he took a Japanese class at seven-thirty in the morning with two other students. Meaning he had ample opportunity to harass me into action in time for me to make it to school.

I pretended to resent his insistence that I get out of bed each morning, but I might not have done it otherwise. As it was, there were days when even James's nagging couldn't convince me to leave the house. Each night I had the best of intentions, but good intentions didn't count for much when I woke up to find that gravity had doubled overnight.

James didn't approve of me skipping, but he was afraid of

me getting into trouble, so he took the initiative to hand in fake letters from Sue and Dom excusing my absence. James might have been an overachiever, but no one could accuse him of being a teacher's pet. He reached his goals through any means necessary. Faking signatures didn't bother him in the slightest. But I felt guilty for driving him to risk it.

When I did attend class, it was getting harder to trudge through. I spent most of the day dreaming of home, and my time at home drifting in and out of sleep. If I wasn't fantasising about either of those things, my thoughts would drift back to the bridge. Contemplating.

My mind went blank regularly these days, too. Enough that James, who'd never acted as though he'd prefer to do anything more than spend quality time with me during lunch, asked me if we could start sitting with our old friends instead of by ourselves.

Suddenly, I was stuck hovering on the edges of a group I didn't belong to day after day. James made valiant attempts to include me in the conversation initially, but I invested no effort into participating. Not because I was sulking—or, at least, not entirely—but because I felt far too self-conscious to speak around them. Here were the class's most outgoing, charismatic guys. Some of them, like Wyatt, had been my friends too, back in the day. Back when I could have passed for outgoing and charismatic, too. That only made it worse. I couldn't prove I deserved the time of day from them, because I didn't have a single interesting thing to say.

None of them minded my presence, even if none of them necessarily desired it. I minded, though. It hurt to know that James was finding me difficult to entertain. Almost as much as it hurt to know that it was my own fault it was happening.

During one of these lunches, while I sat next to James on the end of the lunch table, barely included in the group,

I suddenly became all-too-aware of exactly how out of place I was. Nobody even glanced at me. Their bodies were angled subtly away from me.

Even James wasn't paying me that much attention. He still didn't touch me at all at school. I was uncertain if it was because he didn't want people to know, or if he felt *I* didn't want people to know. I used to think it was the latter. These days I wondered if maybe it was the former. If he regretted being with me. What if he wanted to break up with me but didn't feel that he could?

My heart rate sped up. I glanced at him, searching for a hint that this was true. He was too busy talking to Wyatt to notice. Even Wyatt, who was facing me, didn't notice. Not that that was unlike him.

The room temperature suddenly doubled. Everyone was too close. They were motionless, but they were closing in on me. Trapping me.

I needed to get away.

None of them wanted me there. James didn't want me there.

I needed to stop weighing him down.

I waited for a break in conversation then tapped James on the shoulder. "Hey, I'll be back, okay?"

My voice stayed even, my expression pleasant. The last thing I wanted was for James to catch onto what I was doing and come after me. He deserved to spend lunchtime with his friends. Not to be stuck trying to coerce me into conversation. Thankfully, he didn't notice anything was wrong. He just gave me a smile and a nod and turned back to Wyatt.

As I grew further away from the chatter and activity, my heart rate slowed. Among the deserted hallways I was alone. No one knew I was here. No one expected me to do anything. Everything was okay. I'd remain here alone until I felt okay to go back out.

"Hi, Ashton." The voice was familiar. I whipped around to see Mr. Patricks coming out of a classroom.

I took a step back. Why couldn't I be left alone? Why did there always have to be people? His voice was too loud, and he was approaching me too fast. I fought the urge to bolt.

It's okay, I told myself. *Settle down. He'll leave in a second.*

His smile faltered. "What are you doing out here?"

"Bathroom." I was keeping it together, but only barely.

He needed to leave.

I needed to be alone.

Why was he staring at me?

What was so interesting about me?

"You don't look well. You feeling okay?"

Get out of my face get out of my face get out of my—

"I'm fine. I have to go." I didn't wait for him to answer. I heard his footsteps. *Don't run, don't run.* Was he following me? I looked back. No. He was going in the opposite direction.

Thank God thank God thank God . . .

I kept walking. Into the school yard. Down the hill.

Space. I needed space. I could feel eyes on me. There were too many people. I needed to get away from everyone.

I couldn't return. How could I return? What was I supposed to do? I couldn't be alone with James because he'd resent me. I couldn't be with his friends because I didn't belong. I couldn't be alone because . . . because . . . I just couldn't. I couldn't sit at a table by myself. There was no way in hell.

No wonder James didn't want to be around me. No wonder Elliot had gone. No wonder Sue and Dom didn't want me in their house. No wonder I didn't have any friends left. Why did I insist on making other people put up with me?

What other choice did I have? There had to be a choice. Maybe I could lock myself in a bathroom cubicle each lunch. Then I could be alone without the embarrassment that came with being *that* guy. The one everyone knew was a pariah.

My shoe sank into sand. I paused.

I was at the beach.

How did I get to the beach?

Had I decided to come here at some point? Or had I ended up here by accident?

I couldn't remember deciding to come here. Hadn't I just left the school? It was a fifteen-minute walk to the beach. I hadn't been walking for that long, had I?

Piece by piece my mind peeked out from its hiding place in the back of my head. Back to the present. Well, I was here now. I might as well stay. Being here made me feel calmer already.

I found our rock ledge. Mine and James's. Scaled it alone this time. Sat on the edge, wrapped my arms around myself, braced myself against the wind. My phone buzzed, and buzzed, and buzzed, and buzzed. Texts. Calls. Texts. Calls.

On auto-pilot, I pulled out my phone with hands that felt like they didn't belong to me. I sent James a text assuring him that I was okay. I'd gone to the beach. I hadn't done anything to hurt myself.

Hours passed. Or minutes passed.

Suddenly, I wasn't alone. James's voice called my name. I didn't respond. He called again.

I finally looked up. James threw his arms into the air. "What's going on?" he asked as he approached.

"I wanted some air," I said.

"You can't just leave school, Ash." He scowled while he lugged himself onto the rock.

"Who cares?" I asked, irritated. Why did he always have to follow me? I only wanted privacy. Some space, some freedom from constantly doing wrong. Being wrong.

"I care." James sat beside me. "You'll fail or wind up dropping out. Worse, the school can drag the police into things."

I wasn't worried about any of that. That was a problem for an uncertain future. The only thing I had the energy to feel concern for was the present. "Could you leave me alone please?"

"You want me to go?" James sounded wounded.

"Yeah."

". . . No." He shuffled over a fraction, leaving an arm's width of space between us, but made no move to stand. "I'm staying here."

I didn't bother protesting. To my relief, he didn't try to force conversation. He simply sat by my side, staring into the distance.

It didn't take long for my defensiveness to slip away. It was promptly replaced by guilt and shame, my new best friends. Guilt pointed out how down James looked. How I was causing him to miss class. That he should be with his friends having fun, not babysitting me while I wallowed. Shame agreed with guilt and reminded me how pathetic it was that I'd come out here. How everyone else managed to cope fine with life. How ridiculous it was that I could be this weak.

Why was I so incapable of everything? Every single little thing I attempted failed. Why was I incompetent when everyone else was more than able to manage, and even excel at, life? Why couldn't I just try harder? Why couldn't I do things right?

"What are you doing tonight?"

All I wanted to do was sit in silence and sleep. My life was a constant state of exhaustion, despite the long hours of rest I was getting. I felt so behind, like I'd never catch up to where I needed to be.

"Ash?"

I realised he'd spoken. I tried to focus. "Um. I don't know. Sue and Dom are out."

"Okay. We're going back to yours, then. Come on."

"You have athletics tonight."

"Nah. I'm seeing you tonight."

"No."

He grabbed my shoulders and crouched down beside me, turning me to look at him. He didn't look angry, or disappointed, or annoyed. "I'm seeing you tonight," he repeated. "I don't want to go to athletics. I want to see you. Please?"

There wasn't a point in arguing. So I allowed him to walk home with me. We didn't talk much. He was giving me space. I appreciated it.

Maybe I'd been thinking irrationally at school. I knew how he felt about me, after all. Nothing he'd done provided compelling evidence that he didn't want a relationship anymore. I simply had to pull myself together and become the person he deserved.

I took his hand while we walked.

At home, we made toasted ham sandwiches. I even ate a full one to please James. I didn't taste it, and it sat uncomfortably in my stomach after, but it made James brighten up, so it was worth it.

Afterwards, I plugged my laptop into the TV to set up a film. When it was ready, I turned to see James lying on the couch covered in a blanket, holding his arms out. His dark hair was hanging over his eyebrows, and his full lips were spread into a soft smile, and it hit me that I might very well be in love with him.

I couldn't think of anything less romantic than telling him so at that moment, though, so I tucked the thought away for a better day. A day when I was functioning. I climbed into his arms and let him fold me up into his embrace.

I should be happy. I had James. That usually made me happy. But I wasn't. For no discernible reason, the lump remained in my throat, and the weight didn't budge from my chest. Why wasn't being in his arms numbing the aching? Were things getting worse? What if I could never get rid of this feeling? What if it stayed, dragging me down, forever?

After a while, I excused myself to the shower.

Once I'd turned the taps on to drown out the noise I lunged for the cupboard, snatched up one of Sue's disposable razors and broke it open. I wasn't thinking about the consequences, or anything rational. I was just desperate to relieve some of the pressure that was building and squeezing and suffocating.

I closed myself in the shower to do it. I covered more of my thighs than I ever had before, completely numb to reality. The only lucid thought that crossed my mind was, once again, the bridge. The bridge, the bridge, the bridge. It wasn't until I was sitting on the tiled floor, watching the water run red into the drain, that what I'd done hit me. Along with it came the shame and embarrassment and anger at my own inability to cope.

Now what was I supposed to do? The cuts weren't dangerously deep, but they were still bleeding incessantly. I had no choice but to wait for the blood flow to ease off on its own and pray James didn't notice how long I'd been in the shower.

When the bleeding appeared under control I stepped out and attempted to wrap a towel around myself while also staunching the cuts. No matter how valiantly I attempted to mop myself up, however, thin, pink rivulets of water insisted on dripping down my legs to my ankles. I sprinted to my bedroom and shut myself inside. Never before had I been so grateful for my dark grey carpet.

I pulled on a pair of thick, black sweatpants. My thighs would bleed on and off for the rest of the night if experience was anything to go by. Hopefully the sweatpants, aided by the low light in my room, would hide it.

Oh, the cuts were starting to hurt. A lot. The stinging was all I could focus on suddenly.

With robotic, stiff movements I limped back into the lounge room, bracing myself for James's questioning. Instead, I found him asleep on the couch, his right arm hanging over the edge so his fingertips grazed the carpet.

I felt a surge of affection that was quickly replaced by guilt. I hated how pathetic I was. How incapable I was of giving him what he needed. I demanded all the support and all the attention. What did I give him? What could I give him? How long until he began to resent me?

I gingerly lowered myself onto the carpet in front of him, rested my head on the couch, and tucked my arm underneath his. He stirred somewhat but didn't wake. The simple action supplied me with a world of comfort, and that alone relieved me. It counteracted the agony in my legs more effectively than any painkiller, until I started to feel somewhat human again.

Honestly, he was so beautiful. Like a delicately crafted piece of crystal, reflecting rainbow light. Anyone else would find it simple to handle him with care. I was hopeless, though. I would only break him into shards. I would block his light sooner or later.

Even though I knew he'd be better, happier, with anyone else but me, I was too selfish to let him go. I was addicted to him.

Maybe things would be better tomorrow.

Maybe I'd fix things tomorrow.

TWENTY-FOUR

LOUISE
October 2018

IT WAS MY TURN to be weirdly quiet. Elliot seemed to have calmed down after his outburst, mostly because I promised him I wouldn't speak to James anymore. Which would've been fine if not for the fact that I didn't seem to have any freaking choice but to keep speaking to James because if I didn't he was going to drag Elliot to the police. Awesome.

I didn't want to betray Elliot's trust, but it was way bigger than that now. This wasn't about right and wrong anymore. Screw right and wrong. How the hell did I keep Elliot safe? That's all I wanted to know.

At least I had Saras. I couldn't speak to any of my other friends about this. It would take way too much explaining now. Besides, I wasn't sure I could trust them not to tell Elliot. Like, they were his friends too, and it'd be kind of a bombshell. I could attest to that.

"So, it's obviously suspicious," Saras said. She'd come over my house to talk. We'd attempted to go over everything at work a few times, but it'd proved difficult when Elliot was in the same room as us ninety percent of the shift. Here, sitting in the centre of my worn-out trampoline, the biggest eavesdropping threat was the neighbour's Border Collie, which kept sticking its nose through a small hole in the wooden fence separating our yards. And he didn't strike me as a tattle-tale. "You don't lie to the police unless you have a good reason."

"And you don't hide from your family that your brother jumped off a bridge unless you know for a fact there's no use searching for him," I added.

"Like if you want to give the body time to decompose and hide evidence of murder."

I stared at her, gobsmacked. "*Saras.*"

"What? Are we pretending that's *not* what James thinks happened? What other explanation would he be hinting at?"

Oh my *God*. I did *not* want to think down that road. Elliot was *not* a murderer. Murderers don't have a secret love for pop music, and they don't break out in giggles when they're learning to surf, and they sure as hell don't spend shifts at work pulling faces across the room at you to distract you from customers. Pretty sure that was also a scientific fact. I was full of them.

"We don't know *what* happened," I said. "I was thinking maybe it was more of a fight, like maybe Elliot told Ash to jump or something."

Saras perked up. "Oh. *Oh.* Plot twist." She held up her hands as she stared into the distance. "Elliot, drunk and high, stumbles into the river. Ash sees him and jumps in to save his life, and tragically drowns in the process."

She looked proud of herself. It was a ridiculous scenario,

but I couldn't help thinking at least it was a scenario in which Elliot was innocent. "There's only one way to find out what happened," I said. "Get Elliot talking."

"He'll talk if you tell him James is going to the police."

"Or he'll stall and change the subject and avoid it like he does with *any* problem, and in the meantime, James brings the police to his doorstep."

"Is that such a bad thing?" Saras asked. "If he *didn't* do anything wrong, he can explain it to the police."

"Saras, haven't you ever watched a crime show? If the police find out he lied to them about that night, he's going to have to prove he didn't do something wrong. They won't just take his word that he was with Ash but definitely didn't kill him. Especially not if they know drugs were involved."

The neighbour's Border Collie whined. Saras jumped off the trampoline and made her way over to the fence. She crouched down and patted the exposed muzzle. "That's one way to get your hand ripped off," I said from the trampoline.

"Yes, he's *vicious*," Saras cooed, giggling as the dog slobbered all over her hand. Ew. There'd probably be less bacteria in a toilet bowl. A brief melody rang out from her pocket, and she checked her phone, before rolling her eyes and sighing. "Eurgh. I'll have to head home soon. Mum wants me to visit Nani and Nana with her tonight."

"Tonight? It's only three."

"Mm, but I'll have to go home and change into a *kurta*. If I went around in these, I'd risk giving Nani a heart attack." She gestured down at her tiny denim shorts. Well, at least she pulled them off. If I had legs like that, Abuela would shove me in those shorts herself and show me off at the Spanish club. "Plus, Mum'll probably want me to get dinner ready with her to bring around," Saras added.

Why was it that every girl I knew seemed to be able to cook but me?

And why did I hear that thought in Abuela's accusatory voice?

"That's fine," I said. "Back to the *previous* topic, though . . . what do you think I should do?"

Saras spent a bit longer scruffing up the dog's fur, otherwise known as stalling. "Okay, so, don't read into this too much. But I remembered something this morning."

Uh huh. I got the feeling that I was definitely going to want to read into this. "What?"

She ran a hand along the fence without meeting my eyes. "Well, remember when Joe fired Grace for stealing from the register? And he was rambling about wanting everyone to get a police check before coming back in?"

Vaguely. Grace had only worked at Bruno's for a couple of weeks. I'd forgotten all about her. "Yeah?"

"Elliot acted *really* weird about it. Like, he kept bringing it up for the rest of the shift. '*Do you think he's serious? Can he legally make us do that?*' I remember having to swear on my life Joe wouldn't try anything, considering he pays us off-the-books and he'd get his ass fined or worse if he was caught. Do you think . . . ?"

We stared at each other. Woah. So, it wasn't proof of anything, but it was still a bombshell-and-a-half, considering James thought he had enough on Elliot to involve the police. With each day, I was becoming less and less sure *what* was going on. My Elliot wouldn't have a police record. But then, he also wouldn't drink or do drugs. And, as far as I'd been concerned a few weeks ago, he didn't have a brother.

In all seriousness . . . what if he *had* done something?

I chewed my lip. "Okay. So. What do I do?"

Saras sighed. "Just let James come here," she said finally. "Let them talk it out. Tell me how it goes."

"Are you telling me to do this because you're curious?"

She gave me a patronising look. "Are you trying to tell

me you're *not* curious?"
Good point. "When do I do it?"
"Now. Do it now."

TWENTY-FIVE

Ash
June 2017

Elliot had always appeared so much older than me. But he'd only been sixteen when we'd been placed in care. Sixteen wasn't old and wise, however, as I was quickly discovering. I didn't have the vaguest clue what I was doing half the time.

That was the interesting aspect of age. It always seems so significant until you hit it and realise it's not what you imagined at all. As a child, I would look at sixteen year olds and perceive them as borderline adults. I wanted to go back in time and explain to myself that I was still going to feel very much like a child still when I got there.

These thoughts ran through my mind while Mr. Patricks explained some abstract theory of emotion. Honestly, I couldn't have cared less about the background to the assignment he was about to give us, but at least the extensive explanation made for ample opportunity to drift away.

I imagined Elliot sitting in this classroom two years before. Had he found school as uninteresting as I did, or did he view it as an escape from what we lived through at home? I attempted to put myself in his shoes. Tried to remember what living with Dad had been like, and how much worse it would've been for Elliot to not only have to think about himself, but to feel like he had to protect me. I wondered if he used to worry about me.

Perhaps he'd worried about me for too long. Perhaps he'd reached his limit.

"Take fear," Mr. Patricks said, writing the word on the whiteboard in red. "One of the most basic emotions. In fact, some argue that it is *the* basic emotion—that every negative feeling we have stems from the root of fear. Fear is primal. A new-born can feel fear, even if they don't have a sophisticated understanding of what they have to fear. The unknown itself brings fear. So, you would think fear would be easy to isolate. But even though the experience is common amongst us, the triggers vary. What terrifies one person might elicit no response in another. Let's brainstorm. Give me examples of what makes some of you afraid."

It didn't seem to take much thought. My classmates started throwing out ideas before Mr. Patricks had finished his sentence.

"Guns."

"Heights."

"Spiders."

Myself, I thought. I kept that one quiet.

He wrote them all down, then surveyed the small list. "So, for a start, you can see a pattern here. Fear manifests itself in different ways sometimes. A fear of heights is really a fear of falling. A fear of guns is a fear of a gunshot wound, and a fear of spiders is a fear of a spider bite. Ultimately, these are all the same fear. The fear of harm, or death. Sometimes you need to look past the initial instinct and address what's truly causing emotion. Access the intangible. Ashton?"

I jumped, looking up guiltily. I hadn't been doing anything wrong, but I went straight on the defensive.

"Can you give the class an example of an intangible fear?"

He never called on me to participate. At least, not genuinely. Every now and then he would, in an effort to prove I didn't know what was happening. I guessed this was part of his new "we're best buddies now" mission.

So much for our deal.

Mind you, now that I thought about it, had he ever actually agreed to leave me alone?

A few people looked at me, including Gemma. I could tell from their expressions they were waiting for me to admit I didn't know. Maybe brush off my discomfort with a joke.

Instead, I sat up straighter. "Isolation. Abandonment."

Mr. Patricks nodded, sticking out his bottom lip. "Great. Perfect. Anyone else?"

While the others called out examples, James looked at his lap. "Failure," he whispered, just loudly enough for me to hear. I tried to meet his eyes, but he kept his head down.

Mr. Patricks flicked on the stereo and the opening notes to "Awesome God" played.

James let out a long groan. "*Shoot me.*"

"You know, when this song came out it was supposed to be the original definition of awesome," I whispered. "Like, terrifying and powerful, not super-awesome-cool."

"Wow. That . . . doesn't make me hate it any less. Who taught you that, anyway? Mary and Joseph?"

Mary and Joseph were James's names for my previous foster parents. He thought he was hilarious. "Yep. They preferred their God smiting things. Kept them on their toes, I guess."

"Alright," Mr. Patricks half-yelled over the music. "I want you to write down your three biggest fears. Then exchange them with a partner. You will then rationalise your partner's fears. Break them down, offer solutions, whatever you see fit. Use your objective outsider's perspective to expose the fear for what it is."

The rest of the lesson passed quickly, with James grumbling with increasing conviction as each new song played. I ended up laughing loudly enough to be heard. Gemma turned around to look at us, and I could've sworn she offered me a small smile.

If I was surprised by that, it was nothing compared to the shock of her cornering me in the hallway after the lesson.

"Hey Ash," she said. She didn't seem comfortable, standing with one ankle crossed over the other, with her hands shoved in her jumper pockets. "Do you have a sec?"

I didn't allow my face to betray any surprise. I glanced around for James, who had gone ahead to speak to one of the athletics guys. He was nowhere in sight. "Um, hey. What's up?"

"Not much, same old," she said, tucking a loose strand of wavy hair behind her ear. I recognised the nervous habit.

"How are things with your parents?" I asked.

"Oh, you know. They're them. I didn't come over here to talk about them though."

"Okay, what's going on?" I tried to keep the confusion out of my voice, but it was difficult. She didn't exactly make a habit of speaking to me these days. Suddenly, stupidly, I wondered if she somehow knew about James and me. If anyone had noticed the way I looked at him, it would be Gemma. She had a working knowledge of what I looked like with a crush.

How would Gemma react if she knew? Would she be happy for me? Or would she, like James, think one of them must cancel the other out? As though my feelings for James erased the importance of what I once felt for her.

James's voice was in my ear. *So, you definitely like girls? Or did she make you realise you don't?*

"Just wanted to ask how things are going," Gemma said instead. "You haven't been at school much."

I glanced around. "I've been sick."

"What's wrong?"

"Iron" didn't seem like a good enough excuse suddenly. "Flu."

"Right." She hesitated, her expression sceptical.

She knew about the cutting. It'd started when I was still with her. But it hadn't been too bad or too often, back then.

Out of nowhere, I wanted to tell her everything. Elliot, Sue and Dom, how serious the cutting had become, how dark my thoughts were lately.

I tried to think of a smooth segue, but before I'd settled on one Gemma bounced on her toes. "Well, I'm glad things are all good," she said. "Hopefully you feel better soon."

I paused, then gave her an unconcerned smile. "Yeah. Thanks."

She seemed to be considering continuing the conversation. Ultimately, she must have decided against it, though, because she gave a quick, somewhat awkward goodbye and turned on her heel.

Just like that she was gone in a flash of blonde hair and warm energy, and I was back in the cold.

James came over every night now. Where once he would have attempted to Tetris me around his homework load, now he killed two birds with one stone and brought his laptop over each afternoon. Even though we weren't exactly engaging in quality time together, being in each other's company while we focussed on our own tasks was enough. If I had it my way, he'd never leave. Despite the fact that he monopolised the bed surface with his textbooks and stationary, nagged me to eat, and got annoyed at any study disruptions.

When he wasn't there, it was just me. Sue and Dom were as in the background as ever. Elliot still hadn't contacted me, and I wasn't brave enough to go visit him for fear of rejection. So every night when James left, and during football and athletics practice, my task became to keep myself company. Which mostly involved attempting to entertain myself, giving up, and waiting the night out by sitting in silence.

Sometimes I thought silence was what I wanted. But that wasn't right. Silence left me with my thoughts, and the constant, restless feeling of unhappiness. What I wanted was relief. Relief only came with unconsciousness. If only I could be unconscious constantly, I felt life might be bearable. But that was a contradiction, wasn't it?

After practice that day, James appeared at my house with his laptop like usual, his hair damp and fluffy from the shower and smelling like Shea butter. He was unabashedly thrilled to see me, as though we hadn't been in class together three hours before. "Don't forget we have the parabola exercises due tomorrow," he said.

"When have I ever forgotten *Maths?*" I asked, sitting down at my desk while he made himself comfortable on my bed.

While James took out his graph paper and calculator, I glanced at my laptop. Mr. Patricks had given us an assignment due the next day. "Write a reflection on an emotion." Well, if that wasn't the vaguest assignment I'd ever received.

Somehow, though, the sheer vagueness of the question

gave me the motivation to open up a new Word document. I wasn't entirely sure if there even could be a wrong answer, so I wouldn't have to think too hard. Additionally, I had little else to do while James worked. I might as well attempt some semblance of productivity.

So I began to write. Or, rather, to ramble.

Happiness only exists in polarity, not independently. If it weren't for unhappiness, happiness wouldn't be definable. It would be the status quo. The new benchmark. Maybe it would improve everything and solve all the world's problems if there was only happiness.

But I disagree. I think it would become taken for granted.

When we wake up every day, we don't tend to feel a rush of elation at our overwhelming good luck. If someone living in poverty woke up one day in our positions, though, our little worries wouldn't mean anything to them. They would be overwhelmed with happiness to have what the rest of us have. But eventually—after days, weeks, months, years—the ecstasy would subside, and what had once caused happiness would become accepted. It's all relative.

I'm sure permanent comfort can be achieved, but permanent happiness is a contradiction. And, really, another word for permanent comfort is permanent nonchalance.

Good things can't last by nature. If they did, they would stop being "good." It's probably for the best though. How can you appreciate something, if you don't face the threat of its loss?

James stood up and peeked at the screen, his pointed chin resting on my shoulder. "What are you doing?" he asked.

In one swift movement I pulled the laptop against my chest and swivelled around to face him. "Nothing."

He gave me an odd look. "Um, did I catch you writing erotica or something?"

I hugged the laptop closer. "It's the RSE assignment. It's

not good. I don't want anyone looking."

He bounced back onto my bed to return to his maths problems. "Well, at least you're doing homework."

"I'm bored. Don't get used to it."

"If you let me read it, I'll let you copy my maths."

I shot him an amused look. "That would be far too risky. If I handed up *two* assignments on time on the same day Mr. Patricks might catch on."

When I was certain James wasn't going to attempt to snatch the laptop from my grip, I continued writing. The words came like stormwater, rushing over themselves to get out faster than I could transcribe them onto the page. After all this time, I'd forgotten how easy it was to write when I was interested in the topic. I'd filled the word count before I'd even reached my point. For the first time in years I had to go back and tighten. Thirteen-year-old Ash would have been proud of me. When I was done, I read over the work, contemplative.

I climbed onto the bed and pressed my body against James's. He pushed his work away and pulled me closer, his hand going straight to my hair. "What's up?" he asked.

My body fit right into his. I stared at the wall. Plain cream. Bare. Dull. "The problem with being happy," I said, "Is that you miss it that much more when it's gone."

"Is this a breakup?" James joked. I shook my head, and he traced a finger along the outer shell of my ear. "Good. I'd prefer to stay happy for a bit longer, if that's okay with you."

If James thought I made him happy, he was utterly in denial. At best, I was a cigarette. He might want me, but only because he'd lost sight of how poisonous I was. Perhaps, if he was lucky, he'd be strong enough to quit me one day. He would have his happy ending, at least. But only after I burned out.

Better him than me. Only one of us deserved a happy

ending, after all.

I waited for James to finish the last few maths problems, slowly working his way through the solutions. I knew he double and triple checked every answer.

If there was one thing James didn't stand for, it was falling short of perfection. He approached life like he was sprinting down a hill. As though as long as he concentrated and held full speed, he'd keep his traction. Sometimes I worried about what would happen if he misstepped, however. Would he manage to keep his momentum, or would he hit the ground?

And if he did fall, would I be there to catch him? Or would I miss it, wrapped up in my own problems as I was?

I looked at him. Truly *looked* at him. His deep-set eyes seemed troubled. There was a crease between his brows that didn't smooth out as easily as it used to. His lips were dry from him constantly chewing on them, and his fingers kneaded the back of his neck in an attempt to relax the muscles. Here before me was the personification of stress. A better boyfriend would've noticed it much earlier.

How long *had* he looked like this?

I couldn't say.

"You know you can talk to me, right?" I said.

James looked up, confused. "I'm almost done."

"No, I don't mean now. Just, like, in general. If you need to talk about anything, do. What we have, it goes both ways."

He put his pen down, radiating such gratitude that I wished I'd thought to say it earlier. Instead of replying, he leaned in and kissed me hard, his homework forgotten. Rolling on top of me, his lips moved from mine to my neck and then down to my collarbone. I wrapped a leg around his in response, rising up to meet him in another kiss, deeper this time.

I was lost in the feeling of his hands running down

my body, and I encouraged him by pushing my hands up beneath his shirt, running over his warm, taut skin. It wasn't until he slipped his fingers beneath the waistband of my jeans that I returned to my senses. I yanked back, but it was too late. He'd felt the ridges that snaked up to my hip bones.

His face drained of colour. "No, Ash. No."

"Don't." How was it that every time we attempted to do anything, I managed to ruin it? What was the point of even bothering?

"Let me see."

"No." I curled my body into a ball, protecting my legs. I didn't want to show him, to have to explain to him that I'd ignored his promise of help. It wouldn't achieve anything but upsetting him further. It had nothing to do with him.

"*Ash.*"

"You don't want to see."

He deflated, his hands dropping limply to his sides while I collected myself. "You need help," he said.

He didn't understand. There was no one who could help me. There was nothing that could be done.

James buried his head in his hands. "I don't know what to do. What can I do?"

"Nothing. I'm fine."

"You're not fine. Nothing about this is fine. Please go back to your psych. Please."

"Okay," I lied. "Yeah. I was going to anyway."

James looked so hopeful, it killed me. "Really?"

"Yeah. You're right. I need to talk to someone."

As though talking about things would help. What use would it do me to be assured life would get better? I'd already experienced life for sixteen solid years. I knew what it had to offer. Life *could* be good for some people, the ones who deserved it. But I wasn't one of those blessed ones. I possessed the unique, impressive ability to squander every opportunity that was handed to me. "Help" was for people under the delusion that there was something wrong with them, despite evidence to the contrary. I was under no delusions. There *was* something objectively wrong with me. I was inherently pathetic. My issues stemmed from how painfully aware of it I was.

"Good," he breathed, relieved. "Good idea. I'm glad. Things are getting out of hand."

Things were in shattered pieces. Where would I even start attempting to glue my life back together?

"Yeah. I know," I said.

James tried to touch my leg.

I shuffled out of reach. I didn't deserve comfort. This was all my own fault. If only I could be more motivated, spend less time in a self-indulgent haze of pity, take fewer naps. I'd ruined my own life by acting this way. I needed to be the one to fix it. If "fixing" it was even an option at this point.

Well, at least if it wasn't, I could always just . . . stop.

Swallowing, I shoved the thought away once again. It was starting to weigh more and more, though. That thought.

TWENTY-SIX

JAMES
October 2018

. I TOLD MUM I was spending the night at Rick's house after school. I had zero intention of going to Rick's though. Hell, I didn't even have any intention of going to school. I got dressed in my uniform like any other morning, threw my school bag in the backseat of my car, and got on with the six-hour drive to Conway.

Risky, yeah. A: 'Cause Mum wasn't an idiot, and she'd probably find it a teeny bit suspicious that I'd gone from never seeing Rick at all to suddenly spending the night at his place. B: 'Cause Mum had clearly made some deals with the underworld to keep tabs on me because if I ever did anything I wasn't allowed to do, I swear to God and Satan she knew about it before I'd even decided to do it.

I only had one thing on my side, and that was I was

pretty sure Mum thought I was lying to go to a party. Like the kind of shit normal guys my age do when they aren't too busy driving interstate to solve a possible murder.

Wait, when did I stop classifying myself as normal?

Since Mum was pretty desperate for me to do "normal" things these days, I had a gut feeling she'd ask as few questions as possible when I came home.

Hopefully.

Although . . . maybe I should've told *someone* where I was going. Just in case. Like, for all I knew, Louise was in on the whole thing. Maybe Elliot was using her to lure me over, so he could get rid of me before I found out too much.

Or, *or*, maybe I should stop watching so much *CSI*.

I mean, it was mid-afternoon in a well-off area, all bungalows and dark green lawns dotted with cutesy little gnomes and well-placed hedges. I'm not saying no one was ever murdered in a setting like this, but it wasn't exactly raising the hair on the back of my neck, put it that way.

I found Louise's house without much hassle. Two storeys, dark grey brick with flowerpots on the windowsill, a pretty little letterbox surrounded by storybook rosebushes, and complete with a double garage. Definitely not the house of a murderer.

All the same, my heart was thudding in my throat like someone had gone and turned the bass up too high, and this wasn't even *it* yet. This was only Louise's house. If this is how freaked I was already, I was worried about how I'd handle seeing Elliot.

But like hell was I gonna waste time hanging out in front of Louise's house. Steeling myself, I got out of the car.

TWENTY-SEVEN

Ash
July 2017

I was so tired.

I was so, so tired.

Eventually I stopped trying at school altogether. Not that I'd ever put in much effort, but I'd at least put in enough to pass. Now I couldn't summon the energy to mind if I passed or failed. It made no difference to me, because that was a problem that next-year Ash would have to deal with. And next-year Ash was feeling progressively less real to me.

The only lesson I actually paid any attention in anymore was RSE. And that was mostly because of Mr. Patricks, and his insistence on treating me as though I wasn't an utter failure.

I felt like a naïve child whose affection was easily won by a kind word and a little positive reinforcement. Yet, I didn't mind. It was the first time I'd felt capable of something. These lessons were becoming the highlight of my week, and the sight of Mr. Patricks around the school made me smile rather than grimace. Even if my smiles didn't radiate all the way to the inside of my chest anymore.

Mr. Patricks administered our second assignment before he'd even handed back the last one. James had panicked, because it meant he couldn't employ his grade on the emotions assignment to judge what should be included in this one. I wished he wouldn't worry so much. He spent so much time trying to achieve perfection that he forgot to stop and be proud of what he *had* done right.

Thursday night, James was unable to walk home with me. His coach was going to be absent Friday, so they'd moved practice to Thursday. The guys were heading to dinner after too, he'd told me apologetically, so he wouldn't see me at all that night.

For once, I was surprised to find that I had some energy, despite being by myself. Instead of moping or trying to sleep, I took out the assignment Mr. Patricks had given us that afternoon. It was due the next day. Short notice, so he wouldn't be expecting me to complete it. But I just might complete it. Not because I cared much about grades. Strangely, I simply desired Mr. Patricks's approval. That short-lived burst of validation. No wonder James was addicted to pleasing people.

Write a two-page reflection about your life. What do you like about it? What don't you like about it? What do you live for?

I stared at the question until the words seemed meaningless.

What was good about my life?

James.

Small moments of happiness. They were mostly gone, but I knew they existed, because I remembered them.

What was bad about my life? That would take far more than two pages.

What did I live for?

Well.

I didn't get any pleasure at the thought of my own death. It terrified me, like it scared everyone. But the thought of living through sixty odd more years of what had started to pass for life was undeniably worse.

What *did* I live for?

My mind decided to make up the bullshit Mr. Patricks wanted to hear.

My fingers wrote something else.

I typed it quickly. Five minutes later I was done. It was nowhere near two pages, but I had nothing more to say on the topic. I stared at the words, wondering if I could possibly summon the bravery required to allow Mr. Patricks to read them. They were words I could never verbalise, but instead sat, gathering dust, in the pit of my stomach waiting patiently to be expressed. And now they'd been acknowledged. If someone else read them, they'd be given life.

But at what cost?

"Is this a pity grade?" I asked Mr. Patricks, unsure whether to be apprehensive. I stared at the letter on top of my "happiness" reflection. *A.* It was the first time I'd seen one of those on my own work in years.

"Absolutely not. It was a well-written assignment," Mr. Patricks replied, handing James's assignment to him.

I sank back, the smallest smile touching my lips. I didn't feel delighted, say, the way that I might have if I'd achieved this months, or years, ago. But there was a discernible twinge of something positive buried underneath a heavy blanket of apathy. James's eyes flashed sideways, but he made no comment.

"You have a talent for articulating abstract concepts," Mr. Patricks added to me, before moving on.

The praise left me feeling lighter than I was used to—I'd forgotten how it felt to not let someone down for once—and I stuffed the paper in my bag straight away, like it might disintegrate if I didn't contain it.

"You seem happy," James said. He wore a strange expression.

Happy seemed like a strong word, but all right. "Yes, I suppose. I got an A."

"Cool."

Why did I get the feeling he didn't think it was cool at all? I stared at him in a silent question.

He sighed and slouched. "Sorry, I'm a bit stressed out. I forgot practice was last night, so I didn't have my Phys Ed assignment ready for today, and I decided I'm gonna hand it in Monday, which means I've lost five percent already, and it's better to do that than to hand it up as it is 'cause I'll probably end up with a better grade than if I *hadn't* lost the five percent, but I'm pissed off because if I'd kept track of things I would've been able to draft it properly *and* get it up on time, and I wouldn't have to lose *any* marks."

His words all ran together, increasing in speed as he spat them out. He barely even stopped for a breath. "Don't be so hard on yourself," I said. "You'll still do excellent. I put five pounds on an A, anyway."

"I should've done better. That's all."

"James, give yourself a break."

He glared at the whiteboard. I took the hint and withdrew.

At the end of class, students approached the desk to hand up the newest reflection. James's eyebrows shot up when I joined him at the front of the classroom.

"You're handing something up on time?" Mr. Patricks

asked, holding out a hand. "I'm impressed."

Mr. Patricks acting as though I didn't have the ability to stick to a deadline didn't do wonders for the hesitant self-esteem boost that had accompanied this assignment's completion.

I hesitated. "Actually, do you think I could have a bit longer? I'm not sure it's ready. It's not long enough yet . . ."

But it wasn't the length that had me second-guessing myself. It was the content. I wanted someone, anyone, to understand me, but if it didn't change anything, which I doubted it would, then I didn't know what else to try. My options were running out.

Mr. Patricks softened. "Look, it's a simple assignment. I'll go easy on you, deal? Give me whatever you have, and we'll run with it."

James cleared this throat, a subtle plea not to make things difficult for myself. Hardening my resolve I nodded and handed over the assignment. There. It was done.

"Mr. Patricks?" I said as James handed over his own reflection.

"Hmm?"

I swallowed. "If you do have any questions about it, do you mind asking me? Not my foster parents?"

Mr. Patricks tapped the bunch of papers on the desk to jolt them into a neat pile. "Of course. Everything you have to say in this class will be treated with complete respect. It's a safe place."

"Yes," I said. James was motioning me towards the door now, and I started after him. "Thanks. Thank you."

"Have a good weekend, Ashton."

Back at mine, James worked on his Phys Ed report. I browsed through Tumblr, bored out of my mind but careful not to distract him.

Usually he needed total silence to do his homework. Which is why I was surprised when he spoke. "Maybe I should get you to go over this."

"Me?"

"Yeah. You."

I wondered if he was thinking back to when we were younger. Back when my English teachers used to brag about me. When the seed of my life could've still sprouted into a tree. Before it became a weed. I felt something unfamiliar. Pride. "I can." Then I faltered and shrugged, self-conscious. "But you'd probably fail with my advice, so . . ."

"Well, you got an A on the reflection. It must've been good." He didn't look pleased for me, though. Just annoyed. The pride faded. It hadn't been a compliment after all. Of course it hadn't. Why on earth would anyone pick me, of all people, to instruct them on homework?

I chose my next words carefully, uncertain what he was unhappy about. "I don't know. Maybe. I think I actually put in some effort for once. I found it quite fun." James's expression turned sour. I cleared my throat. "Anyway—"

"I told you you're smart. As soon as you try to do well, bam, you get an A."

That still didn't seem like a compliment.

"Did you not do as well as you hoped?" I asked.

"I got an A as well."

"Okay, fantastic?" I was bewildered now.

"How long did you spend on it?" James asked, clicking and unclicking a ballpoint pen he'd grabbed off my desk.

I shrugged, trying to remember. "Half an hour, maybe? Forty-five minutes?"

"It took me six hours. I was up until two in the morning doing it."

"Sounds as though I got lucky," I said with a forced smile

that James didn't return.

"You didn't get lucky. It's like you said. You put in a tiny bit of effort for once and you did as well as me."

Oh. I started to understand what he was getting at. "Everyone has different strengths," I said. "Don't beat yourself up over taking a bit longer on something."

"I'm not beating myself up. I'm just frustrated."

I gave up my attempts to placate. "I'm not apologising for being good at something for once."

"You're missing the point. I'm annoyed because I have to put in *everything* to do well. It's not easy for me. And then there's you. You pick up on things in seconds, and you can write, and it comes out the way you mean it the first time, but you're too lazy to do well. It's not fair."

That hurt. "Lazy is a bit harsh."

His laugh was cold. "Let's not sugar coat it. You don't give a shit, Ash. You could be something if you wanted to, but you waste it. I'm really fucking jealous of you."

I could tell from the look on his face that he didn't realise he'd insulted me. Usually I'd brush it off but that day I didn't have the energy to detach. "I'm not lazy," I said, despite the aching certainty that he was right. "Life's just difficult at the moment."

James wasn't in the mood to hear it. "Difficult? You don't *do* anything. I would *kill* to have your free time. 'Difficult' is getting to school at seven in the morning to do a language, then classes all day, then training and games four days a week, and spending five hours a night on homework just to keep my GPA, while trying to squeeze in time to see my other friends as well as you, because you won't speak to any of them. You calling your life difficult is insulting to me."

He was missing the point. I didn't feel this way because my life was objectively difficult. My life was difficult *because* I felt this way.

I should have pulled back, tried to figure out what was causing his outburst. A few weeks earlier I would have. But that day his words seemed like an attack. "Just because I'm not ridiculous enough to take on three times more than I can handle doesn't mean I don't have a lot going on," I said testily.

"Giving a shit doesn't make me ridiculous, Ash. You should try it sometime. It's *gotta* be more entertaining than lying around feeling sorry for yourself."

My head swam. I didn't know how to reply to that. Mostly because there was nothing I could say in my own defence. He'd verbalised every angry thought I'd directed at myself in one succinct statement. I hadn't expected James to notice how pathetic I was. Usually he didn't have a word of criticism towards me. If I was even irritating *him*, Saint James, it confirmed everything I suspected about myself. I was an utter failure. And now even James knew. How mortifying.

"It's hard," I said again. "I don't know how to fix everything. I wouldn't know where to start."

James rolled his eyes. "Your life isn't *that bad*, Ash. You have people who love you. You have a future. You're financially stable. There are people who have nothing, you know."

I knew. But I hadn't realised those bitter thoughts had been circulating in James's mind too. I was accustomed to my derisive inner voice. James agreeing with it changed things, though. It meant I was correct. Even after all this time, I'd still naively hoped I was being too harsh on myself.

Suppose not.

James scanned his assignment. It felt like he was making an excuse not to look at me. "I just don't know how you can be so . . . dispassionate."

"Big word," I said, my defensive switch finally clicking into place. The bitterness and sadness deep inside me cheered at the unexpected release. "Are you sure you need to spend six hours with a thesaurus whenever you do an essay?"

It was cruel, and I knew it. I wanted to steer the argument away from myself. James wasn't having any of it, though. The front page of his assignment slid off the bed and drifted to the floor like an autumn leaf, forgotten. "You know," he said. "You keep saying you care about me, but I don't think you do. Aren't people supposed to be *happy* at the start of a new relationship? You've been acting like someone's died."

"Does Elliot not count?"

But even bringing up Elliot wasn't enough to make James scale back. He scowled. "Every time I ask you if you want to talk about Elliot you say no. You say you're *fine*. This isn't *fine*, Ash."

I could barely follow the argument. How many things was he angry at me about? "I don't always want to talk about things, all right?"

"I'm your boyfriend. You're supposed to let me help you."

Was he serious? How was he supposed to help me when he didn't think that I had a right to feel bad to begin with?

"What's so bad, Ash?" he pressed. "*What?*"

I searched for an answer. How did one verbalise omnipresent dread? "I don't know, okay? Just everything."

This only served to anger him further. "What do you want me to do, Ash? I've tried to talk to you. I drop everything whenever you need me to. I don't know what you need to be happy. I should be enough, you know? I should make you happy."

"This isn't something you can do," I said, raising my voice. "You can't try harder until everything's okay, and your boyfriend's all cured. You're already everything you can be, and you're everything I want you to be, but having you doesn't erase everything else."

"So, what you're saying is no matter how hard I try, it won't be good enough for you?" His tone was flat.

"It's not about being good enough." Exasperated, I tried to find the words to explain the tangle of feelings that bound me. There had to be words for it. There were always words. "You're perfect. But having you doesn't magically make me happy."

"You make *me* happy."

"*But you're not like me!*" I cried. "For me, everything always ends up dark. When you come it's like a little candle lights up, but it always snuffs out sooner or later. I can't help it. I want to change it, but I don't know how." Even as the words left my mouth I knew they didn't work. They would have looked fine on paper, but out loud they struck as melodramatic. My throat tightened, and my eyes burned, but the tears, as usual, didn't come. For once, I was glad.

James studied me. He seemed to be swaying between making peace and losing his patience altogether. "Let me help."

"You can't help. This isn't about you. It's about me. And I'm sorry, but that's the way it is. Everything's messed up, and you can't wave a wand and make it better, and neither can I."

"It's not fair on me. It's not fair that I do *everything* I can to help you, and it gets us nowhere. It makes me wonder, you know? If it's a psych you need, or maybe, if you had someone who wasn't me, they'd be able to—"

"Fix me?" I finished for him. "Don't try to make me feel guilty over this."

"Why shouldn't I? You make me feel guilty and inadequate."

"Well, it's all coming out now, isn't it?" I muttered under my breath.

"What?"

"I'm sorry I can't be what you want me to be," I replied, raising my voice. "I'm sorry, okay?"

"Don't apologise, just *try*. You never try! You haven't even booked in with a psych yet. You just sit back and let everything overwhelm you."

He was right. Even this conversation was overwhelming me. I tried to steady my shaking voice. "I do try. I have to try so, so hard at every single little thing I do. I get out of bed, and I feel like I've run a marathon." Instead of calm, I sounded echoey and distant.

James groaned in frustration. "Grow *up*, okay? Sometimes shit happens, and you have to get on with things. If I can't help you then you're gonna have to help yourself. Stop wallowing."

Suddenly I couldn't bother coming up with a response. I wanted silence. To fold into myself and be left alone. Attempting to put everything into words was like trying to stuff an elephant into a suitcase. I could write it. But my mouth wouldn't, or couldn't, form the sentences the way my hands could.

James glared at me. "Great. So now you're not gonna talk to me? You're just gonna shut me out again? I don't deserve this."

"If that's the way you feel, then go." My dismissive voice seemed to come from somewhere across the room. "Just go. Now."

He appraised me with cold brown eyes. *Go on*, I dared him silently. *Do it. Leave. Leave me.*

And he did. With no monologue or fanfare, or even a parting gesture. He grabbed his laptop, gathered the papers, turned his back to me, and left.

My knees gave out. I crashed onto my bed, the springs creaking a warning at the sudden weight. My hand went straight to my mouth, covering it as though pleading with me not to call out after him. *Wait*, a voice inside my head urged. *This is the part where he bursts back in. It's okay.*

So I sat in silence. The clock ticked merrily on the wall, louder and louder. It could almost have been footsteps. Almost.

But nobody came. Nobody.

I wanted to lie down, to curl into a ball and block it all out. Instead I sat, clenching my hands into fists and clenching my jaw harder.

I sent Bea a text. She didn't reply.

Hours passed and still it was just me. Alone. The way it was always going to be. I had myself, and nobody else. Which was unfortunate, because even I despised my own company.

I wandered over to my computer and pulled up the assignment I'd written the night before. The one I'd been afraid to hand in.

Write a two-page reflection about your life. What do you like about it? What don't you like about it? What do you live for?

There's a French term for the latter question. Raison d'être. It means "reason for being." My mum used to say that Elliot and I were her raison d'être. Mum had a reason, now she lacks a being. I have a being, I just lack a reason. I live because of the law of inertia. An object in motion stays in motion unless acted upon by an unbalanced force.

If I were to reflect on my life, I would say it's like being engulfed in quicksand, and as much as I want to get out, I slowly sink deeper, towards an inevitable end. I want someone to pull me out, but I don't know how they can. Their only reactions are to stand on dry land and watch me with concerned expressions, urging me to just walk like they are.

Living is being in the middle of a dark tunnel, claustrophobic and boxed in, and feeling something closing in behind you, and realising you can only beat it by running. But the tunnel never ends, and you come to realise that you can't run forever. You go for as long as you possibly can, hoping to God that you'll see a light before you can't run anymore. You desperately want to live. But everyone has their limit. And when you eventually hit yours, there's nothing more you can do.

Life is temporary. Nothing is certain about it except for the fact that it will end. It can end on your terms or as a surprise. The thing is . . . I don't like surprises.

When would Mr. Patricks read it? Later tonight? Later that weekend, probably. Or maybe never.

Maybe I was screaming into an abyss. Maybe I was screaming over nothing.

Elliot. I had to speak to Elliot. He was the one person I had left who might understand. So I called him.

I didn't expect him to answer. But he did. And I almost cried from relief when he picked up.

"Elliot."

"Hey, Ash," he said. His voice sounded odd. "Listen, I'm on my way out the door, I can't talk."

"Elliot, wait—"

"Sorry, I really don't have time."

"Stop, listen to me for a second—"

"I can't talk right now."

"Please. *Please.* Can we meet somewhere? Can you meet me at the beach? I need to talk to you."

"Another time."

He didn't sound committed, so I pushed harder.

"I don't have anyone else," I said. "I don't have anyone."

He paused. Long enough that I thought he was going to say yes. That he'd meet me. "The beach," I said again, my heart thudding. "I'll wait on the rocks. I don't mind if you're drunk. It'll only take a second."

"No."

"*Please*—"

The only response was a dial tone. He'd hung up on me. He'd hung up on me.

"*Please help me*," I choked out.

But no one heard me.

I shoved the phone in my pocket and drifted to my desk. Grabbing the pen James had been playing with from the bed, I flipped open my notebook to an untainted page. I wrote down two absentminded sentences.

> *I don't belong here. I'm a shadow waiting for the sun to set and erase me.*

At that moment, a cool chill was cast over the room.

I left the book open, displaying my scrawl. At the back of my mind I knew what I was doing. It sent satisfied acceptance through my chest. I was peaceful.

That's when I began to walk.

TWENTY-EIGHT

James
October 2018

THE DOOR WAS ANSWERED by a short, elderly woman with tightly curled black hair and dark mauve lipstick. She was dressed in a smart light-blue skirt-suit with a ruby brooch pinned right above her heart. I wondered if I'd grabbed her on her way out.

"Uh, hi," I said.

What if I didn't have the right house? What if Louise never wanted to meet me, so she gave me a fake address for the hell of it?

"My name's James. Is . . . Louise here?"

Please say yes.

She scanned me up and down. *(Super unimpressed.)* Not the best sign.

Then, finally, "Louisa is home," she said, stepping aside.

"You come wait."

I breathed out a sigh of relief and followed her into the lounge room, where she pointed to the couch. "Sit. We come down soon."

I sat. And she disappeared.

Ooookkkaaaay, old lady. Whoever the hell you are. Nice to meet you too.

On the foot of the couch, someone had placed a bunch of folded up blankets and pillows. Guess that was for my bed. How sweet. I would've thanked someone, if there was anyone around to thank.

The lounge room was neat, and simply decorated. It had a wooden furniture theme—wooden TV stand, display cabinets, bookshelves, coffee table. And plants. A hell of a lot of plants, in pots and on shelves, scattered around the room. I'd never known anyone who kept plants inside. I wanted to test one of the leaves to see if they were real, but before I had the chance, the front door swung open.

A man and a woman walked through the door, lugging in bags of groceries. The man took one look at me then pushed through to the kitchen without acknowledging me. Gee, wonder who Granny's biological kid was. The woman put the shopping bags down by the front door and came right over to me.

"Hi," she said with a large smile. "You must be James."

Finally, someone acknowledged me. I stood up and took her hand. "Yeah, hi. Nice to meet you. Thank you so much for letting me come visit."

She sandwiched my hand between both of hers. "Of course, any time you want to, you feel free to drop by. Louise is just up in her room. She'll be expecting you, go right on up."

It felt weird just wandering up to the room of someone I'd never technically met, but it was one of the least weird things about this whole situation, so I rolled with it. On my way upstairs, I could hear the old woman holding a hissed conversation with Louise's familiar voice.

"Elliot is your boyfriend," the woman said, "and you having a boy sleep here!"

I paused. Elliot was Louise's boyfriend? Why hadn't she mentioned that?

Louise sounded pissed off when she replied. "Elliot is *not* my boyfriend."

"You kiss him—" the woman insisted.

"It is the *twenty-first century*, Abuela, kissing someone—"

"*Créeme. Te casarás con Elliot—*"

"Abuela, I don't speak Spanish, but I can assure you there is nothing going on between—"

Then Louise's grandma glanced to the right, noticed me on the stairs, and started making wild hushing motions, gesturing towards me with wide eyes.

Guess that was my cue. Old Grandma no-manners stepped aside to let me poke my head around the door. Louise, who turned out to be a round-faced girl with an explosion of dark curls and a crater-sized dimple in her left cheek, jumped to her feet. She was a nice-looking chick to begin with, but I was so grateful that she was real, and she was really, truly helping me confront Elliot, that she looked like a goddamn Christmas angel to me.

"Uh, hey," I said, giving her an awkward wave. "Sorry. Your mum told me to come up here . . ."

"No, it's fine," she said. "Abuela was just making sure I wasn't cheating on a guy I am in no way, shape, or form in a relationship beyond platonic with. How was the drive?"

I laughed. Poor Elliot. Friend-zoned like a pro. "Long. Boring. Took about six breaks. Would've helped to have someone to share the driving, but it makes things a bit difficult when I can't actually tell anyone why I came."

Louise smiled back, and I saw her mum in her straight away. I still wasn't convinced she was related to her grandma, who looked like she was ready to grab a broom and sweep me out. "Of course," she said. "Do you want to wait until after dinner to go see Elliot, then? You must be over driving for now."

Oh yeah. *Hell* yeah was I over driving. But was I putting this off for longer than I had to? Give Elliot the chance to hear me coming and mail himself in a one-way crate to Antarctica or something? "No thanks. I'd prefer to get it over with, actually."

Louise, at least, didn't seem to mind. "Right. Okay. Sure."

Her grandma finally piped up. "We have *albondigas* for dinner."

Wait, that was to me. She was offering me food. And she didn't even sound pissed. Well hell yeah. All I'd had to eat all day was a granola bar I'd stolen from the pantry on my way out, so the thought of dinner made me burst out into a genuine grin. Which was a fair achievement, given how nervous I was.

"Sounds awesome," I said, stamping on the nerves *(unadulterated terror)*, and Granny seemed to soften a bit. "Hopefully we won't be too long."

She shrugged and turned to leave the room. "We will wait for you. No hurry."

We waited a few seconds until she was halfway down the stairs, then I turned to Louise. "Thank you so much for this," I started, but *woah*. Her dimples were gone. Girl had turned into Medusa. Maybe I shouldn't have been so hasty to let Granny leave us alone.

"I'm doing this for Elliot," she hissed. "Not for you. I don't know what you think is going to happen when you see him, but just so you know, I'm on his side. Doesn't matter what he says happened. I'm on his side."

Fair enough. I could respect that. "That's fine. As long as you accept that, no matter what he says happened, I'm on Ash's side. Always."

We stared each other down, and I'd like to think we came to a silent agreement. She stopped trying to set me on fire with her eyes, anyway, which was a plus.

Who knew. Maybe we weren't even on different sides. Maybe I'd lost the plot because my boyfriend was gone, and he was never coming back. I wouldn't be *that* surprised to find out that I'd read into clues that weren't there. Okay . . . so maybe *I'd* be surprised, but a psychiatrist sure as hell wouldn't be. They'd say I was just trying to feel like I had some control in a helpless situation. And they'd probably be right.

Either way. Whatever had happened on Ash's last day, it was more than time to find out.

Louise smiled at me, and I smiled at her, and we headed to my car.

———

TWENTY-NINE

Ash
July 2017

I FOLLOWED THE ROAD for a while then veered left, following the creek trail. My iPhone streamed songs at random, changing according to my command every few seconds. I couldn't settle on a song; I hated the sound of all of them. But silence was worse. At least the music muffled my thoughts somewhat.

Eventually the crumbling gravel path led me to the place where the creek met the river. Up ahead, I could see the railway bridge.

Do you remember Mr Olivers?

It didn't take long to reach the bridge. I stepped onto it, balancing on one of the metal ridges like James had done months before. It took a couple of minutes at most to get to the other side. And that's if I dawdled. I had no idea when the next train was due. If I crossed the bridge, the chances of one coming while I was trapped were technically only about ten percent.

So if one does come, I reasoned, *then it's meant to be. The decision isn't yours. Let the universe decide for you.*

Almost as soon as I began the walk, I felt a subtle change in the ground. I ignored it. Only a minute or so to go. The change was tangible now. A soft but steady vibration.

I smiled. An exhausted, bitter smile. There it was.

The river was beneath me now. Quite a drop. Looking at it made my stomach swoop. I kept walking until I'd traversed about a third of its width, stopped underneath the metal arches, and then leaned against the railing to wait. I could see the train now, a speck of light in the distance, approaching rapidly.

There was an eerie calmness to the world. Everything seems beautiful when you're looking at it for the last time. It's a pity it isn't always like that.

I hopped up to sit on the barrier, so I wouldn't be so visible to the driver. I didn't want anybody slamming any breaks.

Ten seconds, maximum.

My mind was clear.

Five seconds.

My fingers squeezed the cold metal. My body tightened. I was ready to pounce.

Four seconds.

I could make out a person in the driver's seat.

Three seconds.

It was a man. He saw me. I braced myself.

Two seconds.

His mouth opened in horror. I was going to destroy him.

One second.

I couldn't do this to him. I couldn't.

With a strangled cry, I threw myself off the bridge instead.

SEEK

THIRTY

James
July 2017

I WAS IN LOVE with Ash. I never told him. But I was.

Ash always had a thing for song lyrics. When we were little, his dad got obsessed with that nineties song, "One Week." And he'd play it all afternoon, every afternoon. I remember complaining about it once when me and Ash were trying to play PlayStation, and he started singing along. Like, the whole thing, even the rap part, word for word. I dunno whether he was trying to prove the song was driving him up the wall too, or if he was just trying to irritate me, but no one else *does* that kind of thing, you know?

Then for ages he didn't sing at all. He tried to kill himself when we were fourteen. It took him forever to act normal again after that. Ash wouldn't talk much about the hospital, and I learned damn quick not to bring it up if I didn't wanna piss him off for days. Then one time I asked Elliot about it, and he told me Ash had depressionandanxiety. Not depression, or anxiety, but this one awful word. Like these twin demon assholes that doubled up to fuck over my best friend as much as they could.

Maybe a year later, we were chilling in my room, and he was lying on my bed, and "Smells Like Teen Spirit" came on my playlist. And I was singing along to it, making up shit as I went like everyone else in the world does when they sing it—because who can figure out what the hell they're saying?—then I realised Ash was singing it right. He was on his phone, not even looking at me. He wasn't even singing loudly. But he had every word spot on. I even looked it up later. Like, I could actually make the words out when he was singing it.

But anyway. I remember just, kind of, stopping and staring at him, and he didn't even notice. And I realised that even though all this stuff had changed, he was still the same person as he was when I first became friends with him. And, like, yeah. That's when I knew I loved him.

Ash disappeared on a Friday night. I think we all expected to know what had happened by the end of the weekend, but we didn't. We spent a few days looking for him, but eventually we had to stop. There was no point. If there was anything to find we would've found it.

We knew something was wrong. Really wrong. But the police, Sue and Dom, they weren't telling us shit. I knew of rumours going around but I cut people off if they tried to bring them up with me. I didn't wanna sit around talking about what-ifs. I refused to go to school at first. I knew I wouldn't make it through five minutes without everyone asking about Ash. Like I knew what had happened to him.

The thing is, I *did* know—depressionandanxiety. I just wasn't letting the thought become real yet. Not when there was technically still reason to hope. I'd already talked to the police. I told them everything, too. About Ash's cutting. How he skipped school and refused to do homework. How he felt about Sue and Dom, about Elliot leaving.

On Wednesday, Mum and Dad forced me to go back to school. By then I didn't mind so much. I wanted to *do* something—*anything*—other than sitting at home giving robotic replies to my parents. Even then, it felt weird to get up with my alarm, sleepwalk through some sort of routine, and come back home to start it again. Pretending to go about life like usual. I wasn't really, though. What I was doing was waiting. Waiting for everything to either go back to normal or to shit. And that depended on what had happened with Ash.

As impatient as I was, though, part of me was cool with the waiting, because it meant not knowing. And as long as I didn't know, I could pretend it was going to be okay. Even though it was less and less likely with every fucking minute, hour, day that passed.

On Thursday afternoon, the first RSE lesson without Ash, I had to sit next to his empty seat and pretend nothing about doing that made me wanna scream the fucking school down.

Mr. Patricks was quiet that day. His stare kept going to Ash's usual spot, like he expected him to appear out of thin air all meek and guilty for making us worry. When Mr. Patricks started the music—a horrendous Amy Grant CD. Who funded this course, *Hillsong?*—no one else seemed to find it funny. It was a joke I'd only ever shared with Ash. I sank in my seat a bit.

"Today," Mr. Patricks said, "we're doing affirmations. Put your name on the top of a new page in your book and give it to the person on your left. When you receive a book, I want you to write something you appreciate about the person whose name is on the top of the page. We keep going until you receive your original book back. Do you think you can all bring yourselves to come up with twenty-five apprecia-tions?"

"Twenty-four," Gemma said, turning around to look at Ash's desk.

I was too busy being pissed off at the timing of this to bother agreeing with her. If we'd done this last Friday's lesson, and Ash had gone home from school with a bunch of nice words in his head instead of the shit I'd decided to throw at him, would the desk next to me still be empty? "Is this in the course outline?" I asked.

Mr. Patricks caught my eye. "It is now," he said, and I got it.

I tore a page out of my exercise book, scrawled Ash's name at the top, and walked it over to Gemma's desk. "Twenty-five," I said, putting the paper in front of her. She looked surprised, but she started writing on it anyway. Usually I tried not to talk to her. She didn't exactly top the list of my favourite people—try number fifty-thousand, two hundred and sixty-seven—but I figured she was one of the only people who came close to feeling the way I did about Ash's disappearance, so she was a temporary ally.

About twenty minutes later, Gemma's book and Ash's paper were passed over to me. Except it wasn't Ash's paper anymore. It was suddenly three pieces of paper, filled to the brim with writing and held together at the corner by two overlapping staples. I didn't have enough time to read the messages, but I could tell straight away people suddenly had a lot more to say to Ash than they did to their other class-mates.

Instead of making me happy, it made me want to lose my shit. A: For everyone not saying any of this to Ash when it might've made a fucking difference. B: 'Cause it was so goddamn *typical* that they'd only remember to give a shit about Ash now it was too late, but they were all too dense to take the chance to pay each other the same kind of attention. Like, why the hell were Ash's affirmations so much longer? Why didn't they all get that anyone in the fucking class could be feeling the way Ash was? Why did they still need to be told to care?

As for me, I didn't write anything on Ash's pages. Anything I wrote on there would feel like a goodbye. Ash would take the piss out of me for writing a sad, sentimental message when he turned up again. Besides. Anything I had to write I'd tell him in person when I saw him. Because I'd definitely see him again, right? Yeah. Sure. I had to. *(You hope.)* I scanned the words written on there without taking them in, then passed it on.

I didn't look at my own affirmation page when it reached me a few minutes later. I wasn't in the mood for anything warm and fuzzy. Gemma skimmed her own page with a grin that faded when she picked up Ash's. I got up and went over to her. "Here," I said. "I'll give it to him when I see him next."

Gemma gave it to me but with one of those *looks*. A patronising, *I'm gonna humour you* look. When they found Ash, I was gonna tell him how I was the only one who'd trusted that he was okay.

The bell rang, but I wasn't in a rush to run off. I was dreading the walk home. Like I needed any more reminders that Ash wasn't here after that lesson. I'd have to go home with my own company. No dawdling. No park. No detour to Ash's.

I'd just grabbed my stuff when I realised I was eye level with Mr. Patricks's waist. "Hey, James," he said. "How are you doing?"

Well how the fuck did he think I was doing?

"Superb," I said, staying in my seat. "Swell. Super. Take

your pick."

"If there's anything I can do to help you, tell me. We have a counsellor here. If you need a break, or an extension on an assignment . . ."

Assignments. For once, they were the last things on my mind. I nodded. "Yeah. Maybe. Thank you."

Mr. Patricks hesitated. "Did you . . ." he trailed off, and I got the feeling he was asking something he shouldn't be. "Did Ashton ever show you his RSE essays?"

"No. Why?"

The moment I answered I knew it was the wrong thing to say. Whatever secret information Mr. Patricks was gonna give me was, for some reason, dependent on me having read Ash's assignments. Whatever the hell that meant. He shrugged and brushed it off. "Just curious. Have a good night."

I meant to walk home. I did. But I missed my street. Instead, I continued without an end in mind.

It was funny, I realised as I wandered around town. That whole time I'd found it so hard to understand what was going on with Ash. Like, why he was so down all the time. As soon as he disappeared, though, I suddenly came up with this whole list of reasons to believe he wasn't okay. I could've written a goddamn thesis on it. I saw everything. Broken family, hardly any friends, no confidence or goals. Finally, I *got* it. Way too late to do anything about it, though.

It's fine, I told myself. *You know now. When he turns up things will be different. You'll be able to help him. The worst bit is over.*

(Liar.)

Somehow I ended up back at school. It was deserted. There were no practices on Thursdays, and it was getting late, so even the teachers would be heading home by now.

I walked through the grounds, and Ash was everywhere. Almost every memory I'd made in this place featured him. Hopefully he'd stop skipping now.

Once he was safe at home. Once he had help.

I reached the top of the grandstand before the football pitch and jumped my way down, a few steps at a time. What if I'd told someone? Sue, or a teacher, or the school counsellor. He would've been so pissed, but he'd be pissed *here*. Safe where I could see him.

(Why didn't *you tell anyone?)*

It was fine, though, 'cause he was fine. He'd only gone missing. I'd learn from this. If anything like this ever happened again I'd tell someone straight away. It was okay, 'cause my mistake hadn't cost anything too big.

(You hope.)

I hit the ground, sending up a cloud of red dirt.

I shouldn't have taken my shit mood out on him. It had nothing to do with him. He hadn't done anything wrong. I'd been tired, and stressed out, and I'd hurt him because I'd felt safe doing it. I couldn't take it out on my parents, or my other friends, or my teachers, so I took it out on the person I knew would forgive me for it straight away. The person who deserved it least. I didn't see it that way at the time, even though it should've been obvious to me. I should've realised what I was doing.

And goddamn it, I should've never left him that night. I'd *left him*. I saw the look on his face, and I knew how he'd feel if I went, and I did it anyway. Just to be spiteful. I deserved to rot in hell for that. *I'll never leave him again*, I thought. *Won't do something that stupid and selfish twice.*

Give me a chance to make it up to you. This can't be it. It can't be over.

On the grass, I slowed down. I should've brought a

jacket. It didn't matter, though. There were worse things than being cold.

I sat, almost in the centre of the field, and waited. Waited for the waiting to be over. I couldn't tell you what irony was, exactly. The only thing I knew about it was that the Alanis Morissette song got the meaning wrong. But I felt like this was probably a good example of it.

My phone began to ring.

I took it out. Mum. This was it. This had to be. He'd turned up. Everything was okay.

"Hey."

"Hi, *anak*," Mum said in a strained voice, and I *knew*.

I stayed silent.

"I need you to come home now."

"Later."

"No. Now, James," Mum said.

"He's dead, isn't he?" I asked.

She hesitated.

"Yeah," I replied for her in a whisper.

"Come straight home, okay?"

"Yeah."

"I'm sorry, *anak*. Are you okay?"

"Yeah. Yeah, I'm fine. I mean, I knew, mostly," I said.

"Okay . . ." she sounded uncertain. "You're coming straight home?"

"Yeah. I'll come home."

"Where are you?"

"At school. On the oval. Just wanted some space."

"You need to come home."

"I will." I didn't even snap at the repetition. I was utterly collected.

When Mum ended the phone call, I made no move to get up. Instead, I pulled out a few blades of grass by their roots. Scattered them. I ran my tongue over my teeth. The corner of my mouth twitched. "He's dead," I whispered to myself, trying it out. "Okay. Alright."

I wasn't even gonna cry, I realised. Maybe this would be okay. Maybe I was weirdly resilient. I could cope with this. I could adjust. People died every day. Life went on.

Then my vision closed in from the sides, and everything went white, and I started screaming. It hit all at once. This agony I'd never come close to experiencing. I'd never known feeling this bad was even possible. I screamed louder, but it wasn't big enough for the feeling that wanted to explode out of my chest. I doubled over, grabbing handfuls of grass and dirt, trying to reattach myself to reality. I was falling, not emotionally, but physically. I was convinced of it. Everything tipped upside down and sideways, and I kept screaming through a raw throat.

My parents found me like that half an hour later. Instead of going nuts at my disregard for instructions, they cried with me. We sat sprawled on the grass, my parents holding me until I didn't have any tears left. Then they pulled me to my feet and walked me to the car, one parent on each side of me.

I'd never told them Ash was my boyfriend. I never even told them how I felt about him.

THIRTY-ONE

Louise
October 2018

"OKAY, SO, HE'S PROBABLY going to be mad," I whispered as James and I walked through the front gate. "Make that definitely. Definitely going to be mad. I'm thinking good cop, bad cop."

"Who's good cop?" James asked. He could poker face like a pro. It was too bad, really. In another life, we probably could've been good friends.

"Oh, you, of course. You're the natural choice," I said, laying on the sarcasm so thick it could've bogged a car.

James made a face. "I'm too charming for bad cop."

I could tell he was joking, though. Of course he was. He hadn't exactly come all this way to challenge Elliot to a game of Scrabble, had he?

We reached the door. Okay. This was it. Too late to go

back now. Maybe I should take a quick time-out to search for a four-leaf clover or something. I needed all the luck I could get if I wanted Elliot to ever speak to me again after this.

I pushed open the door.

"Why is it unlocked?" James asked.

"I texted him I was coming. He always unlocks the door for me."

James blinked, then gave the smallest, saddest smile. "Yeah? Ash used to do that for me, too."

Even though I couldn't have known that would remind him of Ash, I still felt guilty for putting that look on his face. Something about James's expression when he talked about Ash made me want to drop everything and squeeze the sad out of him. But I couldn't. We were in the middle of a delicate mission, here, and I had to focus, damn it.

"Hey," I called out. "Anyone home?"

James followed me through the hallway, arms folded. He looked like he was ready to fight. Which made me think bringing him here was the stupidest idea I'd ever had. At least he didn't seem to be armed. Not that I'd patted him down or anything. Maybe I should've. But how do you even bring that up? Oh, hey, what's up, nice to meet you, can I check your pockets for weapons real quick?

I heard footsteps across the house. "Hey. You didn't bring chocolate, by any chance, did you?" Elliot called out. "Long shot, but I can't be bothered going out, and I'm desperate."

James wasn't next to me anymore. I glanced behind me to find him hanging back, looking at the bookshelf oddly, his forehead furrowed. Was he having second thoughts now? Because it was *kind of* too late for that now.

When I turned back to the hallway, Elliot was standing motionless.

I was going to say something about the chocolate to

try to keep things casual, break the ice or what-have-you, but the look on his face told me there wasn't any point. He stared at James with a half-open mouth, looking right past me like I wasn't even there. I'd expected him to be angry with me. But nope, not angry. He looked terrified. One hundred percent terrified.

"No," James said. "No. No, no, no."

I turned to him. What was he talking about? What did I miss? Then, of all things, he smiled at me in the strangest, conspiratorial kind of way. "This isn't real, is it?" he asked, folding his arms. "I'm dreaming right now."

Huh? Had he lost it? I looked back at Elliot, who still hadn't moved an inch. "James . . ." he said. Like he was afraid if he spoke too loudly James would shatter.

Just as I looked back at James, trying to make sense of what I was missing, he let out a cry and started running.

Before I could even react, Elliot flew past me. James tried to slam the front door on his way out, and Elliot ran into it, staggering backwards. I started after him, intending to help him, but he was back up and running in a split second. *"James, stop!"* he yelled.

"What the *hell*, Elliot?" I cried after him, taking chase.

I was fast, but the guys were faster, plus they had a head start. Halfway down the street, James had doubled over with his hands on his knees. He was either about to cry or throw up. Elliot almost got there first, but as soon as James saw him he shot back up and held out a hand like he was warding off a vampire. All he needed was a stake or garlic, and he'd be set. "Get away from me."

Elliot slowed but didn't stop. "I need to talk to you."

"Get away from me!" James screamed.

I hovered behind Elliot, watching the exchange. But honestly, it was like trying to follow a telenovela without subtitles. Had James seen something in the lounge room?

Something that told him Elliot had hurt Ash, maybe? That had to be it. But what had tipped him off? I tried to picture the scene—the photo frames, and the knick-knacks, and the DVD collection. It must have been something about the bookshelf. Because James had hung back staring at it before Elliot had even come out.

"James, please," Elliot tried.

"*No!*" James's cheeks were red and wet now. Whatever he'd seen, it was bad. "Leave me alone."

Elliot's arms fell at his side helplessly. "I can't."

"You fucking well can; you've proven that," James choked out. He kept backing away from us—from *Elliot*—and neither of us said a word. What the hell was there *to* say?

James practically threw himself into his car. Then the engine roared, and in a blur of colour, he was gone. Just like that.

Seriously, *what?*

I took a step towards Elliot. "What the hell just happened?"

Elliot took in a strangled breath, staring after James. Then all at once his legs gave out, and he sank to his knees in the middle of the road.

THIRTY-TWO

Ash
July 2017

There was only darkness.

Don't ask me how long for; I couldn't tell you. It can't have been long though, because I woke back up with water in my mouth but not my throat. I didn't make the decision to kick up. It came instinctively.

I'd always been a good swimmer, but it was a different experience clothed. My jacket was an anchor pulling me down, my shoes were bricks. I could have given up and allowed my clothes to drown me. If I'd sucked in the water that sat stagnant in my mouth it would have set off a chain reaction, and my lungs would have been waterlogged in only seconds. But instead I kicked, and I fought, and I forced myself to the surface.

I broke the seal of my intended grave with a desperate

gasp for air. I choked, sucking in water and spiralling into a violent coughing fit. My vision closed in from the sides, and my mind faded. I dropped below the surface briefly, and that, too, could have been it. Then clarity sparked, and I was alert. Somehow I managed to wriggle out of my jacket, allowing it to drop to the river bed. In only jeans and a t-shirt I was much less weighed down, and holding my chin above surface went from an impossible task to a feat well within my grasp.

The tide was relentless. It swept me along like a bottle top, weightless. My body slammed into an exposed rock, knocking the air from my lungs with a strangled gasp.

It occurred to me how low the water level was at this time of year. How narrowly I must have missed hitting a rock upon landing.

I wrenched my head out of the water once more and, fighting the tide, struggled over to the riverbank and latched onto a fishing pier. Lugging my drenched body out of the river, I began to sob. My throat raw, I collapsed in a heap on top of the splintered wood and curled up into myself.

It was the first time in years that I'd truly cried. The experience was startling for me, and the tears mingling with the river water on the back of my hands invited a morbid fascination.

I stared down the river to the train track, now some distance away. I could go back. If I threw myself in front of the train, surely I wouldn't survive it. But recalling the paralysing fear I'd felt when falling from the bridge caused me to hesitate.

I don't want to die, a voice inside me begged.

But what else was there?

Perhaps I could stay where I was. Hide under a bush, and stay put, and wait to die naturally. Did I have the will for it? Who the hell knew? But I couldn't go back. Impossible. And there was nowhere else for me to go. I had no one.

As much as I liked the idea of simply lying, I knew I had to move. The train driver would have called the police by now. They'd arrive soon to search for a body, maybe clinging to wild hope that the body would still be moving. The knowledge spurred me to action, finding the nearest footpath and walking away. I didn't have a destination in mind. Home was out of the question; they'd be able to find me there. James wouldn't want to see me. Elliot didn't care about me. I had no one to go to.

Somehow, once again, my legs brought me to the beach. It was apparently their autopilot go-to when I couldn't see any other means of escape.

The seaside wind blew powerful and frigid, and I was soaked through, but I barely felt the cold. I didn't feel anything. Our rock beckoned to me. It was the perfect spot, hidden in the cliff face, so anyone out for a hypothermic swim wouldn't notice a sopping, fully-clothed sixteen-year-old curled up on a ledge planning his death.

I had little idea of my next move. The only thing I was aware of was the desperate certainty that returning home wasn't an option, and the knowledge that I had no one to turn to. That, and the understanding that the kindest, most selfless thing I could do would be to step away from this dance, so James, and Elliot, and Bea, and Sue and Dom, and my dad, and everyone who'd spent so much time and energy on me could be freed from the weight of my existence.

And so could I.

Maybe if I concentrated I could fall into death the way a person falls into sleep. Why did my body have to be so disobedient about this? Why was it so steadfastly determined to survive?

Ash?

I knew that voice.

But I didn't dare to believe it.

The call was distant. Distant enough that I doubted it would come any closer. But then it came again, distinctly nearer.

I leaned up on one hand, swallowing the sobs that hammered at the entrance of my throat. "Elliot?" I rasped.

THIRTY-THREE

Louise
October 2018

I dragged Elliot, all zombie-like, back inside to sit on the armchair across from the couch. "Why do I feel like I've done something really bad?" I asked.

He didn't answer.

Curious, I scanned the bookshelf. An average collection of hard-covers and paperbacks on the bottom few shelves, a couple of vases with cheap plastic flowers, and some pictures of Bea, Elliot, and their friends. I liked those pictures. Mostly because I was in one of them, and that night someone told me I looked like Kylie Jenner. To be fair, my makeup had been flawless.

Nothing on there seemed out of the ordinary.

My phone began to ring. Saras. *Not now, Saras.* I declined the call and turned back to Elliot. I had no idea what to say. "Sorry I threw you to the wolves, but I can explain" wasn't an awesome ice breaker. I could word it better than that, anyway. "I'm really confused, but I wanted to say I'm sorry. He found something out about you. He was going to take it to the police if you didn't speak to him. So I told him he could come and talk to you first."

Elliot stared at his hands and nodded. 'Kay. Guess it was still my turn to speak. "He said you lied about where you were when Ash died, and about speaking to him, and what you did that night, and I think he thinks you did something, and I'm not saying you did, but if you *did* then I want you to know I'm on your side."

Way to ramble.

My phone rang again. *Jesus Christ, Saras,* I thought. *Take a hint.* I declined it again.

"Did something?" Elliot asked.

"Yup. He thinks you hurt Ash."

He started playing with his lip ring. "Would you still be on my side if I did hurt Ash?"

Oh, God. He really *did* do something. My instincts went into overdrive, and the questions I'd been asking myself over the last few weeks had their immediate answer: *Do whatever it takes to cover this up. If he needs you to hide evidence, hide it. If he needs you to lie for him, lie.*

Where the hell had this conviction been when I needed it?

Elliot's phone rang. He ignored it. I checked the caller ID. Saras. What did that girl want? Didn't she know I was in a crisis here? I wondered if something could be wrong. Then I realised she probably wanted to cover a shift. So instead of asking Elliot to answer, I grabbed his hands. "Yes. I promise. I've been a piece of shit for a friend, but I swear I was trying to do the right thing. And I won't let him get you in trouble."

I don't know if he heard me, though. He was too busy

looking outside at the blue car that had pulled into the driveway. "Isn't that Saras's car?"

It was. Suddenly, I didn't think she was trying to cover a shift.

We watched together as she climbed out, slammed the door, and marched up to the house. She knocked, hard, and then burst into the lounge room before either of us got up to answer the door.

She locked onto Elliot with wild eyes like I wasn't in the room. "We need to talk," she said, breathless. "You—I can't, I mean I—I know, okay?"

She seemed totally rattled. Unflappable Saras, who took on all the customer complaints, and told off the kitchen guys if they were slacking, and sassed Joe if he was being an ass. What the hell was going on?

Elliot straightened his back and scanned her up and down. He looked cold. And for the first time, I doubted him. I mean, *really* doubted.

If Elliot had hurt Ash, and we knew about it . . . suddenly, I wished Bea was home. Then I realised. Whatever was going on, Bea was in on it. I remembered the look on her face when I said I knew about Ash. *"What about Ash?"* she'd asked.

What *about* Ash?

Uh oh.

"Elliot?" I asked, shuffling backwards.

He started to stand, but Saras swung to face him, no-nonsense. "No, sit down."

Lowering himself back down onto the armchair, he looked at Saras warily. I think I matched his expression, to be totally honest. She turned to me and pointed sideways to Elliot. "He's been lying to us, Louise."

THIRTY-FOUR

Ash
July 2017

Everything appeared to be floating.

My voice shouldn't have been loud enough for him to hear, but he must have, because seconds later Elliot appeared around the side of the cliff face. His expression dropped as he took me in. Damp, shivering, and swollen-eyed, I had a feeling I wasn't at my best. He launched himself up and over the ledge, with little more trouble than if he'd been climbing a staircase.

"Ash," he whispered, crouching down. "What happened?"

He was truly here.

My breaths came quicker, and I tried to stand but stopped after climbing onto my knees. I heaved a sob. "I need help," I choked. "I need help."

The next half hour was a blur. Elliot somehow managed

to steer me, trembling and weak, over the rocks and halfway across the beach to his car. There, he stripped off my wet t-shirt.

It was then that I felt the blinding pain. My chest was mottled purple, blue, and pink. I was detached enough to be fascinated by it. Elliot, however, looked nauseous, and he wasted no time dressing me in his own jumper, which was far too big for me. When had I hurt my chest? Was it the impact? Or the rocks?

So the jump hadn't been a dream.

I huddled against the door, clasping my hands together behind my neck, and drifted in and out of focus as Elliot phoned Callan.

Ash jumped off a bridge . . . can't come anymore . . . explain later.

A part of me wanted to yelp and beg him not to tell people what I'd done, but I was too grateful to bother.

My brother was here. With me. Not ignoring me. Not shutting me out.

And he'd chosen me over them. He'd chosen me.

Even before he'd known what I did, he came to the beach. For me.

Elliot didn't speak as he drove us home. We'd made it as far as my street corner when Elliot flicked the indicator off and continued straight.

"What's the matter?" I asked, focussing.

"There was a police car outside the house. Did you do something?"

I knew why they were there. The train driver had seen me. "Other than jump off a bridge? No."

"Well, you're lucky suicide isn't illegal here. We're going back to mine."

I was so relieved at the idea of avoiding the police that I didn't even question it.

It was the first time I'd actually viewed the house from within. Simply decorated but well looked after, it appeared more like a cheap hotel room than a home. But it might as well have been the palace of Versailles to me. Elliot stripped the blankets from his own bed, ignoring my protests, and gently bundled me up on the couch. I burrowed into the pile of blankets and pillows, warm in the pyjamas Elliot had given me to change into. By the time he came in with a mug of tea and some painkillers, I'd calmed considerably.

"You okay?" he asked, sitting on the floor in front of me.

"Debatable," I said with a faint smile.

"What do you wanna do?" He blew on his tea. "Do you wanna go back tonight, or tomorrow, or—"

"Not tonight. Not tomorrow. Not the next day."

"Not ever?"

"Not ever. Not for now. I don't know. I can't right now. Please."

Elliot hesitated, then nodded. I was too exhausted to say any more or decide what I wanted to do next. I couldn't think more than a few hours in the future at that point or I'd have a complete breakdown. If only I could escape, somehow. How could I possibly keep sleepwalking through the motions of a normal life? Continue creeping around a house that would never be my home, forcing interaction with people who resented my presence there?

Elliot picked up his phone, and I shot up in a panic. My chest screamed in pain, but I ignored it. "What are you doing?" I asked. "Don't call Sue."

"Relax, *mon poussin*. I'm calling Bea."

"Bea?"

"Well, you can't stay here. They'll find you."

They. I pictured "them" as hound dogs with a scent. Hunting and cornering me. It sent me spiralling into a mild panic.

He held the phone to his ear. Before he could speak, I made out Bea on the other end, talking frantically.

"It's okay," Elliot said, holding up a hand. "It's fine. He's with me."

He glanced at me fondly while Bea replied. It was reminiscent of the way he'd looked at me when we were younger. I recalled a dormant memory of how it felt to trust Elliot. To feel loved and protected by him. When had we lost that?

"How do they know already?" Elliot asked after a pause. "Right. Okay . . . yeah. Look, Bea, he can't go back right now. Can you come get him?"

I stared at the blanket, praying.

There was a further period of silence, and Elliot spoke in a quiet voice. "He jumped off a bridge, Bea. He's alive, but he's not in a good place. He needs some time away. Please. Yeah, I know. No, they're unimaginable pricks . . . They'll find him at my house, I can't. I really can't. Just for a few days? I wouldn't ask if I didn't think it was important."

They spoke for a little longer, then Elliot hung up, satisfied. "She's going to call in sick and leave in the morning. She should be here by tomorrow night."

"A train driver saw me," I said into the blanket.

A train driver that should've kept his stupid mouth shut. I'd put him before myself by jumping off the bridge instead of under his train, and this was how he repaid me? By informing the police? If I'd done what I was on that bridge to do, I wouldn't be here right now. Elliot wouldn't be on the edge of tears, and Bea wouldn't have to skip work, and—

"How's that for timing?" Elliot said. "One train every half hour and you still manage to get seen on the bridge."

"It wasn't a coincidence. I was supposed to jump under the train. But I felt bad."

He stared at me, his mouth twisting. Then he burst out laughing so hard that he fell backwards. "*You felt bad?* Jesus.

Only you."

I didn't find it particularly funny.

"Well, Bea didn't know anything about you jumping," Elliot said. "Sue and Dom called her to find out if she knew where you were. They know you're missing."

They wouldn't have noticed my absence of their own accord. No. The police had approached Sue and Dom, not the other way around. I was certain of that. I guessed it didn't matter. As long as I could stay here. Everything would be fine if Elliot kept me here. I'd be okay.

"It was my fault, wasn't it?" Elliot asked. "You were fine. You were doing so well. I did this."

As though how I felt could be attributed to any one thing.

"I wasn't fine," I said. "I've been cutting for about six months now. This isn't new."

Rather than reassured, Elliot looked stricken. "Why didn't you tell me? I thought you were okay. I never would've left if I'd known."

I don't suppose he realised the implications of his words. That I was only worth his attention if I was mentally ill. Hardly flattering. "Why *did* you leave?" I asked.

He took a long time to reply, long enough that my eyes grew heavy. I almost told him not to bother. Did his answer matter? Would it change anything in the long term? Whatever his reason for abandoning me, he still *had*. Whether it was my sexuality, or one of my many flaws, or whatever. I wasn't going to like hearing any of it. Family was supposed to be unconditional. Whether I truly believed in the word or not.

"Remember when we had that fight?" he asked finally. "When you got rid of my stash?"

"I don't have a clue what you're talking about. Memory's hazy."

"Very funny. Sue heard you going off at me. And I was stupid enough to get some more that night, and when I came home the next day she confronted me."

He had my full attention, although he didn't know it. He was too focused on the ground to see my face. "And she, uh, she said that she'd turn me in for it. I mean, you saw what I had. It would've been bad. Really bad. Then she said she'd keep quiet if I left you behind. She wanted me to give you some distance. Get out of your life for a while. She said if she caught me speaking to you, she'd do it. She wanted you away from me *that* badly."

His words flipped over themselves in my mind as I tried to make sense of them. As they rearranged my reality. "She blackmailed you?"

Elliot looked miserable. "If I get a criminal record then that's it for me. I would've lost you anyway, along with my job, the house . . ."

"Why didn't you tell me?"

"I was embarrassed. Ashamed, I guess. Because we were so close to getting away, and I screwed it all up for both of us."

"I'd rather know you made a mistake than think you rejected me."

"I didn't think. I was too afraid to talk to you in case Sue got angry and followed through. And I didn't have an explanation for what I was doing, so I avoided it. Obviously looking back, I was being a selfish idiot, but at the time all I could think about was how freaked out I was."

"I thought maybe you were doing it because of me and James."

Elliot bit his lip. "I didn't see you and James coming, but it had nothing to do with anything. I'm surprised you didn't tell me. You used to tell me everything."

I avoided his accusing look.

"We used to be so close," he said.

"You used to like me," I said, only half teasing.

"You're the most important thing I have." There was no trace of humour in his tone.

Well that wasn't true. His friends were more important. His friends, his drinking, and his drugs.

"But you won't let me stay with you now."

"If I could keep you here without them finding you, I would. I'll call you every day. Three times a day."

I bit my lip, tears pricking at my eyes. I wasn't sure if I was happy or simply exhausted. Elliot gave me a light punch. "We'll find a way through this," he said.

If there was a way out of this, I couldn't see it. The thick jungle blocking my way forward would have to be cleared, root by branch by vine, if a path were to be created. The task had gotten too arduous for me. It was unfair to expect anyone to take over.

"I'm sorry," I said. "For all of this. I shouldn't be so weak."

"What are you talking about? You're not weak. You're the most put-together person I know."

I stared at the wall. While I was in no mood to participate in his pity session of false compliments—if I denied what he said, he'd only press on.

He pressed on anyway. "You're in school, you have friends and a boyfriend, and a future. What about that isn't impressive?"

"I've tried to kill myself twice. I'm not stable."

"And I only get off my face every fucking night to cope with *my* shit," Elliot said.

We both fell quiet. This was possibly the most open conversation we'd ever had. I didn't have a habit of conversing about deeply personal things. Not even with James.

"Maybe we're as screwed up as each other," Elliot said.

"But we're still going. That's something."

A confession had branded itself into the back of my skull. I'd been so terrified of the answer that I couldn't verbalise the question before. But a better opportunity than here and now might never present itself. "I thought you must resent me," I said. "Because I destroyed our lives and put us in care. We don't have a family because of me."

Elliot shook his head. "We *are* a family. You've been the only person I gave a shit about since Mum died. My family's intact as far as I'm concerned."

I would not get emotional. I would not. "I've needed to feel like I belonged somewhere. I just . . . I guess I miss feeling like I had a permanent place somewhere. Being wanted."

"I want you."

"You won't allow me to live with you," I repeated.

Elliot leaned back against the couch and sighed. "I'm sorry. I really am. But I can't let you keep taking care of me."

It seemed to me like maybe he deserved someone to take care of him. "I don't mind."

"I know you don't. But I do. I'm supposed to look after you not the other way around."

"You're my brother, not my father."

"I'm your older brother, and if I have guardianship of you then I'm responsible for you," he said. "You deserve more than what I can give you."

"I need a family. I don't care about anything else."

"You have a family. Just because we won't be living together doesn't make it any less valid."

I understood what he meant. But to me it *did* make it less valid. Having no one nearby to reach for was loneliness. Independence. Autonomy. I couldn't possibly be left with no one I could trust. Not when my mind was trying so very valiantly to kill me.

Elliot studied me. "Look," he said. "Day by day. We'll get you with Bea, who, by the way, *is* family and wants the hell out of you. We'll take it step by step from there. We won't leave you. Not unless you want us to."

"I'll never want you to."

"Then we never will, I promise. Just stop trying to leave *us*, alright?"

THIRTY-FIVE

Ash
July 2017

SATURDAY EVENING, BEA BURST through the door in a cloud of sugary perfume and took the night shift in babysitting me. Elliot had to go pretend to look for me with Sue and Dom, and James, and anyone else who cared that I was "missing." Small search party, I predicted.

Bea appeared grateful to have an excuse not to join them, actually. Unlike Elliot, she wasn't a natural liar. I doubted she would be able to look anyone in the face without admitting everything. Considering this, I supposed I was lucky her honesty didn't override her sense of familial loyalty. Not everyone would be happy smuggling their cousin out of town under the nose of the police. But she didn't complain once.

In fact, Bea didn't spend any time discussing the day

before with me. It wasn't her style, and I adored her for it. Instead she ordered pizza, drew the curtains and worked with me to create a fort of blankets and pillows.

Elliot found us there, sheltered by linen and watching a comedy, three hours later. Well, I was watching a comedy. Bea had fallen asleep beside me, her head buried beneath a flattened, old feather pillow.

Instead of retiring to his own room, Elliot stole a pillow and a blanket from the fort and set himself up on the couch. The three of us spent the entire night sleeping in the lounge room, sprawled out in uncomfortable makeshift beds, and I couldn't pinpoint a time in recent memory when I'd felt so entirely safe.

When Sunday rolled around, Bea and I left. I was impressed with us for managing to avoid police detection. I laid across the backseat until we'd reached the edge of the town, and I couldn't help but feel like a kidnapping victim. Not that Bea made a particularly fearsome kidnapper, with her short, wavy hair, plum lipstick and striped rockabilly dress. But looks could be deceiving.

At Bea's house there was little need to consider what was happening at home. I didn't concern myself with the fact that each day I stayed missing made my return more compli-cated. Bea had no intention of nagging me into action, and Elliot, who called every day with an update, kept reminding me that my decision to take a break from regular life wouldn't hurt anyone. Not in the long term.

Apart from James, of course. I didn't forget about him. But I made no effort to contact him. Despite the fact that there was a good chance he'd keep my disappearance a secret if I begged him to. Even though assuring him I was okay would save him from what was probably an agonising level of worry. I didn't.

The reason for this is the hardest thing in the world for

me to admit. I believe everyone likes to look back on events and ignore the things they did wrong—or at least reframe them to insist they made mistakes with only the purest of intentions. But if I was completely honest, it wasn't simply fear that prevented me from contacting James. A part of me *liked it*. I relished the idea that he would be worried and uncertain, probably thinking the worst. Partly, yes, to punish him for his harsh words that afternoon. But mostly because I knew that if he'd worried about me, he'd be so happy to see me again that it would negate our argument, and he'd forget all the things he hated about me.

So I left it.

The days crept by, and I survived. More than that. Those days were possibly the happiest I'd experienced in a long time, despite the persistent agony of my bruised chest, and general aching everywhere else. Physical pain didn't bother me the way it should have, however, so I blocked it out easily enough.

Bea took the week off school and work. She told her manager her cousin had gone missing and she needed to assist her family. It made me wonder if my aunt and uncle, Bea's parents, knew I was gone. Not that I particularly liked them anyway, so I guess it didn't matter. Briefly, I also wondered if Dad knew. But I immediately decided I didn't care. Or, at least, not enough to dwell on his feelings.

Living with Bea was an adventure in distraction. Bea was vegan, which involved a lot of cooking and preparation. Which, in turn, resulted in regular mealtimes. At first, the experience of eating three times a day was extremely strange for me. I allowed Bea to steer me, though, uncertain how to decline her enthusiastic offers of food, and unwilling to leave the table prematurely and cut off her lively conversation. It didn't take long to get used to eating proper meals though. Even if I didn't feel hunger pangs yet.

Everything was fine. *Fine.* Until Thursday afternoon, when Elliot called Bea and demanded he be placed on speaker phone. Bea and I sat at the kitchen table with the phone between us like we were in a conference.

"Ash. You didn't mention a suicide note." Elliot's tone was accusing.

Bea whipped her head up to look at me while I tried to process his words. Suicide note? Then I remembered.

"It wasn't a suicide note," I said. "More of a suicide journal entry."

"Yeah well, call it what you want, same conclusion. Plus there was something to do with a teacher and an assignment? Sue told me one of your teachers called her on Friday and said he was worried you were gonna try something, then she couldn't contact you, so she called the police. The police already knew what the driver saw, then they put two and two together, and went to look in your room . . ."

Mr Patricks. Right. *Right.* Oh no. "I didn't think," I said. "I honestly didn't. I'm only remembering these things now because you've brought them up. I was in a trance that day."

"Well, I have bad news."

I went cold. I couldn't possibly handle additional bad news. I wasn't stable enough for it. I braced myself, willing my emotions to shut off.

"Sue called me to tell me the funeral's Tuesday."

Nothing could have prepared me for that.

"The funeral?" Bea repeated. Her voice seemed to echo.

"Yes. *The funeral.* Put it all together: Ash was seen jumping, the suicide note, the skipping school . . . Add in that someone told Sue and Dom about the cutting, and they found his jacket by the estuary, and we're both lying about knowing where he is. Is it surprising they've called off the search?"

"But they don't have my body," I said.

"They don't *need* a body, Ash."

"Will it be an empty casket?"

"Does it matter? Are you listening to me? They think you're dead."

Bea, who was staring at my blank face, spoke up. "Elliot, give him a second."

Elliot apologised, and the three of us fell silent. I don't think my thoughts were even in English. They were a jumbled assortment of vague concepts, with some recurring themes like shock and bewilderment fighting for centre stage.

"The drop wasn't that far," I said eventually. "I can't believe they're assuming this."

"That's what I said to Sue. She said they think you hit your head."

On the rocks. Because the water level was low this year. The rocks I almost *had* hit on the way down. The rocks I'd slammed into when trying to reach the riverbank. "And there are cameras," I said slowly.

"Cameras?"

"On the bridge."

Bea looked confused, but it was coming together in my mind. It wasn't a stretch after all. I'd attempted to die before. They knew about the cutting now—because of James, I would hazard a guess. They knew I'd jumped. And was it so surprising they'd given up on finding me already? With a current like that, I would have ended up in the open ocean before the police had even arrived at the scene.

They'd searched for less than a week, I realised. I'd expected them to still be looking for me. But they'd never been looking for me.

They'd been searching for my body.

A body they'd decided they were unlikely to find.

"What do you want to do?" Bea asked.

My heart was racing, and I fought to control my breathing. As though I had a choice. I would have to go back, now. Immediately. I would be thrown in with a new family. I'd have to start from scratch, navigating a new mine-field of resentment, awkward silences, and unclear boundaries. Alone, this time. I'd never faced this without Elliot by my side.

"I—uh . . ." I stammered, the words catching in my throat on their way out.

What had I done? What was I going to do? What would happen?

"Tell me what you're thinking," Bea pressed.

I stared at my hands. Even I didn't know what I was thinking. Suddenly, I slipped back. I was lying on the rock, soaked in river water, thinking about nothing except my next move. How best to take my own life. I blanched. "I'm thinking," I said, "that I was miserable there. I'm thinking that I tried to kill myself twice in two years, and I won't last another two."

"Do you think it was foster care that made you feel like that?" Bea asked carefully. "Or is this all leftover from when you lived at home? Because if it's the latter, it's not going to make a difference where you live. You need help."

"I think it was everything," I said. "It was all poison."

"Then stay away," Elliot said.

I scoffed. "I can't do that."

"Of course you can. Who's going to look for you now?"

"Guys," Bea interrupted. "Let's slow down for a second. Ash, you need to see a counsellor, or a psychologist, or . . ."

She trailed off at the look on my face. Elliot answered for me. "I think we can assume that's not going to happen."

"Why?"

"I don't want to see anyone," I said.

"Ash's got a phobia of therapy," Elliot chimed in.

"Don't call it a phobia," I said. "I just don't see how it will help. Last time they just dragged information out of me and drugged me up with medicine that made me numb and nauseous."

"Sounds like you had the wrong dose. Or the wrong meds," Bea said. "It took me ages to get used to mine. But now they work perfectly."

"Drugs and psychologists won't be able to help me if I'm trapped alone in a house with strangers who don't want me."

"They *can*, there are fantastic psychs out there—" Bea started.

"We're not gonna make you do that," Elliot said over her.

I slumped back in relief, and Bea bit her lip. "I'm worried about you," she said.

"I've been okay here."

"You've only been here a week."

"Yeah, but I can't remember the last time I went for a week without thinking about dying."

Elliot sucked in his breath, and I felt a stab of guilt. It was the truth though. It was like I'd been living in a dream over this past week. One I wasn't ready to wake from yet. Everything was perfect here. Well, almost. It would have been truly perfect if James had been—

"James," I said, yanked to attention by the realisation. "Oh my God, I need to call James. He—"

"No," Elliot and Bea said at the same time.

I gaped at Bea. What did they mean *no*? James had been told I was dead. He thought my funeral was coming up. I had to call him. No, I had to *go* to him, now, *right* now. I—

Bea took my hand in both of hers. "Slow down for a second, Ash. Decide what you want to do before you contact anyone. The second you call James, everyone's going to find out you're out here, and what we did. We need a plan first."

I wrenched my arms away from her and wrapped them

around myself. I refused to look at her. Eventually, she told Elliot to call back later. After a few unsuccessful attempts to get me to share my feelings, she excused herself. To let me "think."

I spent the time alone fighting a losing battle against the tears that started rolling down my cheeks. How the hell had this happened? How was I supposed to go back there?

My thoughts drifted to the aftermath of my last suicide attempt. I'd gone back to school to find my friends weren't my friends anymore. So what did that mean for James? Would he still stay by my side? Or would this have been the last straw? Surely I'd pushed him too far.

Your life isn't that bad, Ash.

You make me feel guilty and inadequate.

Stop wallowing.

I cringed, staring at the ground.

I'd probably lost James before the jump. And if I hadn't, the jump would've sealed our fate.

The sooner I accepted that, the less it would hurt when he proved me right.

God, I didn't want to go back. How could I face it? How long would I last this time?

Bea came in to start dinner but didn't drag me into conversation. She'd always been the more tactful one of our cousin trio. More mature than most seventeen-year-olds I knew, too. Perhaps part of that stemmed from the fact that she'd been supporting herself for a year now. Elliot and I weren't the only ones with a dysfunctional family. The difference between us and Bea was that, while we'd been rescued from ours, Bea had rescued herself, packing up and moving onto a friend's couch the day she turned sixteen. She never complained, though. She was too sunny for it.

Bea had just served the meal when Elliot started trying to call her. I wanted to answer, but she was firm. Nothing interrupted dinner. The meal was sacred to Bea. Partially because food was her first love. But also, I suspected, because she knew if she gave me an inch with skipping dinner, I'd take ten miles.

I barely tasted the food. Even though I had no appetite, I all but inhaled it in a race to the finish line, to see what Elliot had to say. In case it involved James.

Finally, Bea put down her fork, and I had permission to call Elliot back.

"Bea," Elliot said as soon as he picked up. "Ash and I look alike, don't we?"

I put him on loudspeaker and requested him to repeat the question. Bea slowly looked at me.

Suddenly, I realised what Elliot was getting at. "You can't be serious," I said.

"It makes sense," Elliot said. "If you decide to stay, I don't know what else you'd do. You can't enrol in school as the dead guy across the country. Someone would notice."

"I also can't enrol in school as an eighteen-year-old."

"So, don't enrol at all. As an eighteen-year-old, you'll be graduated."

I couldn't believe Elliot. Even I wasn't impulsive enough to jump on board with this idea. Was he really suggesting I take his name? It was ridiculous. We'd never get away with it.

Would we?

My head was swimming, and I wanted to do it, and I didn't want to do it, and I could *never* do it, not possibly, and it was unthinkable, but imagine if I did. Imagine what life would be like. I'd get to live with Bea.

I'd never see James again, though.

Obviously, that was out of the question.

"We can't," I said.

"Why not?"

"Because . . . well, you need your identification."

I could predict his response before he gave it. "It's pretty easy for me to get another copy of everything. I'll say I lost my wallet. Done."

"But people would find out."

"How? You'd just need to stay under the radar. Don't open bank accounts with it or anything stupid like that."

The more I thought about it, the more I saw that it would be doable. I didn't need a rental contract any time soon if I was staying with Bea. Maybe I could find a job somewhere that paid off the books, if I asked the right people. Really, I could even drive with his license if I wanted to. Not that I did want to.

As long as I didn't run into anyone who knew I was supposed to be dead . . . *technically* it could work.

"So, then what?" I asked. "I just live here under your name, and you stay there using the same one?"

Bea frowned but stayed silent.

"Actually," Elliot said. "If you want to stay with Bea, I was thinking I'd wanna move too."

"What, here?"

"No, you idiot. Then we *would* get caught. Maybe somewhere nearby, though."

Bea and I made eye contact. "Why?" I asked.

"Well . . . I dunno. I don't really wanna be left behind. I wanna be near you guys, so I can still see you. I never wanted to stay here forever, so now's as good a time as any, right?"

Was he serious? Like he could actually bring himself to leave his friends. Ditch the routine of drinking and drugs. "Elliot . . . be realistic," I said.

"What?"

"What Ash means," Bea said, "is you have a life set up in Rokewood Bend. You have your friends, and you have your house—"

"In the last month I almost ended up charged for possession and with a dead brother," Elliot said. "Both because of the life I have 'set up' here. Ash isn't the only one who could do with a fresh start."

As much as I wanted to believe him, I wouldn't. This was certainly just another of his empty resolutions to change things. But I appreciated the thought, either way. As for me, however, whether I could take his name . . . I supposed it would work no matter where Elliot lived. As long as it wasn't in Conway.

Wait, was I truly considering this?

"I think we're going too fast, here," Bea said. "This isn't just hiding from the police for a week, Ash. This is faking a death. What happens if we get caught? You're sure to run into someone you know sooner or later, and then what? How would you explain it?"

"We won't get caught," Elliot said. "Give it a year or two and he probably won't be recognisable anyway. I mean, think of how different you looked two years ago, Bea. As long as Ash doesn't go running up to people if he recognises them on the street, he'll be fine. People aren't exactly on the lookout for old dead classmates."

"That seems awfully optimistic of you," Bea said.

"Only 'cause you're paranoid."

"I'm not *paranoid*, I'm being *reasonable*."

'Their voices sounded distant.

"Can we talk about this more later?" I asked.

"Not really," said Elliot. "I feel like this is kind of an urgent decision."

"And it's also one he can sleep on," Bea said firmly. "We'll call you back tomorrow, Elliot. Okay?"

Bea climbed to her feet and started doing the dishes. That's how I knew she was agitated. That, and the fact that she'd been asked to potentially have her cousin move in with her while pretending to be her *other* cousin until further notice.

"I want to call James," I said after a long silence.

Bea hesitated, up to her elbows in suds. "Look. You can. But if you do, you'll have to go back."

"He thinks I'm *dead*, Bea."

"You can't have it both ways."

"I can't . . . I can't let him . . ."

"You don't have to do this. It's just an idea." The dishes clattered as Bea stacked them. The sound grated on my nerves. "Don't rush into anything, okay?"

Of course not.

But would time make this decision easier?

I could see the light at the end of the tunnel. It was in reach. It was possible. But the last obstacle to overcome was the most impenetrable one. Cut James out of my life? Never, ever speak to him, or even see him, again? It was unthinkable.

But if I did this I would have everything I could want. Out of foster care, living with family, having the chance to start fresh, and meet people who didn't already dislike me before I'd even heard of them. It was terrifying, but exhilarating. And certainly not more terrifying than the life waiting for me if I went back.

But James.

"Maybe we should do a pros and cons list," said Bea over the clanging.

"I think that'll make the answer look obvious. Last time I was there I wanted to die."

"How do you know you won't want to die here, too?"

Ever practical.

"I don't," I admitted. "But I can't see why things would be different if I go back there. Here, I can see reasons to have some hope, at least. You know?"

Bea had been running the sponge over the same plate for

about twenty seconds now. Deliberating.

"What do you think I should do?" I asked.

Bea spent a while considering it. "You really think it could be different here?"

Maybe Bea was right. Maybe it wasn't situational, but just me. After a few more weeks here, who's to say those thoughts wouldn't come back? It was fair enough for Bea to be cautious. It was too much to ask of her. Watching out for me, and checking in on me, and always worrying that one day she'd come home not to me, but my body.

But . . .

"All I wanted was the chance to start from scratch," I whispered. "I wanted to try one last time."

Bea stared at me, and I thought she was about to give me a pep talk about trying to change my life back home.

"Then . . . I think you should stay here," she said instead, surprising the hell out of me.

"Really?"

"Yeah. You know yourself better than anyone. If you're worried you'll do it again if you go back, that's the last thing I want you to do. And if you think there's a chance you could be happy here, then I want to help you."

I mentally replayed her words throughout the rest of the evening. We didn't mention it again, but I highly doubted either of us thought of anything else. I imagined sitting here eating dinner with Bea. Cleaning with her. Falling asleep knowing that my cousin was across the hall and would still be there when I woke up. It sounded like an entirely different existence. It sounded normal.

Even as I thought of all this, I remained cautious. If there was one thing I'd learned, it was that things never worked out the way you wanted them to. And even if they did, the reality was much more of a let-down than it had seemed in the fantasy.

In the morning, I stared out of the lounge room window at people walking past and imagined meeting them. Introducing myself as Elliot Taylor. Being who I wanted to be, rather than who I'd always been.

When Bea joined me, rubbing sleep from her eyes and trying to smooth down her halo of unruly hair, I gave her a hesitant smile. "I think I want to stay, Bea."

She nodded slowly. "Okay. Well. I was thinking about it all night, and I still want you to. But it's conditional."

My heart sank. Wasn't it always?

"Once you get settled and earn some money, you have to see a psychologist. Non-negotiable."

For goodness' sake. I didn't *need* to see a psychologist. I needed to be around family.

But if that's what it took. Well. "Okay. Fine. I will."

She broke into a wide grin, and she meant it. She *meant* it. She wanted me here. "If you're sure," she said. "Then you're staying. That's that."

Yes.

But no. *No.*

How could I do this? How could I agree to permanently cut the ties connecting James and me? Sentence him to mourning what he believed to be my death?

Was I evil? Or just more desperate than I'd ever been?

I picked at a piece of hanging thread on my shirt. "So . . . I'm Elliot?"

Bea smiled incredulously. "Do you think I should call you that all the time, or just in public?"

"Probably all the time. To avoid any slip-ups."

"Good idea. Right. So we're doing this?"

I laughed out loud—at the ridiculousness of it all and at the sudden sense of exhilaration. This must be what having control felt like. "Yes. We are."

"Well then, Elliot, I have good news and bad news," Bea

said, standing up and offering a hand to me.

I took it and allowed her to pull me to my feet. "And what's that?"

"The bad news is your brother's dead. His funeral's on Tuesday."

My smile faded. If I took this leap, that was it. It couldn't be taken back. I would never, ever see James again. "And what's the good news, pray tell?"

Bea wrapped her arms around my shoulders. "You're with me now."

THIRTY-SIX

Ash
July 2017

WE CELEBRATED THE BEGINNING of my new life with my funeral. I wasn't invited, of course.

Elliot insisted on driving to Conway to pick Bea up on Monday, so he could take her to the funeral and bring her back Tuesday night. "You can't expect me to be alone on the night of my brother's funeral," he pointed out.

Elliot and Bea were nervous at the prospect of leaving me alone for almost two days. I assured them I had no intentions of relapsing in their absence, but it took a lot of wheedling on my part to convince them to walk out the door.

Despite my confident assurances, however, I did hold reservations about being alone for so long. Even if I promised myself not to do anything, could I be absolutely certain I wouldn't crumble again with no one to look out for me? It was an odd experience, being afraid of my own mind.

But to my surprise and delight, I found that I coped well with the empty house. With the freedom to wander around from room to room, with nobody to monitor my footsteps, I relaxed instantly. Setting up a film download on Bea's laptop, I took an inventory of the fridge, ran a bath, and settled in for the wait.

Alone, but not lonely.

When Elliot and Bea returned on Tuesday night, they were subdued. I was desperate for information, however, so I bombarded them the very moment they walked in the door. It was morbid, but I was admittedly curious. Being able to evaluate your own funeral was an impossibly rare situation, and I intended to take full advantage of the opportunity.

"How was it?"

"Were there many people there?"

"Did anyone speak about me? Was any of it nice?"

"Did they play any songs?"

Bea handed me a memorial card. A black and white version of my most recent—and easily most hideous—yearbook photo filled the front page. I wrinkled my nose in protest.

Elliot dropped heavily into the couch. "Nah just generic organ music," he said. I must have appeared disappointed, because he added, "Well if you want a specific song let me know so I can organise it next time. Got anything in mind?" Elliot paused. "And heads up, I'm not playing anything from *The Wizard of Oz*."

I darkened. "That's not funny."

"It's very funny. You just need to morbid-up your humour a little."

"That goes well beyond morbid. Anyway, I've already had a serious funeral, so I think next time I want something a touch more exciting."

Elliot nodded, thinking. "Like victorious? Ironic?"

"Ironic would be quite nice. You could play that song 'I Feel So Alive'."

"I think that would've worked better for this one, don't you?"

"Guys, guys," Bea cut in. "Can you stop planning your funerals, please?"

Elliot and I grinned at each other. "I want to make sure my next one is a bit less horrendous sounding," I said. I pinned the card to the fridge with a magnet.

"Stop being so picky," Bea said. "You're not going to be around to know you don't like it, so . . ."

"You know, that's what I used to think. Now, it turns out death is less of a pre-requisite, more optional extra."

"And take this down," Bea went on as she pulled the card off the fridge and threw it in the bin. "I don't want to have to explain to people why I have a copy of my very-much-alive flatmate's memorial card."

"Sue was crying," Elliot said from the couch. "It was hilarious."

"And why do you find that hilarious?" I asked. "Just to clarify."

"Because she must've thought it was her fault." The idea appeared to thrill him. "Good. She should."

I didn't join him in his triumph. It made me uncomfortable to think that I'd hurt her. I didn't do this with the intention to hurt anyone.

"Your dad was there as well," Bea added. "With my parents."

Elliot stiffened. Dad was an awful memory for me, but for Elliot, he was as close as you could get to Satan. If you wanted to see my brother's smile slide from his face, all you needed to do was mention Dad. I could only imagine what it would've been like for him to be face-to-face with him.

My fault again.

It was time to change the topic. Bracing myself, I asked about the person I *actually* cared about. "Was James there?"

Bea and Elliot exchanged an uncomfortable glance.

"Yes, he was," said Bea.

"Is he okay?"

It took far too long for either of them to answer, and my stomach plummeted. Elliot leaned on his knees and sighed. "You know the answer to that already, Ash."

Yes, I did. Of course I did. It was the price I'd chosen to pay. Now I had to live with whatever consequences that stemmed.

I just hoped it would be worth it.

I wish I could say I seamlessly adjusted to life as Elliot Taylor. It'd be a lie, though. Dark thoughts don't disappear overnight. Particularly not after irreversibly severing ties with the person you love.

For the first few weeks I felt like a disassembled jigsaw puzzle dumped from a box to the floor. In the past, whenever I'd felt like this I would gingerly try to put myself together. Inevitably however, after a few pieces had been matched, the puzzle would be stepped on, the pieces scattering.

But life was different now. Putting myself back together was still a painstaking, agonisingly slow process. Now, however, there was nobody to step on me. Instead, I woke up every morning to Bea bustling around, getting ready for school and genuinely happy to see me. I spent the days keeping the house clean, so I didn't feel like I was bludging, and practicing how to cook meals. Real ones.

As time went on, little by little, I was reassembled. For a start, I was eating. Not skipping breakfast and dinner and picking at lunch but sitting down for regular meals. I was even putting on a little weight; after a few weeks I noticed my hollow cheeks filling in. I looked less like a functioning corpse and more like a teenager.

Elliot found friends to take over his lease in Rokewood Bend and transferred stores to work in a small town approximately an hour's drive from Conway. While I was admittedly astounded he appeared to be following through on his promise, I offered no complaint. Particularly not when I realised Elliot was close enough for us to visit one another.

Elliot concocted an elaborate back-story about us being cousins for if anyone ever asked, but he never ended up having to employ it. We simply coexisted an hour away from each other, me in the city, him in a small town, with the same name. As per the plan, I didn't have a bank account, or a car, or a lease, so I flew under the law's radar. Bea persuaded one of her university friends to come over pierce my lip with his own gun one day—honestly, from the guy's appearance it was a miracle I didn't come down with an infection—and voila. I matched my new I.D. card. Wherever it mattered, I was Elliot Taylor now.

Around this time Bea managed to organise a cash-in-hand job interview at a restaurant not too far from home. More shockingly still, I somehow successfully charmed the manager for long enough to *get* the job. And it was an entirely different experience to school. While at school I struggled to listen to a word I was being told, at my job things made sense. The role consisted of simple, straight-forward tasks to be fulfilled. I knew what I was supposed to be doing, and why, at all times. I even made *friends*. People who didn't have a history of shutting me out. Who didn't expect the worst from me before I had a chance to influence their opinion of me. And I found myself talking. Smiling at strangers. Relaxing.

I started to find myself with compelling reasons to get

up each morning. A routine. Goals to meet and the accompanying pride of accomplishment. Bea eventually prodded me to attend a psychologist, and, mindful of my promise to her, I followed through. And to my unending surprise, it wasn't a tense, fraught experience like the last time. Some of the exchanges with this psychologist and I made a certain amount of sense. In fact, they made a lot of sense. Gradually, but still perceptibly, I was beginning to regain a sense of control.

I thought of James constantly, of course. He was in my thoughts while I ate breakfast, beside me as I walked to work, laughing with me while I joked with Louise and Saras. His voice whispered encouragement while I learned volleyball with Liam, Rachael, Nikki, and Jacob, and affection while I lay in bed each night. James was the one regret I had left. I'd given him up for a second chance at life, but he was a hell of a price to pay.

Despite that, I found that I was happy. Properly happy; not just on a temporary high. Remembering the bridge didn't make me frustrated at my own failure anymore. It made me grateful—dizzyingly, terrifyingly grateful—that I hadn't died.

I'd lived. And here I was. Living.

My old life felt as though it had happened to someone else. For the most part, I could push it out of my mind. It occurred, and it was somewhat bittersweet, mostly horrible, and completely in the past. It influenced the present, sure, but it was separate. Over.

At least, that's what I thought. Until one evening in October, when I trotted downstairs to greet Louise and found myself face-to-face with James, standing in my kitchen.

THIRTY-SEVEN

Louise
October 2018

Saras and Elliot stared each other down in some secret, wordless battle. It was pretty obvious they both knew what was going on. Which, I'm sorry, but how? How did I end up being the *only* person out of the loop, here? Eventually, hopefully, one of them would figure it was time to enlighten me.

Saras did the honours, still watching Elliot with narrowed eyes. "Your name's Ash, isn't it?"

Hah, okay, *what?* Yep, I had to be dreaming. This would be weird even for a dream, sure, but it made more sense than the alternative. Because this couldn't be real. This couldn't be happening.

Again, Elliot didn't tell her she was wrong. *Come on, Elliot*, I urged silently. *What are you waiting for? Tell her! Tell her it isn't true.*

"How did you find out?" he asked instead.

"I found James's last name through some digging, then I found his Facebook, and he had pictures of you on it. And I figured unless Elliot's dead brother was actually his identical twin, something was going on."

Woah, woah, woah. Slow the *hell* down. "What *is* going on?" I asked. "Can we rewind?"

"His name is Ash," Saras said. "Elliot Taylor isn't a real person."

"Well, he is," Elliot added. "But yes. My name's Ash."

Surely they'd both taken some serious drugs this morning, right? There was no way this was real. Nope. "So, what?" I asked, my voice shrill. "You faked your death? Is that it?"

He couldn't be Ash. Why would anyone fake their death? That shit didn't *happen* in real life. And if he was Ash, then who was Elliot? Was Elliot the one who was dead?

"I did try to kill myself. But I survived."

Saras glanced at me. I didn't say anything. I was numb.

So, instead, Not-Elliot spoke.

He told me everything I'd been begging to hear for over a month now. And, despite my bewilderment, and fear, and outrage, I listened.

I'd promised myself I would, after all.

I'll admit that it took me a whole evening to process Elli—no, *Ash's*—confession. Saras and I had gone off together and talked the whole thing over. What it all meant. If we could forgive him. If we should tell our friends or our co-workers.

In the end, we decided it wasn't our place to tell them. Even if he was lying about his identity to our boss, which was *seriously* not cool. As for if we could forgive him—we were divided.

Saras took the whole thing personally. She was really big on loyalty, and honesty, and transparency. Which was the reason she'd been so uncomfortable about me talking to James to begin with. She said she understood why Ash had done it, but that she didn't feel the same around him anymore. Which I understood.

After Saras went home, I sought out Abuela. Not to tell her about it, but just to be around her. Something about her made me feel like I was in control. We sat on the couch together, her reading her Spanish tabloids and me pretending to browse Instagram, and I thought.

It took me a while to figure out where I stood on the whole thing. On the one hand, it hurt that he hadn't trusted me enough to tell me. But at the same time, I got it. Even I wasn't *totally* confident I'd never slip up, now that I knew the truth. And if I did, I could destroy everything for him. Things had been easier before I knew. I couldn't deny that.

Then I realised that, when I met him, he'd recently tried to kill himself for the second time in his life. He'd cut himself off from everything he knew. From the person he loved.

He'd changed so much from that point. I'd just figured he was shy when he moved here, but it was way more than that. So, he might not have trusted us with the truth, but he'd trusted us with his new life. His final attempt to live. Yeah, he'd lied—about so much—but he'd told the truth wherever he could. About his parents, and his likes and dislikes, his hometown, and his cousin. I *knew* Ash. I might not have known his name or his past, but I knew his present. Most of it, anyway.

That's when I saw things through his eyes. In one afternoon he'd seen his old best friend and boyfriend, possibly lost him forever all over again, and been forced to admit a year of lying to two of his new friends, only to be abandoned by them. He knew he'd lost James. He must be worrying he'd lost Saras and me, too.

As soon as I realised this, I jumped in my car and drove straight to his. He was out of the house before I'd climbed out of the car. My friend. My caring, hilarious, idiotic friend. He touched the porch wall, looking hopeful.

He wasn't Elliot. He was Ash.

I could handle that. Or I could learn to, anyway.

When I hugged him, he squeezed me back fiercely. "I'm sorry," he whispered. "I'm sorry, I'm sorry."

"I know," I said. "It's okay."

THIRTY-EIGHT

James
November 2018

LOU CASTELLANO:

He told me everything. I had no idea, I swear. Are you okay?

LOU CASTELLANO:

I can't even imagine how you must be feeling. Trust me, he's not exactly sitting around laughing either. (Notice how I wrote "he"? It's going to take me awhile to not call him Elliot.) My point is, as horrible as this all is, he needs to talk to you, James. Please let him talk to you. He's falling apart. He keeps crying out of nowhere. He's never, ever done that before. I don't know how to handle it!

LOU CASTELLANO:

He wants me to tell you he didn't plan it. It just happened. And I believe him. He told me everything, and I think he's finally telling the truth. He didn't want to hurt you.

LOU CASTELLANO:

James?

LOU CASTELLANO:

James.

LOU CASTELLANO:

Ash wants me to leave you alone. He says you have every right to be angry, and to never want to talk to him again.

Look. I get that you're hurt. I get it. But ignoring him, and ignoring me, isn't going to fix this. You know, the reason I thought he was the Elliot you were looking for was the look on his face when I played your video. He went white, and he started shaking. Does that sound to you like he hasn't been thinking about you? Does it sound like he didn't care about you? He deserves the chance to explain himself.

If I'd asked you two weeks ago what you would do to be able to see Ash one last time, you would've told me you'd do anything. Your chance is right here. There's nothing in the world he wants more. Don't be stubborn, don't be a coward, and don't pass up your chance.

I was in the car and driving before I had the chance to talk myself out of it. I almost turned back about five times a minute, give or take, during the entire drive, but each time, I decided that I'd started the trip and I may as well see it through. My Type-A personality in full swing again. So I drove the whole freaking way. Six-point-five hours, if you counted the whole twenty minutes I let myself have as a stretch break. Because reason wasn't a thing anymore, apparently.

It wasn't 'til I was actually in Conway that what I was doing hit me. I was exhausted from the drive and feeling irrational and emotional. It was way too late to turn around. I'd never make it all the way home. I'd done the trip here and back the last time I came to Conway, and basically made it home on pure adrenaline and panic. Even then I'd almost fallen asleep on the highway more than once.

So if driving home was out of the question, theeennn . . . what the hell did I do now? It was eight at night. What had I expected, to turn up at Ash's house, yell at him, and leave? Like, "hi, I hate you, bye forever, and this time I *mean* it, too"?

(Ooh, you sure showed him!)

What the hell was I *doing?* I considered calling Louise, but I hadn't even told her I was coming. Not to mention I hadn't said a word to her in two weeks. Well, shit.

I pulled over to the side of the road and tried to get a grip. Mostly, I tried to figure out why I'd done this to begin with. Stupid, stupid, *stupid* me had been acting on impulse. That was something I didn't *do*. I had no plan. All I knew was that I couldn't sit at home hating Ash from a distance. Louise was right. I had to find closure somehow. I *had* to.

So, dreading every second, I drove to Ash's house. My mind freaked the hell out when I parked, so my body got out of the car and walked to the front door without it. That's how it felt, anyway.

Bea answered the door, all curled hair and hoop-skirted

and made up, like she always was. I had to fight from slapping her in her stupid smug-ass face for keeping this from me all this time. "*James*," she said, her voice breathy and high pitched. "Hi."

I wasn't in the mood. "You know why I'm here."

"Ash is at work," she started, and I turned to go. Screw this shit. I shouldn't have ever come, and—"Wait. *Wait*. You can't leave. He'll murder me."

"I don't know if I want to talk to you," I said, pausing with my back to Bea. "And I *really* don't know if I want to talk to him."

"You drove six hours to *not* talk to him?"

Yeah, yeah, yeah. It didn't make sense. I got it. Maybe I'd been possessed. That was the only explanation for coming all the way out here. I wasn't ready to talk to Ash.

(Hah. You will never be ready for that.)

But what goddamn choice did I have now? I tipped my head back and turned around. Bea relaxed into a smile and ushered me inside. "I'm so glad you came. Ell—I mean Ash . . . he's been a wreck."

Aw, diddums. "I didn't come to make him feel better. I came because . . ."

Why? I still hadn't figured that out. To demand answers? Or prove to myself that this was all real?

Was it just to hear his voice again?

Bea nodded. "You can stay on the couch tonight. I'll get some blankets."

I didn't necessarily want to stay the night, but I hadn't given myself much choice, had I?

(Super-awesome forward planning, James.)

Together we set up a sleeping area, and I'd just taken off my shoes and sat on top of it to wait for Ash when his key turned in the lock of the front door. All the tension that'd left my body returned times a billion.

"Elliot," Bea called out, starting to stand.

"Hey. Sorry I'm late. Saras went home sick, so me and Louise had to stay to—" he rounded the corner and froze as he caught sight of me. "Count the registers," he finished in a faint voice.

Bea gave him a perky smile. "Look who I found. We're having a sleepover. Surprise."

Ash and I stared at each other. It was the first time I'd really seen him in over a year. Sure, technically I'd seen him weeks earlier, but I'd been in way too much shock to pay much attention to how he looked.

He was all sweaty and tired-looking from his shift, but despite this he was still way more put together than he'd been the last time I'd seen him, in year eleven. *(Hotter, you mean.)*

His dark hair was still long on top, but now the sides had been shortened, and he wore it brushed back, instead of the wavy mess I remembered. He had piercings now, too; one in his lip to mimic Elliot's, and small black plugs in his earlobes. He wasn't worryingly scrawny anymore either. I'd obviously found him attractive when he was thin, but seeing him like this, with the gauntness gone from his cheekbones and the swell of muscles beneath the sleeves of his shirt . . . Well, shit. I had to force the fog from my head.

Neither of us spoke. What was there to say? How the hell did you start a conversation like the one we were about to have?

Bea looked between us, then went to Ash and grabbed his hand, dragging him by force into the lounge room. "You. Sit," she said. "I'm going to be in my room. If I hear anyone murder the other, I'll come back, otherwise . . ."

Good luck. She didn't say it, but it was on her face. He lifted his hand, then turned his attention to the ground. I thought for a second he was gonna force me to kick off the conversation, and I was wracking my brain to come up with a good place to start—*Crap, crap, crap, what the hell do I say?*—when he surprised me by speaking up. "I didn't think you'd come back. I didn't think I'd ever see you again."

"Me neither," I said. "I don't know why I did come, to be honest."

He sucked on his lip ring, his eyebrows drawn together. I knew the general look. Even after all this time, it was coming back to me like we'd been best friends—boyfriends—only days before. He was trying his best to keep himself together. Well, that made two of us. "Right. So . . . what have you been up to over the last year?" he asked.

Wow. No matter how hard he tried, he couldn't make *that* question sound casual. I gave him a tight-lipped smile, and he lowered his eyes. At least he wasn't stupid enough to mistake it for friendliness. "Hmm, let's see," I said. "I spent last year falling apart, then spent this year trying to put myself back together."

Ash picked at the couch. "Was it that bad?"

"Put it this way. By the start of upper sixth I'd dropped out of football and athletics, had a B average, and pretty much no friends left."

"Is this a bad time to tease you about Bs not being the end of the world?" Ash asked with a weak smile.

"It's a terrible time."

"Thought so."

The silence that followed was anything but comfortable. Then I went and made things worse. "You know, things were shit enough when you were dead, and I had to remind myself all the time that you'd been hurting, and that I couldn't be pissed at you for abandoning me. But I don't know how to cope with this. Knowing you were out there the whole time, and you just didn't give enough of a shit about me."

"It's not that I didn't care," he said. "But—I thought you'd adjust. You know, get over it?"

"*Get over it?*" I asked. The hell was that? Was having a boyfriend kill themselves something you were supposed to casually move on from, like a fucking stubbed toe?

"I didn't mean it like that," he said hastily. "I just . . . thought you didn't need me."

My vision went blurry, and I swallowed, looking anywhere but at Ash.

Weeelllll, gee. *This* had been an awful idea.

What the hell had made me think I'd get anything out of coming here?

To my relief, I managed to cut any tears off before they fell. For whatever reason, I didn't want him to think that I still gave a shit. If we were playing the *I barely think about you* game, I wanted to win it.

Ash looked pensive. I'd never been much good at reading his mind. That hadn't changed with time.

He stood up without warning. "You want a drink?"

I did. "No thanks."

"Okay. Well I'm getting one, so can we move this to the kitchen?" Ash gave me an indifferent stare then left the room.

It was funny. Two years ago, I used to dread Ash's cold front. I'd always blamed myself when he turned frosty, trying to spot some pattern to it so I could stop doing whatever it was I did to make him angry. But now I could see what had been staring me in the face back then. He wasn't switching off because I'd pissed him off. It was a defence tactic for when he felt vulnerable.

Feeling like the world's biggest idiot for only now figuring that out, I followed him. He stood at the counter and started making two hot chocolates. I felt like a shot of vodka or fifty might've worked better, but I appreciated it.

Even if I had said I didn't want one.

I slid into a chair and leaned my elbows on the dining table. "You screwed up Mr. Patricks," I said because I knew it would hurt him, and I felt like being a shit person. "He's never been the same. Still at school, but yeah. He's a lot less friendly now."

Ash focussed on pouring almond milk into the nearest mug, still passive. I felt a surge of anger. Defence mechanism or not, what right did he have to act like none of this mattered?

"You destroyed me," I said.

Ash winced, spilling milk onto the counter. Good. At least I knew he was listening.

"It was like a nightmare I kept waiting to wake up from," I went on. I needed him to know. "For the first day I was convinced it wasn't real. Like, real life can't be *that* bad, you know? That's what I thought. Then I'd remember that it was real, and I'd dwell on these scenarios. Like, what if I'd turned back? What if I'd never left, or I'd called you, or been near the bridge when it happened? All these things I could've done to change it, and I didn't. I was too busy sulking at home. And it made me feel so helpless. I had the chance to save you, and . . ."

He sucked in his cheeks and nailed his stare on me while I spoke. When I trailed off, he returned the milk to the fridge and slammed the door. "It was nobody's fault," he said. He grabbed one of the steaming hot mugs and placed it in front of me. "I mean, if you have to play the blame game the whole thing goes back a lot earlier than us, or what happened with me and Elliot. But there's no point trying to pick it to pieces like that. At the end of the day, I was depressed, and, for a hundred reasons, I gave up."

He lowered himself into the chair in front of me, and I ran a finger around the rim of my mug, not meeting his eyes.

Did he even *get* how bad it'd been? Why did he sound so casual?

"I'll never forget when Mum told me you were dead," I said. "Ash, you were everything. My whole life, it was us. And then bam. I'd already said the last thing I was ever gonna say to you, you know? And I was expected to keep living, and I didn't know how to do that without you." My voice was high-pitched and choked, and I was mortified. Again with the fucking crying.

"I'm sorry," was all Ash said. "I'm so sorry."

"Sorry doesn't fix it."

"No," he agreed. "You know, I can't explain how it felt to know you were out there, and I could never see you again. We ended on nothing. I wasn't sure if we were technically still together at the end or what. But I was convinced that you were better off without me. I used to drag you down so much. You were so popular and talented and smart, and all I ever did was dampen it."

"You did not."

"I thought I did," he pressed. "I'm trying to make you understand why I did it. I honestly thought I was the worst thing that could've happened to you. But letting go of you was the hardest thing I ever had to do."

I didn't have it in me to feel sorry for him. Maybe one day I'd be able to, but right now all I felt was bitter and furious.

And hurt.

"It's taken me every bit of self-control that I have every day to not contact you," Ash said. "I used to consider making a fake Facebook account or something, so I could talk to you again."

I snorted. "That's so creepy."

"I know! I know it is. It's like I was addicted to you though. And the withdrawals never went away. It never even got easier. Even now. You'd think after *over a year* I would've moved on."

I clutched my mug like I'd fall apart if I let it go. "Yeah. Over a year."

Ash hadn't been my first crush. That honour went to Prince Eric from *The Little Mermaid*—I had my type sorted out even at seven years old. He hadn't even been my first human crush. But pretty much from puberty onwards, I defined myself by the unrequited love I had for my best friend. It'd made me feel like a tragic hero. Even though saying that makes it sound like I liked it. Actually, I would've done anything to make him like me back. I was obsessed. I used to read into every word and every look, and sometimes I was able to convince myself he was trying to tell me he loved me too.

Then.

He kissed me.

He goddamn fucking well kissed me, and everything was more perfect than it ever should've been. In real life, unrequited love stays that way. It just *does*, and everyone knows it, even if they wanna deny it.

With those odds I would've bought a lottery ticket, but any jackpot would've seemed like a shit deal in comparison to Ash. When he was there, I slowed down and saw where I was instead of where I wanted to go. It was like, holy shit, maybe life can actually be like those sappy, sentimental assholes say. I swear I hadn't even known how happy I could *be* 'til then.

But then he took it. He took everything.

Ash stared at me. "James?"

"Hmm?"

"Can I—would you mind if I . . ."

I took a sip of hot chocolate. Ash looked serious, and I had a feeling I wanted to put off whatever was coming next for as long as I could. "What?"

He exhaled. "I don't want it to be weird. It's—I want to hug you, I guess. Would that be weird?"

There was a long silence while I considered it. I wanted to be left alone almost as strongly as I wanted to grab onto him and make sure he was real. Finally, shaking, I opened my arms and took him in. It felt like time travel, like I'd been pulled through some invisible trap door and planted in the place of my younger self. After all this time, he felt the same, in ways that I'd forgotten. How his heart beat, the smell of his skin, the pressure of his arms.

Then he was sobbing against my chest, and I caved and joined him. The two of us sat there crying our eyes out for a solid five minutes. It hurt. And it didn't feel like it'd ever stop hurting. I held onto him with an iron grip like I'd never fucking let him go. The way I should've done the last time I'd held him.

I tried to speak, but the words came out jumbled.

"What?" Ash asked.

"I loved you," I repeated in staccato syllables. "I had to say it. I spent four hundred fucking days wishing I had the chance to say it."

Ash tucked his head under my chin. "I loved you too."

I flinched. That felt dirty. "You don't need to feel obliged to say that."

"I don't. I did love you. I wasn't very good at it. But that doesn't mean it wasn't real."

I let out a laugh that ended in a miserable keen. "Why did you have to . . .?" I trailed off and growled in frustration. "Fuck. I hate you so much."

"I know," he replied. "I know."

THIRTY-NINE

JAMES
November 2018

THAT NIGHT I SLEPT on the couch, and Ash went to his own room.

When I woke up in the morning, he was passed out on the armchair. His legs hung over one of the armrests and his torso was twisted at an awkward angle.

The curtains covering the lounge room window were open a crack. It was bucketing down outside. The temperature in the room had plummeted overnight. Ash had no blanket and was only wearing a thin t-shirt and sweatpants. His arms were covered in goosebumps.

Well, I wasn't a monster, even if I hated him.

I checked the time. Eight in the morning. No point dragging him up yet. As gently as I could, I placed my own blanket over him and tucked it around his body. Obviously not gently enough, because he opened red-rimmed eyes as I pulled away. "Thanks," he said, rubbing his face.

"What are you doing out here?"

He shrugged, self-conscious. "I woke up early and came out to see if you were still here. Guess I fell asleep again. Sorry."

"It's fine." I hesitated. "I probably should go home soon. I think we both said everything we needed to say last night."

"Yeah," he said. "Almost."

"Almost?"

"I actually have something I wanted to show you, if that's okay?"

I helped him to his feet. "Sure."

Ash's room was filled with books, furniture, posters, and clothes I'd never seen before. I stood awkwardly in the doorway, trying to remind myself that *these* were his things now—that all the decorations I remembered had been given to charity or thrown out by Sue and Dom—while he kneeled down and rummaged through one of his desk drawers. He grabbed two hardcover notebooks and brought them to his bed.

Without a word, he handed me one of the books. I opened it to the first page and Ash kneeled behind me, reading over my shoulder.

> *Dear James,*
> *Elliot told me he saw you at my memorial. He told me how upset you were.*
> *I regret it. But I don't feel like I can turn back now. I've taken it too far. Elliot's started looking for houses in the next town. Bea and I have been setting up my room. And it's so exciting, but I'm dying, James. I haven't seen you in two weeks, and I feel like I've lost half of what makes me me.*

How am I supposed to pick myself up without you?
Who even am *I without you? Do I have an identity*
outside of you? I hope so.

I glanced at Ash, who handed me the other book, already open. Swallowing, I went back to reading.

Dear James,
Some things have been so easy to let go of. I've had
barely any slip-ups. I suppose it's easy to forget the things
I want to forget. And I'm so used to being called Elliot
now that I catch it before I mention his name. But when
it comes to you, it's a struggle.

Even after a year so much still reminds me of you. I'll
start telling a story to Louise, or Jacob, or someone, and
I'll have to completely dial it back. Your name's always
on the tip of my tongue. How can I just not ever mention
you? We were so twisted up in each other our whole lives,
like different strands making up the same rope. And now
it's all unravelled and I can't call myself a rope at all
anymore.

I guess on the plus side of things, if I don't mention
you, I don't have to worry about revealing too much
information. There's not much about my past to even talk
about if I have to leave you out of it.

I flicked through the rest of the book, finding each page filled with similar letters. Was he for fucking real? I looked at Ash, wide eyed. "You were writing to me?"

"It kind of felt like I was talking to you. I couldn't handle having no contact with you."

"How many letters are there?"

He picked up the leftover notebook. "I dunno. Maybe a couple hundred? I haven't counted."

"A couple *hundred?*"

Ash blushed. "It's a bit weird, hey? I'm sorry."

"How long did you do this?"

Ash took the book from my hands and opened up one of the last pages. The last entry.

> *Dear James,*
>
> *I saw your video today just before work. You look the same. Different, but the same. I had to spend the whole shift pretending I was fine. Then I went home and played the video over and over again, just to hear your voice. I don't think I've ever cried so hard in my life.*

Ash took it away from me and closed the book, and I ran a hand through my hair, more than a bit overwhelmed. "It bothered you that much?"

Ash gave me a funny look. "Yes, James, it bothered me. Are you surprised? Shocked?" He gathered the books in a pile and put them on the desk.

"After I saw you, I had this image of you starting over again here, with new friends and Bea, and being super happy. I figured you must have hated me after everything I said to you. Otherwise, like, how could you leave me there, alone— knowing I was out there—without ever trying to contact me?"

"With great difficulty," Ash said, gesturing towards the books. "Bea had to delete your number out of her phone because I talked about calling you that many times in the first few months."

I stared. A lump formed in my throat. "I wish I'd known about these earlier," I said, lifting a shoulder in the direction of the books.

"Would it have made a difference?"

There was a crack of thunder, reverberating loud enough to shake the house. Apparently even Zeus was pissed off at this shit. I jumped, and Ash hopped up to close the window.

"You were thinking of me," I said while he wrestled with the windowpane.

Slamming it shut, Ash raised an eyebrow at me. "Duh."

"The whole time."

"What's your point?" he asked, blinking as a flash of sheet lightning lit up the room.

"I dunno yet. I'm trying to figure that out."

We dawdled around the house. Procrastinating.

I didn't want to leave yet, but I felt like I'd be saying I forgave him if stayed. Something something rocks and hard places.

Eventually, while we sat on the loveseat on the front porch, deliberately as far away from each other as we could, Ash said, "You know, if you left now you wouldn't get home 'til almost midnight."

"Yeah. Good point."

"You should probably stay tonight and leave tomorrow morning. So you're not driving at night."

Subtle, Ash. If he thought I wasn't gonna see right through that, he'd forgotten how well I knew him. But he'd said what I wanted to hear, so I didn't call him out on it. I just shrugged.

The storm drizzled to a stop. The air smelled like rain, and the wind had that nice sort of chill to it you only appreciate when you can't remember winter. Ash took out his phone.

"What's up?" I asked him.

"Louise. Everyone's catching up for lunch."

"Everyone?"

"Our friends."

Okay, so it shouldn't have surprised me so much to hear him say that. There was no reason for him not to have a group of friends. It's just that back at home he'd only had me, so I guess I'd figured things were the same with him and Louise.

(Not jealous, James, surely?)

"Can I come?" I asked.

Ash hesitated. I could read his mind. He was afraid I'd call him "Ash." Or, worse, outright tell everyone the whole story. "I'll be careful," I said. "I'm just curious."

He still looked a bit suspicious, but he stood up. "Fine. Sure. Let's do it."

Conway was to Rokewood Bend as the Sun is to Earth. I'd never visited before, and even though I'd seen photos and stuff, it was way more overwhelming to walk around in it than I'd thought. I ended up hanging back and letting Ash lead. Which was weird.

He knew the exact bus stop and route, and within five minutes we were chilling on the backseat. I watched him while he made himself comfortable. He tucked himself into the corner of the window and rested his head on the back of the seat in front of him.

He looked different; you couldn't deny that. The piercings, his clothes, his haircut, his toned limbs. But it was more than his looks. He seemed kinda peaceful. Content. He sat straighter, his eyes seemed sharper.

When he caught me staring, he gave me the world's most adorable, self-conscious smile, which made me worry about the status of my grudge. His being cute didn't magically erase what he'd done. *Focus, goddamn it,* I thought.

It only took ten minutes to get to our stop. Ash gestured down the road when we got off the bus, towards a large restaurant on the corner of the street; bordered by floor to ceiling windows that basically stood in for bricks and mortar.

The word "Bruno's" flashed in giant cursive letters above a sliding glass door half-hidden by the enormous, brown umbrellas that sheltered three of the ten outdoor tables. Well, it was eye-catching. "That's where Louise and I work."

"Aren't we going there?" I asked when he turned his back and started heading down the opposite end of the street.

"Hell no. I had to call in sick today. Joe'd murder me."

"You didn't have to call sick for me."

He ignored me.

We headed into a fifties-themed diner, just far enough down the road that Ash didn't have to worry about an accidental sighting from his boss. I spotted Ash's friends straight away, they were sitting around a red pleather booth towards the back of the diner. It was hard to miss Louise's thick curls sticking over the back of the booth, not to mention her high-pitched laugh. Girl had grown on me. Another chick with warm brown skin and shoulder-length dark hair noticed us first, and she called out to Ash. Not with his name, though. With Elliot's.

Yeeaahh . . . This was gonna take a lot of getting used to.

Louise turned around as we got closer, and her mouth fell open. "James," she said. "I didn't know you were visiting."

Then they all turned to look at me. Two guys and three girls. Ash was the third guy, apparently. How freaking tidy. They could all pair up. Super cute.

"Yeah," I said. "Thought I'd check out the city. Broaden my horizons a bit."

"James is Elliot's friend from home," Louise said to the group. "James, this is Liam, Jacob, Rachael, and Nikki."

"He's like a Liam two-point-oh," Jacob, a short guy with uneven front teeth, said.

Liam, a guy with coiffed hair and freckles who I guessed was probably of Chinese descent, rolled his eyes at me. Oh joy, a race joke, this would be fun.

"Shut up, Jacob," Rachael snapped, while Ash grabbed a couple of chairs from a nearby table and set them up on the foot of the booth. "You're not funny."

Ash crossed his legs underneath him and passed me a menu. "You'll be pleased to know there's actual dairy here," he said to me.

Rachael made a show of wincing. "Guess you've been subjected to the soy-milk torture?"

"Unfortunately. I'm still standing though, so."

Louise raised her eyebrows at this. "How long have you been here?"

"Uh . . . since yesterday."

"*Yesterday*," she repeated, directing the words at Ash. I guessed he hadn't told her I'd shown up. Not that he'd had much of a chance.

Ash looked unconcerned as he flicked through the menu. "Found him hanging around the house after work last night. Thought I'd let him crash on the couch."

"So, you're proof Elliot actually had friends before he came here," Liam said with a good-natured grin. "We thought he might've been home-schooled or something. He never talks about anyone from home." He must have realised that might offend me, 'cause he followed it up with, "I've heard your name thrown around a few times, though." Hah, well *that* was almost definitely a lie, but the thought was sweet, anyway.

"Yeah, we haven't stayed in contact," I said carefully. "He's changed a bit."

"We've corrupted him," Nikki, a girl with frizzy curls and a slouchy grey sweater, said. "Sorry about that."

"I call it an improvement," Rachael said.

"Well, there's the piercings, for a start," I said. I touched my lip and looked at Ash, who twisted his own lip ring in response. "He used to have a massive phobia of needles. He cried when we got our vaccinations at school."

Ash shot me a dirty look, and the guys cracked up laughing.

"So Elliot has a sensitive side?" Nikki asked, leaning across the booth to poke Ash in the arm.

"Negative," Ash said with dignity. "James just likes to imagine one, so he can justify being friends with me. Like people who think their cats love them."

"Wait," Liam interjected. "I'll have you know Hercules's love for me is more real than any human-based love you guys think you have. You're just jealous you don't have a cat."

"Why the hell would I want a cat?" Ash asked. "They're smarmy-faced little fucks that lord it over everyone, and you fall for it like the gullible slave they've trained you to be."

Smarmy-faced little *what*, exactly? Can't say I'd expected to hear that come out of Ash's mouth. These guys weren't kidding about corrupting him. Not that I was delicate about the word fuck. I'd said worse things to five-year-olds in my time. But still.

"Say that to my face," Liam said.

"I *am* saying it to your face."

"Say it to Hercules's face."

"I would, but he *doesn't understand English*, Liam."

It didn't take me long to realise I didn't hate his friends after all. Even if I did resent the fact that they'd had him for the last year when it was *me* who needed him.

Actually, it was super weird to watch him around these guys. The Ash I remembered never spoke up in groups. He used to shrink away if people looked at him, going all red if anyone teased him. This was like seeing Ash the way he'd been way back in the day, before the first time he'd tried to kill himself, before foster care. Back when we'd shared a group of friends. When he was confident. I'd never thought I'd get to see this Ash again.

It was like by becoming Elliot, he was able to erase everything he didn't like about who Ash had turned into. But it wasn't sustainable. He had to know that.

God, this was such an Ash thing for him to do. All action, no foresight. What'd happen when he ran into someone from Rokewood Bend? It was only a matter of time. Or, even if he got lucky and that never happened, how was he planning on going through life with only a driver's license? Was he gonna work at a freaking B-grade restaurant for the rest of his life? Would he never get into a serious relationship or would he hide the fact that he had a brother from his partner? How many laws would he break before getting caught?

And what would happen if his new friends found out he'd been lying to them this whole time? Would they all be as forgiving as Louise? Or would he be left alone? Back where he started?

And, most of all, where did I wanna be when this all happened?

FORTY

Ash
November 2018

THE WORLD WAS BLACK, and the air was cold, and someone was hissing my name. It took me several groggy seconds to piece the scenario together. I was sprawled on the lounge room floor on top of a blanket. It was either extremely late, extremely early, or on the very cusp between the two.

"Ash," James whispered again from his vantage point on the couch.

"What?" I buried my face in Bea's spare pillow.

"I wanna ask you something."

Groaning, I checked my phone and squinted against the blinding screen. "What's the freaking time?"

"Louise's grandma said you and Louise kissed. And I just texted her asking about it, and she said you said you didn't date friends."

I rubbed a palm across my eyes. "What? Don't text people stupid shit in the middle of the night!"

"I'm sorry, I was curious."

"Well, stop that."

"So you won't date friends anymore?" James asked. "Was I that bad?"

I resisted the urge to ignore him and go back to sleep. Why should I feel guilty about Louise? What was I supposed to do, remain steadfastly committed to him even though he didn't think I existed anymore? Besides. "We kissed six months after I moved here," I said. "We were drinking. It didn't mean anything."

"She's pretty."

"She is."

"Do you like her?"

"She's just a friend."

"You said that about me once."

It was either far too early or far too late for this. Either way, it took an exceedingly large level of patience for me to keep my tone measured. "I'm tired, James. Can we talk about this tomorrow?"

He laid back. "Sorry. I'm just a bit surprised to find out you were already moving on after six months." He laughed at this, as though his hurt was a trivial punchline.

I turned off my phone and plunged us into darkness. "I wasn't. It was just a kiss."

He didn't answer. Instead, he pretended to be asleep. With a sigh, I rolled over.

James sighed in response.

God only knew what his problem was.

"I think I'm turning into a plant," James said, pushing away his coffee. Bea, sitting across the table from him, tutted.

With a shrug, I grabbed his mug and began to drink from it, pulling myself up to sit on the kitchen counter. "Sounds interesting," I said. "Out of curiosity, how does one know when one is becoming a plant?"

He slumped in his seat and surveyed me with puffy, dark-circled eyes. "Well, I've lost my appetite, and I just turned down coffee. The logical conclusion is I've started drawing my energy from the sun."

I pretended to consider this. "Right. It *is* plausible. But there are two notable flaws. One, you barely get any sun. Two, you clearly don't have any energy."

"I don't have any energy *because* I haven't been getting any sun," James said dully.

"Oh, of course," I grinned. He didn't return it. Well, one thing was for sure, there was nothing quite as awkward as sharing a joke with someone who wanted nothing to do with it.

Bea took a sip of her own coffee. "Come on, dude. You'll survive. It's just soy milk."

James curled his lip at her like she'd said, "it's just a rotting human corpse," and she folded her arms. "When you choose to live under my roof, you live by my rules, and my rules are no animal torture."

"I bet you regret coming to avenge my death now, don't you?" I asked.

James shot me a resentful glance. "Shut up, Ash."

"No, I'm serious. It's comforting to know if anything ever happened to me, you'd hunt my murderer down and kill them."

Bea took one look at James, who was gritting his teeth, and jumped up to place her now empty cup in the sink. "Are you staying again tonight, James?" she asked. "I need the lounge room. I'm having some people around after work."

James and I glanced at each other. Inwardly, I begged

him to say he was staying longer. Or at least admit he was considering it. "Nah, I have to get home," he said. "It's getting hard to convince my parents I came up to go to a concert."

I didn't purposely allow my disappointment to show, but I apparently had little control over my own facial muscles. It didn't go unnoticed, either. James averted his gaze, and Bea gave me a sympathetic shrug as she headed out the door to work. I couldn't hold it against James, I supposed. I was just grateful he'd come back, and that he'd afforded me a chance. Still, it sent a panicky jolt through my chest to realise he'd be leaving soon. What if I never saw him again? Was this it now? Forever?

We were left hanging in an uncomfortable silence. I filled it by placing my own cup in the sink with more force than I meant to. I anticipated that James would seize the opportunity to start packing, but he didn't. He just sat.

I stood before him, and he looked up at me, apprehensive. "Do you think you might come back sometimes?" I asked. "I don't want to think this is the last time I'll see you."

He rolled up the sleeves of his oversized navy jumper, shrugged, and hung his head, his hair falling over his brow. He looked stunning.

"For the record, I told Louise I couldn't date her because she was my friend," I said. "But that wasn't the problem. The problem was she wasn't you."

He took a long time to reply, and I wondered if he was thinking what I hoped he was thinking. Then he stood up.

He kissed me gently, like he was afraid if his touch were too firm I'd dissolve. It was more skin-to-skin contact than anything. I placed a hand on his arm and kissed him back, deepening it until I could taste him again. Though I'd never forgotten his voice, I'd completely forgotten how he tasted. The déjà vu was a sensory overload.

Suddenly, he broke away from me, pursing his lips. "I'm sorry," he said. "I can't."

He left the room before I could protest, and I was left blinking away tears. It was okay. I'd lasted well over a year without him, and I could do it again. It was the only way things could've gone, really. I was okay. I was fine.

When I was sure I wasn't going to break down sobbing, I went after him. He was on the back porch with his legs drawn up, glaring at the plum tree as though it had personally offended him. Wordlessly, I sat beside him.

"I can't see you again," he said. "How could I hide you from my family? From everyone at home? It's a stupid idea."

Yes.

He was correct.

But.

But I wanted it.

"I don't know how I can be in your life without expecting something more," he continued. "And you can't give it."

Something more? And what did that refer to? A relationship? Openness? Honesty? Or did he expect me to somehow alter the past?

"If you wouldn't come to see Elliot, would you come to see Ash?" I asked.

James's face darkened. "Isn't he gone?"

He was, I supposed. And I'd done that. But that didn't mean he had to be lost forever. In reality, I woke up every morning and chose to be Elliot. There were alternative options available to me. I could still choose James. If I was brave enough to face the fallout that would come with it, that is.

If I was brave enough.

"I'm not sure," I said.

James's shoulder pressed against mine. A strong gust of

frigid wind blew our way, and he inched in, almost imperceptibly closer. "Well, I can't promise anything," he said. "And I'm not asking anything. But if something changes . . . let me know. And we can talk then. Okay?"

"Okay."

"Okay."

No.

Not okay.

And I wasn't going to let it go. For once I was going to voice my true feelings.

"I have to say something to you." The words were firm. Their decisiveness surprised me.

James waited while I braced myself to continue. What was I doing? What if this pushed him further from my reach? Instinctively, I didn't want to justify myself. I wanted to apologise, and beg for his forgiveness, and say I couldn't do anything right. Like I used to. But I wouldn't.

What I had done was wrong, but only because there'd been no right answer.

"I didn't choose to leave you," I said. "I chose something that involved leaving you. But I didn't choose to leave you."

"So you're playing semantics?" James asked.

"I was suffering. I was in pain. I was exhausted. I felt like I had nothing to keep trying for. The most appealing option at that point was to die. But I didn't. I took one last shot. I didn't know if this was going to fix anything. But I did it so that one day, if you did look for me, there'd be someone here to find. Coming here was the hardest, most terrifying thing I ever did. But if I didn't, I would've killed myself. I *would have*. I did the only thing I could've done to save my own life. I'm sorry it hurt you. I'm sorry it hurt Mr. Patricks, and Sue, and Dom, and Gemma, and anyone else. I didn't do it to hurt anyone. It must've been so fucking horrible for you. I acknowledge that. But I don't accept that I should have to pay for what I did for the rest of my life, when all I was trying to do was stay alive."

I stopped when I realised I was borderline shouting. I didn't intend to raise my voice like that. James appeared taken aback, grabbing onto the hem of his jumper with white knuckles.

"I'm sorry," he said.

"Don't apologise."

"No, I'm sorry," he repeated firmly. "I was angry at you for being sick. I thought it'd be like in the films, where romance cured you or some shit. But it didn't happen like that, and I guess I took it personally."

Oh, screw the past. I was so sick of him dwelling on the past. Last year he only cared about the future, and now he only cared about last year. When would he learn to pay attention to the present?

I walked away from him. For once, I was the one to lead.

To my surprise, he followed me. "Ash." I'd made it to the lounge room before he caught up with me and grabbed my arm. "*Ash*. You're right."

I shook him off. "About what?"

"You did the right thing."

It was what I wanted to hear, but it was an empty victory. Because how could it have been the correct path when I'd left a trail of destruction walking it?

"Thank you," he said. "For staying. Alive, I mean."

To my horror, this summoned the tears I'd so diligently worked to prevent. I turned my head to try to hide them, but it was too late. "What's wrong?" he asked, his voice softening.

I wiped my eyes hastily, but more tears replaced the ones I erased. Great. They had backup. After all the years I spent complaining about my inability to cry, my body had decided to pay me back a hundredfold for the sake of irony these days. "I used to wonder what would happen if I ever saw you again," I said in a choked voice. "And I always pictured you being happy to see me. But then when you actually did, it was like you wished I *had* died."

His mouth hung open. "That's an awful thing to say."

"It's an awful thing to feel." I was flushing with embarrassment, but I refused to back down. For once, I wanted him to know.

James sat down heavily on the carpeted floor. "Ash . . ." he trailed off, his own voice breaking now. "I'm so glad you're okay. Please don't think I'm not. I can be hurt and happy at the same time. Which is what's been so confusing. I don't know what's more important to me: how mad I am or how grateful I am."

I sat down to face him, crossed-legged. "What did staying mad at someone ever achieve?"

He gave a shaky smile. "Good point."

"Don't go home yet," I said. "Please."

James hesitated. "Bea's having her friends over though." I glanced towards my bedroom before I could stop myself, and James shook his head. "Nope. No. Bad idea. Awful idea."

"We won't do anything," I wheedled. "We'll just sleep. I don't want to say goodbye yet."

"Ash . . ."

I started to reach for him but pulled my arms into my chest instead. "Sorry. This is kind of emotional blackmail, isn't it?"

He stared at my hands and tapped his fingers on his thigh. "We can't do anything. It'll get too messy."

"I promise," I said in a voice so hopeful that he ended up laughing.

"Okay, fine. *Fine.* One more night. But any longer and Mum will want proof of what I'm doing, and if I say I'm visiting you, I'm worried she'll send the cops for me."

FORTY-ONE

Louise
November 2018

I CAN'T SAY I was expecting it when Elliot—Ash, I mean—and James came to visit during my shift. It took me a few minutes to even notice they'd walked in. I'd just gone back to the bar to fill a drink order while Saras wrapped up a phone call when a familiar voice made me look up.

"Hello, Saras. I believe you tried to add me on Facebook."

James was leaning his elbows on the counter and flashing Saras a toothy smile. Ash gave me a quick greeting, then glanced at Saras. Okay, so things weren't awesome between them, exactly, but they'd cooled off. As for me, I held out hope Saras would soften. It was still early days.

Saras started putting the reservation in the system. "Oh, you noticed? What, was I not worthy to be an official friend?"

"Well, actually, I only figured out who the hell you were when someone mentioned your name at lunch," James said. "I might have to make it official now, though."

Saras gave him the smallest of small smiles. James was like that, I was learning. A natural slayer of ice queens. You just couldn't look at his grin and stay aloof. "I mean, if you want," she said. "I got all the information I was after either way."

"So, is that how you found Elliot?" James shot Ash a sideways look at the mention of his brother's name. Ash grinned back, and—wow. I'd never seen Ash look at anyone the way he looked at James. Kind of like how I pictured I'd look at Zayn Malik if I ever met him. Unabashed awe and admiration.

"Uh huh. I Googled 'James, Rokewood Bend', and found your last name through some football article. Then your Facebook was public for the world to see. Better hope no one ever decides to stalk you for real."

James looked impressed. "I'll make a note of that. Well, I'm glad I had someone competent babysitting Elliot. I hope he wasn't too much trouble."

Saras pursed her lips. "Hmm. About that . . ."

"I've yet to be fired," Ash said. "I refuse to accept I have flaws until that day happens."

"Would you like me to organise it?" Saras asked. "I can put in a good word, if you'd like?"

"I wouldn't want to be a bother."

"No bother." Saras raised her eyebrows, but she was mostly joking. I think. Ash knew it, I figured, otherwise I doubted he'd have taken the bait. Either she was softening a bit, or she just didn't wanna seem like a mega-bitch in front of James.

"Can I get you guys a drink?" I asked.

James rested his head on folded arms, like he was too exhausted to hold himself up, and looked at me sideways. "Yes, please. Coffee, please."

"You never used to like coffee," Ash said.

James glared at him. "I've been through stuff. I think it's impressive it's my only vice."

I set about making a coffee for James and a hot chocolate for Ash. He'd liked them more than coffee as Elliot, and, as far as I knew, he liked them as Ash.

"I didn't know you were in town, James," Saras said.

"I visited a few weeks ago. I figured it's an okay place. Thought I'd hang here for a bit."

"Don't blame you. I've seen your town on Facebook. Looks small."

"Small isn't good advertising. We like to call it cosy or quaint. Nice to know you've had a good look at my page, though."

"Of course I have. I wanted to see if I could find anything to blackmail Elliot with."

I looked up from the coffee. "Hey. I still haven't seen your Facebook. I want to see the embarrassing photos."

James lit up and took his phone out. Saras rolled her eyes and took over the drink making so I could look. Let me point out that no one could ever accuse Saras of not being a gentlewoman.

"It doesn't go back *too* far," James said while he flicked, "But we have a few. I scanned Ash—" he broke off, realising his slip-up, "—*his* year five photo a couple of years ago. Isn't he *so cute* with braces?"

"Watch yourself," Ash muttered. "I have photos of you too, you know."

"And here's year ten formal. He took Gemma. She's this heartless harpy he used to date."

"She's not a heartless harpy, James."

"Debatable."

I looked up from the photo of a pretty, petite blonde girl in a cotton candy dress to find Ash rolling his eyes and laughing, while James nudged him with his shoulder. I wished I could take a photo of it. Ash looked happier than I'd ever seen him. I had to say, I hoped these two could find a way to get through this.

James reached out and flipped to the next photo. Before he could narrate, I pulled the phone closer. "Who's *that*?" I asked.

"I don't know, I can't see it, can I?"

I showed him the picture. Ash was sitting crossed-legged on a park bench, surrounded by Autumn trees. James was perched on the back of the bench, between Ash and a really, *really* hot guy.

"That's . . ." James paused, unsure what to say. He looked around, but no one was listening outside our group. "Elliot. Like, *Elliot*."

As in, the real Elliot. Ash's older brother. Right. *Right*.

I stared at the picture. I'd spent over a month there imagining an absent brother. What he might look like. How we might have gotten along. What his personality was like.

In a weird way, I guessed this guy *was* the absent brother. Older, and oh-God-so-much-hotter, and with a different story to the one I'd imagined. But either way.

Saras came over to look. "Ooh. He's cute."

"No," Ash said. "*No*. Don't even think about it."

"Why not?" I asked.

"He's my *brother*."

"He's an alcoholic drug addict," James added.

Ash shot him a cold look, all the familiar affection vanished. Even I could've told James that was a dumb line to cross. "He's not," Ash said. "Don't call him that."

"It's the truth."

"It's not. He's different now."

James didn't look convinced. I looked back at the photo, tapping the dimmed screen to brighten it. "Do you ever see him?" I asked Ash.

"About once a month. He lives in Kinsale."

Kinsale. That was doable. But a guy like that would surely have a girlfriend.

Wait, slow down, Lou, I told myself. *You've never even met him. He might be the most boring person ever. Don't you turn into Abuela on me; you do not judge a guy on his gorgeousness.*

"Can I meet him?" I asked.

The voice in my mind groaned.

Ash sighed and looked to the ceiling. "I guess."

James and Ash left twenty minutes later. To do what, I didn't know. Hopefully, to try and sort their shit out. I liked James. I could get used to having him around.

Saras called me over once they were gone. "What do you think?" she asked.

I shrugged. "I think they aren't over each other."

"If I was James, I'd never forgive him. Ever."

Yup. And maybe he still wouldn't. Time would tell.

FORTY-TWO

Ash
November 2018

We put on a film before bed, turning the volume up to drown out the chatter of Bea and her friends in the lounge room. It quickly became difficult to concentrate on the plot, however. Each time I glanced at James he was either studying his hands or staring at the wall, lost in thoughts I desperately wished I could overhear. I wondered if he was thinking the same thing I was: that we used to 'watch films' as background noise to our make-out sessions.

Something moving caught my eye. A mosquito. I tracked it around the room with narrowed eyes. James continued to stare ahead with a glazed expression, not even noticing the sudden stiffness in my shoulders.

I picked up one of James's shoes from the ground and, in one swift movement, smacked the mosquito against the wall.

James winced.

"What?" I asked, dropping the shoe back down on the floor.

"Nothing," he said too quickly.

"What was that?"

"*Nothing*. I just wasn't expecting it."

I stared at him, a slow smile spreading across my lips as I realised. "Do you have a complex about killing insects now?"

"No."

"Have you been avoiding killing insects in case they were me?"

"Shut up, Ash."

"*Oh my God.*" I burst out laughing. "Wow."

"It's bad to kill things, okay?" He turned red. "They could have feelings."

"They could be your ex-boyfriend."

"Well, *just in case*. It's not like I *actually* thought it. It's just in case."

"Right."

When I finished laughing, I sobered quickly. As much as I'd known my death would be hard for James, I'd somehow never predicted just how badly it would affect him. James was the capable one. He had a million things in his life that weren't me. I'd rarely seen him even buckle under weight before, let alone crumble.

I'd thought I'd escaped by doing what I did. But I hadn't ended the race. I'd just passed the baton onto James.

"Can we turn the film off?" James asked. "I have a six-hour drive tomorrow, and I'm kind of dead."

It didn't escape me that he was already establishing the fact that he was going home soon. Fair enough, however. His visit had been significantly extended, after all.

"Fine." I switched the television off with the remote. "I'm pretty tired too. That half-hour trip to Bruno's took it out of me."

He sent me a dirty look and assaulted me from afar with a pillow while I headed to the bathroom.

I remained in the shower twice as long as I normally would have, scrubbing every inch of my skin until I was swollen and red. Well, everywhere except my thighs, at least. They were still riddled with faded white ridges, and I imagined they probably always would be. I still hadn't decided whether I considered them shameful, or a symbol of what I'd overcome. Motivational posters would say the latter. Maybe in time I'd agree.

When I finally stepped out, the mirror was fogged with steam, and I had to rub it with the towel for several seconds before I could examine my image. My hair was fluffy and unruly. It was when it was clean. Hardly the most flattering style. I regretted washing it now.

I pulled on my sweatpants and a t-shirt and leaned against the towel rack, forcing myself to steady my breathing pattern. I was about to sleep in the same bed as James, for eight uninterrupted hours. I'd never been so eager and apprehensive in my life.

James perched on the end of my bed, his legs crossed at the ankles while he scrolled through his phone with an agitated finger. I hesitated in the doorway, hugging my arms around myself.

Without looking up, he flicked on the bedside table lamp. "I shower in the mornings."

I switched off the ceiling light and James's figure was engulfed by warm, soft shadows. Wow. Had he always been so beautiful? I remembered being attracted to him, intensely so, but this . . . *this* was another thing altogether. Now that we were alone, I could properly appreciate the way he'd grown into his own limbs. I stared at his exposed upper arms, trying to remember what it was like to touch the gentle slope of his biceps. His skin looked impossibly soft.

Oh no. I was staring at him like an idiot. I climbed beneath the covers on my side of the bed and plugged my phone in to charge.

"I do have to go home tomorrow," James said to the wall.

The wall didn't reply, so I thought I should. "It's fine, James. You stayed longer than I expected, anyway."

"Hmm."

I had no idea what he wanted me to say, or if there was anything I *could* say. Surely I'd inflicted too much damage for either of us to reverse, no matter how much I wanted it. He couldn't even look at me, for goodness' sake.

"Goodnight," I said in a small voice.

"Night."

He plunged us into darkness. I remained motionless, attempting not to annoy James with my tossing and turning. I entertained myself by indulging in self-pity. I was nowhere near sleep. Lying on my back, I allowed my head to roll to one side, so I could watch James. He was on his left side, his back to me, but his breathing gave away his alertness. Not only was he awake, he was wide awake.

He'd thrown the covers off his body despite the room's chill. His t-shirt had bunched up at the back, and one of his socks had slipped down, exposing his ankle. I was either sexually repressed or a nun because these innocent patches of skin made me want him so fervently that I felt dizzy.

It was an all-encompassing physiological response— more intense than any yearning I'd ever experienced. Everything about him—his scent, his warmth, his proximity— absolutely paralysed me. It was all I could do to fight to quiet my breathing.

I shifted onto my own side, resisting the urge to stroke a hand down his back. After all this time, I'd been so certain I'd get over him. How wrong I'd been. If anything, I needed him more. Who knew feelings could continue growing without contact to nourish them?

Was it possible that he felt the same, or was he simply trying to fall asleep, unperturbed by my presence? The realisation that he might pass out on me, leaving me here like this, was enough to make me desperate. I bit the inside of my cheek to stop myself from begging him to acknowledge me. *Come on, James,* I thought. *Roll over. Please.*

I changed position again and couldn't stop the small noise at the back of my throat as I did. I wasn't sure whether to pray that James hadn't heard it, or that he had. He rolled over onto his back and snuck a peek at me from the corner of his eye. One look at me, and he swallowed. "We can't do anything," he said. "You promised we'd just sleep."

I screamed internally and ran a hand down my thigh in the hopes it might indirectly kill some of the aching. It made it worse. "I'm not doing anything." The thickness in my voice gave me away.

"I'm going to sleep."

I gave a weak nod, and my heart sank as he rolled back towards the wall.

The tension hung thick between us. His sock had slipped off further with his movements, exposing his heel. It couldn't have been comfortable, but he made no attempt to fix it.

He was on edge.

Ever so gradually, I inched forward without touching him. I mimicked his posture, allowing the curve of my body to run parallel to his. He stopped breathing.

I'd just accepted that he was going to ignore me when he looked over his shoulder. "Fuck sleep," he hissed before grabbing for me, kissing me with a desperate fervour, so forcefully my head bumped into the bed frame.

I put my hand up as a buffer and James grabbed my wrist, pinning it in place above me. There was the smell of

Shea butter, and the taste of his mouth, and the familiar way he moved his lips.

I'd never left. I'd never managed to detach myself from him. I felt like I'd rediscovered myself. A part of myself I'd forgotten I needed.

I kissed him back until it was all I was aware of. The only thing that existed. Like it used to be. "James," I said, pulling back breathlessly.

Insecurity crossed his face. He thought I was asking him to stop. "What?" he asked, rolling off me.

"I still love you."

Why did I sound so surprised?

He tilted his head, studying me long and hard. I'd never felt this exposed. I swallowed.

"I love you too," he said.

And just like that, with four words, I felt every regret and every tear and every mistake erase itself and become meaningless. He loved me. He *loved* me. James still loved me.

He touched the corner of my mouth. "We're so screwed, aren't we?"

I laughed. "*So* very screwed."

He cupped my face and looked at me through the darkness before lowering his head to press a long, soft kiss on my lips. "You're beautiful," he whispered.

Suddenly, I remembered him whispering those same words to me, alone in my bedroom a million years before. And I remembered the silent reply I'd traced into his back, too afraid and self-conscious to verbalise it and give it life. Words that, in hindsight, were probably all he wanted to hear all along. A validation.

"I need you."

FORTY-THREE

Ash
January 2019

"I STILL CAN'T BELIEVE there's only one public school," Louise said. She stood by the car with folded arms and looked down the main street, wrinkling her nose. She'd been so eager to see Rokewood Bend, and now that she was here all she could do was judge it.

"Only one public secondary school," Elliot—the *real* Elliot—corrected her, climbing out of the driver's seat. "There's two primary schools."

"And no university," Louise said.

"Who needs uni, anyway?" Elliot asked. "I'm doing fine without it. So is Ash."

Louise, to her credit, didn't use the opportunity to put Bruno's down to make her point. I appreciated it. "Doctors do, Elliot," she said instead. "And lawyers." She'd only met him for the first time the night before, when he'd driven up from Kinsale, but she'd probably said his name at least a hundred times since then. I had the feeling she was trying to train herself into calling someone else my old name.

"If you have a country of doctors and lawyers, who's gonna drive the bin lorries?" Elliot asked, leaning against the car. He watched Louise with a cocky half-smile, raising one eyebrow. I knew that look. He was flirting with her. I had to suppress a laugh.

"As long as it's not me, I don't care," Louise said, stretching her arms out in front of her.

I looked around, my muscles tensing. It was time to hurry up and get this over with, before one of the people walking down the street recognised me. As if Louise read my mind, she said, "Are we waiting for James, or are we going to get this out of the way?"

"Waiting for James," Elliot and I answered in unison. He gave me a knowing smile, and I shrugged. Was it any surprise that I wanted extra moral support before uprooting my life once more?

Thankfully, at that moment, James appeared around the corner. The butterflies gut-punched me. Even though we'd remained in contact since he'd left Conway, I hadn't seen him since then. Two months of only his voice on the phone to assure me his return to my life hadn't been a wonderful dream. He pulled me into a tight hug when he reached us. "I can't believe you're doing this," he whispered against me, and I gave a shaky laugh.

He offered Louise a warm greeting as soon as he pulled away, and then turned to Elliot. "So," he said. "At least I know why you wouldn't speak to me at Ash's funeral."

Elliot looked sheepish. "It's good to see you."

"You too. How have you been lately, anyway?"

To anyone else, it would've sounded like a harmless

question. But our little group knew what James was really asking. "I've been good," Elliot said. "I met some great guys in Kinsale. A better crowd there, you know?"

Elliot caught my eye and smiled at me. He was telling the truth, as far as I knew. He was hardly a born-again Christian now, and he hadn't sworn off alcohol, but his activities seemed to be firmly planted in the realm of legal these days. I couldn't be happier about it.

James opened his mouth, then closed it.

Elliot must have noticed. "What's up?"

James's hand brushed against mine. Like he was trying to seek comfort from me, the way I'd used to do with him back at school. A lot could change in a year. "I'm glad you're doing better," he said, "but I'm also glad Ash has been living with Bea instead of you."

"James—" I started.

"No, Ash, I wanna say this. He wasn't there for you. He was supposed to look out for you, but he didn't. I was the one who dropped everything in the middle of the night when you needed me. *I* made sure you got out of bed in the morning. *I* dragged you to school when you wouldn't go. *I* made you eat when you didn't want to. Me. Not him. And I'm not saying I mind. I'd do it for the rest of my life if you needed me to. But you," he turned to Elliot, "should've done it too."

Louise looked in the direction of the ocean, suddenly highly captivated by the view. Elliot glanced at her, biting his lip, then nodded to James.

"Sorry to bring this all up now, man," James said, "but I've been bottling that up since last year."

"No," Elliot said. "It's fine. You're right. I don't have any excuses. But thank you. I owe you a lot."

I wanted to step in and defend Elliot. I'd forgiven him for everything long ago; as far as I was concerned, he'd been struggling with demons just as I was. But I'd have that discussion with James later. Rebuilding that bridge wouldn't happen overnight. James would understand eventually, though.

We fell into silence. After a few awkward seconds, Louise turned to Elliot brightly. "Do you think you'll visit more after this? Our friends would want to meet you, I think."

Yes, sure Louise, that's why you want him to visit, I thought, giving James a sideways grin.

Elliot leaned against the bonnet of the car and crossed his legs. "I probably should. Best to keep an eye on this one," he said, nodding at me.

James held out a hand to me. "Before we do this, do you think we can go talk alone for a second?"

I looked to Elliot and Louise. Elliot beamed. "Go do your thing," he said. "We can grab a coffee or something while we wait. Do you drink coffee?" He directed this last part at Louise, who touched her hair.

"Chai?"

"Good enough."

They began to walk down the street without even a second glance at us. James gave me an incredulous look before leading me in the opposite direction. He was steering us towards the beach. It was only a few minutes' walk from the main street, after all.

"How are you feeling?" he asked as we walked.

I took in a deep breath and swung my arms. "A bit terrified. But, you know. Fine."

"I didn't wanna ask this before but . . . have you broken any laws? Is this an awful idea?"

I crouched down and hopped onto the shallow rocks at the top of the cliffs. "I'm almost certain I haven't," I said. "Bea and Elliot checked it out too. It's not illegal to run away, and it's not illegal to provide a false name in social situations. I worked cash in hand, I didn't drive, I didn't enrol anywhere. No contracts, no bank accounts . . ."

"Lucky you basically turned into an Amish vegan," James grinned, jumping down a particularly large rock. I gingerly lowered myself down the same one. We continued until we'd reached our ledge. James kneeled down to give me a leg up. Once I'd pulled myself firmly onto the flat I reached out and helped him up, and we sat with our legs hanging over the side as though we were sixteen again.

"So what happens next?" he asked. "Are you going to go see Sue and Dom?"

"Yes. Definitely. I want to apologise to them."

"Why?"

I shrugged. "They weren't that bad. In hindsight, I think they might've even cared about us. They didn't deserve what I did."

"What about Mr. Patricks?"

Hearing his name gave me a chill. Out of the mess I'd left behind, I especially regretted dragging him into things. I should never have handed in that assignment. He didn't deserve to feel responsible for what happened. "I don't know. Would he want to see me?"

James took my hand in his and bumped his foot against mine. "I can't think of anyone who wouldn't wanna see you."

Well, I found that rather unlikely. I inhaled a deep breath of salted air and attempted to remain calm. The idea of facing everyone couldn't have scared me more. But I had to do it. I refused to keep running away from this.

I ended up lost in thought and barely noticed as James took off his backpack. To be fair, I was so preoccupied with what I was about to do that I hadn't realised James had taken his backpack from the car in the first place. He only caught my attention when he pulled out a few crumpled sheets of paper.

"I brought this for you," he said. "I thought you should see it."

I took the sheets carefully. The staples sat loose in the corner, like the pages had been handled dozens of times. The writing, scrawled all over in no real order, had multiple authors. Different ink, different handwriting.

"Ashton," I read aloud, picking one at random, "I never got to know you well, but I always wanted to. I remember being in a reading group with you back in primary school. We were at the top of the class, the only ones who were reading adult books already, but you never rubbed it in anyone's face. You were the only one who got most of my jokes. You never made me feel like I needed to dumb anything down, or lower my voice, or anything. I remember when I told you I loved Stephen King, and you told me about the Bachman books, and now they're some of my favourites. Whenever I read them, it reminds me of you. Not in a creepy way. I hope you'll read this. Sarah."

I lowered the pages, stunned. James gave me a gentle smile. "It was this exercise Mr. Patricks had us do back in RSE after you—" he started before lowering his eyes, shrugging. "Everyone else got to read theirs, so I took yours home for you. I figured if I left it with Mr. Patricks, it'd get lost."

From the worn, well-handled look of the pages, I'd bet that wasn't the only reason James had brought it home, but I didn't say so.

"I remember that stuff with Sarah in primary school," I said finally. "I didn't think she would, though."

"Yeah. I think you didn't realise a lot of things. They all wanted you around, Ash. The whole time."

A lump formed in my throat as I shuffled through the pages. Entry after entry after entry. James sat, patiently watching me read for a while longer, then cleared his throat.

"So," he said. His voice had gone funny. "I'm moving."

I looked up. "Yeah? Where to?"

"Conway. I got into Holstenwall uni."

It took me a few seconds to process this. I gaped at him, then spread into a slow grin. "Really? Are you *really*?"

"Well, they do a good teaching course there," James shrugged, and I tackled him backwards in a bear hug.

"Oh, my God. You're serious!"

"I'm serious."

We shuffled away from the ledge and I slid into his lap and kissed him with a crushing force. He kissed me back without hesitation. His whole face had lit up. I could tell he'd been dying to share the news with me. I wondered how long he'd kept it a secret for.

"Does this mean . . . um," I faltered, suddenly uncertain of myself, but he seemed to know what I was getting at.

"I wanna be where you are," he said, brushing my cheek. "If you can't be here, I don't wanna be here either."

"It's going to be hard," I said. "Things will be weird for a while. I'll have to tell everyone at home what I did. And everyone here's going to know. Your parents will probably hate me."

He looked unperturbed. "It's gonna be ridiculous to sort out," he said. "*You're* ridiculous. Which is why you need me on your team. I don't do things halfway, remember?"

"Oh, I remember."

He kissed me again. For a while all I was aware of was the taste of him, and the sound of the waves crashing into the rocks, and the smell of salt. All too quickly, however, it was time to go back. Despite the fact that I was able to get down from the ledge alone, I allowed James to assist me to the ground. It was nice to be helped.

Elliot and Louise were waiting for us by the car. Well, they were supposed to be waiting for us, anyway. In practice, though, they were so wrapped up in their own conversation they didn't notice us approaching until we were right by their side.

Louise put an arm around my shoulder. "You ready?"

"Yeah. I'm ready."

In a group, we walked a few doors down until we reached the police station. I held Louise's hand in my right, James's fingertips resting against my wrist, and Elliot's eyes firmly fixed on me.

"We'll be right here," Elliot said.

"You'll be fine," James said.

Louise squeezed my hand.

After we walked through the automatic doors, I broke away from them. A few people were seated around the room, but the path to the front window was clear. A woman held up a finger while she shuffled some paperwork, and I took a deep breath. It sounded like a foghorn in my hyper-aroused ears.

She lowered the stack of papers and leaned forward, smiling at me through the window and lacing her fingers together. "How can I help you?" she asked, speaking through three little holes in the window.

I could feel the others watching me as I took a small step forward. Then I took a second step, more confident now.

I lifted my head and looked at her straight on. Her eyes went wide and flashed with sudden recognition as I spoke.

"My name is Ashton Taylor."

ACKNOWLEDGMENTS

CONTRARY TO POPULAR OPINION, shiny, polished books aren't brought by the stork one morning to an excited writer's doorstep. There are approximately one billion people involved in the process of taking an idea and turning it into what you're holding in your hand/on your e-reader.

Firstly, thank you to my amazing agent, Moe Ferrara. I cannot overestimate how much of an impact you've had on my writing. From your countless pages of edits, to the hours of phone calls and Skype calls (even if they do usually take place at six in the morning for me--you've probably never heard my voice when I'm not half asleep and mildly crabby). From the start you have believed in me, invested your time in me, celebrated with me, and encouraged me when I'm down. More than this, though, is your apparent ability to effortlessly "get" my characters, and talk with me about them like they're good mutual friends of ours. Thank you for everything so far, and everything to come!

To the entire team at Amberjack, thank you from the bottom of my heart. For taking a chance on me, for putting in the hours upon hours of work into editing and polishing this book, and for being the ones to put it in the hands of readers. Thank you in particular to Amberjack's Managing Editor, Cassandra Farrin, and my editor, Cherrita Lee. Your notes are always spot-on, and you have a way of identifying and articulating issues that I was aware of on some level but could never quite pinpoint alone. Without your insight, and the expertise of the entire team, this book wouldn't be what it is.

Thank you to the multiple clinical psychologists, police officers, and the coroner who helped me with timelines, procedures, and legalities throughout the writing process. Your time and assistance was invaluable to me, and the fact that you were all happy to help me with my weird/creepy plot-related questions without (to my knowledge, anyway) putting my name on any watch-lists could not be more appreciated.

Thank you to Mum and Dad, and all the friends who have volunteered (read: were coerced/bribed) to read my various short and long stories over the years. In partic-ular, thank you to Laura, who has read everything I have produced since 2006. I'm sorry I made you guys read through the objectively awful things I produced while I had my training wheels on. Without the lot of you, I would've never learned to ride this bike at all.

To my amazing critique partners, all of whom are some of the most amazing people I've had the opportunity to meet, whether online, in person, or both: thank you for laughing with me, crying with me, suffering in solidarity, and celebrating our triumphs. For never complaining if we needed to spend two hours finding the perfect word to slot into a sentence, and for being available seemingly 24/7 (do you guys ever sleep!?). For loving my characters when it seemed like no one else ever would, and above all, for being unashamed book nerds with me.

To my partner, Cameron. For nodding convincingly at three in the morning while I'm explaining a convoluted plot idea that's popped into my head. For giving up your access to entire rooms every evening so I can write without distraction. For bringing me Nutella and Pepsi Max when I'm at my breaking point. Thank you for choosing me, even though I spend the majority of my time daydreaming about the romance between various figments of my imagination.

Finally, to the people who needed this story, for any reason. You are strong. You are loved. You are worthwhile. Even if it doesn't always feel that way, it remains true.

SUICIDE PREVENTION HOTLINES

THE FOLLOWING PROGRAMS PROVIDE free, confidential, 24-hour phone support for people in distress, prevention and crisis resources, and self-help information for friends and family.

The National Suicide Prevention Lifeline is available to anyone in suicidal crisis or emotional distress in the US. They can be reached by phone as well as online chat. For emergency situations, contact 911.

1-800-273-8255 | https://suicidepreventionlifeline.org/

Samaritans is a charity aimed at providing emotional support to anyone in distress or at risk of suicide in the UK.

116 123 | http://www.samaritans.org/

Lifeline is a charity that provides support to anyone in need of crisis support, suicide prevention, or mental health support services in Australia through phone and online chat.

13 11 14 | https://www.lifeline.org.au/

ABOUT THE AUTHOR

S. Gonzales is a twenty-five-year-old Young Adult author from Melbourne, Australia. When she isn't writing (and she's almost always writing), she can be found ice skating (Level: At Least She Tries), performing in musicals (Level: Average to Exceptional, depending on whether you ask an unbiased observer or her mother) and consuming copious amounts of Pepsi Max (Level: Unchallenged Reigning Champion).

S. has been writing since the age of five, when her mother decided to help her type out one of the stories she had come up with in the bathtub. They ran into artistic differences when five-year-old S. insisted that everybody die in the end, while her mother wanted the characters to simply go out for a milkshake. Since then, S. has been completing her novels without a transcriptionist.